CHILDREN
of
RAGNAROK

THE RUNESTONE SAGA

Also by Cinda Williams Chima

CINDA WILLIAMS CHIMA

CHILDREN of RAGNAROK

THE RUNESTONE SAGA

BALZER + BRAY

An Imprint of HarperCollinsPublishers

Balzer + Bray is an imprint of HarperCollins Publishers.

Runestone Saga: Children of Ragnarok
Copyright © 2022 by Cinda Williams Chima
Map © 2022 by Kevin Sheehan—Manuscript Maps

Library of Congress Cataloging-in-Publication Data
Names: Chima, Cinda Williams, author.
Title: Children of Ragnarok / by Cinda Williams Chima.
Description: First edition. | New York : Balzer + Bray, [2022] | Series:
    Runestone saga ; 1 | Audience: Ages 13 up. | Audience: Grades 10-12. |
    Summary: Desperate to escape her demon master, runecaster Reggin
    Eiklund flees to the Grove, while Eiric Halvorsen, falsely accused
    of murdering his modir and stepfadir, journeys to the Grove at the
    behest of a powerful jarl interested in restoring magic to the world.
Identifiers: LCCN 2022006022 | ISBN 9780063018686 (hardcover)
Subjects: CYAC: Mythology, Norse—Fiction. | Magic—
    Fiction. | LCGFT: Fiction. | Novels.
Classification: LCC PZ7.C4422 Ch 2022 | DDC [Fic]—dc23
LC record available at https://lccn.loc.gov/2022006022

Typography by Laura Mock
22 23 24 25 26   PC/LSCH   10 9 8 7 6 5 4 3 2 1

First Edition

*To all those warriors of the written word
who fight back against the gatekeepers
who come between young people and the stories
they love and need. Teachers, librarians, parents,
book lovers—thank you for holding the line.
Politicians and petty despots—make your name elsewhere.*

THE LOST TEXTS

The Lost Texts of the Jotun

–ON THE CREATION–

In the time before memory, the jotun Ymir
Existed in the void.
He was the first of the jotnar
And from his body
Was built the Nine Worlds
Linked by the tree Yggdrasil.
The Innangard worlds of Asgard and Midgard.
Asgard: fortress of the fierce Aesir gods.
Midgard: home of the humans.
All of Innangard was ruled by the warlike
Aesir and Vanir, gods
With a hard hand.

All else was Utangard,
Beyond the boundary–
Alfheim: home of the elves.
Nidavellir: the cavernous home of the dwarves.
Jotunheim: land of creative chaos and freedom.
Hel: dwelling place of the dead.
Muspelheim: land of elemental fire, home of Surt the fire-jotun.

Niflheim: world of darkness and elemental ice.
Vanaheim: original home of the Vanir gods.

Wild, uncivilized, dangerous.
Creative.
Free.
Seething with magic.
An endless temptation to those
Within the boundary.
A dangerous playground
For the young gods.

The jotnar devised spellwork to charm wolves and all the beasts
On the land and under the sea.
Soft rains to quench the flames of Muspell and
The warm sun to wake the flowers
And trees and every good growing thing.
They turned the Utangard into a garden.

Jealous, the gods crossed the boundaries,
Killing the jotnar, stealing the treasures of the outlands:
The mead of poetry, silver and gold and precious stones,
The runes of magic and
The women of the Utangard
Who knew prophesy and the ways of magic.

Heidin came as emissary to the gods.
She brought many gifts to Odin's seat:
Garments woven of dew and dreams.
Spellsongs to ensnare the stars.
Spellwork to charm wolves and all of the beasts

On the land and under the sea.
Soft rains to quench the flames of Muspell and
The warm sun to wake the flowers
And trees and every good growing thing.
She turned the barren worlds into a garden.
These things she gave the gods.
She offered good counsel, prophesy, and healing
And brought the wisdom of the dead to serve them.
The gods of Asgard were frightened.
They shaded their eyes against her brilliance.
Called her witch and sorceress.
Envied her power.
Repaid her largesse with treachery.
Three times they slew her in Odin's Hall.
They stabbed her and burned her, and yet
Still she lived, and took their bloody answer back to the Utangard.
This was the beginning of the end of the world.

–ON RAGNAROK–

Odin Allfadir called the seeress
From her bed beneath the stones
And demanded a foretelling.
The spakona warned
That the web was woven.
The price of foretelling
Is obsession with that
Which cannot be altered.
Still, the allfadir put down his silver
And demanded answers.

The seer spoke of the end of days,
Of the mighty gods brought low.

Brodirs shall fight and fell each other,
And systirs' sons shall kinship stain;
Axe-time, sword-time, shields are sundered;
Wind-time, wolf-time, ere the world falls;
Neither gods nor men each other spare.
This is the fate of the Asgardians.

After hearing the volva, Odin wandered the Nine Worlds in disguise
Seeking that which would
Prevent the fall of the gods.
He gave an eye
And drank from the well of knowledge.
Nine nights he hung
From the windswept tree
And stole the runes—
the tools of old magic.

The one-eyed god roamed the Midlands, the world of men.
Stirring battle-lust, he claimed the dead
to build his armies in Valhalla.
Heidin weaves her webs and bides her time.

Asgard fed the ravens with
The blood of jotnar, elves, dwarves, and men.
The green forests fall to feed a storm of arrows
And the earth yields up the stuff of swords.
Heidin throws the bones and bides her time.

The time for reckoning arrives.
The sun turns black, earth sinks into the sea,
The hot stars down from heaven are whirled;
Fierce grows the life-feeding flame,
Till fire leaps high about heaven itself.

Now do I see the earth anew
Rise all green from the waves again;
The cataracts fall, and the eagle flies,
And fish he catches beneath the cliffs.
Then fields unsowed bear ripened fruit,
All wounds are healed as Heidin returns.
The jotnar meet on Ithavoll
And regard
The bones of the Midgard Serpent.
They recall
The calamity of Ragnarok,
The betrayal of Heidin,
And Odin's faithless quest.

There they will find once more
The golden game pieces
In the grass,
Which were theirs
In the earliest days.
The Lady mounts the golden throne.
The mighty past
they call to mind,
And the ancient runes
Now come home.

1

SUNDGARD SAGA

ON A MORNING LATE IN autumn, the year he turned five, Eiric Halvorsen was milking the cows in the summer barn when he heard his modir calling him.

"Eiric! They're home!"

He scrambled to his feet, nearly kicking over the steaming bucket in his haste. He did not have to ask who was home. Most other vessels had already returned to the village of Selvagr for the winter, but his fadir and grandfadir had sailed off alone in late summer and had not returned. Several times a day, his modir climbed the headland and looked out to sea. As the days grew shorter and darker and colder, he'd seen the shadows of worry gathering in her eyes.

By the time he'd put the milk out of harm's way, released the cow from her cross ties, and run down to the beach, the little ship was already pulled up on the sand, and his grandfadir Bjorn was wading back and forth, unloading. There wasn't much—none of the usual gold, silver, tools, and trade goods they brought back from summer raids.

Something else was wrong. His fadir, Leif, stood at the water's edge, holding a little girl by the hand. His modir, Sylvi, faced them, her arms crossed over her chest, a dangerous light in her eyes.

Eiric wanted to greet his fadir and grandfadir, but the tension was so thick he didn't dare.

The stranger had golden skin, chestnut eyes, and hair the color of comb honey. She was taller than Eiric, so he knew she must be older. In her ragged moss-colored tunic, she resembled a landvaettir—a forest spirit from Bjorn's stories.

Was this the only treasure they'd brought back after weeks on the water?

Bjorn hung back as Leif led the little girl up to Sylvi. "This is my dottir, Sylvi," he said. Leif was always a man of few words. He spoke better with his blades and fists. "Her name is Liv."

"Liv is not my name," the little girl said, her voice quivering. "My name is Heidin. I brought the gift of magic to Asgard—and they betrayed me. I have returned to make them pay."

Leif ignored her. "I met her modir the summer after you and I were married. Now her modir is dead." He gave Liv a little push toward Sylvi.

"She's not dead," Liv announced to everyone. "I don't need another modir."

"Nor do I need another mouth to feed," Sylvi snapped, looking at Leif.

Leif stood his ground. "Please, Sylvi," he said. "She doesn't have anyone."

"I don't *need* anyone," Liv said, clutching a pendant that hung from a chain around her neck. But Eiric saw the tears pooling in her eyes, threatening to spill over.

Maybe Sylvi noticed that, too. She hesitated, stormy faced, biting her lower lip.

"The girl has magic in her, Sylvi," Bjorn said, finally speaking up. "And this world could use a little magic."

Eiric edged closer so that he could see the magic for himself. One side of Liv's face was puckered and scarred, to the point that she could scarcely open her left eye. Her left arm, also, was shiny with scar tissue. Had magic done that?

If that was magic, he wanted no part of it.

"She's been through a lot, as you can see," Bjorn said to Sylvi's silence. "She needs a safe haven."

Sylvi glared at Bjorn, a look cold enough to freeze milk inside a cow. "This is your fault, Fadir," she said. "You promised me you wouldn't go back there."

Then she turned back to Leif. "If I accept this child," she said, "then you must promise me you won't return there."

"Sylvi, I—"

"You must promise," she repeated. "Or sail away with your dottir for good."

"All right," Leif said. "I promise."

"Both of you must promise," Sylvi said, looking at Bjorn.

"I promise," Bjorn said, not meeting her eyes.

"I've heard promises before," Sylvi said. "To make sure that you keep it, you must give me the sunstone."

"No!" Bjorn protested. "That's not right. Since when does a dottir tell her fadir what to do?"

"Since her fadir breaks his promises," Sylvi said.

"I gave you the farm when you married," Bjorn protested.

"Aye, you did," Sylvi said. "So I ought to be able to decide who lives here, who I cook for, spin for, plant for, make butter and cheese for. I'd rather live proud and penniless on the streets than be shamed in my own home."

"All right," Bjorn said finally. "The stone is yours."

Sylvi extended her hand. "Now."

Eiric edged closer to the young stranger. "What's a sunstone?" he whispered, hoping she might tell him when the adults would not.

"Shut up, barbarian," she said.

Bjorn fished in his carry bag and drew out a sealskin pouch. Reluctantly, he dropped it into Sylvi's hand.

Now Sylvi shifted her gaze to Leif. "And the amulet."

The girl clutched her pendant with both hands. "No," she said.

"Let her keep it," Leif said. "It's the only thing she has from—"

"If she wants to join our household, then that is the price. You say she has magic in her. I cannot risk an eight-year-old sorceress with a grudge in this house."

It took both Bjorn and Leif to wrest the pendant from Liv. She ran back down the beach to the water's edge, gripped the prow of the longboat, and attempted to push it off the sand and out into the bay. In the end, Leif slung her over his shoulder and carried her back to Sylvi, setting her on her feet, but keeping one hand on her shoulder to prevent another attempted escape.

"Give it back," Liv said to Sylvi. "Give it back, or you'll be sorry." Something about the way she said it made the threat convincing.

"You leave my modir alone," Eiric said, stepping between them.

"Such a wee fierce warrior," Liv said, appraising him.

"Eiric," Sylvi said, quelling him with a look. "Liv has lost her modir and she is far from home. Think how frightening that must be."

"I am not frightened," Liv said, glowering. "You detain me at your peril."

Sylvi stowed away the sunstone and the pendant, then knelt next to Eiric, putting her hand on his shoulder but speaking to the stranger. "Hello, Liv. Welcome to Sundgard."

"My name is Heidin," Liv said.

Sylvi searched her face. "You have an old soul, and no doubt countless names. But here at Sundgard, your name is Liv." She paused, and when Liv said nothing, continued. "This is my son, Eiric. He could use an older systir."

Suddenly, Eiric found himself pinned by those chestnut eyes. Liv lifted her chin and looked down her nose at him. After a long moment, she seemed to reach a decision. "He does look like he needs help," she said. "I will stay here for now."

From that day forward, the farm at Sundgard became the richest, most productive farm in all of Muckleholm.

2

HOME FIRES

THIS SAGA BEGINS JUST AFTER the winter solstice the year Eiric Halvorsen turned sixteen, and his systir, Liv, was nineteen years old. The year their brodir, Ivar, was born.

If Eiric had the gift of prophesy, maybe things would have turned out differently. But he had no such gift. And maybe it wouldn't have mattered if he had. His grandfadir Bjorn always said that when a man is born, his fate is already woven into the fabric of the world.

If Bjorn really believed that, then why had he insisted on burning charms of protection into the gunwales and tiller of the boat they'd built together? Why did he continue to honor the gods and insist that Eiric do the same?

If the people of Selvagr really believed that, then why banish a man for doing what the fates impelled him to do?

But in those days, Eiric did not believe in prophesy, or the gods, or much of anything at all beyond the value of an axe in his hands. He'd been in the forest most of the day, chopping and splitting logs from a downed tree, then walking back and forth, a mile each way, dragging the split logs to the wood bin next to the house. By the time he was finished, he was sweating, exhausted, but now he knew there would be enough fuel to last until the morning on one of the coldest, darkest nights of the coldest year anyone could remember. Some compared it to Fimbulwinter, the bleak cold season before Ragnarok.

It was also an excuse to be out of a house where the tension was as thick as day-old porridge.

The problem was his stepfadir.

His fadir, Leif, had died a few years ago. His modir's fadir, Bjorn Eiricsen, had followed Leif to the other world two years later. The trouble began when his modir, Sylvi, married Sten Knudsen the year after that.

Sten was the son of Gustav Knudsen, the richest and most powerful man in the village of Selvagr. Sten was tall and handsome, with flaming-red hair and muscles built working in his fadir's tar pits.

The marriage hit a serious reef almost right away. Sylvi brought to the match her farm at Sundgard that Bjorn had bequeathed to her. It had been in her family for generations. It was widely thought to be the richest land and the best location in the jarldom. Elsewhere, crops withered, livestock sickened, and cows went dry, homes were struck by lightning, and apple trees bore sour and shrunken fruit, but not at Sundgard.

There's something about Sundgard, people said, casting envious eyes.

The Halvorsens weren't rich, but in a barren, impoverished land, a fertile farm was worth a fortune.

Sten had assumed that the farm would come to him as Sylvi's dowry. Instead, Sylvi gave him a bag of silver coins Bjorn had brought back from one of his raids and kept the farm in her own name.

"I didn't marry you for a bag of silver!" Sten had shouted in one of their first rows.

"Are you saying that you married me for my farm, then?" she'd snapped back.

It didn't take long to find out that Sten was brutal, violent, and impossible to please, even when he was sober. When he drank, he was even worse. He doled out beatings on a regular basis. Eiric took the brunt of them, but his modir and systir were sometime targets. Winter was the most dangerous season, when bad weather kept them all inside.

Sylvi told Sten she was divorcing him, but he refused to move out, and she would not move out herself, leaving him in possession of the farm. So life in the longhouse became a standoff, punctuated with episodes of violence.

Then their modir became pregnant with Sten's child. After that, he never laid a hard hand on Sylvi.

From then on, Eiric and Sten couldn't be in the same room for any time at all before Sten would begin finding fault with him. Eiric longed for coasting season, when he could board his boat and leave Sundgard—and his stepfadir—behind.

When he'd stalled as long as he reasonably could, Eiric carried an armload of wood into the house. Liv was at the loom, sliding the shuttle through the upright warp, forking the weft tightly against the fell of the fabric. Though the brief winter daylight was almost gone, his systir seemed to be able to work by feel.

His modir was seated close to the fire, making a pair of socks for the new baby, her bone needle glittering in the firelight. When Eiric replenished the fire, it blazed up, and he could see the outline of her swollen belly pressing against her overdress. The baby would be coming soon.

He didn't see Sten at first. It wasn't until his stepfadir gripped him by the shoulders and swung him around that Elric realized his mistake.

"It stinks like a sty in here, boy," Sten growled. "When was the last time you cleaned out the stalls?" The winter barn was attached to one end of the longhouse to permit easy access during the cold season. When that task was neglected, it was readily apparent in their living quarters.

"I cleaned the barn out yesterday," Eiric said. "I don't smell anything."

"I said it *stinks* in here," Sten shouted, slamming Eiric up against the wall. Sten leaned in so they were face-to-face, his ale-stale breath in Eiric's nose, his food-encrusted beard inches away. "You're eating us out of house and home. The least you can do is earn your keep."

Since Eiric made it his business to stay out of Sten's way, it came as something of a shock when he realized that he was now taller than his stepfadir. When had that happened?

Sten still outweighed him by half, but after a year out of the tar pits, his middle was going to fat.

Eiric looked into his stepfadir's eyes and smiled.

Sten noticed. His eyes narrowed, and his mouth twisted, as if he realized that it was only a matter of time before Eiric began to hit back in earnest.

"Leave him be, Sten," Sylvi said, looking up from her work. "I'll have the nattmal on the table as soon as I finish this row. We'll all feel better after we've eaten."

"Do you expect me to sit down to a meal when that stench is making me half-sick?"

Eiric was tired and sore, and in no mood to listen to Sten. In fact, he was never in the mood to listen to Sten.

"If it stinks in here," he said, "it's not coming from the barn."

That was his second mistake.

With a roar, Sten backhanded him across the face so hard that

Eiric lost his footing and landed flat on his back on the dirt floor. Blood poured from his split lip. He had to turn his head to keep from choking on it.

Instantly, Liv was up on her feet, wading in. "You leave him alone!" she said. "Who spent all day chopping wood? Who fishes all summer so that we have something to eat all winter? He does a lot more work around here than—"

"Shut your mouth, witch!" Sten growled. "Always skulking around, muttering under your breath. A face like yours could turn a man to stone. Everybody in town knows you're bad luck."

"You should hear what they say about *you*," Liv spat back. "Every day, you look more and more like—"

"Enough, Liv!" Sylvi shouted desperately. "Go back to your loom. The light is almost gone."

Eiric rolled to his knees, then stood, blotting the blood from his face with his sleeve. The rage rose in him like a geysir as he faced his stepfadir, fists clenched.

"Eiric," Sylvi said, dumping her work from her lap and struggling to her feet. "Go to the boat shed."

"Leave the boy alone," Sten said. "If he wants a fight, I'll give him one. It's time he learned that I'm the head of this household now."

"You're not the head of this household," Eiric growled. "You're nobody. You're an unwanted freeloader on my modir's farm. If you had any pride, you'd get out."

Sten lunged forward, but Eiric sidestepped him, sticking his foot out so that Sten tripped and crashed headfirst into the table. It helped that his stepfadir had no doubt been drinking all day. He lay there, groaning and cursing, temporarily unable to rise.

"Eiric Halvorsen," his modir said, her voice low and trembling, "I told you to go to the boat shed, and I expect you to obey." She paused, put her hand on her swollen belly, and then whispered, "Please."

Eiric went, seething.

The boat shed was cold and dark. Eiric dumped kindling and touchwood into the firepit and ignited it with flint and steel.

That's one thing you're good at—starting fires.

Even after the fire was burning well, Eiric lingered, warming his hands, staring into the flames. He was angry at Sten, disappointed in himself, and frustrated with his modir's apparent submission to his stepfadir's bullying.

He wished he could be somewhere—anywhere—else. Bjorn claimed that in the southern ocean, the weather was warm enough to sail all year long. He wished he knew which one of his grand-fadir's chants would take him there.

He wished he were a year—even two years—older. Then he would have hopes of recruiting his own crew, one large enough to sail the langskip.

Sylvi always said, *If wishes were fishes, our nets would be full.*

At sixteen, Eiric was bigger than most men. By law, he was old enough to marry. When he went to the village of Selvagr, girls pointed at him and whispered, but he'd learned to look for sweet-hearts farther from home. The village was too small, and memories too long.

These days, he scraped away the red hairs that sprouted on his chin and upper lip and combed and braided the locks of his fair hair. He was still outgrowing his clothes. His modir and systir couldn't keep up with the spinning, weaving, and sewing to keep them all clad. It was a long way from sheep and flax to a shirt and trousers.

People said that he favored his fadir, who'd been tall, broad shouldered, fair-haired, and blue eyed. Leif Halvorsen had come to

Selvagr when he'd signed on as crew with Bjorn one summer.

"As soon as your modir laid eyes on Leif, she would have no one else," Bjorn had told him. "I warned her that he was not the kind of man who stayed in one place, or with any one woman for very long. She told me that she'd rather spend one season with Leif than a lifetime with any other man. When he returned to Sundgard the next summer, she married him."

Leif went coasting with Bjorn every summer after, but he always came back. He was gone coasting the summer Eiric was born.

By age eight, Eiric was big and strong enough to handle an oar or bail all day. He'd joined the crew then, and had spent every summer on the water since, learning the tricks of seamanship and navigation. Eiric was proud and hotheaded even then, and the crews gave him no quarter for age or lineage. He sparred with axe, spear, lance, and lausatok, a form of weaponless grappling that meant a man was always ready for a fight.

It was only when he went to sea that he learned the gods and jotnar from his grandfadir's stories had slaughtered each other centuries ago. Men were limited to the Midlands, where they struggled to survive, and Hel, where they went to dwell when they lost that battle. It was then that he began to grow up.

After Leif and Bjorn died, Sylvi begged Eiric not to sign on with a vikingr crew, which would keep him away all summer. He didn't like crewing under someone else, anyway. So, for the next two summers, Eiric left the longboat in the shed, hired a single crew member, and took his little karvi out to fish the banks in the Archipelago, with a little coasting thrown in. Sometimes Liv crewed for him. She had an instinct for reading the wind and for anticipating what Eiric wanted before he knew himself. He wished she could crew for him all the time, but Sylvi needed her help on the farm.

Finally warmed through, Eiric abandoned the fire, sat down on the workbench, and picked up a toy horse he was carving for the new baby. It was nearly done. He just had to tease the mane and tail out of the rough wood and rub flaxseed oil into it. He picked up his draw knife and began to hone the rough edges.

His stomach growled. Sten was right about one thing—Eiric was always hungry, and now he'd missed the nattmal—the evening meal.

As if called by the thought, the door to the boat shed eased open and Sylvi entered, a bowl of steaming porridge between her mittened hands. She set it down on the bench next to him. It was topped with a large piece of smoked fish and a hunk of oat bread.

"I knew you'd be hungry," she said.

"I am." He was still too angry to risk saying more than that. He broke up the fish with a spoon, stirred it into the porridge, then took a big bite.

His modir settled heavily onto the far end of the bench. She was pale and sweating, despite the cold. "You need to leave here before the baby is born."

Eiric practically choked on a mouthful of bread. "What?"

"Sten plans to kill you so that his child will be in line to inherit the farm." Sylvi's voice was low, matter-of-fact. Chillingly so.

"He told you that?" Eiric felt as if he were breathing underwater, unable to get enough air.

"When Uncle Finni visited two weeks ago, I overheard the two of them talking. That is why Sten has been trying to pick a fight with you. He sees you as the major obstacle to his plan. With you out of the way, he thinks Liv will be more manageable."

"If that's what he thinks, he doesn't know Liv," Eiric said, his dinner all but forgotten.

Sylvi winced, lips tightening as if she were in pain.

"Are you all right, Modir?" Eiric said, setting his porridge aside, ready to spring up and do something—like call his systir in.

Sylvi took a breath, released it, and ignored the question. "Ulff Stevenson has said more than once that he'd take you on as an apprentice. You can live above his shop." Stevenson was the blacksmith in the village.

"I'm not going to move into the village and leave you and Liv here with Knudsen," Eiric said. "If I leave, you leave with me."

"No," Sylvi said. "This is my farm. If we leave it, Sten gets what he wants. He won't bother Liv if you're living nearby. He knows you'll come after him if he does."

"It hasn't stopped him so far," Eiric said bitterly.

"No," Sylvi said. "When you're–" Her voice hitched, and she doubled over.

"Modir?" Eiric said, by now thoroughly alarmed. "Let me take you back to the house, where it's warmer."

She shook her head and slowly straightened. "When you are older, the three of us will handle Sten in a way that won't be traced back to us. What I want is for you and Liv to survive until then."

"I'm sixteen," Eiric said. "I'm big enough. I'll kill him."

"No," she said, gripping his hand so tightly that it hurt. "Promise me that you will not try. That's what he wants. He is still stronger than you, and a more experienced fighter."

"Not when he's drinking," Eiric said.

"Make no mistake, Sten is still dangerous when he's drunk," Sylvi said. "He will find a way to kill you. It does not have to be a fair fight. That is why you have to leave now."

If I'm not big enough now, Eiric thought, I will be soon.

As if she'd read his mind, she said, "Even if you succeed, you'll go before the Thing council for murder. Sten's fadir and brodirs are on the Thing, and most of the other members do business with them. You'll be outlawed, and then Sten's family will kill you. He's not worth it, Eiric."

"Why did you marry him?" Eiric demanded, his frustration boiling over. "We were doing all right."

"No," Sylvi said bluntly. "We were not. It's a big farm, too big for Liv and me to manage on our own every summer when you go vikingr."

Vikingr. A word that used to mean much more than it did now. That meant coasting, raiding, adventuring—where a band of men blooded their blades in common cause. Where one man could prove his worth each and every day.

A word that meant more than fishing.

"You should have said something," Eiric said, guilt washing over him. "I could have stayed home."

"You are no farmer, Eiric," his modir said. "You are too much like your fadir and grandfadir to stay home for long. You have always been more interested in what's over the horizon than what's behind you." She paused, as if debating whether to go on. "Bjorn always claimed that he was descended from Njord, god of the sea. One of the Vanir gods. But he also said that the wise man honors all of the gods."

"I suppose that's why he always insisted that I honor them," Eiric said. "Though I don't see the point if they're dead."

For a long time, Sylvi said nothing. Then she reached out and fingered Eiric's pendant—the one his fadir had left him. "I gave this to Leif when we married. Your fadir traces his ancestry to the Aesir gods—the warriors. You are much like your fadir, but you have something of your grandfadir as well. You have a choice. Choose carefully."

"I don't understand," Eiric said.

"Fighting is not the only way to win." She tousled his hair in a way that said that if he didn't understand it, she wasn't going to explain further. "Tell me you will go to Stevenson."

"I'll think about it" was all he could offer.

"Think quickly." Sylvi mopped her forehead with her sleeve. Her skin appeared pale, clammy, and she took quick, shallow breaths. "If I don't survive this birth, here's what I want you to do."

"Modir!" Eiric said with growing alarm. "Do you—"

"There's a stone set into the floor under my sleeping bench. You'll find a small chest underneath. Take my jewelry that's in there—my brooches, my silver armband, and the amber necklace—for your systir. Return the rest to the barrow and never speak of it again. Do not tell Liv."

Why shouldn't he tell Liv? "I don't understand what—"

"Swear to me, Eiric Halvorsen," Sylvi said, each word a steel-tipped shaft, "that you will return the rest to the barrow and never speak of it again."

"I swear," he said.

"If anything happens to me, Sundgard goes to you and Liv. Don't let the Knudsens take it away from you."

"Nothing will happen to you," Eiric said.

"I need your oath."

"I swear, Modir," Eiric said, feeling the weight of the oath settling on his shoulders. Oaths were a serious business in the Midlands, not to be taken lightly.

"Help me up," she said, extending her arms. Eiric lifted her to her feet. Then he saw that her overdress was soaked through and there was a puddle between her feet. "Let's go back to the house. Your baby brodir is coming."

3

IN GUNNAR'S HALL

REGINN EIKLUND STOOD IN THE doorway of Gunnar's Hall, looking down the crowded street to the quay at the foot of the hill. The harbor resembled a shorn forest, studded with trading ships with their masts taken down and secured to the gunwales.

It was the Disting, the blessing of the plows, the gathering of the goddesses, and the festival of new beginnings. Here in Langvik, the largest port on the big island of Muckleholm, it was also the Feast of Ships. Though ice still bobbed in the harbor, the festival signified the beginning of the shipping season.

For most, even those who cared little for goddesses or plows, it was the first excuse since the Yule to drink themselves senseless.

It was Reginn's sixth night at Gunnar's—and so it would be her last.

Tomorrow, there would be a long walk to another town. Or a tight berth on another sea crossing.

Her master, Asger, liked harbor towns because there was so much coming and going. Always a new crowd. Always a quick getaway. Had they been to Langvik before? The venues all ran together after a while.

A week was as long as they'd stay anywhere. It was as if Asger was on the run from unseen demons who might catch him if he lingered too long in one place. Unfortunately, Reginn's demon followed her wherever she went.

Reginn could hear Gunnar the hallkeeper bustling around behind her, excited about the commerce he expected to come through the door. With the holiday, nearly all the town's lodging places were at capacity, including Gunnar's.

He'd been happy to accept Reginn's offer of singing and flute playing and healing and foretelling during the weeklong festival. Especially because she'd offered to perform for bed and board and tips alone.

She hadn't seen Asger all week, which might mean he had business elsewhere. Or he might have been here all along. He was like one of those lizards that could change colors to match its surroundings. Any one of the patrons could have been him, glamoured to resemble a sailor, a farmer, a herdsman. She never knew when he would appear out of nowhere, and she would feel the kiss of flame on her skin.

"Why do you do that?" Reginn said, when she plucked up the courage to ask. "It gives me the shivers."

"Just keeping you honest, meyla," Asger would say, pinning her with his ember eyes, his hair flickering like flames around his head. He always called her "meyla"—little girl.

There's nothing honest about any of this, Reginn thought. Except, maybe, for the music. Of all the talents she claimed (and there were many), only the music was true magic.

Well, and maybe the healing.

Asger would be here tonight for sure. He never missed the last night of an engagement, when the money really rolled in and it was time to collect her takings.

Some patrons were already knocking back cups of mead and

ale, but this was a brief respite before the madness began. First, the nattmal, a supper consisting of lamb-and-barley stew. Then more drinking and entertainment. Reginn wasn't looking forward to another night in a boisterous alehall, fending off patrons who assumed that she offered services beyond spellsongs, healing, and prophesy.

She straightened her overdress and adjusted the belt hung with decorated pouches, baubles, remedies, and charms that she would sell to customers before the night was out. She carried her bone flute in a separate bag, attached to a leather strap that crossed her body from shoulder to hip. Tools of the trade, along with her wits.

They were all she had. They were all she'd ever had.

Tablet-woven braid straps secured her dress at the shoulders. More braid decorated the hem of her linen tunic. Fine red leather shoes peeked from beneath her skirts. Her untamable hair was the color of oak leaves at midwinter, streaked with copper and red. She wore it gathered into a long plait, with a gold brocade fillet over it.

Like any player on the stage, she was dressed for the part—a prosperous spakona, or seer, one well worth consulting.

Still lingering in the doorway, Reginn breathed in the sea air and dreamed of faraway places. Places Asger Eldr would not find her.

She nearly lost her footing on the wooden stoop as a harried servant wearing buff livery jammed past her and into the hall.

"What's your hurry?" Reginn muttered under her breath.

The servant threaded his way through the taproom until he found Gunnar. After a brief conversation and a bit of hand-waving, the servant elbowed past her again and descended into the street.

Whatever the servant had said, it left Gunnar beaming, all but skipping across the taproom. That was a tall order for someone as bulky as he was.

"We've got important guests tonight," Gunnar told Thurston, the innkeeper's thrall. "You'd better step lively."

Reginn couldn't help herself. "I don't know how he could work any harder than he already does," she snapped.

That was true. Reginn had never seen Thurston slacking—not once over the past week, which was more than she could say for herself. Thurston was Gunnar's sole thrall, and he had to make up for a master who talked big and worked very little.

Thurston was popular with the regulars—many called out greetings as he threaded his way between the tables. If people returned to Gunnar's Hall, it was because of Thurston.

Nobody came back for the mutton stew.

Gunnar was still going on about his prospective guests.

"All right," Reginn said, knowing that Gunnar wouldn't shut up until she asked the question. "Fine. Tell me. Who's coming?"

"The keeper," Gunnar said with barely concealed pride.

"That *is* an honor," Reginn said, nodding. "What does she keep?"

"She keeps *nothing*," Gunnar said, disappointed that he wasn't getting a bigger reaction. "She's the high priestess of the Temple at the Grove."

"So—she still practices the old faith?" Reginn said. Hardly anyone worshipped the gods anymore. Wooden shrines to them had been torn down and burned for fuel, though the stone ones still stood. Amulets and images had been melted down and repurposed. The gods no longer poked into human events, so what was the point of honoring them?

"It's not about the gods," Gunnar said, like someone making it up as he went. "The temple dedicates are called wyrdspinners, and they are the last of the vala."

The vala were magical practitioners, healers, and seeresses, like Reginn claimed to be. Her modir, Tove, had taught her the vardlokkur—their spellsongs—before she sold Reginn to Asger.

"So this keeper—she works the alehalls and longhouses?" Reginn said.

"Oh no," Gunnar said, horrified. "She's the real thing. Her emissaries come every year, but she rarely comes in person. When she does, it is said that kings and jarls from Groenland to Frakkland seek her counsel."

That got under Reginn's skin. It wasn't so much the implication that Reginn was running a rig as the suggestion that the keeper was not. *She's just another player with a better script, better costumes, on a bigger stage.*

"Well," Reginn said, "I'm not a jarl or a king. That's probably why I haven't heard of her."

"Probably," Gunnar said, missing the barb completely. "When the wyrdspinners come, they ask only to be allowed to visit the poorhouses, orphanages, and slave markets, collecting orphans. Most people are glad to be rid of them, and it means fewer mouths to feed around here."

That was true enough. Times were hard—had been hard for as long as Reginn could remember. Livestock often did not survive the brutal winters, and crops withered in summer. Fishermen came home with empty nets. Pestilence blazed through towns and villages, leaving modirless children in the streets, while the old often walked into the forest to die.

It was a good time to sell remedies and talismans, at least. And to predict a future that was better than the present.

Reginn herself had been a foundling, until Tove took her in. Which raised a nagging question in her mind. "What do they want with orphans?"

"They seek the gifted to serve in their temple."

"How can they tell that they're gifted?"

Gunnar shrugged. "How would I know? But the ones they choose are lucky. It's said the temple is like a palace, with floors inlaid with gems and fixtures of gold and silver. The fish leap out of the sea at the spinners' beckoning, and fruit trees drop cherries and apples into their baskets, so that their tables groan with cheese, butter, skyr, fish and game, and berries of all sorts."

They're sure to love your mutton stew, then, Reginn thought. Out loud, she said, "Where's the Temple at the Grove?"

"Nobody knows," Gunnar said. "It's on an island hidden by magic. If a ship is blown off course and wrecks on its shore, the entire crew is eaten up by sea monsters. Nobody lives to tell the tale."

"How do you know?" Reginn said.

Gunnar appeared stumped. "How do I know what?"

"If nobody lives to tell the tale, then how do you know about it?" Reginn knew the hallkeeper was getting annoyed, but it was her last night, so she didn't care.

Gunnar rolled his eyes. "That's what people say."

Reginn changed tack. "Did the keeper come here for the festival?" That might mean some unwelcome competition.

Gunnar shook his head. "She did not mean to come here at all. Her ship was badly damaged in a storm off the coast. They brought it into the harbor for repairs. They didn't know about the festival until they found out that all of the inns were full."

"You'd think if she was any good, she could predict the storm was coming and stay out of the way," Reginn said with a shrug. "Or at least realize that it's the Disting."

Gunnar's eyes widened in alarm. "I don't want to hear that kind of talk from you while she's here," he said.

"Don't worry," Reginn said. "I'll ask her about the temple and the sailors instead. She should be able to clear that up." She knew this would generate an explosion for sure.

Gunnar did not disappoint. "No!" he all but shouted. "I don't want you speaking to her or her attendants about anything while she's here. Just keep your mouth shut and do your job."

But I can't do my job with my mouth shut, Reginn might have said, but Gunnar hustled away.

How can I be so bold with Gunnar and yet so timid when it comes to confronting Asger? Reginn thought.

Because there's an ocean of difference between Gunnar and Asger.

"I thought you'd want supper before the rush."

It was Thurston. Of course. He pointed to a small table where he'd set out a bowl of stew and a cup of ale from the cask.

"Thank you," Reginn said, ambushed by his thoughtfulness. She sat, pulled the bowl toward her, and took a bite while Thurston stood there awkwardly. He obviously had something to say.

She glanced around, sniffed the air. What were the chances that Asger was already here? If he saw her sitting with Thurston, he might—

No. He wasn't here. And if he were, she'd tell him it was business. Though that hadn't always worked in the past.

"Please. Sit with me," Reginn said. "You should have some supper, too."

Thurston shot a quick look toward the corner where Gunnar was holding forth, then dipped up some stew and some small ale and sat across from her.

"I wanted you to know—I've been watching your performances this week, and I've never seen better," he said. "You know all about herbs and healing. And—your music—your voice, and especially the flute—" He put his fist on his chest. "That song about the lady of the bogland—it goes right to the heart."

"Oh," Reginn said, both mortified and pleased that Gunnar's

thrall felt the need to leap to her defense. "Well, thank you."

"It reminds me of the pipes at home," he said. "They say scent stays in memory the longest, but for me it's music." He paused. "I'm going back there one day."

"Oh!" Reginn glanced at Gunnar, who was drawing off cups of ale.

Thurston followed her gaze. "I am saving my money," he said, touching the slave collar around his neck. "I mean to buy my freedom. But first, I need a telling. I need to know whether I should approach Gunnar now or later."

"No," Reginn said, deeply embarrassed. "You don't want to make a decision based on what I tell you."

"But–" Thurston hesitated, his eyes fixed on her face. Even his fringe of eyelashes was reddish, Reginn realized. "That's what you do every night. Right? Tell people what the future holds."

"Yes, but–"

"I can pay." He pulled a leather pouch from under his coat and shook it so Reginn could hear that it jingled.

Reginn sighed. Took another look around. Then gave in, digging an object out of her carry bag.

See, Asger? It is *business.*

"Here," she said. "Hold this."

"What is it?" Thurston asked suspiciously. "I haven't seen you use that before."

"A sheep's knee bone," Reginn said. "It's used to answer yes-or-no questions. We'll ask the question, then drop it. The answer will come in the way it lands. If the hollow side is up, that means no. If it's down, that means the answer is yes."

Cautiously, Thurston took the bone in his hands. Reginn closed her hands over his and sang the summoning of the vaettir–the spirits of the dead.

"Answer me, dear vaettir, the questions I will ask. "Will Thurston buy his freedom tonight?"

She waited a moment, then repeated the lines.

Thurston began to glow, all the way to the tips of his roughly shorn hair. It was as if light were leaking through his skin so that Reginn could see the bones beneath.

Before they even dropped the bone, a voice answered, echoing inside her head.

> *He will find freedom*
> *As freedom comes to all of us.*
> *He will buy his freedom,*
> *But he will pay the gods' price.*
> *He will find his freedom in Helgafjell.*

Helgafjell. The land of the dead.

Reginn yelped, causing Thurston to drop the bone. It landed on the floor, bounced once, and came to rest.

"So," Thurston said, kneeling down to look at it. "What does it mean?"

Reginn laced her fingers together to hide her shaking hands. Looked around to see who might have been whispering in her ear. "It means nothing. Nothing. When it lands like that, it means that the spirits don't want to answer."

"Oh," Thurston said. "Could we try it again?"

"No," Reginn said, scooping up the bone and returning it to her bag. "The vaettir do not like being summoned a second time on the same question. But I wouldn't say anything to Gunnar today."

Thurston nodded. "If you say so," he said, obviously disappointed.

"Promise me," Reginn said, looking into his eyes.

"I promise," he said.

"Now, we'd both better get to work," Reginn said. "Gunnar's been looking daggers at us this whole time." She stood, keeping a hand on the table so she wouldn't fall over.

"What do I owe you?" he said, sliding his fingers into the pouch.

"Nothing!" she said. "Save it for someone who can give you better answers."

4

CROSSING THE BORDERLANDS

REGINN REFILLED HER CUP, THIS time from the cask of mead. She drank it down, then filled it again. After that last episode, she needed something to calm her nerves. She had no idea what had happened, but one thing she knew—she didn't want it to happen again.

One of her modir's favorite sayings was this:

Those who cast nets for the spirits risk being pulled into the deep.

Which seemed an odd saying for someone who made her living casting those nets and hauling in dreams.

That was probably as unreliable as anything else Tove had told her.

Still, Reginn worried. Had she somehow put events into motion that were better left alone?

He will find his freedom in Helgafjell. The land of the dead.

He would die enslaved.

No, she thought. I will not have it.

Squaring her shoulders, she made her way to the corner that Gunnar had roped off to serve as a kind of stage. Word of Reginn's performances had spread, and the house had been packed since the first night. Tonight would bring in more coin than the other nights combined. Tonight was the play that could be made only once.

She scanned the crowd, a sea of eager faces, bodies leaning forward, all trying to catch her eye, all hoping to be chosen for a telling. She always played to that—her gaze lighting on one person, then another, like a dragonfly on a thistle.

Who would be the one to die tonight?

She didn't see Asger. That didn't mean he wasn't there.

Just then, Gunnar escorted two guests to a table just beyond the rope, evicting the current occupants over their strenuous protests. The newcomers wore ankle-length blue cloaks, even indoors, like armor against the everyday folk they'd been forced to mingle with.

Or maybe, Reginn allowed, they were just cold.

Underneath, they wore fine gowns studded with gems at the neckline and belted at the waist.

These must be the important visitors Gunnar had described. What was it he'd called them? Wyrdspinners?

From their belts hung mysterious pouches, charms, and amulets, and they carried distaffs of wood, iron, and bronze nearly as tall as they were. Reginn judged that their jewelry would be worth a fortune as chop silver and gold. She dropped her arms, trying to conceal the cheap baubles and gimcrackery that hung from her own belt.

The younger of the two women was striking. Her face was like sculpted bronze set with eyes the color of hoard amber. Around her neck, the spinner wore two pendants on a gold chain—one the figure of a woman wrought in gold, silver, and precious stones, the other a crystalline pendant that caught Reginn's eye because it glowed with a pale blue light.

The other woman moved with a stately grace. She was considerably older, her face like leather tooled with the imprint of wisdom, framed by a lambskin hood lined with white fur.

She must be the keeper, Reginn thought.

As if called by the thought, the hooded woman looked straight at Reginn, pinning her like a mouse under a cat's paw. She cocked her head as if to say, *Yes. And you are . . . ?*

Me? I'm nobody. I'm in over my head.

Reginn drew the younger spinner's attention, too. She appraised Reginn through narrowed eyes before turning to their servant.

He set a small cask on the spinners' table. Skillfully, he tapped it, releasing the contents into two cups, which he served to the spinners.

By craning her neck, Reginn could see that the cups contained wine the color of garnets. A rare find in a land all but empty of vineyards.

With the spinners served, the servant stood against the wall, awaiting their pleasure. A brace of guards in the same livery took their place by the front door.

Reginn had performed in halls and alehouses the length and breadth of the Archipelago, but she couldn't ever remember somebody bringing their own servants and their own guards.

Not to mention their own wine.

Then again, ordinarily, these kinds of people never came to the venues she played. They stayed in private homes, with jarls and merchants.

Panic welled up in Reginn like a geysir. Her breath stopped up in her lungs, her heart pounded in her ears, as if she really were drowning.

Through sheer force of will, she resisted the urge to flee through the door.

She might not believe in some of the gifts she claimed, but she believed in Asger Eldr's ability to find her, sooner or later, if she ran. And then there would be hell to pay.

Reginn took a deep breath, then released it slowly. *Remember—same play, bigger stage, better costumes for the part.*

She reached for her flute.

Methodically, she unwrapped the instrument from the soft leather that protected it. That familiar ritual calmed her. Without a word of introduction, she raised the flute to her lips and began to play.

The pure, high notes pierced the din in the room, stilling conversation. The younger blue cloak looked up and stared, as if ambushed, her spoon halfway to her mouth. With a clatter, she dropped it back into her bowl. She closed her hand around the crystal pendant that hung at her neck so that the light leaked between her fingers—this time a warm amber glow.

Almost immediately, Reginn's heart quit hammering, and she found her breath again—enough to fuel the notes that made the songs.

This. This was her gift—the only true magic she knew.

Tove had taught Reginn to play when she was very small. She'd rapidly progressed beyond anything her modir attempted. Music was an escape—a constant for a girl who had no control over anything else in her life.

Tove was always vague about the origins of the flute but claimed that it predated the gods. She said that it was made from the bones of Ymir, whoever that was. All Reginn knew was that its voice was brilliant, the play subtle but true. If only she could figure out how to sing and play the flute at the same time.

When she finished, the blue cloaks put their heads close together and whispered. Were they talking about her?

The evening went on, smudged by mead and ale into a clamor of shouted requests, curses, calls for food and drink, the clank of silver dropping into her tip bowl, the scent of sweaty bodies, and the rush of cool, fresh air when the door opened and closed.

She should have seen Asger by now. It was long past time for the wink and the nod that would tell her the game was on.

After a short break, Reginn called for clients to receive the gifts of healing and foretelling. Reluctantly, she brought out the sheep's knee bone again, worried that the voice of doom would return.

The lucky chosen asked yes-or-no questions, and Reginn cast the bone, gave them their answers, and collected their tips. Some went away happy, some confused, others disappointed in the answers they received.

For healing, she had several different options, depending on the client and the problem. For rashes, blisters, abscesses, and the like, she had a supply of unguents and creams that she applied directly or dispensed on a small wooden stick or in a twist of linen. Sometimes, she provided healing runes inscribed on more small sticks.

She was least confident in the entertainment value of this part of the act. Healing wasn't quick; it wasn't showy. It was important only to those who sought a cure.

When she looked at the spinners, though, they seemed to be arguing with each other, rather than paying attention to her. While the keeper spoke, the younger one tapped her fingertips on the table, her lips pressed into a tight line. When it was the younger woman's turn, the keeper folded her arms and listened with her chin tilted up.

Finally the older woman stood, scooped up her elaborate staff and the cask of wine, and stalked toward the stairs to the sleeping loft. The younger spinner gazed after her, lips pursed, fingers drumming on the tabletop.

This drama engaged Reginn to the point that she nearly missed it when a commotion arose by the bar. Several patrons were huddled around someone lying on the floor, shouting conflicting advice.

"Give him air!"

"Bring him water!"

"Take him to the stable to sleep it off."

There it was. The rig. Finally.

Reginn set aside her flute and stood, trying to peer over the heads of the crowd. Gunnar elbowed his way into the middle to see what was what. He knelt down, disappearing for a few moments, then rose, his face gone shark's-belly gray, a body cradled in his arms.

"What's going on?" Reginn called. "Is something wrong?"

Gunnar didn't respond, only forced his way through the onlookers toward the remaining blue cloak. He squatted before her, rolling the body onto the dirt floor.

"Please," he said to the wyrdspinner, raising his hands in supplication. "Revered lady. Can you help him? This boy—he seems to have taken ill."

The blue cloak frowned, as if unhappy to have all this attention focused on her. Finally, she clutched at her skirts and knelt down to have a look.

It took Reginn a moment to process what was happening.

No, Gunnar. This is my *rig. Don't be handing it off to out-of-town talent.*

Reginn stormed from the stage, pushing her way through the crowd until she stood next to Gunnar.

Just in time to hear the spinner say, "This boy is dead, hallkeeper. There's nothing anyone can do."

Just in time to see that the boy on the floor was Thurston.

Reginn fell to her knees next to Gunnar, her head aboil with confusion.

So *Thurston* was the one Asger had chosen to play opposite

Reginn in this bit of theater. *Thurston* was the one he'd chosen to die.

Because that was the game. Asger would enlist someone to "die" during Reginn's performance. The illusion was helped along by Svefnthorn—thorn of sleep—a rune that Tove had taught Reginn when she was just a little girl. The symbol was carved into a stone pendant that Asger gave to the "victim" to wear against his skin. It caused a deathlike sleep that ended only when the pendant was removed.

The effect was startlingly real. The color that had stained Thurston's cheeks earlier in the evening was gone, leaving a deathly pallor. When Reginn placed her hand in front of his mouth, she could feel no breath coming and going.

She was oddly disappointed. If Thurston was working with Asger, why hadn't he said anything?

While Reginn was having this debate in her head, Gunnar was pleading with the spinner. "Please," the hallkeeper was saying. "I've fed and housed the boy for six years, and it's only now that he's begun to earn his keep. I'll never get my investment back."

"I'm sorry," the spinner said. "Once a person crosses the borderlands into death, there is no coming back. Raising the dead is the province of the gods, not of mortals. It can't be done."

"Maybe not," Reginn said loudly, "but at least you could *try*."

As soon as the words were out of her mouth, she regretted them. The blue cloak stared at her, as if astonished, then smiled a smile that was more of a pat on the head. "By all means, spellsinger, have a go at it."

With that, she rose amid a rustle of skirts and returned to her seat.

Gunnar focused on Reginn, taking a different tack than before. "Will *you* try to bring the boy back? As you can tell, he means the world to me. I love him like a son."

An idea kindled in Reginn's head, flaming up higher and higher. It might be the best rig ever. Or the worst mistake she'd ever make.

"Very well, hallkeeper," she said. "You say you love him like a son. Are you willing to pay a price to see him restored?"

Gunnar blinked at her, as if startled by her mercenary attitude. "Of course," he said. "I mean, within reason."

"I cannot work magic on a thrall," Reginn said. "The vaettir would be offended if I disturbed them on his behalf. You must free him first."

For a long moment, Gunnar was speechless. "Why would I do that?" he bellowed. "What good is that to me?"

"But . . . you said you loved him like a son," Reginn said, all wide-eyed confusion. The patrons crowded around them murmured agreement.

Taking no chances, Gunnar knelt again, pressed his fingers against Thurston's wrist, peeled back his eyelids, then shouted in his ear to see if he got a response.

Nothing.

"Fine," Gunnar growled. "If he lives, I'll free him."

"Remove his collar, then," Reginn said.

"Look, there isn't time to—"

"Remove his collar, or I'm not going to waste my time," Reginn said. "Please hurry. With each moment that passes, the boy wanders farther into the borderlands."

Still grumbling under his breath, Gunnar groped for the ring of keys at his belt. He selected one and unlatched the tarnished collar so that it plopped to the floor. "There," he said. "I hope that you and the spirits are satisfied."

"We'll see," Reginn said. Once again, she glanced around for Asger, and once again, he was nowhere to be seen. The wyrdspinner sat alone at the table she'd shared with the keeper, her chin resting on her hand, watching the proceedings with faint amusement.

Reginn's confidence took a nosedive. What was it about the spinners that intimidated her? Well, for three, they were rich and fancy and famous.

She leaned forward and took Thurston's hands, then nearly dropped them in her surprise. They were uncommonly cold, heavy, as lifeless as two pieces of raw meat. She and Asger had been running this rig for almost a year, and none of the other "corpses" had ever seemed quite so dead before.

What if she was wrong? What if Thurston wasn't Asger's chosen at all?

"Thurston," she said, swallowing hard. "This is not your time. Come back to us." As she spoke, she unlaced his shirt, expecting to find the runestone hanging from a chain around his neck. It was not. She gently patted him down, seeking the small stone carving Asger would have given him.

Nothing.

She patted him down again, a little more thoroughly. Still nothing.

"Are you a witch or a pickpocket?" Gunnar grumbled.

Third time's the charm, Tove liked to say, but in this case, it wasn't. No runestone. The worm of worry in Reginn's middle became a writhing snake.

When she leaned in close to Thurston's face, she breathed in an odd, sweet smell. Like cherries. There were red stains on his tunic as well. Had he gotten into something he shouldn't have?

Was it possible that her divination had been true, and Thurston really was dead and gone, and Reginn had put herself into a predicament?

Beads of perspiration collected on Reginn's forehead. Most of the patrons still seemed to expect a miracle, their faces rapt and eager. A few rolled their eyes, elbowed each other, waiting like jack-als around an injured animal, ready to come in for the kill.

Where was Asger? He would find a way to get them out of this.

All she could think to do was stall for time, dig deep in her bag of remedies and tricks, and hope the fates smiled on her.

"The boy has passed nearly beyond my reach," she said. "I will sing the old songs to entice the spirits and ask for their assistance. I ask for your help, too."

A murmur of confusion rolled through the crowd.

"Will you see the boy live?" Reginn cried in a voice like a clamoring bell.

"Yes!" they shouted.

"Do any of you know the vardlokkur?"

More confusion, and then a couple of women shyly raised their hands. Women were often reluctant to admit it, for fear of being targeted as witches.

"Good," Reginn said. "You don't have to be perfect, just loud. If you don't know it all, then join in on the parts you know. The more who participate, the more likely it is that the vaettir will hear and respond."

The wyrdspinner's smile had transitioned to a puzzled frown, as if to say, *What are you up to, girl?* Once again, she closed her fist around her amulet. It glowed brighter than ever, still the color of comb honey.

Vardlokkur—the haunting songs used to summon the vaettir for aid or prophesy. Reginn hadn't heard them in so long, she wasn't sure she remembered them properly. But the big advantage, to her mind, was that they were long. Likely nobody in Langvik knew them all the way through.

And so she began, and as she did, the old songs brought with them a cascade of memories. Snuggled next to the fire in some long-forgotten town. The scent of burning peat in her nose. Her modir's hands guiding Reginn's fingers on the flute. The heartbeat of her drumming. The landscape of Tove's face in the flickering lamplight.

The absence of Asger.

Reginn's voice soared as she remembered, rising and falling as she wove her webs in the air. Other voices joined in, adding threads to the web.

Maybe she imagined it, but it seemed that the room became more crowded as shadows settled in around her. She heard the murmur of ancient voices.

Leave us be, spinner, we who have gone before you.
The Wyrdweb will not be unraveled by such as you.

Maybe I shouldn't have drunk so much ale, Reginn thought. Not to mention the mead. But performing always made her thirsty. She kept singing.

The voices came again. It wasn't so much like hearing, but more like the knowledge was soaking in through her skin or welling up from a source deep inside her.

Be patient, wandless youngling. Soon enough, you will know
what we know.
A view of the future only clouds the present.
Be careful what you ask for.

But Reginn just kept singing. The audience, the walls around her smudged, dissolved away, until she sat in the open on a high seat, surrounded by the stone ships that carried the dead to the afterlife. The midsummer daylight faded as the bloody moon rose.

Spinner! We are done with the mortal world.
We are tired and want only to return to our beds of ash and
bone.
The web is finished; it cannot be rewoven.
And now we sleep.
Leave us in peace. Do not disturb us again.

Reginn kept singing. Now shadows flew into her face, clamored in her ears, and the stench of death assailed her so that her eyes watered and she could scarcely breathe. Did that mean the doors between the worlds were opening?

Tove's words came back to her. *No matter what they say, no matter what they do, keep singing until they ask you what you want. The old songs are protection from those who would do you harm.*

Reginn kept singing, feeling like a fool. And then it came.

What is it you want, spinner?

Now, under pressure, Reginn couldn't think how to phrase the ask.

There is one among you that I would have back.
The boy, Thurston, crossed over before his time.

Back came the reply.

There is no mistake.
This is his time.
The Wyrd is the wyrd.
It is woven. It is done. Let us sleep.

Reginn resumed singing, though her throat was getting raw with the effort.

Hear me, vaettir.
The web is never really finished.
Once off the loom,
It can be stretched, or dyed,
Or fulled, or a border added.
It can be cut and sewn and shaped.
The web is not quarried stone. It breathes.

Finally, the spirits spoke once more.

If you want the boy back,
Then call him to you.
We will not stand in the way.
Now leave us in peace.

Success? Maybe.

Now she had to carry on with the game. But how to call him?

Reginn always spoke best through music. Thurston had just told her that "The Lady of the Bogland" was his favorite song. It was a song thralls had brought with them from the green lands to the west. A song older than the gods she knew. Maybe that was the key. Maybe that would call him back.

Reginn picked up her flute and began to play. Truth be told, it was one of her favorites, too—a song so sweet and pure that it still raised goose bumps every time she played it. Each note was a glittering sliver that pierced her heart.

She was so caught up in it that she didn't realize what had happened until the crowd around her sucked in its collective breath.

She looked down at Thurston and realized that his eyes were open, an expression of confusion on his face.

The flute fell from Reginn's nerveless hands, plopping onto the floor. A surge of relief all but swept her away.

It took you long enough.

"Reginn," Thurston whispered.

With that, those gathered around began to applaud, stamp their feet, and cheer.

"Thurston!" someone shouted. "Hey, Thurston. Welcome back! What's it like, being dead?"

"Get him a drink!"

"Get us all a drink and we'll have a toast."

"Stay back," Reginn ordered as they crowded in closer. "Give him some space."

"What's going on?" Thurston said, propping himself up on his elbows.

"Take it slow," Reginn said, "and see how you feel." She pressed a hand against his back to prevent him from toppling over. The warmth had returned to his body.

The blue cloak rose and swept toward them, the crowd parting like waves before the prow of a great ship.

She stood over them for a long moment, her lower lip caught behind her teeth, both hands wrapped around her staff. The glow from her pendant bronzed her face.

"Congratulations, youngling, on your journey into the realms of the dead and back again," she said to Thurston. She turned to Reginn, her expression grave. "I would speak with you, spellsinger, in the morning. Before you leave." With that, she walked toward her room, back straight, her skirts swishing. The guards left their post by the door and followed her.

How does she know this is my last night? Reginn wondered.

Why does she want to speak with me? Is she going to chastise me for being a fake or a cheat?

Yet the foretelling *was* true, in a way. Thurston *had* found his freedom in the land of the dead. Maybe she was better at this than she'd thought.

"I had the most peculiar dream," Thurston said as someone thrust a cup into his hands.

"It wasn't a dream," Reginn said. "You have been to Helgafjell and returned a free man."

5

NAME DAY

EIRIC'S NEW BRODIR WAS BORN the same night his modir warned him about Sten. When the baby was just a few hours old, he began to tremble and shake, arms and legs flailing. It lasted only a few minutes, but it was frightening.

Sylvi quickly wrapped the baby in a blanket and put him to her breast, confirming his place in the family, but the damage was done.

Sten glared at the child. "That's no child of mine," he said. "That's a fiendling or a wight."

Sylvi only hugged the baby more tightly. "He is your child, and no one else's," she said. "He will mend. It's just that he still has one foot in the other world."

In the days that followed, the shake spells continued. Sylvi tried various remedies to calm them, but nothing seemed to work.

Liv insisted on calling in Emi, a thrall in the household of Sten's fadir. Emi was a healer and midwife who claimed the gift of magic as well. Liv and Emi had been close since childhood, when their common interest in seidr—magic—brought them together. These days, the two of them were constantly scratching symbols in the dirt. It had led to trouble more than once. Knudsens did not like to see their servant engaged in activities that didn't put money in their pockets. Townspeople did not like seeing two women whispering together.

Eiric argued against calling Emi in. "Sorcery won't make Sten any smarter, but if Emi comes out here, our business will be all over town. And anyway, we can't afford it."

But Liv was smitten with anything to do with spells, runes, and incantations, so she traded the ring that had been their grandmodir's for Emi's services. The witch sang over the baby, inhaled spirits, and fed him potions from a little cup, but the episodes continued. In between, he ate and slept like any other child.

Eventually, Emi, being out of ideas, proclaimed that the baby's condition was not an illness but a blessing from the gods to be celebrated. With that declaration of victory, she departed.

Sylvi did her best to hide the baby's "blessing" from Sten, but that was hard to do because the seizures came without warning. Each time it happened, Sten became enraged, shouting, "Who's the real fadir, Sylvi, because it wasn't me!" Or to Liv: "You bewitched him, because you didn't want to share bread and board with a child of mine."

Then he would stalk out to the summer barn, where he could drink and fume undisturbed.

By law, their stepfadir had nine days to recognize and name his child. Every day, Sylvi would carry the baby to Sten and try to put him in his arms, and every, day Sten refused to accept him. Sylvi grew more and more distraught.

Eiric was perplexed. Was Sten really stupid enough to reject a baby that might give him a claim to the farm?

Yes, apparently he was.

On the eighth day, Sylvi begged Eiric to ride to the village and bring Emi back for another try. After traveling the several miles to

Selvagr in the bitter cold, he learned that Emi had left to serve as midwife for a birth on the far side of the peninsula. So there was nothing to do but ride all the way back again.

When he reached the longhouse, it was dark and cold, the fire nearly gone out. Eiric added wood to the firepit, stirring it so that sparks spiraled up toward the smoke hole. "Hello?" he said.

There was no answer.

He pushed back the curtain to his modir's sleeping bench, but she wasn't there. Neither was the baby.

"Liv?" he said. "Where is everyone?"

The house wasn't that big. It didn't take long to realize that he was alone.

Where could they be? His modir wouldn't take a newborn out on a night like this.

He stepped back outside.

"Eiric!" It was Liv, cheeks pink with cold, running toward him from the boat shed. "I fell asleep, and now I can't find Modir and the baby. Do you know where they are?"

"I hoped you would know," Eiric said.

"They could be in the summer barn with Sten," she said, pointing. Smoke was rising from the vent in the roof.

Eiric knew Liv didn't believe that–Sylvi never went into the summer barn in the wintertime, and she certainly wouldn't risk taking the baby in there.

"Go in the house and warm up," he said. "I'll be right back."

When Eiric walked into the barn, Sten was slumped on a bench by the fire, drinking ale from a wooden cup. From the looks of things, he had been there for some time. The bucket of ale he'd drawn from the barrel was nearly empty.

That was bad and good at the same time. Sten was more likely to lash out in a rage, but he'd be less likely to land a blow.

He didn't even look up when Eiric came and stood in front of him.

"Where is Modir?" Eiric demanded. "She's not in the house."

"How should I know?" Sten snarled. "She's not in here."

"The baby's gone, too, and I know she wouldn't take the baby outside," Eiric persisted.

Sten finally lifted his bleary eyes to look at him. "I gave the fiende back to the gods," he said. "He won't trouble us anymore."

Eiric felt as if the air had been squeezed from his lungs, leaving him breathless, his heart pounding. It was tradition that if a fadir didn't claim and name a baby within nine days of birth, the child could be given back to the gods. In other words, carried into the woods and left to die.

Eiric flexed his hands, wishing he could grip his stepfadir by the neck and drag him out of the barn. But he knew that would end in a fight that would take up precious time.

He ran out of the barn, back toward the house. Liv was waiting outside, a tall figure in one of Leif's old cloaks.

"I think Modir is in the woods with the baby. I'm going to go look for her."

"I'm coming, too," Liv said.

"Come on, then," Eiric said, pulling off his knit hat and pushing it down over Liv's ears.

Liv showed him where she had followed tracks a little way into the forest. Sten's large, deep tracks, going and coming. And a set of smaller, shallower tracks, leading away from the house.

They ran, ducking under low-hanging branches, their breath freezing on their faces and hair. Liv ran like a deer. Sometimes it was all Eiric could do to keep up with her, weighed down as he was with a deepening sense of dread.

They found their modir curled up under a tree, dusted with

snow. Her eyes were open, her face pale as chalk.

Liv cried out and flung herself on top of Sylvi.

Eiric knelt next to Sylvi's body, stroked her cheek, checked for breathing. There was nothing. Her skin was icy cold.

"Modir! Wake up!" Liv pleaded, brushing the snow from her hair, kissing her forehead. She pulled a feathered bone rattle from the pouch at her waist and shook it. The clatter made Eiric want to scream.

"Stop it," Eiric said, his voice thick with grief and rage. "We're too late. She won't wake up. She's gone."

"No!" Liv said fiercely.

"Liv," Eiric said. "You can't raise the dead."

"How do you know, brodir?" Liv growled. "You have no idea what I can do."

And then he heard it, faint, like the cry of a cat. Liv heard it, too, because she cocked her head, listening. She reached under their modir and pulled out a red-faced, squalling baby. Liv cradled him in her arms, wrapping him in her cloak.

Sylvi kept her baby warm, Eiric thought. She kept him alive. But how long can he live without a modir?

Liv stayed on her knees for a moment, the baby in her arms. Then she scooped up a handful of snow and sprinkled it on him.

"Liv?" Eiric said, confused. "What are you doing?"

"This is his name fastening," she said. Addressing the baby, she said, "Your name is Ivar Eiricsen. You are named for Ivar, son of Ragnar. He was a sickly child who grew up to be a great warrior." She reached out a hand to Sylvi. "This is your modir, Sylvi; I am your systir, Liv; and this is your brodir, Eiric. Welcome to the family."

She didn't mention Sten at all.

Eiric cleared his throat. "Do you think it's a good idea to—"

"This is how we keep Modir in the world," Liv said. "Ivar carries your bloodline, too."

She fished in the pocket of her gown and pulled out two small, engraved stones. Eiric recognized them as some of the weights Liv and Sylvi used to keep the warp taut on the loom. She tucked one into Ivar's blanket. "A name-fastening gift," she said. She carefully set the other stone on their modir's chest. "She will need possessions to take into the next world," she said, answering Eiric's unspoken question. "We will give her a proper funeral as soon as we—as soon as we can."

She stood, cradling Ivar, and said briskly, "Let's go back to the house."

Eiric followed Liv as she strode back the way they'd come. His mind seethed with mingled grief, anger, and worry about what would happen when Sten sobered up.

Liv had saved this baby, who posed a threat to their lives and legacy, from the fadir who'd meant to kill him. The baby that had cost them their modir.

His modir's words came back to him. *If anything happens to me, Sundgard goes to you and Liv. Don't let the Knudsens take it away from you.*

And his own response: *Nothing will happen to you.*

He recalled Sten's words when Eiric pleaded with him to help him find his modir. *She can go to the gods, too.*

In the end, it was an easy decision. *Sten wants Ivar dead. Sylvi died to save him. We honor her by making sure she didn't die in vain. We honor her when we protect each other and her legacy.*

He understood what he had to do.

When they emerged from the woods, the house was still dark, meaning Sten was probably asleep in the summer barn.

Probably.

When they passed the wood bin, Eiric scooped up another

armload of wood. "Wait here until I call you in," he said.

As he'd guessed, Sten wasn't there. Once Liv was in, Eiric dropped the crossbar into place to secure the door. He replenished the fire while Liv wrapped Ivar in a fresh blanket. Then Eiric saw to the livestock in the winter barn, making sure those doors were secure as well.

Sylvi was everywhere, and nowhere. Here was the chair by the fire where she'd knit socks for the baby and nursed him after he was born. There was the basket of unspun wool and drop spindles she'd picked up whenever she sat down.

"Is there anything you need?" Eiric said to Liv, who stood, Ivar in her arms. "Do we have anything to feed a baby?" He looked around the hall, as if something might magically appear.

"I'll thin the leftover porridge with some milk," Liv said, setting the baby down next to the fire. "It will at least fill his belly. Tomorrow I'll ride to the village. Hilde Stevenson just lost a baby. She might be willing to nurse him."

Liv reheated the porridge that Sylvi had made that morning while Eiric fetched cups of Sylvi's fruit wine. They ate quickly, huddled together by the longfire, the warmest place in the longhouse.

Eiric dug beneath his sleeping bench and pulled out the axe his grandfadir had left him, followed by the sword that had been his fadir's. On his deathbed, Leif had asked for his sword. When Eiric brought it to him, he said, *This sword is Gramr—given by Odin, won by Sigurth, mended by Regin of the dwarves, and used by Sigurd to slay the dragon Fafnir. Now it is yours. It brings good fortune to those who honor the gods.*

He looked up to find Liv watching him from her bench against the opposite wall, Ivar tucked in the crook of her arm as she spooned porridge into him.

Eiric sat back on his heels. "Sten has to go. When he finds out that Modir is dead, he'll kill both of us and claim the farm. There's no one but us to stop him."

Their eyes met for a long moment. "Heill, brodir," she said. "This is not a good day to die."

"I did not choose the day," Eiric said. He rolled up in his blanket on the threshold, his sword and axe to either side.

Somehow, he slept.

6

RED, RED WINE

AFTER THURSTON'S REVIVAL, THE HALL was swept up in a frenzy of celebration. Gunnar tried to join in, but anyone could tell his heart wasn't in it.

Business was good, as usual after a resurrection. Reginn sold out of her remedies, runesticks, herb bundles, talismans, and simples. She was besieged with requests for readings and healings, all of which she declined. She was done for the day—exhausted from drink, or drama, or from grappling with the vaettir, the spirits of the dead.

Thurston took some of his saved-up silver and bought a round of drinks for everyone. That did not diminish his popularity one bit. But when asked to tell, and retell, what had happened, he had next to nothing to say.

It was only when people asked what had caused his untimely death that he averted his eyes and said he didn't know. It was an obvious tell for a lie—obvious to Reginn, anyway, but the non-answer seemed to satisfy the patrons at Gunnar's Hall.

Gunnar kept the hall open until business dwindled to a trickle, undoubtedly trying to recover some of what he'd lost that night. Thurston returned to his post at the washtub, finishing up his chores without complaint.

This seemed to spark some hope in the hallkeeper that Thurston might want to stay in bondage awhile longer. For old times' sake, maybe.

"You know, Thurston, I've always looked on you like a son, having none of my own," Gunnar said. "People say I saved your life, buying you off the wharf as I did, nursing you back to health, and so on. I removed your collar while Reginn worked on you 'cause the spirits won't intervene on behalf of a thrall. But that doesn't have to change things between us. How would you like to stay on here, doing honest work and being assured of a roof over your head and plenty to eat?"

Thurston stopped scrubbing. He looked at Gunnar. "Are you suggesting that I put the collar back on?"

"Well—ah—yes, since I'd want people to know you are under my protection and that you belong here to the—to the inn."

"Thank you, sir, for the kind offer, but I'll be leaving in the morning," Thurston said. "I did not come back from the dead to live enslaved. There are so many places in the world that I want to go and other trades I would like to try my hand at beyond washing dishes and clearing tables."

Gunnar scowled. "Very well. Finish up here tonight, boy, and you can leave in the morning, if that's your choice. Mind, don't be taking more than the one suit of clothes."

"I only have one suit of clothes," Thurston murmured.

"And don't be crawling back to me in a few months, begging for a second chance," Gunnar said. With that, the hallkeeper retreated to his quarters behind the kitchen hearth.

For a long moment, Reginn and Thurston stood looking at each other, waiting to make sure the hallkeeper was really gone.

Then Thurston tossed his washrag aside and fell to his knees before Reginn. "Gracious lady. There's no way to repay you for all you've done for me," he said. "We're practically strangers, and yet, in one evening, you saved my life and then made that life worth living by making me a free man."

"I . . . saved your life," Reginn said, shaking her head. "No. That's not possible. Now get up and tell me what really happened."

Thurston blinked at her like a redheaded owl. Slowly, he got to his feet, his cheeks pinking up. "I don't know what you—"

"You really gave me a scare," Reginn said. "I assume that Asger put you up to this?"

Thurston wrinkled his brow. "Who's Asger?"

"Well, I don't know what name he would have used with you," Reginn said. "But he's the one would have given you the runestone."

"What is a runestone?"

"You know. The thorn of sleep." When Thurston's lost expression didn't change, Reginn plowed on. "You'd remember Asger, even if he didn't give his name. He can take on whatever look he likes, but his skin is so thin, you can see the bones through it, and he has eyes the color of red amber from under the sea. He's sleek as a ferret, quiet as a whisper, and his hands—his hands—they—"

She stopped when she realized she was giving a child's description of a monster.

Thurston stood, hands on hips, head cocked to one side. "I never saw the man you describe," he said. "I don't know what you're talking about. Nobody gave me any stone."

"But . . . he must have." Reginn rubbed her aching forehead. None of this was making sense. Unless—it was some kind of trick. One of Asger's tests of loyalty.

"Did Asger tell you to pretend you never met him, and he never gave you the runestone, and that I really brought you back from the dead, and—and—"

Somehow, she found herself gripping Thurston by the front of his tunic, glaring into his startled face.

She was trembling—she couldn't help it—and it was only her grip on Thurston's shirt that was keeping her upright.

"Reginn," he said softly. "Do I seem like the kind of person who could pull that off?"

She took a deep breath, and then another. When she let go of his shirt, he took hold of her elbow and guided her to a bench. "No," she said, sitting. "I suppose not."

"Can I get you anything to drink? To eat?" he said.

"No," she said. "I—I've probably had too much ale as it is."

He sat down next to her. "You must be worn out," he said.

"You say it wasn't a runestone," Reginn said, back on topic. "What was it, then, that put you on your back?"

Thurston looked down at his hands, then picked at a scab on his thumb. "I'm embarrassed to tell you," he said. "It was all my fault. I should have known better. I'm sorry I put everyone through that, even though it all came out well in the end."

"How was it your fault?" Reginn said, on firmer ground now that Thurston was on the defensive.

"It's just—I never tasted wine before," he said, his cheeks stained pink with embarrassment. "I'm not a thief. I didn't figure it to be stealing because they said to go ahead and clear the table, even though the one cup was still full."

Prying a story out of Thurston was like pulling a crab out of a snail shell—all but impossible.

"The only food or drink I had all night was when you and me sat down together," he went on. "I figured since she didn't want it, it wouldn't do any harm just to taste it."

All at once the puzzle pieces snapped into place. "You're talking about the blue cloaks' wine."

He nodded. "Once I started, I ended up drinking the whole cup. I didn't mean to, but that's what I did. People talk about the mead of poetry—I think it must have tasted something like that." Thurston smiled a dreamy smile, his eyes focused on something far away. "I went numb all over. I remember hearing a thunk as the cup hit the floor, and then I went down. I don't remember anything after that until I heard you playing 'Lady of the Bogland.'"

"Are you saying the wine was poisoned?"

"Maybe. It didn't taste off, if that's what you mean. Anyway, they brought their own wine, so how could it be poisoned?" He shook his head. "No. More likely it was because it was magicked. Meant for spinners. Too fine for my sort."

"Hmm," Reginn said, unconvinced. "Let me see your shirt again."

Thurston stood, shifting from foot to foot while she ran her fingers over the red splatters on the front of his tunic. Wine, it looked like. Wine the color of garnets. She sniffed. Wine the color of garnets that smelled of cherries. There was no taint of any of the poisons that she knew.

Had there been something in the wine that mimicked the death sleep of Svefnthorn? Something that had worn off on its own?

"Where's the cup?" Reginn said. "Is there any wine left in it?"

He shook his head. "Most of it spilled on the floor when I fell. After I woke up, I went ahead and washed the cup. I was—I was ashamed of what I'd done, and I didn't want anyone else to get into it."

He took a breath, then said, "Now. I've answered your questions. Will you answer one of mine?"

"Depends," Reginn said, knowing what was coming.

"Who is Asger, and what was the plan you keep talking about?"

"That's two questions," she said.

"Answer the first one, then."

"Look," she said. "I don't owe you any answers, but here's one." She opened the neckline of her tunic to display the thrall collar beneath.

Thurston gaped at it, and no wonder. It was likely the finest thrall collar ever made—of fine gold, inset with fire agates and rubies.

"What is that?" he whispered.

"I would think that you, of all people, would recognize it."

"You're a thrall?" The disappointment in his eyes all but broke her heart.

"I am, and Asger is my demanding master. You know the rules. There is nothing to be done."

"You . . . freed me," he said. "And then saved my life. And yet you remain enslaved?"

"At last, the boy understands," Reginn said, rolling her eyes. "That, it seems, is what the fates decreed for me."

Thurston bit his lower lip and said, "I'll offer him a trade—me for you."

"No," Reginn said.

"He'd have to take it," Thurston said. "I'm big; I'm strong; I'm a hard worker."

"I promise you, Thurston, he will not make that trade, but he *will* kill you for offering."

"What kind of a monster is he?" Thurston said.

"Not the kind of monster you want to tangle with," Reginn said. "The best advice I can give you is to leave right away and put as many miles between us as you can." When he still didn't move, she added, "Thurston, I've done a lot of bad things in my life, and not many good ones. Freeing you was a good thing. Don't ruin it by getting yourself killed."

"So it's goodbye, then."

She nodded. "It is." She stood.

He stood, too. "Why are you so scared of him?"

"Let it go," Reginn said. "Good night."

7

A GOOD DAY TO DIE

EIRIC AWOKE TO A POUNDING on the door. He sat up slowly, realizing that he was still holding on to his weapons. He looked for Liv. She was standing next to the firepit, rocking from foot to foot, their baby brodir in her arms. He could see her eyes glittering in the firelight.

"Sylvi!" Sten shouted. "Open up the door!"

Eiric slid his feet into the shoes that Sylvi had made for him and stood. Assessing his weapons, he put the sword Gramr aside and picked up the axe. Liv laid the baby in their modir's bed and scooped up the staff Bjorn had left to her.

"Sylvi!" Sten pounded again. "Don't you lock this door against me or it'll be the worse for you."

Liv strode to the center of the room, staff in hand. Pointing at Eiric, she put her finger to her lips.

"Go away, Knudsen," Liv said. "Leave Sundgard and never come back."

"I'm not talking to you, girl," Sten said.

"You have no place here," Liv said. "Go back to Selvagr."

"Let me speak to Sylvi." Sten pounded again. "Sylvi! We'll make more babies, wait and see." He paused, and when there was no response, said, "I'll break the door down if I have to."

"Sylvi is dead," Liv retorted.

This stopped the conversation for a long moment.

"Don't lie to me," Sten said finally.

"She's dead, and it's your fault, you dung-eating . . . troll." Liv was usually good with words, but she seemed to be having trouble coming up with something foul enough. She closed her eyes, smacked the butt of the staff into the dirt floor, and murmured under her breath.

"You're the monster, witch girl," Sten snarled. "Your face would turn a man to stone. Always whispering and giving me the evil eye. I'm thinking you're the one that ruined that child."

"I don't care what you're thinking," Liv said. "My modir is dead, and you are trespassing. You need to leave right now."

"She's not even your modir," Sten said. "Sylvi never should have taken you in."

"I was about to say the same of you," Liv said.

This generated another frenzy of pounding. Maybe Sten's fist was getting sore because it finally slowed, then stopped.

"If Sylvi's dead, then let me in to see the body," Sten said, his tone shifting to conciliatory. "If it's true, then I'll go."

"Sylvi's in the woods, where you left her baby," Liv said. "You'll have to go look for her there."

"Where's the boy?"

"He's in the woods waiting for you," Liv shot back.

Perhaps prompted by all the shouting, Ivar chose that particular time to begin to wail, a high, desperate cry.

With a roar, Sten threw himself against the door so hard that it shook, rattling the crossbar. "You have that fiendling in there, don't you? And I'll bet Sylvi is hiding in there, too. Open this door, or I'll burn this place down around you."

"You do that, and I'll see to it that you burn for the rest of your days," Liv said.

It was hard to tell whether Sten believed that, but Eiric heard his footsteps walking away and then returning. Something slammed into the door, cracking it and sending splinters flying.

Sten had fetched the axe from the woodpile. It wouldn't take long for him to get through the wood.

Liv stood in center of the room, staff in hand, so that she would be the first thing Sten would see. She nodded at Eiric, and he stepped to one side, waiting for Sten's grand entrance.

Each time the axe crunched into the door, the crack grew wider. Now Eiric could hear Sten's labored breathing as he swung the blade, his growled curses. Ivar wailed and wailed.

Eiric gripped his axe as rage boiled up inside him. Life at Sundgard had been hard before Sten's arrival, but at least they could count on each other. Now their losses were mounting with no end in sight. It was all Sten's fault.

By now, Sten had opened a sizable hole and was working on enlarging it until he could get through.

"I'm warning you," Liv said, pointing her staff at him. "Don't come in here."

Sten put his shoulder to the door one last time, and it exploded inward, sending him staggering toward Liv. When he'd regained his footing, he fixed on her and raised his axe.

Eiric could tell Liv was scared, but she spread her arms, raising the staff, and he would have sworn that flame flickered over her skin, sending sparks up toward the ceiling. Light flooded into every corner of the room.

No, Eiric thought. That's impossible.

Sten backed away, his axe held loose in his hands, his eyes as big as the haymaking moon.

"Don't. Try. Me," Liv said, in a voice that rang like a bell.

All at once, Ivar stopped crying.

The sudden silence pressed in on Eiric, raising gooseflesh on his arms.

Sten gathered courage from somewhere, took a step toward Liv, and raised his axe again. "I'm finally going to cleanse this farm of Halvorsen's litter of demons and vermin," he said, "beginning with you."

"Actually," Eiric said, "you'll have to begin with me."

This caught Sten mid-lunge, and he all but stumbled in his efforts to change direction. Eiric swung his axe two-handed at his stepfadir, aiming for his head, but the blade glanced off Sten's shoulder blade instead, leaving a deep gash but doing little other damage.

It didn't slow him down much, either. While Eiric was off balance, Sten swung at him, failing in an attempt to cut off Eiric's arm, but cleaving skin and muscle under his rib cage.

They faced off again, both bleeding. Sylvi's words echoed in Eiric's head. *He is still stronger than you, and a more experienced fighter.*

"So, boy," Sten said, with a satisfied smirk. "It's about time. I was beginning to think your modir had gelded you and you would never grow to be a man."

He's trying to make you angry, Eiric thought, so that you make a mistake. Well, two can play at that game.

"And I thought you were going to leech off your wife and her children forever," Eiric said. "What kind of a man does that?"

"This is my farm. Mine."

"Maybe you should have settled that with Sylvi before you married her," Eiric said.

Sten's eyes narrowed and his ears turned red, signaling the rage building in him.

Liv was edging along the wall toward the door. Anyone else would think she was making a run for it, but Eiric knew she was going after the sword, still lying where he'd left it.

Eiric needed to keep Sten busy so he wouldn't notice. "Look, Knudsen, you haven't lifted a hand since you moved in."

"Why should I put work into a farm that isn't mine?" Sten said.

"So you admit that it doesn't belong to you," Eiric said.

"I admit nothing!" Sten shouted, and surged forward. His axe whistled past Eiric's head, nicking his ear and slicing off hair as he spun away, spraying droplets of blood in a wide circle. Eiric buried his axe in the back of Sten's thigh, wrenched it free, then danced sideways, away from the door.

Sten howled and charged at Eiric like a wounded bull. He swung the wood axe, meaning to take Eiric's arm at the shoulder. Instead, the blade slashed along the length of it, from his biceps to his wrist. The wound immediately began spurting blood, making it difficult for Eiric to maintain his grip as his axe grew slippery with it. Even more worrisome was the fact that his hand was not responding as it should. It was his weaker hand, but he was no longer confident that he could manage a two-handed stroke.

Eiric realized his mistake. Sten had had all night to sober up. Eiric wasn't used to fighting his stepfadir when he was sober.

Sten came on, smelling victory, and Eiric retreated until he somehow stumbled over a beer bucket and went down on his back, sending his battle-axe flying across the room.

He scrambled to his feet and backed away as Sten advanced, looming over him like a jotun—a monster out of Bjorn's stories. Eiric drew his knife, a laughable weapon against Sten's longer reach and better weapon. When Eiric came up against the wall of the winter barn, he knew it was over.

Sten grinned and raised his axe, savoring the moment. "I've been waiting for this for a long time, boy."

His eyes widened and his mouth gaped, his expression one of hurt confusion as the tip of a sword protruded from his chest. The axe slipped from his fingers as he grabbed for the blade, cutting his hands in the process. Blood bubbled from his mouth. Finally, he sprawled forward, facedown in the dirt, propped up a bit by the steel blade.

Cheeks flushed, Liv planted her foot on Sten's buttocks and yanked Gramr free, landing on her own backside.

Eiric stepped over Sten's body and extended his good hand to help his systir up. "Well done, systir," he said. "Under the rib cage and up through the—"

"Just shut up," Liv said. She was shaking, her teeth chattering. She leaned against Eiric as if to keep from toppling over.

For a few long moments, they clung together, breathing hard, both blood-spattered survivors.

Finally, Liv pulled back. "I was wrong, brodir," she said. "This *is* a good day to die—for Sten Knudsen."

"Yes," Eiric said, head swimming from his dance with death and loss of blood.

"Now," she said, "you've fed enough blood to the gods of battle. I need to bind you up before you join Sten in the afterlands."

8

LIMITED-TIME OFFER

THE NEXT MORNING, REGINN WAS in no hurry to leave her bed in the loft over the alehall. She needed time to think. She also hoped to give Thurston time to be on his way before she made an appearance.

Gunnar was up earlier than she'd ever seen him, moving slow, muttering about ungrateful servants and treacherous witches, commentary no doubt intended for Reginn's ears. He replenished the fire and put the porridge on, then sat down by the longfire and promptly fell sound asleep.

Soon after, Thurston emerged from his cramped quarters in the shed, carrying a haversack. He must have seen Gunnar sleeping by the fire because he moved soft footed. He peered at the porridge, gave it a stir, thrust a few pieces of dried fish and day-old bread into his sack, and heaved it onto his back. He walked purposefully to the door, then turned and looked straight up at Reginn's loft. He lifted a hand in farewell, then walked out the door.

"Safe travels and good fortune, Thurston," Reginn murmured, relief and regret warring inside her. Knowing that he was someone who might have been a friend.

Brushing that aside, she studied what to do if Asger didn't show up that day.

She knew better than to show herself on the streets of Langvik. She'd be assailed by every grief-stricken widow and parent in town, wanting her to reassemble their loved ones out of ashes and bone. She never felt more like a fraud than when she had little ones tugging at her skirts, offering their pitiful treasures in their grubby hands, crying, "Laeknir! Heal my brodir," or "Please, bring my modir home!"

Reginn was fresh out of miracles and running low on remedies. She needed to replenish her supply of talismans, herbs, and tonics. She'd seen some likely looking upland meadows and ravines on her way into town that might provide some of what she needed. And, surely, by the end of the day, Asger would come.

Unless he's dead.

She smothered that spark of hope before it could grow into a flame.

Just then, the two blue cloaks emerged from their rooms at the back, trailed by their guards, their liveried servant carrying their bags. The keeper followed the servant out the door, while the younger woman spoke to Gunnar. He pointed up at the loft.

"Spellsinger," the spinner called, looking up at Reginn's hiding place. "A moment of your time, please."

That's when Reginn remembered that the blue cloak had asked to speak with her this morning.

Reginn was in no mood for a lecture from a wyrdspinner or anyone else. But there seemed to be no way around it.

"I'll be down in a minute," she said. She loosed her tangled hair, combed it with her fingers, and rebraided it. She pulled her dress over her chemise, then yanked on her stockings and shoes.

When Reginn reached the bottom of the ladder, she saw that

the blue cloak had taken a table in the farthest corner. The spinner motioned for her to sit down opposite her. With the spinner's hood pushed down, Reginn could see that her hair was mingled colors of amber, copper, and bronze, drawn into a twist low on her neck.

"I'm Modir Tyra," she said. "Headmistress at the Academy at the Grove. What's your name?"

"Reginn Eiklund," Reginn said, resisting the temptation to add *spellsinger of the Archipelago* or *speaker to the dead*.

"Eiklund," Modir Tyra said, brow furrowed. "That means 'of the oak grove.'"

"My adoptive modir always told me that she found me in a forest," Reginn said.

"Really?" Tyra's expression said that she wasn't sure whether to believe it or not.

Deciding that a preemptive strike might be in order, Reginn said, "Look, if this is about last night, I didn't mean to be rude. It's just that I–"

The headmistress raised her hand to stop the speech. "It's not important, youngling. You were worried about your friend. And much as I hate to admit it, you succeeded where I would have failed."

Reginn considered this. "Well, maybe so."

"And in the process, you have opened my eyes to new possibilities." She paused, as if expecting Reginn to say, *Such as?*

When Reginn didn't, she continued on anyway.

"That is why I wanted to speak with you. We–the keeper and I–believe that you have a rare gift. A very old magic. Do you know anything about your lineage?"

"My lineage?" Reginn repeated stupidly.

"Sometimes these gifts run in families," Modir Tyra said.

"Well," Reginn said, "I guess I come from the kind of people who would leave a baby in the woods."

Tyra laughed. "There are plenty of those kinds of people here in the Archipelago," she said. "We are wondering where you received your training. Clearly you've had instruction in the use of herbs and healing agents. You play the flute beautifully, and your voice is a spell in itself. Who taught you?"

Reginn tried to think how to make her "training" sound more like something and less like nothing. "I suppose you could say that I served an apprenticeship. I received much of my training from my foster modir."

"Ah," Tyra said, nodding. "The one who found you in the forest?"

Reginn studied the headmistress's face for any sign that she was making fun of her. Seeing none, she nodded.

"So your foster modir was gifted as well."

"A little, I suppose," Reginn said.

"Where is she now?"

Well, that's a good question, Reginn thought. You're the famous seeress—you tell me.

"I haven't seen her since I was seven."

"Oh!" Tyra studied her, eyes narrowed, as if she could see through Reginn's skin. Then said softly, "Is she the one who sold you into bondage?"

Reginn stared at her, open-mouthed. There was no need to feel for her slave collar and make sure it was still concealed under the neckline of her underdress. She was absolutely sure that it was.

A shiv to the heart, and Reginn hadn't seen it coming.

How does she know? she thought. And then answered her own question. She's a spakona, stupid—a seer. Probably saw it in my aura or something.

"Look," Reginn said, "I said I was sorry for being rude, and we agree that it's good that Thurston survived. I have things to do, and

I'm sure that you do, too. I think we're done here."

Reginn shoved her chair back but, quick as thought, Modir Tyra reached out and pinned her hand to the table. She looked soft, but she was surprisingly strong.

"Let go of me," Reginn said, her voice low and dangerous, her other hand finding the knife at her belt. Shiv for a shiv.

"Give me a few more minutes," Tyra said, releasing her hand, "and then we can go our separate ways if you so choose."

Reginn leaned toward the spinner and said, "I'm not going to sit here and be picked apart by you. I am not one of your students."

"No, you are not," Modir Tyra said, "but you could be."

For a long moment, Reginn sat, ambushed into silence. "Wh–what do you mean?"

"The keeper and I are inviting you to join us at the Temple at the Grove, to study alongside some of the most brilliant and gifted students in the known world." The spinner sat back, resting the heels of her hands on the table and smiling as if she'd presented Reginn with a gift.

Reginn had learned that presents can be used in lots of ways–to entice, to distract, and to ask forgiveness for the unforgivable. In Reginn's experience, presents always came with strings attached.

"Where is it?"

"Where is what?" Tyra said, looking confused. Clearly this was not the enthusiastic reaction she'd been looking for.

"The Grove. The academy. Is it very far?"

"It's on the island of Eimyrja, across the strait from Vigrid, the site of the final battle."

Vigrid. That sounded vaguely familiar. "What battle?"

"Ragnarok–the war between the gods and the jotun. We keep watch over the graves of the fallen."

That didn't sound enticing.

People still sometimes called on the old gods, and built altars to them, and swore by them, but as far as Reginn knew, the old gods had never lifted a hand to help her.

Maybe because, as Tyra said, they were dead.

"We have built a world in which magic is celebrated and the natural world is cherished and protected. We call it New Jotunheim."

"Jotunheim?" Reginn didn't even try to hide her surprise.

Tyra laughed at her expression. "Why would we name our paradise after the land of savages and beasts—the former hunting ground of the gods, where they went to kill the jotnar and carry off women?"

Reginn nodded wordlessly.

"History is handed down by the victors," Modir Tyra said. "It's no wonder that it's biased. Odin Allfadir dabbled in magic, but he only used it to fuel his pointless squabbles with the other gods, to trick the jotnar, to seduce women, and to build up his armies in Valhalla. The end result was Ragnarok, the destruction of all of the gods, leaving humans to fend for themselves in a world ravaged by their excesses."

Tyra stopped, took a breath, seeming to realize that the conversation had taken a turn. "Don't misunderstand the role of the Grove. We are not a monument; we are not priests or worshippers; we are practitioners—the living repository of magic. These days, most of our students come to us as babies. Their gifts are varied in strength, breadth, and purpose and manifest as they grow older. We nurture those gifts."

"Why choose me?" Reginn said.

"We have no one like you, Reginn Eiklund," Tyra said bluntly. "But it's more than that. It's personal for me. Like you, I was older when I came to the Grove. I know what it's like to be betrayed by those closest to you. That is why, despite your age, we would be pleased to have you join us."

Despite your age. Meaning that she'd be in with a bunch of students who'd been together since they were toddlers. Who had a fifteen-year head start on her when it came to whatever they were teaching at this school. The notion of being the stupid one in class was not appealing at all.

She could read and write the runes of magic, at least, something few could claim. Runes had a higher purpose than taking notes or proving to somebody else that you knew something.

She was smart—or, if not smart, clever, which was often just as good and sometimes better.

Reginn felt like every part of her was at war with the others. Her stomach churned; her mind swarmed with worries and possibilities.

She was not used to following rules, beyond the few ironclad rules that Asger had laid down. Neither was she good at keeping to any kind of schedule, because she'd never had a schedule to keep beyond *Be at the alehall in time for the nattmal.*

Asger had handled most everything else. This was the longest she'd been away from him since he'd come into her life, and she felt better, stronger than she had in a long time. It was as if her confidence and power had grown in his absence.

What if this was the way out she'd been looking for? This might be the only opportunity she'd ever have to do something different with her life.

She'd never stayed in one place for a month, let alone a year.

Her first instinct was to say no and be done with it—so she could stop grappling with mingled terror and hope.

That's the coward's way out. Don't close this door without thinking things through.

"I—I don't know what to say," Reginn managed. "It's a great honor to be asked, for sure. Could I have some time to think about it?"

Tyra nodded briskly. "Yes, but don't delay too long. The keeper is already aboard our ship, and I'm going there myself. We will sail before dawn tomorrow, when the tides are in our favor. You'll need to give me an answer before then. Come to our ship."

She stood, took a step toward the door.

"Wait," Reginn said.

The spinner turned back.

"The thing is, I'm concerned about my master. What he'll do if I leave."

"The temple would be more than willing to pay your redemption price so that you are free to accept this opportunity."

"He won't take it," Reginn blurted. "He won't make any kind of deal with you."

Modir Tyra appraised her. "Given the right offer, I'm sure he will. If he refuses, I can guarantee you one thing—he will never find you where we're going."

With that, she picked up her carry bag and was out the door.

9

BLOOD FEUD

LIV WRAPPED EIRIC'S WOUNDS IN linen, managing to stop the bleeding, but she continued to fuss over his left arm, the one Sten had slashed to the bone.

"This isn't right," she said. "You need a healer with more experience."

"It's fine," Eiric said, attempting to demonstrate by making a fist. He failed. "What I mean is, it will be fine once it heals."

"It's not fine. And given your habit of getting into fights, you're going to need two working arms. If you end up crippled, I'm the one who's going to have to listen to your whining. You'll be the one getting drunk in the summer barn."

Eiric knew better than to argue. So he led out two of their best horses (the second was for Hilde Stevenson, the wet nurse, if she could be persuaded to come back to Sundgard). He discovered that saddling a horse was all but impossible with only one functioning arm, so Liv had to do most of it while he held the baby.

Liv mounted, and Eiric handed Ivar up to her. It was still brutally cold, so she carried him in a sling underneath her warmest cloak.

The trip to town was risky for several reasons. Knudsens aside, Liv had long been a target, due to her scarred face, sharp tongue,

unusual height, and now her connection with Emi. Seers and healers had once been respected in the Archipelago, but in hard times,
people looked for someone to blame.

When Liv was still small, Leif had interrupted a pack of boys
attacking her at the market with sticks and stones. Leif beat several
of them within an inch of their lives before they could escape.
That story kept hecklers away for years after.

But Leif was long gone.

"Be careful," Eiric said. "You don't know who might be waiting
between here and Selvagr. Times are hard."

Liv leaned down from her horse so that she could put her hand
on Eiric's shoulder. "Mind, brodir, with me in the village, Sten's
brodirs might decide that this is a good time to come after you."

"I'll be careful," he said, though to be honest, he was not in the
mood. "While you're gone, I'll prepare Modir to travel to the next
world."

"If everything is ready before I return, go ahead and light the
pyre," Liv said. "I'll watch for the smoke from the harbor so I know
when she's safely away."

"If that's what you want," Eiric said.

Liv gave him a long look, then turned her horse's head toward the
village and dug in her heels. Eiric watched until she was out of sight.

After Liv left, Eiric spent the rest of the day clearing the battlefield. He rolled Sten's body onto a length of sailcloth and dragged
it far into the forest. There he dropped it into a fissure so deep
that no one would find it but the worms and beetles. He rinsed
his battle-axe and sword in the spring, oiled the blades, and leaned
them against the wall next to the door, in easy reach.

The entire time, he struggled with his injured arm. His arm was
still strong enough to support a heavy load, but his hand was numb,
and he didn't have the dexterity in his fingers that he'd had before.

Maybe it would just take time.

He carried stones to a spot overlooking the sound where his modir liked to sit on summer days, spinning wool and watching the ebb and flow of the tides. It was also a good vantage point from which to watch the path along the shore that led from the village or the boats that rounded the headland. He swept the snow away, then laid the stones out in a rough outline–the outline of a boat half the size of his little karvi.

He returned to the site where Sylvi had died. She lay stiff and frozen. He carried her back to the gravesite, setting her down gently at the center. She wore no jewelry–her hands had been so swollen from the pregnancy that she'd removed her rings months ago. Where would they be?

Then he recalled what she'd said on the night Ivar was born. *There's a stone set into the floor under my sleeping bench. You'll find a small chest underneath.*

Eiric walked back to the house and knelt before the bed that still carried his modir's scent. When he groped underneath, his fingers found the outlines of a large, square stone just under the dirt. Using a pry bar from the barn, he managed to lift it up and set it aside.

In the hollow below, he found a small, elaborately decorated chest made of bronze inlaid with silver. Fantastic creatures, ships, and unfamiliar landscapes were etched into its surface.

The chest was locked, but he broke the clasp with the tip of his knife and lifted the lid.

Inside he found some familiar pieces–the armband Sylvi had been married in, her amber necklace, two oval brooches, and several rings in silver and gold.

He chose a ring and a brooch his modir favored, then set out her other fancy pieces on her sleeping bench. He'd offer them to Liv when she came back, then sell what she didn't want.

As he went to close the lid, he realized that the box seemed too heavy to be empty. When he shook it, it rattled. He measured the distance between the inside and the outside with his fingers and realized that there must be a hidden space or compartment inside.

After several minutes of poking and probing he heard a snap, and the floor of the chest popped out to reveal a space underneath.

Inside were two items he didn't recognize at first. One was a pendant cast in gold and silver and set with amber—a figurine the size of his palm, which looked to be one of the old goddesses. Familiar.

Then he remembered. It was the amulet Liv had been wearing when she came to Sundgard. The pendant Sylvi had taken away from her. When he went to pick it up, it scorched his hand, startling him so that he nearly dropped it. Holding it by its chain, he carefully set it back into the compartment.

The other was a leather pouch. Inside was an oblong crystalline stone on a gold chain. Another pendant? It looked too large and heavy for comfortable wear. He fingered the rough surface, turning it this way and that. A thick gold bail secured the chain to the stone. A red stone had been set into the other end, resembling a drop of blood.

It was the sunstone Sylvi had taken from Bjorn more than ten years ago.

When he brought it close to the fire, he could make out faint runes etched into the gold. When he ran his fingers over the engraving, a voice whispered, *Come back to me.*

An old hunger kindled inside him, a wistful longing for new horizons and faraway places.

Then he remembered the oath he had sworn to his modir.

Swear to me, Eiric Halvorsen, that you will return the rest to the barrow and never speak of it again.

It was never wise to break an oath to the dead.

Eiric stuffed the stone back into the pouch, put it back into the compartment, and closed the chest. He set it back into the niche and covered it with the stone, wondering if he was doing the right thing. Wondering if he should return Liv's necklace to her.

The oath hung heavy around his own neck.

Back at the gravesite, Eiric put the jewelry beside Sylvi's body and covered her with her favorite blanket—the one she'd woven of flax from their fields and wool from their sheep. He set the two loom weights Liv had contributed on top. Then it was back and forth to the woodpile, carrying kindling as well as the split logs he'd hauled out of the woods not even a fortnight ago. Carefully, he stacked the wood around his modir's body until it was totally enclosed.

By then, the wound in his side had broken open again, and new blood seeped through the bandages. Every part of him hurt. Still, Liv's words resonated.

If everything is ready before I return, go ahead and light the pyre.

He knew what had gone unsaid. *Act now. Don't wait. The web of our lives may ravel out at any time.* The past few days had proven that.

He pulled his flint and strike-steel from his carry bag and nestled touchwood into the crevices in the pyre. He struck steel to stone, kindling the touchwood on the first try. He lit the wood in several different places. Before long, smoke rose high into the sky.

"Be at peace, Modir," Eiric whispered, guilt like a stone in his gut. "You deserved a better son."

As he turned away, he spotted two horsemen approaching along the coast trail, riding hard. Though they were still too far away for Eiric to make out their features, he knew in his bones that it was his uncles, Finni and Garth, come to check out the situation at the farm. And to take action if it wasn't to their liking.

By the time Sten's kinsmen rode into the home yard, Eiric stood in the doorway of the longhouse, his axe in his hands, his sword leaning against the wall. He'd positioned himself so that his injured arm would be less noticeable.

They dismounted, tied their horses to the corral fence, and walked toward the house. By now, the winter sun had dropped behind the house, putting the doorway in shadow, so they didn't see Eiric at first. They were almost upon him when he spoke.

"Greetings, Uncles," he said. "Have you come to pay your respects to my modir?"

They jumped, visibly startled, and took two steps back.

"She's up yonder," Eiric said, pointing to the plume of smoke on the headland.

They stole a quick look at the pyre, then focused back on Eiric, taking in the blood-soaked linen wrapping his middle, his bandaged arm, the blood spatter covering his clothing. He'd cleaned up the battlefield, but he hadn't spent any time on himself.

"Boy," Finni said finally. His stepfadir and his uncles always called him "boy" as if he could be diminished with a word. "What's all this?"

Eiric had decided that in this case, the less information, the better. "Sylvi froze to death in the woods."

They both stared at Eiric, temporarily speechless, as if they didn't know what accusation to make.

"Where is Sten?" Garth said. "We would like to offer our condolences."

"You can offer your condolences to me, Uncle. I am the only one here in need of them."

Finni and Garth looked at each other. "What do you mean?" Finni said. "Where is Sten?"

"Why are you covered in blood, boy?" Garth growled. "What have you done?"

"What I had to do," Eiric said. "Sten tried to kill me. He failed." He'd decided to leave Liv out of it entirely.

"I don't believe you," Finni said.

"Really?" Eiric said. "I heard that you and Sten discussed the plan weeks ago."

The expression on Finni's face told him everything he needed to know.

Now Garth weighed in. "What my brodir means is that if Sten set out to kill you, then you would be dead."

"I'm not dead," Eiric pointed out, in case they'd overlooked it.

"Not yet," Garth said.

"We'll just take a look for ourselves," Finni said, striding forward.

Eiric raised his axe, and Finni stopped just out of arm's reach. "No," Eiric said. "You won't. I wish I could offer you hospitality, but we welcomed Sten in, and that was a mistake. My modir burns on the headland because of him."

"You cannot keep us from looking for our brodir," Garth said.

"You can look for Sten all you like. Just not here."

"You won't get away with this," Garth said. "We'll burn you out and salt your crops, and—"

Finni already had him by the arm, pulling him away. "Let it go, brodir. We'll talk to Fadir, and he'll bring the boy before the Thing."

"That's three months away!" Garth said.

"We can wait," Finni said. "This farm isn't going anywhere." He turned back toward Eiric. "Enjoy these next three months," he said. "The council will name you vargr—outlaw—and then we will hunt you down."

10

HEROES AND VILLAINS

AFTER THE WYRDSPINNER LEFT GUNNAR'S Hall, Reginn huddled by the hearth under the innkeeper's poisonous glare. She was afraid to leave for fear Asger would show up and find her missing. By late morning, when he still hadn't come, she asked Gunnar if she could stay until her master came to claim her.

"Take your belongings and get out, witch," Gunnar growled. "You've cost me enough already."

"I can pay," she said. She had silver in her pocket for a change, since she'd done well at Gunnar's and Asger hadn't shown up to take it from her.

Yet.

"Get out before I throw you out," Gunnar said.

It didn't make sense because, as far as Reginn knew, he had no more thralls to lose.

Reginn spent the daylight hours hiding out farther up the shoreline, in the forests and meadows she'd spotted earlier. There she was able to gather henbane, poppy, butterbur, and hemlok. She even tried to take a nap, but her mind just galloped on through a maze of worries.

That was the problem with hope. Hope was like that itch on

your skin that gets worse when you scratch it. As soon as you start hoping for something, you think of all the ways it could go wrong.

There were so many times she'd run away, so many times she'd thought she'd gotten free of Asger Eldr. It might take a day, it might take a week or a month, but he'd always tracked her down and slaughtered anyone who'd given her shelter. The thought of going through that again turned her insides to water.

So it was that late that evening, Reginn found herself walking back down the muddy street along the harbor front in Langvik, her carry bag over her shoulder.

She peered in at Gunnar's to see if Asger might be there, but she did not see him, and there was no telltale scent of ashes.

Fortunately, the harbor was nearly empty of ships, since those here for the festival had left for other adventures. That meant that other lodgings would be looking for customers as well. She did not want to have to share a bed with a fisherman still stinking of fish and sweat.

She was nearly at the end of the quay when she spotted a small ship at anchor in the harbor—a passenger vessel of the kind the seafarers called a knarr. It displayed a flag emblazoned with a crosshatch symbol, like a net or a web. Reginn recognized it as the same signia that had been on the livery of the spinners' servant.

This, then, must be the ship the wyrdspinner had spoken of. Reginn stood at the edge of the quay, the wind off the North Sea fingering her hair, wondering what it would be like to sail out of Asger's hands and into a new life.

Ship of dreams.

She shivered, and gooseflesh rose on the back of her neck. Her middle went wobbly, and her mouth went dry. Someone was watching her.

Asger?

She spun around and looked up and down the street. She might have seen a flicker of movement as someone ducked out of sight.

It couldn't be Asger, she thought. She never saw Asger until he wanted to be seen.

She breathed in—then let the breath out slowly, trying to slow her pounding heart. If it was Asger (and it probably was), there was no point in trying to get away.

There was no way dreams of escape could live in her head when Asger Eldr occupied such a large part of it.

Reginn booked a room in the lodging nearest to the spinners' ship. First, the hallkeeper offered her a place in his bed in the loft. When she declined, he mentioned a shared bed in a dormitory room just off the common area. When she showed him a little more money, he remembered that an alcove near the rear door was available and that the nattmal was about to be served.

The room was small, but serviceable, and the sleeping bench comfortable once she cleared the vermin out of the bedclothes with a runestone. She pinned the herbs she'd collected on the wall, though she knew they were unlikely to dry properly inside.

By the time that was done, her stomach was growling. All she'd had to eat that day was a handful of not-quite-ripe bilberries and some cheese she'd filched from Gunnar.

Reginn was a talented thief. At times she'd earned at least half of their income that way.

She could smell food cooking and hear muffled conversation from the hall. There seemed to be a good crowd, despite the exodus of people from the town. She hoped that meant the food here was better than at Gunnar's.

The common room was nearly full. As was her habit, she surveyed the custom before she chose a seat. Most appeared to be locals grabbing a cup after a day on the docks or in the markets. A pair of sunburned men shared a table in the corner, peat-cutters by the stink of them. A young couple held hands across a table, gazing into each other's eyes.

A young man sat alone, an empty bowl beside him, a cup within the circle of his arms. Something about him made her take a second look.

He was unusually tall, broad shouldered, and well made. His fair hair was dressed in the coaster style, the top pulled back in a leather thong, the rest hanging free. He wore a heavy gold ring on his right arm. A sword leaned against the wall in easy reach, and an axe lay on the table, close to his right hand. Reginn could see the kiss of the sun on his bronzed skin and hear the rush of the sea in his veins.

The tables and benches closest to him were empty, as if no one dared to get too close. Still, he drew considerable attention and whispers from the other patrons.

Reginn crossed to the mealfire, where the young cook was doling out pork stew that smelled better than anything that came from Gunnar's hearth. "Who's the boy yonder?" she said.

The cook didn't have to look to know who Reginn meant. "That's Eiric Halvorsen," she said with a delicious sort of shiver. "He comes from a family of coasters. They own the finest farm on Muckleholm." She leaned closer, speaking in a whisper. "He murdered his own modir and stepfadir just after Solstice. He'll go before the Thing in Selvagr before long. By all rights, he'll be outlawed. Others say they won't dare."

Reginn stole another look. She loved gossip as much as anyone. After all, sagas and songs were tools of the trade. "What's he doing here?"

"I hear he came to buy tar," the cook said, giving the pot a stir. Fortunately, most of the patrons already had first helpings, so she had time to talk. "His stepfadir's family owns the tar pits in Selvagr, and since the murders, they won't sell to him. He must be getting his ship ready for the season."

"He's a coaster himself?"

She nodded. "His modir's family never strays far from the sea. People say that his grandfadir, Bjorn Eiricsen, descends from the line of Njord, god of ships and sailors. They've gone vikingr nearly every summer for generations."

Reginn knew the type. They'd come boiling into the alehalls in spring as the ice in the fjords broke up, with empty purses and big plans. Shipowners looking for a crew, and second and third sons seeking a place on a longship. In fall, if they were lucky, if they survived, they'd return with silver to spare, stories to tell, and baubles to bestow on any willing girl.

Like everything else in the Archipelago, it seemed that the takings dwindled every year. Many had taken to fishing to put food on the table.

"Now," the cook said, leaning in, "here's what's interesting. Word is that his fadir, Leif Halvorsen, descends from Thor, Odin's son, a great warrior. Others say not Thor but Baldr, the handsomest of all the gods."

"Really?" Reginn said, wide-eyed, even though a person couldn't throw a rock in the Archipelago without hitting somebody who claimed to be a descendant of the gods. Not only was she good at telling stories, she was good at listening to them, too.

But there was more. "They say he's got a girl in every port in the Archipelago."

"Do they?" Reginn murmured. "Does he? Good for him."

"They say he's dangerous because he's so charming," the cook whispered, her cheeks pink. "He'll carry you away on his ship, and when he's done with you, put a collar around your neck and sell you in the markets."

Reginn had the sense that the cook might risk it if the coaster offered the least encouragement.

At that moment, Eiric Halvorsen looked up and caught them whispering and staring at him. He raised his cup, as if in a toast, and drank deeply. Then extended his empty cup. The cook rushed to refill it, leaving Reginn to help herself.

Reginn filled her bowl with the chunky pork stew and drew a cup of ale. As she passed through the room, heading for a bench in a dark corner, several patrons pointed at her. She heard a murmur of "spakona," "laeknir," and "spinner." Seer. Healer. Witch.

Skita. This town was just not big enough. She should have known she'd be recognized.

Look at Eiric Halvorsen instead, she thought. He's prettier and more famous than me.

Reginn kept her head down, avoiding eye contact until she reached the sanctuary of her corner.

I need an invisibility runestone. A "keep away" runestone. A "closed for business" runestone.

She sat on her bench and wolfed down her first bowl, using her belt knife to cut some of the meat into smaller pieces.

"Excuse me. Revered lady."

Reginn looked up to see an old man, face seamed with weather and trouble, unable to meet her eyes.

"I'm told you can raise the dead," he said in a voice husky with age. "My sweet Hilde has been gone these three years, and I don't know what I'll do without her. She was the best wife a man could have. If there's anything you could do for her . . ." He extended something toward her, cradled in his hands.

An arm ring of gilded bronze, and the gilding was thinning in some places. A treasure to him but something Asger would fling against the wall if she took it in payment.

"It sounds like she worked hard," Reginn said gently, closing her hands over his. "You should let her rest in peace."

"I know it's selfish, but I can't help wanting her back."

"Of course you want her back," Reginn said. Then, against her better judgment, she fished a runestone out of her remedy bag and pressed it into his hand. "This may help ease your grief. Keep it with you always in remembrance of her."

"Thank you, lady," he said, disappointed and grateful at the same time. "May the gods bless you all of your days."

I'm still waiting for that first blessing, Reginn thought, as the man ducked his head and backed away.

Several other people approached her while she ate, and she always gave them something—a kind word, a runestick, a cream to soothe away the itches. Twice, people at other tables sent a cup of ale over to her.

What would it be like to have a permanent stall in a small town, where people could come to throw down the bones, to seek remedies, runestones, and a kind hand? Where she could help bring other people's babies into the world and then protect them as they grew.

Tove always warned against becoming too comfortable. *Everything will be fine for a while, and then they will come for you.* She'd probably hoped that Asger would be the solution to that problem.

By now, even Halvorsen had noticed the attention she was getting. He sprawled back in his chair, long legs crossed at the ankles, turning his cup between his large hands, watching her through narrowed eyes.

Jealous? she thought, raising her cup to him. He answered the toast, looking amused.

The need to get out of this town warred with the necessity of waiting for Asger. Still, after two bowls of stew and three cups of ale, Reginn felt better than she had since leaving Gunnar's that morning.

She yawned. *Better stop with the ale now.* Free ale was a dangerous thing.

She was half dozing when a familiar voice cut into whatever dreams she was having.

"Hello, meyla."

The voice in her ear and the whisper of heat on her skin caused her to lunge sideways in a panic so she all but fell off the bench, sending her cup crashing to the floor, where it shattered.

There was only one person who called her that. *Little girl.*

"Asger!" she said, the bile rising in her throat as she caught the scent of char.

"I thought I would find you at Gunnar's Hall," Asger said. He claimed the seat next to her, then shifted his lean body, seeking a comfortable position. He had too little flesh on him for suitable padding. "The hallkeeper said that you had left." He laced his gloved fingers and rested his chin on them, looking at her in that way that said he was disappointed. "I thought we agreed that you would stay there until I came." His voice was silk on steel.

Reginn struggled to control her breathing, to keep her voice from trembling, both of which were admissions of guilt from Asger's point of view.

"You were late," she said, then instantly regretted the element of accusation. "I mean, I thought you would be there for my performance on the last night—like always. And then"—she knew she was taking a risk—"and then nobody showed up with the runestone. When you didn't come, I wasn't sure what to do."

"Had you considered staying where you were, like I told you?" Asger said, his black eyes flickering red, signifying that he was in a dangerous mood. "I am the one who makes the decisions. I am the one who sets the schedule. Therefore, I am never late."

Reginn peeked at Asger out of the corner of her eye. He didn't look well. His skin was always pale, but now his face was chalk white against his soot-black hair and smoldering eyes. He was usually meticulous about his appearance, but now his boots were scuffed and his linen shirt needed laundering. He appeared more cadaverous than ever, and Reginn would have said that was impossible.

"What happened?" she said. "Where have you been?"

"Where I have been is not your concern," Asger said. "We were discussing why you were not where you were supposed to be."

As if she were a piece of furniture that had been moved while he was gone.

"Once my engagement was over, Gunnar wouldn't let me stay."

"What do you have for me?" Asger said, thrusting his hand toward her so that she reflexively flinched back.

Reginn dug out her purse, heavy with hack silver and coin. Asger took it, undid the ties, and dumped some of its contents onto his palm, feeling the weight of it.

"You've done very well," he said, as if surprised. Then, quick as thought, he circled her neck with his free hand, pressing against her windpipe, his thumb running along her chin. She could feel his heat through the leather. "Is this all of it?"

"Yes. Of course," Reginn said hoarsely, eyes watering as she breathed in the scent of leather and flame. "Why would I steal from you?"

"Why indeed?" Asger said, stowing the purse away.

Reginn often wondered what Asger did with all the money he collected from her. He did spend freely on her clothes—he seemed to delight in dressing her up, buying her presents with the money she earned.

His own clothes were finely made, but basic, since his habit of shedding sparks meant that they needed frequent replacement. He always wore a black wool coat over a linen shirt, a black leather belt with a silver buckle that carried a scourge, narrow black wool trousers, and fine leather shoes.

A sword in a black leather scabbard hung from a baldric that slanted across his body. A sword that flamed when he bared the blade. His only ornamentation was two silver amulets on a heavy chain, bearing runes Reginn didn't recognize. That was probably for the best.

It was good that he wore black, because when he shook his head, cinders flew, and he always carried the scent of char—the scent of destruction, of devouring, of burning. People instinctively kept their distance, as one might circle around a snake in the path.

"Excuse me, spakona," somebody said.

Reginn turned to see a young woman standing a safe distance away. She looked from Reginn to Asger and back again, the sight of them causing her to lose her words.

"I'm sorry," Reginn said, "but as you can see, I'm busy right now."

"Please, my lady," the woman said. "I'll only take a moment of your time. My nephew was at the alehouse last night and saw what you did for Gunnar's thrall, Thurston. He said it was a miracle that you brought him back to life when the blue cloaks couldn't."

Reginn sensed Asger's keen attention, like an ember against her skin. She thought about claiming that the woman was mistaken, that she had the wrong person, but Asger already knew enough to put the lie to that.

The woman continued on, adding fuel to the fire. "Not only that, but you made Gunnar set him free. We've been saying for a long time that Thurston deserves better. He was the only reason we ever went to that place. I just want to say, bless you, my lady, and thank you."

Having done her damage, the woman backed away and rejoined her table.

"What was that all about?" Asger said.

Reginn shrugged. "I guess her nephew must have seen my act last night."

"I *heard* what she said," Asger said. "I want to know what it means. What's all this about blue cloaks? What, exactly, did you do that was so impressive?" He paused, then added, "In my absence."

"When you didn't come yesterday, I decided to carry on with the act anyway, because it always brings in so much money. So I talked Gunnar's thrall into doing the bit with me." She hesitated. "Turns out, he had a real talent for it."

"How did the blue cloaks become involved?" From the way he said it, she knew Asger had heard of them before.

"There were two blue cloaks in the dining room when Thurston went down. Gunnar was hot to have his thrall back, so he asked one of the blue cloaks to save Thurston. She said that she couldn't, that nobody could raise the dead.

"So then he asked me to try."

"How did you convince Gunnar to free him?" Asger said.

"Well, Gunnar kept begging me to try to save him, and I told him that the magic wouldn't work on a thrall, so he needed to set him free."

"Why would you do that?" Asger said. "How was that your business?"

"Well. He just—it seemed like—" Reginn was usually quick-witted, but she always lost her words in Asger's presence.

"Did you, perhaps, wish that someone would do the same for you?"

"No, of course not," Reginn said, swallowing down the truth.

"Were you planning to run away together? Run this rig on your own?"

"No!"

"Don't lie to me, meyla," Asger said. "You know you can't lie to me." Slowly, methodically, he began to remove his left glove, pulling on each finger until he could slide the whole thing free. Then he began to work on the other one.

"I'm not lying," Reginn said desperately, eyes fixed on his hands. "Please. Why would I lie?"

"That's a good question," Asger said. "Is it possible that you've gone into business for yourself?"

"No-no-no, I—"

Asger closed his hands around her wrists, and the pain sliced through her like a hot steel blade. It was as if he'd fastened his teeth into her and was bleeding out her soul.

Reginn sucked in a breath, then bit back the scream that crowded into the back of her throat as all her muscles went rigid.

Don't scream don't scream don't scream . . .

Asger didn't like screaming. Especially in a crowded room.

She couldn't help it. She released one gasping cry that stopped conversation in the hall before she melted back into herself, trying to get into that place in her head where the music drowned out whatever was going on in the physical world. That was a delicate balance. If she went too far, she would pass out, taking her beyond Asger's reach.

Asger didn't like that, either.

The list of things Asger didn't like was too long to navigate.

"Tell me the truth, meyla." Asger's voice pulled her out of her safe haven. "You know I've warned you about . . . entanglements." His touch drew the strength from her, leaving her weak and floppy as a rag doll. He was so empty—a yawning cavern of need—that he threatened to consume her entirely.

He was always like this after they'd been apart. Hungry.

Reginn tried to dive deep again, dancing on the edge of consciousness.

"Enough!" someone said. "Let her be."

The torment continued, until suddenly the pain was gone, and Asger with it, leaving Reginn in a trembling heap on the floor. She heard sounds of a struggle and then a thud as something hit the wall.

Gods, Reginn thought. Not another hero. More than anything, she wanted to remain where she was, her tears soaking into the dirt floor of the hall. Or, better yet, to crawl away and hide. But she needed to try to stop this if she could. Planting her hands on the bench, she used it to pull herself onto her knees.

The woman who had approached her earlier took her hands and helped Reginn to her feet, wrapping an arm around her shoulders.

"Thank you," Reginn said. "But please, stay away. He'll kill you."

The woman looked into her face, and whatever she saw there caused her to kiss Reginn on the forehead and move away.

Turning, Reginn saw Halvorsen's broad back between her and the rest of the hall. And beyond him, Asger coming to his feet, shedding all traces of fatigue like a snake dropping its skin to reveal something sleeker and more deadly. He was always like this after contact, as if her pain nourished him.

"Now get out of here and leave her alone," Halvorsen said. "I'm not going to let you hurt her anymore."

"Is that so?" Asger said, cocking his head. "Did she tell you that I was hurting her?"

Halvorsen shot a look back at Reginn, who hunched her shoulders miserably and picked at her dress with nervous fingers. "Let it go," she said. "No harm done."

"You see?" Asger said. "She's telling you to mind your own business. I suggest that you follow her advice."

"No!" Halvorsen said. "Whether you've hurt her or not, I can tell she's scared to death of you. Now, why would that be?"

"It is not uncommon for a thrall who misbehaves to fear punishment from her master," Asger said.

"A . . . thrall?" Halvorsen looked from Asger to Reginn.

"Ah," Asger said. "She always neglects to mention that." He turned to Reginn. "Meyla," he said, as if he were coaxing a small child, "show the hero your collar."

Reginn ripped at the neckline of her overdress, sending her brooch flying so that it pinged against the wall. Spreading the opening, she displayed the gold slave collar underneath.

"Rather fine, don't you think, for a disobedient thrall?" Asger shook his head. "I treat her well, and yet she still requires a great deal of discipline."

Halvorsen stepped in close to Reginn and tilted her chin up with a calloused hand as if to get a better look. His eyes were blue green under reddish brows, and there was a shadow of red stubble on his face. He smelled of sweat, and rage, and the sea.

"What do you want?" he said.

No one—especially not Asger—ever asked her that.

"I want you to leave," Reginn whispered. "Step away while you still can. Otherwise, he will kill you, and I will pay in a hundred different ways."

"You all know the rules regarding thralls," Asger said, breaking into their whispered conversation. "Meaning, there are no rules. She is mine to keep or dispose of in any way I please. For instance, I can do this." He gripped her arm and wrenched her away from Halvorsen, all but dislocating her shoulder.

"You know that anyone who interferes with a master's rights

to the full enjoyment of his thrall is subject to penalty, including possible outlawry," Asger said.

Gripping Reginn by the hair, he pulled her upright, stowing her in the crook of his arm. With his free hand, he unfastened the coiled lash from his belt and snapped it, sending sparks flying across the room. The length of the lash glowed an angry red orange.

The crowd retreated, an ebb tide of would-be heroes. All except Halvorsen, who stood his ground, though he kept his eyes on the flaming lash.

"What kind of demon are you?" he whispered.

"I am what you might call a refugee from another world," Asger said, displaying his sharp-toothed smile. "I'm out of place here, I admit, but I mean to remedy that." He snapped the whip again, as if to emphasize his point.

What does that mean? Reginn thought. Remedy it how?

Then again, it wasn't like they'd ever had a conversation about Asger's hopes and dreams.

"Perhaps we can strike a bargain," Halvorsen said, fingering the purse at his waist. "I'll pay her redemption price."

"No," Reginn said. "There's no way to win this. Walk away. Don't undo the one good thing I've done." She'd saved Thurston, but now Halvorsen would pay with his life.

"Interesting," Asger said. "What are you talking about, this 'one good thing'?"

"Nothing," Reginn said.

"Now, meyla, you wouldn't have brought it up if you didn't want me to know," Asger said. "And you will, of course, tell me eventually." He turned his attention to Halvorsen. "She is correct in one respect—I'm afraid I cannot make a deal for the girl. She is too precious to me."

"You haven't heard my offer," Halvorsen said with calm confidence. Clearly, he wasn't used to taking no for an answer.

"There is nothing that you could offer me that would make me change my mind," Asger said.

"How about this—free her, and I'll let you live," Halvorsen said. "Plus, I'll pay her redemption price."

The crowd murmured, shifted.

Asger stared at Halvorsen in astonishment, then laughed softly. "Ah, meyla," he said. "The heroes always find you, do they not? Your friend may have the advantage of size, but I'm afraid he's not very bright."

With that, he thrust Reginn aside and slashed at Halvorsen with the whip, aiming for his eyes. The coaster just managed to raise his arms in time, or he would have been blinded. As it was, he screamed as the flaming lash raised blistered welts across his forearms.

And yet he stood his ground, even though his sword still leaned against the wall.

Asger pivoted and drove in again, striking once, twice, three times, the lash cutting Halvorsen's shirt to smoking ribbons. Finally, the coaster barged through the pain, throwing a hard elbow to Asger's face, breaking his nose, sending steaming blood spattering everywhere. Before Asger could recover, Halvorsen took hold of him at neck and waist and flung him headfirst out the door. Snatching up his sword in one hand, his axe in the other, the coaster stormed out after him. He returned a few minutes later.

"He's gone," Halvorsen said, extending a hand to help Reginn to her feet.

"No," she hissed. "He is *not* gone. He'll come back. You need to leave now, and put as much distance as you can between us before it's too late."

Around them, the other patrons cheered and stamped their

feet, though Reginn noticed that the hallkeeper peered out the door, then shut it and threw the bar across.

As if that would keep Asger out.

Reginn returned to her bench in the corner and huddled there, head swimming with misery and remorse.

Halvorsen escaped his admirers and joined her, clunking two cups of mead on the bench between them.

"What's this?" she said, pointing at the cups.

"You deserve at least one of these," Halvorsen said. "You took as much punishment as me."

"I doubt that," Reginn said, eyeing his blood-streaked shirt and his blistered arms, thinking that he must have a high tolerance for pain.

Taking in her scowling disapproval, he said, "I'm sorry I interfered, but it's not right for him to treat you that way, even if it is within the law."

"He won't rely on the law," Reginn said. "He'll deal with this himself."

"And I'll deal with him, if he comes back," Halvorsen said, his jaw set stubbornly. He seemed to be in the mood for a fight.

"I don't want you to deal with him," Reginn said. "I want you to go."

"Then what?" Halvorsen said. "What do *you* intend to do?"

"I'll wait for him," Reginn said. "If I'm here when he comes, that may appease him enough that he won't come after you."

"No," Halvorsen said. "That's a terrible idea." Tilting his head back, he drained his cup in one go while Reginn watched in amazement. Though some might call him a beardless boy, there was something about the coaster that drew the eye. It wasn't just his physical size. If you were looking for someone to be on your side, he'd be the one you chose.

It wouldn't matter. Not for her. She needed to persuade him to save himself.

If it wasn't already too late.

"They call me spakona, someone who can predict the future," Reginn said. "People pay me for that service, but I'll give you a reading for free. If you're here when Asger comes back, you will die, and it won't help me."

"I've learned that if you give in to bullies, they get worse," Halvorsen snapped. "I'm done with that." Reginn could tell that there was a story there, but she didn't want to ask, didn't want to get to know this boy only to see him murdered.

"I did not ask to be rescued," Reginn said. "To be honest, it's arrogant for you to ignore what I'm telling you and assume that you know better than I do." She hesitated, then plunged on. "The last thing I need is another Asger."

Halvorsen stared at her for a long moment, and then a smile twitched at the corners of his beautiful mouth. "You are right," he said, inclining his head. "I know better. I'm sorry."

It was Reginn's turn to be surprised. There was more to this coaster than met the eye. He had tried to help her, which was more than most would do. She could tell by the way he moved that he was in pain, and she knew from experience what Asger's lash could do.

"Come back to my room," she said. "Let me see to your wounds. If those burns aren't treated, they'll fester by tomorrow." She handed him the other cup of mead. "Better drink this, too," she said. "I think you'll need it."

11

THE SEER

EIRIC HALVORSEN FOLLOWED THE THRALL back to her curtained sleeping bench in the rear of the hall, chased by a few catcalls and obscene suggestions from the handful of drinkers still lingering. He wondered what he'd gotten himself into.

He was in trouble enough. He couldn't afford to get into it with a slaveholder over a thrall.

Everywhere he went, if there was even a chance for a fight, he'd step into it. And, right now, he'd prefer a fight he could win.

The laeknir—the healer—reminded him a little of his systir, Liv. They shared the same fierce, take-no-prisoners attitude. But while Liv was long limbed and rangy, this girl barely reached Eiric's elbow. Liv's hair was a bronzy gold, but the healer's hair was all the colors of autumn in the Westlands.

Liv wore serviceable clothes suited for life on the farm—an overdress made from wool from their sheep, an underdress made from linen she'd woven on the smaller of their two looms. An apron over all as protection from day-to-day dirt.

The thrall's clothes were fine in comparison—her overdress edged in tablet-woven braid, her shoes of red leather, matched brooches of amber set in silver. When she'd walked in, he'd taken her for a fine lady and did not look again.

As the evening wore on, he'd noticed other things.

She was kind. He could tell that she was bone weary by the way she moved, by the fact that she'd sought refuge in the corner farthest from the hearth. And yet, when people approached her, she listened, she treated them kindly, and she always sent them away with something.

She was powerful. Those who recognized her seemed to be in awe of her. They'd called her seer, healer, sorceress. And yet she married power with compassion, something rarely seen in the Archipelago.

Everything had changed when the demon arrived. Eiric had seen how she flinched when her master spoke to her, how she writhed under his touch, the desperate fear in her eyes when she begged Eiric to leave. *If you're here when Asger comes back, you will die, and it won't help me.*

It offended him to see her pinned under the demon's boot.

The seer's "room" was just an alcove in an alehall, but she'd made it her own. Bunches of herbs hung overhead, and the complicated scent of her was everywhere.

She fetched a linen cloth from her remedy bag, spread it over her pallet, and said, "Sit, Halvorsen."

So she knew who he was.

Eiric sat. "Call me Eiric," he said, as she rummaged for more supplies. "What's your name?"

"Reginn," she said. "Take off your shirt and shoes."

The demon was gone, and she had regained her footing.

Eiric slid his feet out of his shoes and set them aside. His linen shirt was stuck to his wounds in several places. Wincing, he pulled the fabric free and yanked it over his head. His skin was crisscrossed with angry, blistered welts.

"Does he use the lash on you?"

She nodded. "Not often, these days. I try not to give him cause to use it. Besides, it leaves marks, as you see, and he doesn't like that."

"I should have killed him," Eiric muttered.

"Yes," she said, "you should have, but you'd find that it's harder than you think."

"What is it he calls you? Meyla?"

"It means 'little girl.' He's called me that since I was small."

"Were you born into thralldom?" Eiric said.

Reginn shook her head. "My modir sold me to Asger. She wanted to make a new start."

Eiric looked down at his hands. He didn't know what to say. "How old were you?" he said.

"I was seven," Reginn said. "Tove was a traveling seer, performing many of the same routines that I use. Asger insisted that she teach them to me before the deal was made."

"So she was gifted as well?"

Reginn laughed. Bitterly. "Maybe. A little."

Eiric chose not to pursue that. Instead, he asked a thornier question. "What did he want with a seven-year-old? Was he a—" He stopped, face flaming, unsure how to continue.

"It wasn't like that. He's not—he doesn't—his touch is incredibly painful. That's why he wears gloves all the time. The only difference between that and the lash is that the lash leaves a burn." She shook her head. "It was always about magic, about megin. That's what attracts him. He seeks it out. At first, I think he thought that Tove might be enough—until he met me." She swallowed. "I've been good at bringing in income, but otherwise, I've been a disappointment."

"But you *have* magic," Eiric said.

"Maybe," Reginn said. "If I were truly powerful, you'd think I could get myself out of this mess."

"What *is* he, exactly?" Eiric said.

"I don't *know*, exactly," Reginn snapped back. "Sometimes, when he's in his cups, he's called himself a refugee. Once, he said he was an eldrjotun, a son of Muspelheim."

"Muspelheim?" Eiric said. It sounded familiar. Maybe Bjorn had mentioned it?

"It's the realm of fire, in the old stories," Reginn said. "One of the Nine Worlds, home of the devourers, the fire demons."

"Fire demons," Eiric said, his usual skepticism returning. "Do you believe that?"

"I believe what I see," Reginn said, returning her attention to his wounds.

When the air struck them, it was as if someone were running a lit taper up and down his chest and back. He couldn't help it. His breath hissed out through his teeth.

"Here," she said, handing him a stick painted with symbols. "Use this."

He turned it over in his hands. Was he supposed to bite down on it while she cleaned his wounds? Not wanting to show ignorance but worried that he would embarrass himself, he finally said, "What is this?"

"It's a runestick," she said. "It's very old magic."

"Oh," he said. Then felt compelled to add, "There are no healers where I live."

This wasn't exactly true. His modir, Sylvi, had had some remedies she swore by. Most people knew how to straighten and lash a broken bone or cut into an infected wound to release the poison. There was Liv's friend Emi, a thrall who served as healer and midwife in his home village. She put on a good performance, but her skills were questionable.

If he was wounded during his summers at sea, the plan was

simple: use enough pressure to stop the bleeding, clean it out, bind it up, and hope for the best. The fates would determine the outcome.

"Not many people know the runes or how to use them." Reginn took the runestick from him and said, "Hold out your hands."

When he did, she laid the runestick across both his palms and used her own hands to close his fingers over it. Her hands were small, but he could feel the strength in them.

"It will help with the pain," she said, letting go.

And it did. He wasn't asleep, but he sat as if in a trance while she cleaned the burns on his chest and applied ointment to them. He was acutely aware of every time she touched him, but it somehow didn't hurt. Her hair had come loose from its plait, and when she leaned toward him, it brushed his face and neck, raising gooseflesh.

At one point, Reginn fingered the silver pendant his fadir had left him. "You're wearing Thurisaz. Thor's rune."

"Is that what it is?" Eiric craned his neck so that he could get a look at it. "It's a mark my fadir favored."

"That explains a lot."

"Why? What's it good for?"

She traced the rune. "Destruction of enemies, curses, binds and fetters, awakening of the will to action." Then, biting back a smile, she said, "Chaos, destruction, and violence."

He flipped it over. "My grandfadir's mark is on the back."

She studied it. "That's Yngvi," she said. "Symbol of Freyr, the god of summer, fertility, and"—she paused, appraising him—"masculine potency in particular."

"Well, yes," Eiric said, feeling the sting of her wit again. "That makes perfect sense."

"It's uncommon to find Thor and Freyr together," Reginn said.

"My fadir and grandfadir honored different gods," Eiric said. "What about you?"

Eiric hesitated, reluctant to offend her. "I just don't think about them much, to be honest." He shrugged.

Reginn surveyed the battered landscape of his chest and shoulders. She ran her fingers over old scars and the fresh evidence of his last fight with Sten.

"You're marked like a warrior," she murmured, sitting back on her heels. "Are you that hard to get along with?"

"I say what I think. I don't go looking for fights, but I don't walk away from them, either." In a physical fight, at least, a man could tell who won.

A smile crept onto her face. "Gods, Halvorsen, you'd better either hone your skills as a fighter or develop a sweeter personality. Otherwise, I can safely predict that you will not live much longer."

Eiric laughed. This bold girl was so different from the downbeaten thrall cowering under her master's hand. He knew that she was a performer, but still—the transformation was remarkable.

Apparently done with his front, Reginn knelt behind him on the pallet, her knees pressing into his hips. "I need to do something with this hair," she said.

Do whatever you want, Eiric thought. Hack it off, color it blue, tie it up with a ribbon. After two cups of mead, under the spell of the runestick, he was feeling very cooperative.

Fortunately, she did none of those things. She untied the leather binding his hair, combed through it with her fingers, then followed with a comb. Finally, she bound it up again so that it wasn't in the way.

To his embarrassment, Eiric found this process arousing. He was glad he was facing away from her. To be safe, he pulled the blanket over his breeches and up to his waist.

Easy, Halvorsen, he thought. Just because you're in bed with a girl doesn't mean she's interested in you.

Although. He had to admit, in the past, it had always been a very good sign.

She was back to business then, giving his back the same treatment as his front. Her hands were like small birds, alighting for a moment before they took flight again. By the time she finished that, the flames she'd lit inside him had dwindled to coals, and he'd gotten his pulse under control.

Finally, she knelt before him. Frowning, she gripped his bad arm at elbow and wrist and traced the pink, knotted scar Sten had left him with on that last fatal day. "This looks recent. What happened here?"

"Family quarrel," Eiric said. Her head jerked up, understanding flooding into her face, and he knew that she'd heard about Sten. "My stepfadir thought I'd lived long enough. I disagreed."

She looked at him, chewing her lower lip, and Eiric could tell she was sorting through questions. "Go ahead," he growled, his mellow mood evaporating. "What have you heard?"

"I heard . . . that you killed your modir and stepfadir," she said.

"That's the story Sten's family is pushing," Eiric said, surprised that it had followed him all the way from Selvagr. "It's true: they're both dead." That was all he meant to say, but somehow her silence required him to fill it. "My stepfadir left my baby brodir in the forest to die."

She sucked in a quick breath. "Why would he do that?"

"Ivar was not the perfect son Sten was planning on," Eiric said. "He had shake spells. It's the fadir's right to give a baby back to the gods before his name day. When my modir found out what he'd done, she went into the woods looking for her baby on the coldest night of the year. The baby lived, but she froze to death."

Reginn closed her eyes, released a long breath, opened them again. "I'm sorry, Halvorsen. Your modir must have been a brave woman. Not all modirs stand up for their children that way."

Even Eiric could hear the pain beneath the words. Her own modir had let her down.

He didn't want to tell her the truth of it—that he wished his modir had made a different decision and survived.

When he didn't respond, she said, "What happened with your stepfadir?"

"When he found out Sylvi was dead, he knew he might lose any claim to our farm, which he'd been after all along. There were two things in his way—me and my systir. He came after us, and we killed him."

"'We?'"

"To be fair, Liv dealt the killing blow. She saved my life."

She cocked her head, as if surprised that he would admit that. "And yet you're the one going before the Thing?"

"That's the way it works in Muckleholm."

"What are your chances?"

"Sten's family controls the council, so . . . ." Eiric shrugged. "I'll be declared vargr—an outlaw—in the end, and Sundgard will go to Sten's family. No doubt they'll toast him every midsummer from here on."

Why was he telling her all this? These were more words than he'd said since Solstice. There was something about her that drew out the truth like a poultice on a festering wound.

As if recognizing his discomfort, Reginn very deliberately returned her attention to his arm. "It's still not right, is it?" she said.

"No," Eiric said. "I think this is as good as it will ever be." Not good enough.

"Maybe," she said, drawing her brows together.

Using her fingers and a pot of oak gall ink, she painted more runes down his arm. She took hold of it again at elbow and wrist, exerted gentle pressure, then released it.

She moved on to his torso, fingers whispering across his skin.

"That tickles," he said at one point, laughing, gripping her wrists. She flinched, then settled. For a long moment, they looked into each other's faces, the air between them thickening. The healer's gaze dropped to his lips. The flames rose up again.

She sat back on her heels, cheeks flushed, and surveyed her work. "Is that better?"

"Much better, thank you," Eiric said. "I hardly notice it anymore." Which wasn't entirely true.

"Good."

For a long moment, they sat in awkward silence.

"I'm going to try to get some sleep," Reginn said finally, looking down at her hands.

"May I stay?" he said, lifting her chin so that he looked into her eyes. They were lit with—hope? Desire? Interest, at least? And then the embers flamed out.

"You'd better go."

"Maybe I can help," Eiric said. "I'm not afraid of him."

"You should be," Reginn said. "I don't want another dead hero on my conscience."

Another dead hero, Eiric thought. She's been through this before.

"Look," he said. "My ship is in the harbor, and I sail with the tide in three hours. Come with me. Our farm is near Selvagr. You could stay there, for now at least. As I said, we're in need of healers."

She raised both hands, palms out, and he could already see *no* in her eyes.

"I have no . . . expectations or demands," he said. "You would come as a free woman. I think you would get along with my systir, Liv. You have much in common."

Reginn lifted her chin and thrust her thumb under her slave collar. "How, exactly, do I come as a free woman?" She shook her head. "If I go back to Sundgard with you, Asger will burn the place down. You'll be dead, and your systir, Liv, will be without a roof over her head. If she survives."

She leaned in and put her hand on his thigh. The effect was incendiary. "I honor your courage. Now, honor me by listening to what I have to say. Some things cannot be mended by a brave heart and a strong blade. Heroes have no place in some stories. Leave now, and live." She stood.

"All right," he said, disappointed, but he'd been disappointed before. Still savoring the memory of her hands on his skin, he found his shoes, then stood and slid the ruins of his shirt over his head. Liv will not be happy, he thought. That's two shirts in a month. He strapped on his baldric, then swore as it pressed against his wounds.

"You might want to use the waist strap only for a while," Reginn said. Standing on the bed, she adjusted the shoulder strap so that it didn't impinge on his burns.

"Thank you," he said awkwardly, finding himself eye to eye with her again.

She studied him for the longest time until he squirmed under the scrutiny.

"What is it?" he said.

"May I ask a favor, before you go?"

He nodded. "Of course."

"May I kiss you? I've never kissed a man, and I don't see much hope of it in the future. From what I've heard, you're good at it."

Once again, this girl had unsettled him. Eiric enjoyed kissing, and he liked to think that he had some skill, but now he felt like the reputation of his gender rested on his blistered shoulders.

"Halvorsen!"

He looked up to find her glaring at him.

"It's not a hard question. May I kiss you, yes or no?"

"Yes," he said, because, of course, there was no other answer.

She placed her hands carefully, circling the base of his neck but avoiding his shoulders. She leaned forward, her cloud of hair brushing his skin, and kissed him gently on the lips. She broke it off momentarily, studied his face, then kissed him again. This time, she slid her fingers behind his head and pulled him close, pressing her small breasts against his upper chest. He could feel the rapid beating of her heart, like a covey of birds under the skin.

She pulled back, a little breathless, and said, "So. How was that? Is there anything you—"

"Yes," he said. He pressed her back onto the bed, cradled her face between his hands, and kissed her on the mouth, long and slow and deep and fierce, until every part of him was burning.

This time, when they broke apart, her cheeks were rosy and she took quick, shallow breaths.

"I think I've got the hang of it," she said, running her tongue over her lips as if to savor the taste. "Thank you for that. Now. I've let you stay too long already. You'd better get back to your ship before I lose my good sense."

Eiric sat back, his own breath coming quickly. In his experience, *goodbye* was not what followed a kiss like that. "Good sense is overrated," he said. "It gets in the way of so much pleasure."

"There's the coaster I've been hearing about," Reginn said with a sad smile. "But you do have to go. Just know that this is the first time a man has touched me and it hasn't caused me pain."

Eiric had no words.

"I wish you fair winds and following seas," she said. Then, extending the runestick toward him, said, "Please take this with you. I have a feeling that you're going to need it."

Always send them away with something.

Eiric took it from her and stowed it in his carry bag. Then, carefully, slid Gramr into his scabbard. "I hope, when we meet again, you'll find a role for a hero in your story," he said. "Or a friend, at least."

He pushed between the curtains enclosing the sleeping bench, threaded his way through the alehall, and emerged into the cold night air. He scanned the dark street.

He is not gone.

Eiric recalled what he'd said to Reginn. *I'm not afraid of him.*

Well, maybe he was. A little.

He drew his axe, carrying it close to his side as he strode down the middle of the street all the way to the quay.

He half expected to find his little dragon ship burned to cinders, but she was still afloat, bobbing in the shallows at the landward end of the wharf.

Eiric gave her a quick look-over before he committed, scanning the fish hold for intruders. He saw only the casks of tar he'd put aboard that morning.

He cast off before he leaped aboard, letting his momentum carry her a little way from the dock. It was still two hours before he'd see the most favorable tide, but he did not intend to close his eyes with his ship tethered to the shore. Sliding a pair of oars into place, he rowed *Dreki* out to the middle of the harbor and dropped anchor.

For a few minutes, he sat midships, staring back toward shore, absently flexing his bad hand. That's when he realized that the usual numbness and tingling pain were gone.

He flexed it again. Still a little stiff, but much improved from what it had been since the fight with Sten.

She'd healed him. He wished that he could do the same for her. For as long as he could remember, his size, his strength, his sailing and fighting skills had been admired by his friends and sweethearts and respected and feared by his enemies. None of those gifts had been of any help in contending with Sten Knudsen and his family. And now, he had absolutely nothing to offer this girl.

Rolling up in a blanket, he lay down in his usual berth at midships, but the sting had returned to his wounds, and he couldn't seem to get comfortable. His mind swarmed with images of the seer, with regrets and worries and the dregs of lust.

Heroes have no place in some stories.

Finally, he retrieved the runestick from his seabag and cradled it between his hands. It was only then that he fell into a fitful sleep.

12

WHEN THEY BURN YOU

Create a fortress inside you—a place of refuge you carry with you always. That way, when they burn you, you have someplace to go.
—Tove

Linen burns more readily than wool.
—Tove

IT WAS WEAKNESS THAT HAD moved Reginn to ask the coaster for a kiss, and now she was paying the price. Try as she might, she couldn't drive the memory of it from her mind.

To be honest, she didn't try very hard.

To be very honest, she wallowed in it, reliving every delicious second, the heat of it burrowing through her again and again. His fingers pressing against her scalp, his thumbs on her cheekbones, the rasp of stubble against her skin. His mouth—gods, his mouth. His tongue, the scent of him. The honest pleasure he took in it. The way he looked at her—really *focused* on her with those blue-green eyes, as if she were the only treasure in the world.

The violent history written on his body—some of it quite recent—and yet his willingness to put himself at risk again for her sake.

The fact that he listened when she said no.

Reginn had told him that she didn't need a hero. That didn't prevent her from wanting one just the same.

The hero was gone, but she had this—the memory of him that no one, not even Asger, could take away.

It took another hour and a bowl of mead filched from the cask in the common room before Reginn found sleep.

She had no idea what time it was when she awoke, realizing that she needed to visit the privy. She took a moment to put on her shoes before she slid from her bed, landing silently on the dirt floor. She could hear snoring all around her.

As she left her alcove, she froze like a rabbit under the gaze of an owl as she caught a whiff of char. Asger?

She sniffed the air again. Now she smelled nothing but the dying hearth. Shaking her head, she slipped out the back door to the privy, located a hundred feet away.

Now she smelled nothing but the privy.

She was walking back toward the alehouse, had nearly reached it, when she heard a whoosh and the building erupted in flames.

Reginn's first thought was of Asger. The patrons of the alehall had disrespected him. He couldn't abide that.

Still, it was hard to believe that he would set the hall on fire with her inside.

You weren't inside. You were in the privy. The back of her neck prickled as she realized that he must be watching her.

Then it hit her. "My flute!"

It was her last tie to Tove. It was also the link to her most important gift—the gift of music. She'd already lost so much. She would not leave it to burn while there was breath in her body.

She charged forward, knowing that if she hesitated, she would lose her courage. Just outside the door, she took a moment to plunge her head and shoulders into the rain barrel. When she straightened, water streamed down her body. At first, the door resisted, but when she put her shoulder to it, it gave. She went down on her face as a torrent of flame exploded through the now open door. As she crawled forward, she thought she heard someone behind her, screaming her name.

Inside, the smoke was an impenetrable wall, thick enough to chew but impossible to breathe. Reginn began to cough, her eyes burning, blurry with tears. It was incredibly loud; the roar of the flames mingled with the sound of people screaming.

She knew she must be close to her sleeping bench, but she was already disoriented, starved for air. How long did she have before she lost consciousness?

In a fire, stay low.

So she continued to crawl, following the wall with her hand to make sure that she didn't lose her way. Finally, her questing hand met fabric. The drapes around her sleeping bench.

Parting them, she slipped between them.

Inside the alcove, the smoke was not as thick—not yet—though the scent of smoldering wool told her that this little haven wouldn't last long. She dragged in air as she slid the baldric carrying her flute over her head and fastened the belt with its pouches of runestones and remedies around her waist. She painted the rune Raidho on one arm, for a safe journey, and Uruz on the other, for strength of will.

The bucket of water she'd used to clean Halvorsen's wounds still stood next to the bed. She put on her coat, and then stripped the blanket from the bed, soaked it in the bucket, and wrapped it around herself, protecting the flute as well.

When she crawled out of the alcove, her heart sank. She'd dallied too long. A wall of angry orange flame rose between her and the back door.

Front door, then, Reginn thought.

The screaming of horses just ahead told her that she was going the wrong way—toward the stable attached to the far end of the longhouse. There had to be another door there—else how would the horses get in and out? She climbed over the half wall that divided the main hall and sleeping quarters from the stalls. The center aisle was blocked with fallen timbers, so she climbed into the stalls, dodging this way and that to avoid the plunging hooves of the panicked horses. As soon as she got past the obstacle, she began opening the doors of the stalls, hoping the horses would show her the way to the door. They plunged down the center aisle to the end, smashing through a pair of large double doors, escaping into the night. Reginn charged after them, sucking down the fresher air that poured through the gap. Behind her, fed by the draft, the flames' roar became deafening, as if screaming in frustration at seeing Reginn close to escape.

She heard a crack overhead, a whoosh of flame, and then something smashed her flat on her back in the aisle. It was another timber, pinning her down. No matter how much she squirmed and twisted, she could not free herself. She even leaned forward and tried to dig herself out, clawing at the dirt floor under her limbs, hoping to hollow out enough space to get free.

That might have worked, but she'd be dead long before she succeeded. The air was a bit clearer, here on the floor, but what with the smoldering sod walls, that wouldn't last long. Would she burn to death, or suffocate? A good question.

Fine seer you turned out to be.

And then, through the murk, she saw two red points of light, coming closer. A shadow deepened around them and became a silhouette haloed in flame. Slender, silent, light-footed. Familiar. Even amid the choking smoke, she could pick out the scent of leather and char.

Asger.

"Meyla," he said. "It never occurred to me that you were foolish enough to run into a burning building. I never planned for that." Sliding his hands under the burning timber, he heaved it aside. Then scooped Reginn into his arms, cradling her against his smoldering coat. By now, there was another wall of flame between them and the stable door. Asger rammed his shoulder against the side wall, bursting through the sod and into the fresh air.

It was bedlam along the harbor front. Hallkeepers and business owners were racing back and forth across the pier, scooping up buckets of water and wetting down their roofs to prevent flying sparks from catching. Fortunately, the few remaining ships were anchored far out in the harbor, out of range of the flames.

Once outside, Asger kept walking, up the quay toward the long dock, eating up the distance with angry strides. Everyone else was running the other way, toward the fire, to help or to gawk. The glare of the flames concealed, then revealed his face. There was no evidence of the broken nose, aside from the heat of his fury.

"Let me down," Reginn said. "I can walk."

Asger set her on her feet, but took hold of both her wrists, turning her to face him. "What were you thinking? Were you trying to save your hero? Was he that important to you?" His voice shook.

Reginn was lost for a moment, and then she understood. Asger thought that Halvorsen was with her—sharing her bed. *And now he thinks he's dead.*

Good.

"He was kind to me," Reginn said. She did not have to fake the tremor in her voice.

"Am I not kind to you?" Asger said. Not waiting for an answer, he took hold of her arm again and walked on, practically dragging her down the waterfront. Their speed discouraged conversation.

Not that Reginn had anything to say.

This end of the quay was all but deserted, since most of the ships had already set sail. The sunrise was just beginning to gild the horizon.

Once they reached the long dock, Asger turned onto it, passing several larger vessels until he reached a small boat of the sort used to carry cargo out to ships at anchor in the harbor. A scrawny young man stood next to it, so focused on the drama down the shore that he didn't see them coming.

"That's Beau," Asger said, pointing toward the crewman. "He's too stupid to live."

Proving Asger's point, Beau yelped and practically jumped into the harbor when Asger tapped him on the shoulder.

"This is the girl," Asger said, nodding at Reginn.

Beau looked her up and down, taking in her once fine spakona garb, now blackened and torn in several places. His eyes lit on the pouches and amulets at her belt, the runes painted on her fore-arms. He swallowed hard. "You want *me* to take *her* to the *Fossegrim*?" He gestured toward a sleek warship at anchor far out in the harbor.

Asger went dead still, something he was good at. "That's what we agreed upon."

"But . . . what if she . . . ?"

"Are you really frightened of a *child*?" Asger rolled his eyes in disgust. "You'll keep her locked in the hold on the way to the ship. Once you are alongside, you hand her off to Jarl Karlsen—no one else. He will pay you half. Then return to the dock and wait for me. I have some business to attend to before we sail. Once you ferry me over, you'll get the rest."

Reginn scarcely heard what else he said, because another ship had caught her eye, anchored a little closer in. The ship that had flown the crosshatch blue flag. The flag was down now, and the crew was manipulating the rigging, as if preparing to get underway.

Reginn eyed the position of the two ships relative to the dock. They would have to pass close to the wyrdspinners' ship to reach the warship.

Hope rose in her like a full-moon tide. If only she could find a way to cross the expanse of water between them.

Then she deflated like a pricked toad. If only she knew how to swim.

It doesn't matter. He'll find you, and hurt you, and destroy everything else.

Asger lifted her into the small boat and climbed in after her. Still gripping her hand, he half dragged her to the hatch that opened into the hold, tucked under the decking at the bow. He unfastened the latch and hauled it open.

"Don't lock me in," Reginn pleaded. "I promise I'll be good."

"Meyla, you've proven to me that you cannot be trusted," Asger said, attaching a heavy chain to a ring on her collar. He pushed her through the opening, into a space that was scarcely large enough to stand up in.

There was scarcely room to sit down, either. She was surrounded by jars and barrels—salted fish, ale, cheese, and other shipboard foods and supplies. All around her, she heard rustling and squeaking. Mice, probably.

She'd faced worse than mice.

Reginn looked up in time to see Asger wrap the chain around the mast and lock it. Then he tossed a skin of water through the hatch and sat cross-legged on the deck beside it.

"Look," she said. "I'm chained up. I'm not going anywhere. Don't lock me in. You know I'm not good in tight spaces."

"Maybe not," Asger said, "but it seems that you *are* good at capturing the hearts and minds of fools." Each word was honed to a point, tipped with bitterness.

"Give me a light stick at least," she said. "You know I'm afraid of the dark."

Sometimes, at her performances, she sold Asger's light sticks. She wasn't sure how he made them, but somehow he captured flame in a glass rod that could be used to light a person's way.

Deep in thought, Asger didn't respond.

She wanted to keep him talking, to keep him from slamming the door and maybe persuade him to allow her to stay up on deck. She groped for a topic.

"Did you have anything to do with the fire at the alehall?" she asked.

Asger blinked, as if he'd all but forgotten that she was there. Then snapped, "Don't waste my time by asking me a question if you already know the answer. I have told you before that I will *destroy* anyone who intrudes between me and you."

"Who is Jarl Karlsen?" she said.

"Let's just say that Karlsen and I share some common interests, and he can provide resources that I haven't had before now."

"Where are we going?"

"Up the coast. To a place called Selvagr. That's where Karlsen's high seat is." Asger came up on his knees, as if he might shut the hatch and leave. Then settled back again and began to remove his gloves.

"Please," Reginn said, breath hitching. "Not now."

"I need your help, meyla," Asger said. "I need your strength more than you do." He gripped both her wrists for what seemed like an eternity while she writhed and whimpered. When he finally let go, she lay gutted and gasping, while he pulled on his gloves again.

Then, just for a moment, he rested his gloved hand on the small of her back. Reginn flinched. He removed his hand.

"Why do you have to go back to town?" Reginn whispered. "Did you forget something?"

"So many questions," Asger said. "No, meyla, I did not forget anything. I intend to find out exactly what happened at Gunnar's Hall between you and the ginger and the blue cloaks. The 'one good thing' you mentioned."

"Please, Asger," she said. "Leave it go."

"It's time that you learned that you cannot keep secrets from me. That you cannot create alliances against me."

"I know that now. He's gone. We'll never see him again. Let's move on."

"Yes," Asger said, showing his teeth in a savage smile. "The ginger is gone." With that, he tossed something into the hold. A light stick. And followed with something else, a wad of cloth.

He lingered for a moment longer. Reginn could feel the pressure of his eyes, but she did not meet his gaze.

"I am sorry," he said, "that I cannot take what I need without hurting you."

With that, he stood and slammed the hatch down. The boat shifted as he stepped off onto the dock. She heard his footsteps retreating, and then he was gone.

She rolled the light stick between her hands to kindle it. Then unwrapped Asger's other "gift."

It was Thurston's bloody shirt, still smelling of char.

She shrieked and dropped it into her lap. She closed her eyes, rocked, and tried to retreat into her inner sanctuary.

But there was nowhere to go. She could not unsee it. She could not unhear Asger's words.

The ginger is gone.

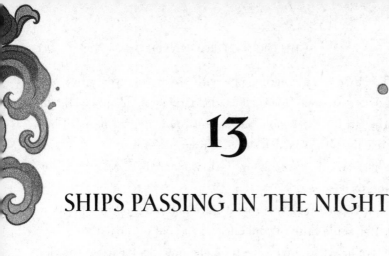

13

SHIPS PASSING IN THE NIGHT

EIRIC AWOKE TO A GENTLE rocking as the outgoing tide rushed past his ship. He sat up and was immediately sorry. His pounding head and blistered skin brought back the events at the alehouse.

So it wasn't a dream. Not that he'd really thought it was. Most of his nightmares did not include kissing at the end.

He looked shoreward. The alehouse stood, a dark hulk at the edge of the quay. By now, Reginn must be sound asleep inside. Was she dreaming of kissing, too? Or were her dreams darker, prowling with demons with ember eyes?

He searched for the runestick and saw that it had slipped from his fingers and fallen to the deck. Unstrapping his leather-wrapped ship's tools, he used an auger to drill a hole at one end of the stick so that he could slide it onto the chain next to the pendant.

He studied the pendant, the symbols on each side. What was it she'd called it? Thurisaz. And Yngvi. Corresponding to two very different gods. He ran his thumb over the engraving, smiling as he recalled what she'd said about it.

He scanned the harbor. Two other ships were at anchor near the harbor mouth, probably preparing to sail with the tide as well. One carried blue banners emblazoned with an unfamiliar device.

The other was a longship, one with twenty or twenty-five sections. Forty oarsmen at least. It carried Jarl Harald's banner. Harald was the jarl for the region, but up until now he had been all but invisible in Selvagr. Which suited Selvagr just fine.

What's he doing in Langvik? Eiric wondered.

Not his business.

He unclipped the yard from its rack and moved it into position so that he could raise the sail once he was out of the harbor.

Before he set to rowing, he took one more look back at the alehouse. Just in time to see it explode into flames.

14

LEAVING THE OLD GODS

THE THING, OR COUNCIL, MET four times a year in the village of Selvagr–at the winter and summer solstices and at the equinoxes in the spring and fall. Eiric Halvorsen was to stand before the Thing at the vernal equinox to answer for the murder of his stepfadir.

In the time between Eiric's return from Langvik and the meeting of the council, Liv scoured the farmhouse, the barn, and even the boat shed looking for valuables that might buy off the Knudsens at Eiric's hearing. At least, that's what she said she was doing.

"Are you looking for the Halvorsen Hoard?" Eiric said. "You know, the one that doesn't exist? You have Sylvi's jewelry. We never had so much silver that we needed multiple places to hide it."

Liv sat back from where she was rooting through Sylvi's spinning supplies and mopped cobwebs from her hair. "There has to be *something*," she insisted. "There has to be a way out."

Eiric's conscience pricked him. Was she looking for the pendant and the sunstone–the two items Sylvi swore him to secrecy about?

Liv had sewn Eiric a new shirt to wear to the hearing, since he'd ruined two in a matter of weeks. She never saw the one Asger did for, since Eiric had thrown it overboard before he left Langvik Harbor and made up a story about a mishap in the tar pits.

He'd said nothing at all about what had happened in Langvik—the pain was still too fresh. It was his fault the demon had burned down the alehouse with Reginn inside. He should have left well enough alone.

Then, when he went to try on his new shirt, Liv said, "By the gods, Eiric. What happened to your back?" She circled around him. "And your chest. It looks like you've been flogged." She ran a light finger over his skin. "These look like burns."

"They're healing up," Eiric said. "It just looks bad." Knowing that she wouldn't be satisfied with that, he said, "I got into some trouble in Langvik."

"What kind of trouble?"

"I got into a fight over a girl." Which was, technically, true.

"We don't have troubles enough, brodir?"

"I don't want to talk about it."

Now her eyes fixed on the runestick. "What's that?" Before he could take evasive action, she had hold of it, turning it in her hand. "Where did you get this?"

"From the girl." When Liv shook her head, puzzled, he added, "The one that the fight was about."

"This is very old magic," Liv said, fingering the runestick. "Lost magic." She looked up at Eiric, her eyes alight with interest. "I would like to meet this girl."

"She's dead," Eiric said bluntly. "Like I said, I don't want to talk about it."

"Oh." She looked at him, her face solemn and sad. "I'm sorry."

"I only met her the once," Eiric said. He snatched up the new shirt and pulled it over his head. "Thank you, Liv," he said, extending his arms so that she could adjust the sleeves. "It's perfect."

"It will do," she said, studying him through narrowed eyes. "Now. You know that our grandfadir Gustav, and Uncle Finni and

Uncle Garth, will speak against you."

Eiric nodded. His stepfadir's family would attend the hearing, demanding justice. Or, in lieu of justice, the farm at Sundgard. Thus, there were three loud voices to speak against Eiric.

The only witness—the only voice who could speak for Eiric besides himself—was his systir, Liv, but as a woman, she was not allowed to be a witness in legal proceedings.

This did not sit well with Liv. Maybe it was because she had been born in a faraway place, but she would not accept the rules of the jarldom just because that was the way it had always been. "A ten-year-old boy could testify, and I cannot? How does that make sense?"

"It doesn't make sense," Eiric said, "but we have to deal with what is, not what should be."

"If I don't help, we will lose the farm," Liv said, displaying scant confidence that Eiric's testimony would win the day. "Maybe Bjorn will come," Liv said. "He could tell the council what his intentions were."

Eiric stared at her, worried that his systir was losing her mind. "Bjorn is dead," he said. "Our grandfadir died more than a year ago. He's not coming."

"I'll summon him," Liv said. "Maybe he'll come." With one fore-finger, she drew a symbol on her other palm, then displayed it to Eiric. He could have sworn a rivulet of light ran across her hand. He blinked, and it disappeared. "I cast a net for him," she said.

"You cast a— are you talking about sorcery again?" Eiric bit his tongue to keep from saying more. Then said more anyway. "What's this all about, Liv?"

She looked up at him with an expression that said he was on thin ice. "What's what all about?"

Since Sylvi's death, Liv had spent more time than ever with Emi, practicing chants to entice spirits, reciting incantations, pounding powders. Eiric couldn't make sense of it. Liv had always been the most practical person in the household. Now she focused on the practice of magic with the same single-mindedness she brought to every other task.

"Lately it seems like you're spending all your time on magic," he said.

"Really, brodir?" Liv said, her voice deceptively calm. "Do you mean when I am not milking the cows, or churning butter, or cooking meals, or spinning wool, or sewing your shirts, or weaving a sail for your boat?" She raised an eyebrow.

Eiric quickly retreated. "I'm not criticizing, Liv. I just wondered why . . . the sudden interest. Healers are still important, of course," he said, the memory of Reginn pinching him. "Sorcery only seems to make you a bigger target."

"Emi is my friend," Liv said. "My only friend. Modir is gone. Emi is the only person I can talk to."

"She's a thrall, Liv," Eiric said, the memory of Langvik an open wound. "If she gets into trouble, you won't be able to protect her. Not many people believe in the old ways these days."

"They do where I come from," Liv said.

"How do you even remember?" Eiric said, stress and worry driving his temper. "You were only eight years old when you came to Muckleholm."

"I can feel it," she said, flexing her hands as if squeezing magic from the air. "It's all around us. You could feel it too if you weren't so willfully blind to it."

"Liv, if the gods do exist, what good does it do us?" Eiric said, his voice rising, the heat building in him again. "Is there any evidence that they care? Modir is still dead, and our stepgrandfadir and stepuncles are going to take our farm away from us."

"I'm not counting on the gods," Liv said. "I'm talking about seidr–sorcery."

"Bjorn always said that when we are born, the Norns have already woven our fate into the fabric of the universe. If there isn't anything you can do to change it, then why try?"

"The web is not off the loom yet," Liv insisted. "What if you could unravel bits of it and reweave it? What if you could add a bit of lace or a new color? What if you could take something drab and make it beautiful? What if you could see the future and avoid trouble that is coming your way?"

"If you can do magic, then conjure up a sack of gold we can use to pay off the Knudsens," Eiric shouted, his rage and helplessness driving him. He paused, calmed himself with an effort, then added, softly, "All I'm saying is that there are no miracles anymore. The gods are not walking among us, pitching in now and then. We are not going to be saved by magic or anything else."

"Give up on magic if you want," Liv said in a voice like steel. "If men give up sorcery, they still rule the world. They sit on the councils; they make the laws; they sail away and make their fortunes or die. Their lives go on much the same." She snatched up her distaff, the one she used to spin flax, and shook it in his face. "That is why magic is so often the province of women. It is the power we wield in the world, our ability to shape and change and control it. We would be foolish to give it up."

15

SHIP OF DREAMS

FROZEN BY GRIEF, REGINN FELT the boat rock as the crewman boarded and pitch again as he cast off. Finally, she heard the creak of the oars and felt the swells beneath them that meant that they were underway.

Still, she didn't move, stricken by the voices clamoring in her head.

Tove: *Your fate is already woven into the fabric of the universe from the moment of your birth. There is no use trying to change it. What will be will be.*

That should have relieved her guilt, but it did not. It only made her feel helpless.

From the vaettir—a warning she had not heeded.

He will find his freedom in Helgafjell.

Leave us be, spinner, we who have gone before you.

The Wyrdweb will not be unraveled by such as you.

She ran her fingers over her slave collar and the attached chain. Why had she ever thought she could be anything more than a puppet—a thrall who danced to Asger's tune? How could she still believe in the magic of the runes when they'd offered Thurston no protection?

Hopelessness swept over her.

If she tried to escape, she would drown.

If she tried to escape and survived, Asger would find her and make her pay.

Your modir sold you to a demon.

How can you expect to do better?

And then, another voice.

You are Reginn of the Oak Grove.

You are the meeting of fire and ice

The underlayment of all other magic.

You make your own choices

And live with the consequences.

We do not help the weak and timid.

We are here for the bold.

Those words sizzled through her, breaking the spell of helplessness.

What was it Thurston had said? *I did not come back from the dead to live enslaved.*

And Modir Tyra: *I can guarantee you one thing—he will never find you where we're going.*

No choice was without risk, but there was always a choice. Reginn just hadn't seen it until now.

How much time did she have? She didn't know. The warship was far out in the harbor, and Beau was a slacker. Hopefully it would be enough.

She picked up her dagger. Gripping it in her left hand, she extended her right forearm, clenched her fist, and cut into the flesh. Blood welled around the blade. One cut up, another down, on a slant.

The rune was Uruz—strength of will. Courage. She layered another on top—binding them together. Sowilo, meaning success and solace.

She continued until she was nearly faint from pain and loss of blood, then finished with a rune of healing. Her arm was now a cobweb of puckered pink scars.

The next step was more than risky, but she had to get free of the chain. Reaching up to her neckline, she fingered the link that attached her collar to the chain. The weakest link.

She unfastened her overdress, slipped out of it, and stowed the brooches in her carry bag. Then she spread her dress over the planked deck and used the waterskin to wet it down.

She set the light stick on the damp overdress, carefully positioned the blade of her dagger, and struck a sharp blow to the glass at one end, cracking it. She held the stick upright and struck it again, taking the tip off.

Immediately, she felt the heat of Asger's flame leaking from the light stick. Gritting her teeth, she raised the rod until it touched the iron loop that connected the chain to her collar.

As both chain and collar heated, the pain became all but intolerable. When Reginn dribbled water over the collar, steam boiled up. Finally, she slid the waterskin between the collar and her neck to provide some protection. When she removed it, a stream of molten gold that had been dammed up by the waterskin poured down between her breasts.

The collar was melting.

Stifling a scream, Reginn dropped the light stick and leaned forward so that the molten gold fell onto the overdress instead. She wrapped her hands in Thurston's shirt, gripped the collar, and with a strength she didn't know she had, wrenched it off. It plopped onto the wool, now an open coil still attached to the iron chain.

She stared at it with revulsion. Blisters were already forming around her neck and down her front. But she remembered something Asger had said as he fastened the first collar around her neck.

Gold is gold.

The metal was still hot, still a little soft. Using the tip of her dagger, she managed to pry the link open and remove the chain. She wrapped the collar in her overdress and stuffed it into her carry bag. *A girl never knows when a little gold will come in handy.*

The scent of burning wood reminded her of the light stick. She'd dropped it, and now the flames had found a purchase on the sloped walls.

When they burn you.

Fighting down panic, she strapped the bag over her underdress, then banged on the hatch and shouted, trying to get the oarsman's attention. The creak of the oars continued, and so did her banging and shouting. Eventually, the rowing stopped, and she heard Beau's voice through the hatch.

"Stop that," he said. "It won't do you any good."

"The ship's on fire," she screamed. "Something went wrong with the light stick. Let me out! We've got to put it out or the whole boat will burn."

"Don't give me that," he snarled. "Your master told me not to believe anything you—" He stopped. Sniffed. "I smell smoke." Even through the door, she could hear the panic in his voice. "I can't swim."

"Neither can I," Reginn snapped back. "And I'm chained to the mast. Let me out so I can help you put it out."

She heard Beau fumbling at the latch. The air was getting harder and harder to breathe.

"Please hurry," she said before she was overtaken by a fit of coughing.

The oarsman finally managed the latch and yanked the door open. Reginn scrambled out, followed by billows of poisonous-smelling black smoke. Something in one of the casks had caught fire—probably tar.

"Hey," Beau said, frowning. "I thought you were chained up."

"Not anymore," Reginn said, swiping at her burning eyes. She scooped up a bucket, dropped it over the side, and hauled it up, full of water. She emptied it through the hatch, then thrust it at Beau. "Here, keep filling this with water; pour it into the hold and wet down the deck."

Meanwhile, Reginn scanned the ocean around them. They were a little ways past the spinners' ship, about halfway to the *Fossegrim*. The crew on the spinners' ship was hauling in the anchor and raising the sails. In just a few minutes, they would be underway.

As she watched, a tall figure appeared on deck and advanced to the rail. Somehow, Reginn knew that it was Tyra. The spinner shaded her eyes, obviously looking for something. She fixed on the burning boat, came up on her toes, and extended her arms, as if to summon her.

"The fire's spreading," Beau shouted. "Are you going to help or what?"

Reginn turned to see that the flames had burst through the decking in the bow and were roaring toward midships.

We are here for the hold.

Reginn climbed onto the gunwale and balanced for a moment, judging the distance she'd have to swim.

"Hey," Beau shouted. "I thought you couldn't swim."

"I can't," Reginn said. "I'd rather drown than burn." With that, she launched into a shallow dive that she hoped would take her as far as possible from the burning oarboat.

She smacked into the sea, her momentum driving water up into her nose and mouth, setting her to coughing, flailing, and panicking. The water was numbingly cold. Her swimming adventure might have ended right there, but she finally realized that she could lift her face out of the water to suck in a breath.

A memory came back to her–Asger, Tove, and Reginn were camping beside a clear, cold stream that flowed down from the snowpack in the mountains. Tove was trying to teach Reginn to swim, and Reginn was fighting it.

"Lie flat," Tove had said. "Dig a hole in the water in front of you and push it behind you."

Reginn kept her body as flat as she could, trying to mimic the shallow-draft longboats the bold Northmen sailed clear across the western sea.

She kicked her feet, pulled herself forward with her arms, raising her face now and then to make sure she was on course. Fortunately, she was still in the harbor, and the swells were not too large. The next time she looked forward, she saw that a small craft had been lowered from the side of the spinners' boat. Two oarsmen were propelling the boat toward her.

But she was growing weary, her lungs starving for air, her clothes and her carry bag a constant drag on her. She thought of trying to cut away her underdress but feared she would sink if she stopped moving. She flipped onto her back and coasted a little, looking back at the oarboat. By now, it was totally engulfed in flames.

She hoped that Beau had made the jump as well. Better to drown than burn.

When she turned around again, the spinners' boat was close, but she saw then what she hadn't seen before. The jarl's warship had also birthed a boat, this one a narrow blade with eight oarsmen. It was rapidly closing the gap between them.

Reginn lunged forward, kicking and pulling harder than before. In minutes, she was alongside the spinners' boat. One of the crew extended an oar, pulled her close, then gripped her by both wrists and wrestled her aboard.

Reginn lay gasping, leaning against the gunwale.

"Are you all right?" one of the oarsmen said, kneeling beside her.

"Row!" Reginn said, pointing toward the jarl's oarboat, which was on a course to intercept.

The oarsmen went at it with a will. Despite her exhaustion, Reginn would have joined in had there been an oar to spare. From her vantage point, she could see Modir Tyra at the rail, looking back and forth from their boat to the jarl's longship. They were close—close enough for Reginn to make out Tyra's features in the growing light, her knuckles whitening as she gripped her staff.

But not close enough.

Tyra scanned the decking nearby, as if looking for help or witnesses. Apparently seeing none, she raised her staff and rolled it between her hands like a spinner collecting fiber on a distaff. The head of the staff began to glow, as if ensnaring the light of the dawn stars. She kept her eyes fixed on the head of the staff until, seeming satisfied, she snapped it toward the approaching longboat. Tendrils of light spun out from the head of the staff, bathing the jarl's crew in an unearthly glow. Then it poured out over the water, creating a brilliant path across the surface of the harbor. The longboat crew stared as if transfixed, their quarry forgotten, and then, one by one, let go of their oars and slipped into the sea, following Tyra's lighted path to nowhere.

The empty longboat coasted on for a distance, then slowed and stopped, turning so that the waves slapped uselessly against the lapstrake hull.

Reginn watched, mesmerized by this display, until their small craft bumped against the side of the spinners' knarr. The ship's crew deployed a rope ladder. Reginn's oarsmen gestured, and she climbed up the side, flipping over the gunwale and flopping onto the deck. She lay there, shivering. Overhead, she heard the captain calling out orders to his crew, the rattle of metal as the wind filled the sail. She felt a lurch as the ship got underway.

Then Tyra was kneeling beside her. "Are you hurt, dottir?" she said.

Dottir? No one had called her that since Tove left.

"N-no," Reginn said. "J-just cold."

"Why would Jarl Karlsen send a boat after you?" Tyra said, looking to starboard, where the jarl's warship seemed to be preparing to give chase.

"He knows my master," Reginn said, wondering how Tyra knew who he was. "We were to sail aboard his ship."

"Let's get you out of the wind," Tyra said grimly, "and out of sight." Gripping Reginn's hands, she helped her to her feet, then draped her blue cloak over her, whether to hide her or to warm her, Reginn didn't know. It felt good to be cared for.

Tyra led her midships, where they descended into the cargo area. It had been adapted into a seating and sleeping area, half-covered by a canopy.

"I'll find you some dry clothes," Tyra said, looking her up and down, then rummaging in a chest full of clothing. Moments later, she tossed a wad of linen to Reginn.

"Change into this," she said. "I'm going on deck to see what's happening."

Huddled under the canopy, Reginn unstrapped her carry bag and stripped off her sopping underdress. It took her a minute to sort out the spinner's clothing. It was a pair of loose, knee-length trousers and a soft linen shirt. Like men's clothing but made of the softest, most finely woven fabric she'd ever touched. She pulled the underclothes on over her naked body and thought, This must be what is worn in the halls of the gods.

As she ran her fingers over the sleeves, she heard the keeper's voice from overhead.

"Tyra, you know better than to take these kinds of risks."

"Don't worry, Amma," Tyra said. "We'll outrun the barbarians."

Barbarians? Reginn thought. Is that what the wyrdspinners think of us?

"A knarr will never outrun a warship," the keeper said. "We will have to intervene, and that will ignite their curiosity."

"It doesn't matter," Tyra said. "They'll never find us."

"Barbarians have found us before, and they will find us again if we kindle that desire in them," the keeper said. "Taking a half-grown thrall from an ally of the jarl's might do that. That is one reason we select our acolytes as infants. They have no history, no relationships in the Archipelago."

Reginn sat on a sea chest, hunched her shoulders, tried to make herself smaller.

"She was on her way to Karlsen. There has to be a reason. Do you really want him to gain control of her?"

"If he was interested before, your actions have confirmed that he is on the right path," the keeper said. "They'll wonder who we are and why we intervened."

"She has gifts that we need," Tyra said stubbornly.

"We *have* what we need," the keeper said, her voice edged. There was a pause; then the keeper continued. "Tyra, this obsession of yours will be our undoing. Let go of it, or I will–"

Then came the voice of a crewman, interrupting. "They're going to overtake us, Highest," he said. "What are your orders?"

Reginn imagined the jarl's men boarding the ship, slaughtering the crew, and then yanking her out of the hold. And the spinners–what would happen to them? Would the jarl respect their position as vala?

Barbarians, the keeper had called them.

Fighting off the temptation to burrow behind a sea chest and hide, Reginn climbed to the deck, not wanting to be trapped below if they were boarded.

But when she emerged, it was to see the keeper standing in the stern of the ship, her cloak whipping about her, facing their pursuers, staff in hand. Tyra stood beside her, uncloaked, with her own staff. As Reginn watched, the keeper spun the staff in her hands, light collecting around the distaff end.

The wind picked up astern, freshening into a gale that ripped away the warship's sail, sending it kiting out of sight. The oarsmen kept rowing, now close enough that Reginn could see the fright in their faces.

While the keeper called the waves higher, Tyra slammed the butt of her staff into the deck and then pointed the head of it toward the oncoming boat, enveloping the ship and its crewmen in brilliance. The ship slowed as the oarsmen eased off, and the helmsman looked around as if confused. A curtain of fog descended between the ships, obscuring the warship from sight.

Their own ship forged ahead through the glittering waves as the rising sun portended a fair day.

By now, Reginn was shaking, her teeth chattering. She had never seen magic like this. Her little runecharms and spellsongs seemed rudimentary in comparison.

Modir Tyra and the keeper left their positions at the stern to return to their quarters midships. As they passed Reginn, the keeper's cool gaze brushed over her, making no promises.

She doesn't want me at the Grove, Reginn thought. She thinks I'm more trouble than I'm worth.

Reginn was determined to prove her wrong.

Asger Eldr strode down the waterfront, burning with excitement and anticipation. His visit to Gunnar's Hall had proven fruitful.

After he'd soothed Gunnar's hurt feelings with Karlsen's silver, the hallkeeper was happy to tell him the story of the thrall and the witchling who had sung him back to life.

At first, Asger had been skeptical. After all, his meyla had said she had found her own partner when Asger's choice didn't show up. She had considerable experience convincing a roomful of people that they were seeing something magical. And if she and the ginger had something going, Asger had to admit that it was a genius way to free the boy from his fettered status.

But . . . what if it were true? What if Reginn could speak to the dead, even bring them back to life? More importantly, what if he could convince Karlsen that it was true? It would provide Asger with the status he yearned for and the tools he needed to reshape the world around him to suit his purposes.

But when he reached the quay where Beau should have been waiting to ferry him to the ship, he found Rikhard Karlsen instead, pacing.

"What is it?" Asger said.

"Who was she?" Karlsen demanded. "Who was the girl?"

Asger blinked at him. *Who* was *the girl?*

"What do you mean?" Asger said in a low hiss. "Where is she? What's happened?"

Karlsen held up a charred piece of planking. "Your thrall apparently set fire to my oarboat once it left the quay. She leaped off the boat into the water, and another ship picked her up. We sent our ship's boat after them, but the crew went mad and dove into the water. We gave chase, but lost them."

"You. *Lost*. Them?" Asger said, feeling the flames rising at this litany of failures. "How is that possible?"

"Those aboard the ship conjured a cloud that confused and blinded my helmsman and left my ship adrift," Karlsen said.

"Because of your thrall, I've lost a boat and a crew. The question is why."

"She's . . . gone?" Asger whispered.

"Yes," Karlsen said impatiently. "I've never seen magic like that. This might be the break we have been waiting for. Now I need to know everything about her—what her gifts are, who her allies might be, and why it was so important to them to retrieve her. And, of course, we need to find out where they are now."

She has no allies, Asger wanted to say. *I've made sure of that.*

He wanted to lash out, to char this self-important jarl to ashes.

It was an impulse he had to resist. Asger was dangerous, but the jarl was dangerous in a different way. Plus, it appeared that Asger would need allies, too, if he was ever to reclaim what was his.

16

THING

SUNDGARD WAS THE FARTHEST FARM from the village, situated as it was along the cliffs overlooking the sound. On the day of the spring council meeting, Eiric and Liv rose before the sun in order to ride to Selvagr and arrive by midday.

Eiric carried a bag containing the gold arm ring Bjorn had left him, Liv's heavy gold necklace, and a small gold game piece inscribed with runes worn down by handling. Leif had brought it to Eiric after a summer at sea.

"Keep this," his fadir had said, "and maybe one day we'll find the game that goes with it."

For years, Eiric had carried it everywhere as a kind of talisman, a charm of protection, but he no longer believed in its power.

Eiric and Liv hoped that if the Knudsens demanded compensation for Sten's death, these would suffice. His axe was stowed across his back through his belt, within easy reach in case negotiations took a turn for the worse.

Not that it would provide more than a temporary reprieve if the worst happened.

Liv carried her staff and a knapsack filled with food for the journey. She also had several boning knives secreted around her person.

Completing the party was Hilde Stevenson, Ivar's wet nurse, carrying Ivar in a sling. Hilde was the dottir of the blacksmith Ulff Stevenson, married just two years when her husband died of a fever at summer's end. She'd had a baby at the solstice, but it was stillborn. She'd moved in after Sylvi died, seeming to welcome the distraction of caring for Ivar and helping on the farm. She was in the process of sewing Eiric yet another shirt.

Sten's family had insisted that they bring Ivar along to demon-strate that he was alive and healthy. Eiric suspected that they hoped that would make it easier to take custody of him when the Thing ruled in their favor.

Eiric hadn't risked traveling to Selvagr since Sylvi died just three months before. Even though there had been no ruling on Sten's death, there was always the chance that Eiric's stepfadir's family would exact their own blood price for their kinsman, preempting the council proceedings. Liv was a force to be reckoned with, but with Eiric gone, she would be unlikely to hold on to the farm.

During the long ride through the birch forest, Eiric startled every time the winter-sered branches rattled in the wind or a flicker of movement caught his eye. His stepgrandfadir and uncles would know that they would be traveling this road to arrive in the village at midday. There was still time to intervene before the council met.

There were no incidents along the way, so perhaps the clatter of branches and the rustling of leaves signified nothing more than the last flailings of a dying winter when spring is on the way.

He should be readying his ship for sailing, not contending with what passed for justice in Selvagr.

Eventually, they emerged from the trees, having reached the rocky shoreline of the sound. They then followed the beach toward Selvagr, and away from the open sea.

As they neared the village, they passed more and more small

farmsteads along the path. When they rounded a headland, Eiric saw that a new longhouse was rising on a choice spot on a high bluff overlooking the water. The foundation pillars had been pounded into the ground and the vertical posts fastened in between, but only the center roof beam had been raised. It was surrounded by several smaller structures—barns or other outbuildings. Workers swarmed over the site like scavengers over a shipwreck. It was already clear that, when finished, it would be the largest and finest dwelling in the village.

There hadn't been much building in recent years. If anything, the population was dwindling as people left, seeking better fortune elsewhere. Fish had fled the nearby waters, and more and more farms were falling into ruins. The tar pits seemed to be the only business that was thriving.

"Whose house is that?" Eiric pointed as Liv came up beside him. Despite the risk, she had continued to travel to and from the village and was more up to date on the news.

"Harald Karlsen has sent his son Rikhard to manage his holdings in Selvagr," Liv said.

"I saw his ship in Langvik," Eiric said, feeling that gut punch of loss that always accompanied the memory of that night.

"It was probably Rikhard. He brings Harald's ship in to Selvagr sometimes. He doesn't spend much time at home these days. Some are saying the two quarreled, and either Harald sent his son away, or Rikhard thought it best to put some distance between himself and his fadir."

"What do nobles have to quarrel about?" Eiric muttered.

"The same as the rest of us," Liv said. "Money, property, family, power. Anyway, that's his house going up."

Eiric studied the house, wondering if it was being built with Jarl Harald's money.

"They say Rikhard makes his own way," Liv said, answering Eiric's unspoken question. "Every summer, he funds several ships on raids to the west and south. Every fall, they come back with a hold full of riches. Everyone wants to join his crews. Some in the village are hoping to find work on his farm," Liv said, "but I've heard he'll bring his own people."

The village market was busy with midday shoppers and browsers, though there wasn't much on offer this early in the season, this late in the day. The fresh-fish monger was sloshing buckets of water over her display tables to wash away the fish bones and slime. The cheesemaker was all but sold out.

It was just as well. The Halvorsens might own the finest farm in the Archipelago, but like most farmers, they were land rich and money poor. Especially these days, when nobody had any silver. The best they could hope for was a barter arrangement. They couldn't afford to be spending money at the market with the farm at risk.

They sat down under a tree, and Liv opened the carry bag full of food. They all went at it with a will, including Ivar, who latched onto Hilde's breast as if he never intended to let go. It was like they all understood the need to fuel up for the battle ahead.

Their arrival didn't go unnoticed. Reva and Astrid, the tanner's dottirs, huddled together, pointing and whispering. It seemed that whenever they weren't smearing brains and codfish oil on hides, they were pointing at Eiric and whispering.

They were nearly finished eating when Eiric saw his two stepuncles, Finni and Garth, stalk through the market, scowls on their faces. He remembered what his modir had said that night in the boat shed when she'd tried to persuade him to leave the farm.

Sten's fadir and brodirs are on the Thing, and most of the other members do business with them. You'll be outlawed, and then Sten's family will kill you.

His modir had warned him, but he hadn't listened.

"It must be time," Liv said. She stood and took the now-sleeping Ivar from Hilde's arms. Eiric slung the bag with the jewelry over his shoulder. They followed after their uncles, leaving Hilde sitting under the tree with the remains of their food supply.

The Thing at Selvagr met at the Knudsen longhouse, since it was the largest house in the village (for now, anyway) and because Sten's fadir, Gustav Knudsen, was the head of the council.

When they arrived at the Knudsens', Emi met them at the door. She pulled back the blanket to peer at Ivar's face, then gently stroked his cheek.

"He thrives," she said, smiling. "You have taken good care of this child of the gods."

"He may not be ours for long," Eiric said crossly. He was in no mood to entertain the notion that anything about their situation was a blessing.

Emi pressed a bundle of herbs into Liv's hands. "Put this in your pockets for luck," she said. "They're already in the alehall. They've been in there for a while already." Emi picked up a tray of cups, then led them around to the rear of the longhouse to the hall, housed in a separate building.

When Eiric and Liv entered the hall, the conversation stopped abruptly.

Was that a a sign that the verdict was already in?

The council members were seated on benches arranged in a semicircle around the longfire. Opposite the council, on the other side of the firepit, stood the bench for the petitioner. Or the accused. Their uncles were there, and their grandfadir, grim faced as hired mourners at a wake. Aside from Emi, the only semifriendly face belonged to Ulff Stevenson, Hilde's fadir. The blacksmith who'd offered Eiric an apprenticeship a lifetime ago.

What if he'd taken it? What if he'd left before Ivar was born, as his modir had wanted?

In addition to Sten's family and Stevenson, the final member of the Thing was Calder Olafsen, the tanner, fadir of the very eligible Reva and Astrid. Calder's dottirs might point and whisper about Eiric, but the tanner had made it no secret that he had hopes of marrying them off to Sten's bachelor brodirs.

Stevenson nodded at Eiric and Liv, while the rest sat, arms folded, heads tilted back, looking down their noses at them like butchers appraising a haunch of venison.

There's no way to win this, Eiric thought. I may as well pack my rucksack now.

Eiric and Liv sat side by side on the petitioner's bench, Liv with Ivar on her lap.

With that, Uncle Finni launched his first volley. "Why is she here?" he said, pointing at Liv. "Women are not allowed to testify at the council."

"I came to help my brodir Ivar, because you insisted that he be here," Liv said.

"He's not your brodir," Finni said. "He's a Knudsen."

"Where were you at his name-fastening?" Liv said. "Your brodir denied him and left him in the forest. We claimed him and named him, and so he is ours."

"You are lying, witch," Garth said.

"Liv is not lying," Eiric said, realizing that his crafty systir had found a way to testify after all. "I was there, too. She's telling the truth."

"Why should we listen to either of you?" Garth fired back.

"If you're not going to listen to us, then why are we here?" Liv said.

While Garth grasped for a response to that, Gustav said, "Give the child to me, then, and leave us."

"Why not let Liv take Ivar outside?" Eiric suggested.

"Quit calling him Ivar!" Finni shouted.

"What's his name, then?" Liv said.

They all seemed stumped.

"We'll make that decision in due time," Gustav said. "The boy stays here. Give me the child."

With a faint shrug, Liv sauntered over to Gustav and handed off their brodir.

Ivar had seemed to be sound asleep, but now his eyes snapped open. Seeing Liv's retreating back, he began to howl.

Ivar was a lusty howler.

It was all Eiric could do not to laugh out loud, dire as the situation was.

Gustav's expression was that of a man who has accidentally picked up a hive of bees or a bag of skita and doesn't dare drop it. He looked around wildly, then tried bouncing the demon child on his knee. Ivar kept right on screaming as if someone were ripping off his toes, one by one.

Gustav stood, then, dangling Ivar like a wad of soiled linen. He tried to hand him off to Garth, who raised his arms to fend off his fadir.

"Blood and iron, Knudsen," Olafsen said finally. "Give the baby back to the girl. I don't care whether she stays or goes, but I can't abide this any longer."

Gustav gave Ivar back to Liv, and the squalling diminished to a few hitching sobs as he gripped Liv's braid in his fist.

"You'd think just seeing that girl's face would set him to howling," Garth muttered, intentionally loud enough for everyone to hear.

"He knows his family," Liv said, settling onto a bench by the fire, Ivar on her lap.

"All right," Gustav said, trying to regain his footing, "but if she disrupts the hearing, I'll—"

With that, the door slammed open.

"Rikhard!" Gustav blurted, eyes wide with surprise. "When did you come back?"

Eiric swiveled to view the newcomer.

He was tall—not so tall as Eiric, but few men were. His long wool tunic was decorated with woven braid, his belt was threaded through a silver buckle, and a showy sword rested at his hip. His linen trousers were wrapped knee to ankle with more wool. He had fine leather shoes on his feet, heavy gold on his arm, and his cloak was secured with an ornate brooch.

Eiric realized, too late, that he was staring, but then everyone else was, too.

There were more gold rings on Rikhard's fingers. Eiric couldn't help noticing how clean his hands were. Calloused, yes—but clean, the nails trimmed and buffed. He resisted the urge to tuck his own hands under his cloak.

The jarl's son's bleached hair was cropped short in front and reached only to his collar elsewhere—shorter than that of most men in Selvagr. He was beardless, displaying only a reddish stubble. Maybe that wasn't a matter of choice. Eiric was shocked at how young he was. Close to his own age, and yet Liv had said that he owned a number of warships.

"I returned last night," Rikhard said, moving toward the center of the room. Ten men filed in after him, all heavily armed, many with swords. The eyes of everyone on the Thing grew bigger.

This must be Rikhard's hird, his personal guard and circle of advisors and liegemen.

"Ah," Gustav said. "So. To what can we attribute the honor of your visit here at our council?"

"My ships are beached on the other side of the headland. I intend to sail from here this season, but I am in need of tar for repairs before I set out."

"Of course, of course," Gustav said with evident relief. "We are grateful for the trade. I will send my man over later today to assess your needs."

"Good," Rikhard said. He strolled over to the ale cask, pulled out a silver cup, and filled it without so much as a by-your-leave. He turned, leaned against the nearest pillar, raised his cup, and said, "I bring news. My fadir, Harald Karlsen, is dead."

The members of the Thing looked at each other, no doubt hoping that someone else would ask the obvious question.

So Eiric asked it.

"My condolences," he said. "What happened to your fadir?"

Rikhard studied Eiric over the rim of his cup, as if noticing him for the first time. "We haven't met," he said. "Who are you?"

"My name is Eiric Halvorsen," Eiric said. "We own a farm at Sundgard."

"Sundgard!" Rikhard said, eyes narrowing. "You live at *Sundgard*?"

"Yes," Eiric said. Clearly, the jarl had heard of it. How and why? Was his presence here more than happenstance? "It's been in our family for generations," Eiric added, shifting his gaze to those sitting in judgment of him.

A murmur went through the council, but the members held their peace.

"Well, Eiric Halvorsen of Sundgard, my fadir had an accident." He paused. "He ran into a sword."

"Whose sword?" Eiric said.

"My sword," Rikhard said. "I have replaced him as jarl for the region."

Everyone sat frozen as the new-minted jarl took a seat on a stone bench just outside the council circle and his men arranged themselves along the wall, hands on their weapons.

Did Rikhard think the Thing was going to launch some kind of rebellion against the change in regime?

Knudsen raised his cup. "All hail, Lord Rikhard," he said. "I know your fadir would be ... proud ..." He stopped, flushing, as if unsure how to carry on.

"No doubt he *would* be proud of you if he were still alive," Eiric said. Liv handed him a full cup, and he raised it, then drank.

Already, this meeting had gone on longer than he'd expected. He'd thought he'd be banished before noon and dead before sundown.

"So," Gustav said, licking his lips, his gaze flitting around the room. "If there's nothing else, we were having a meeting about some minor local ... issues. Nothing that would be of interest to you, lord."

"You're wrong," Rikhard said. "As I will be responsible for the jarldom, I am interested in everything that goes on. I want to get to know the members of this council and understand how this works." He gestured, a graceful flick of his fingers. "Proceed."

17

ROUGH JUSTICE

ANY FOOL COULD TELL THAT Sten's family had no interest in showcasing their rush to justice in front of the new jarl. They shifted on their benches, looked at each other, then at the armed men lining the walls. Clearly, if the jarl wanted to stay, there was no dislodging him.

Finally, Gustav rose, crossed to the ale cask, and drew another cupful. Then turned to face the jarl. "Actually, it is a hearing of evidence regarding a murder." He hesitated, as if debating saying more. "My son—and his family—were killed."

"I'm sorry for your loss," Rikhard murmured.

Encouraged, Gustav continued. "So you can see that this is a private matter, and not one of interest outside of Selvagr."

"On the contrary, I am intrigued," Rikhard said. "Is it customary to have the family of the deceased decide the guilt of the defendant?"

"It is customary for the *council* to make these decisions," Garth said through clenched teeth. He was the most hot-blooded of Sten's brothers and, as usual, seemed to be having trouble holding on to his temper. "As we are the duly elected members of the Thing, it is our duty to make this decision."

Finni put his hand on his brodir's shoulder to shut him up. "Our greatest concern is for the safety of the accused, if the hearing was made public," Finni said.

Eiric had no idea what game the young noble was playing, or if it would matter in the end when the final verdict came down, but he was enjoying the evident discomfort of his accusers. At least, this way, Sten's family might have to work a little harder to make their case.

"I am the defendant," he said, "and I would welcome witnesses to this proceeding. Particularly witnesses who are not related to the dead man."

Rikhard flinched a bit, as if he'd forgotten that there was a defendant in the room. He gave Eiric an appraising look, his blue eyes narrowed, then turned back to Gustav. "There you are. The defendant has no objection." He tented his fingers and looked from person to person. "So. Carry on."

Gustav nodded gloomily, as if his appetite had been ruined for the feast ahead. "Eiric Halvorsen, you stand accused of murdering your stepfadir, Sten Knudsen, and your modir, Sylvi Eiricsen, in an effort to claim the farm at Sundgard for yourself."

Liv came to her feet, eyes blazing. "*That* is an unforgivable lie," she said. "We had nothing to do with Modir's death."

"Be quiet, girl," Garth said. "Your brodir will have his time to speak."

"That is the accusation," Gustav said, sailing forward. "What evidence is there against the boy?"

"I am Finni Knudsen, brodir to the dead man," Finni said. "I spoke to my brodir often during the weeks prior to his death. He was so happy—looking forward to the birth of his son.

"He often spoke of raising the boy at Sundgard, teaching him about farm life, and how a child would bring him and Sylvi closer. They both wanted many more children."

Finni sighed, shook his head. "Then, as Sylvi's time came near, Sten grew worried. Sylvi's older children were becoming more and more hostile toward him. They wanted no part of a brodir who might compete with them for their modir's favor. They saw Sylvi's new family as a threat to their own legacy. Sylvi was worried, too—"

"Modir was worried, all right," Eiric said. "She was worried that, once Sten had an heir of his own, he would murder the two of us." He turned to Ulff Stevenson, who was watching the testimony, shoulders hunched with discomfort. "In fact, just before Ivar was born, she tried to persuade me to go to Selvagr as apprentice to you."

Stevenson stared blankly at him for a long, heart-stopping moment, then nodded, recollection flooding into his face. "I remember. We spoke of it several times. I agreed to take you on. But you never came."

"That night was the first time she mentioned it to me," Eiric said. "Then Ivar was born, and he was sickly, and—"

"Let the witness finish, boy," Gustav thundered. "Go on, Finni."

Finni nodded, darting a look at Rikhard. "After the baby was born, Sylvi kept him close, worried about what the Halvorsens would do. Until one night Sten was working in the summer barn, leaving Sylvi and the baby alone. She must have fallen asleep and awakened to find the baby was gone—likely taken by the Halvorsens. She went out into the woods to hunt for him. She wasn't properly dressed, and she froze to death."

Finni paused for dramatic effect. "And then, when Sten came back to the house, Eiric Halvorsen laid in wait and murdered him."

"How do you know all this?" Rikhard said abruptly.

Finni blinked at him. "What do you mean?"

"How do you know this is what happened? Were you there? Were there any witnesses?"

Finni gaped at him, his mouth opening and closing with nothing coming out. "Of course I wasn't there. If I'd been there, I would have stopped it. But it's not that hard to figure out. The witch came into town with a newborn baby, looking for a wet nurse."

"So I came looking for a wet nurse for the baby we tried to kill?" Liv said, offering Ivar her knuckle to bite on. "Does that make sense? Why would—"

"When she refused to answer our questions," Finni all but shouted, "Garth and I knew something must have happened to Sylvi and Sten. We rode straight for Sundgard and found the boy had built a funeral pyre for his modir. Sten was nowhere to be found."

"Did you ask Halvorsen where Sten was?" Gustav said.

Garth nodded. "He said he was gone and that we should look for him elsewhere."

"So you thanked him for the information and departed?" Rikhard asked, lips quirking with amusement.

Garth and Finni looked at each other. "No, we . . . ah . . ." Finni said, making the mistake of beginning before he'd decided on the end.

"What makes you think he was murdered?" Eiric said. "Have you found a body?"

"No, we haven't found a body," Finni said. "He's disappeared."

"Men disappear for lots of reasons," Eiric said. "Maybe he was distraught over his wife's death and—"

"We guessed Sten was dead," Garth said, raising his voice, "because the boy had obviously been in a fight."

"What do you mean?" Olafsen said.

"He was covered with fresh wounds when we arrived at the house," Garth said, "and wrapped in bandages. Yet he acted like nothing was wrong. He didn't offer any explanation."

"I didn't owe you an explanation," Eiric said.

"It's clear to us that Halvorsen murdered Sten and his wife,"

Finni said quickly. "He denies it, so that's why we decided it was best to bring the dispute to the Thing."

"Do you have anything to say before we vote?" Gustav said, glaring at Eiric as if daring him to delay the verdict.

Eiric stood, planting himself as for any other fight, not meaning to waste time with a long speech. "When our brodir, Ivar, was born, he suffered from shake spells. Sten claimed the child wasn't his and took him into the forest and left him to die."

"As was his right," Olafsen put in.

"If the child wasn't his, it was not," Liv said.

Garth could stand it no longer. He lurched from his seat, shouting, "If you cannot keep your mouth closed, then you can wait outside." He reached for Liv's arm, meaning to haul her to her feet, but somehow his feet got tangled together, sending him sprawling.

He scrambled to his feet, swearing, to find Eiric in his path.

"Sit, Uncle," Eiric said softly.

Garth pointed a shaking finger at Liv. "The girl's a witch! When I went to–to help her up, she knocked me down."

"Maybe you should keep your hands to yourself," Rikhard said, in a manner that brooked no argument. He nodded to Eiric. "Continue."

"When Sylvi realized what he'd done, she went looking for her baby. We found them together. Sylvi was dead, but the baby still lived." He swallowed hard. "Sten refused to welcome him into the family. So we named him and claimed him ourselves."

"Why would you do that?" Stevenson said, looking lost.

"Modir died for him," Liv said. "She wanted him to live. We did it for her."

This time, when Liv spoke, Garth spoke up again. "How old are you, anyway?"

"I'm nineteen," Liv said, a familiar defiance in her eyes.

"Why aren't you married?" he said. "No man will have you with that face?"

"I could ask you the same question," Liv said, "but I really don't care." Eiric could tell that his systir was losing patience with the proceedings.

Gustav seemed eager to return to the business at hand. "The boy tells a good story, but don't forget—he's had three months to work on it."

"Use your common sense," Garth said. "Why would Sten reject the baby he'd wanted for so long? Why would he risk the health of the woman he loved?"

"Because he's stupid?" Liv murmured.

"It's time to vote," Gustav said.

"There's a problem," Liv said.

"For the last time, hold your tongue, girl," Gustav said.

"There's a problem," Liv said, louder.

This time, they ignored her and took their vote. When all was said and done, the vote was just as Eiric had expected—four to one to convict. Stevenson was the only one who voted against it.

Gustav managed to put on a somber face. "Eiric Halvorsen," he said, "it is the finding of this council that you are guilty of the murder of Sten Knudsen. You are proclaimed a vargr, an exile from this place. The farm at Sundgard is forfeit. Any freeman who encounters you in this region after three days' time is entitled to kill you without—"

"There's a problem," Liv shouted.

Gustav tried to ignore her. "—is entitled to kill you without penalty and so—"

Liv stood. "I said, there's a problem. My brodir did not kill Sten Knudsen. I did."

18

DEVIL'S BARGAIN

WHEN LIV SPOKE UP AT the Thing, it was as if she'd kicked over a beehive in an alehouse, throwing the entire proceeding into chaos. Eiric glared at her, but she refused to look at him. Instead, she went and stood in front of Gustav.

"I killed Sten, but neither of us is guilty of murder. You've seen Eiric's wounds. I killed Sten because he was trying to murder my brodir and because I knew if he succeeded that I would be next." Liv extended her forearm and walked around the fire circle. "Carve the mark into my skin and call me vargr from now on and hunt me down and kill me if I return to this place. But leave my brodir be."

This did not suit the Knudsen agenda at all. Banishing Liv would not make it any easier to claim Sundgard.

"Is this true, boy?" Finni sneered. "Are you going to let your systir take your punishment for you?"

"Liv said that neither of us is guilty of murder, and that is true," Eiric said.

"He's already been banished," Garth said. "It's too late to undo it."

"Isn't it customary in situations like this for the accused to offer compensation to the family of the dead man?" Stevenson said. The blacksmith was clearly casting about for a solution that would avoid banishing anyone. That made him the only one in the room.

"We are not admitting guilt," Eiric said, "but in view of your loss, we can offer some compensation." He pulled the carry bag from under his seat and shook the gold armband, the game piece, and the necklace out onto the bench. They clattered as metal met stone.

"What the hell is that?" Garth demanded, clearly unimpressed.

"These are artifacts brought back by our grandfadir from his voyages," Eiric said. "The metal alone would bring a good price, but the objects themselves are priceless, created by master craftsmen centuries ago." He felt like he was hawking trinkets at the market.

"What would we want with a bunch of old jewelry?" Finni said. "That won't bring our brodir back."

"Neither will banishing this woman," Rikhard said.

Everyone stared at him, having all but forgotten that he was there.

The jarl rose from his bench and crossed the room to where the armband and necklace were displayed. He picked up the game piece and ran his fingers over the engraving, lips moving as if he could read what it said. Then examined the necklace and the armband.

"Where did these come from?" he asked Eiric. His face displayed nothing, but something in his voice and the way he moved suggested tightly reined excitement.

"I don't know for sure," Eiric said. "My grandfadir was a coaster and vikingr for years."

"Could I speak with him?" Rikhard said. "Perhaps he would remember."

Eiric shook his head, puzzled at the sudden change in topic. "No, he died more than a year ago."

"Would he have left any maps, drawings, anything?" Rikhard persisted.

Now Gustav was losing patience. "This is all very interesting, but we've already said that we're not interested in jewelry."

Rikhard swiveled to face him, arms folded across his chest. "Really, Knudsen? What, specifically, are you interested in? What would you consider to be adequate compensation?"

"Well . . ." Gustav hesitated, biting his lower lip, sliding looks at his sons. "Sten loved the little farm at Sundgard. That's where he died. It would mean a lot if we could keep it in the family."

"No," Stevenson said. "You can't ask for their farm. That's their livelihood. It's been in Sylvi's family for generations."

"Right," Eiric said, grateful for Stevenson's support. "It has never been in your family, so you wouldn't be keeping it, you'd be taking it."

"If it helps," Gustav said, "Garth would be willing to marry the girl." He jutted his chin toward Liv.

"I have no interest in sharing a bed with this man," Liv said, pointing at Garth. "If such a thing were to happen, he would be wise not to close his eyes. Besides, the farm belongs to Eiric. He carries Sylvi's blood; I do not."

Eiric could see Liv's strategy. Admit guilt for the crime and leave the farm in the hands of the person best able to protect it. A trade of her life for Eiric's and the preservation of Sundgard.

By now, all the Knudsens were scowling. It was plain that they wished Sten had worked a little harder to remove these two stubborn obstacles to their plans.

Finni shrugged. "They don't have anything else that we would want."

"What about silver?" Eiric found himself saying. "Or gold?"

Now everyone was staring at him. Including Liv, who looked as if she thought he'd lost his mind.

"Are you saying you have funds enough to pay a *blood price*?" Olafsen raised an eyebrow.

"Not now," Eiric said, desperate to delay the inevitable. "But I could have it in a year."

"Or we could all be dead in a year," Garth said, shaking his head. "No. We've waited long enough for justice. We want compensation now."

"How much?" Rikhard said, his voice rich with irony. "What would it take to ease your grief?"

Gustav and his sons put their heads together, then named a high sum, one they were no doubt reasonably sure that Eiric and Liv could never meet.

"And we want it now," Garth said, shooting a smug look at Liv.

"Is tomorrow morning soon enough?" Rikhard said.

This was met with a brief, stunned silence. "I don't understand," Gustav said.

"I will advance the money to the defendant now, with the farm"— he crossed the room and scooped up the artifacts—"and these items as surety," Rikhard said. "He can repay me with a year of service. That way, you receive payment now, and if Halvorsen's service is satisfactory, he retains the farm. Everyone's happy."

Except nobody was happy, it seemed, but Rikhard. He would receive a year of service from Eiric, which would never be judged satisfactory by Rikhard's measure. In a year, he would own the farm, having stolen it right out from under Gustav's nose.

That's the way rich people do it, I suppose, Eiric thought.

"That's not right," Gustav said, coming off the bench in a rage. "Why should you get the farm, and not us?"

"We don't want your money," Liv said to Rikhard. "Banish me, and leave the farm—and my brodir—alone."

Eiric focused on Gustav. "We've offered you compensation for a crime we did not commit," he said. "That's more than fair. You should take it and let us go in peace."

The only one there without a stake in the outcome was Stevenson, and he looked as blindsided as the rest, everyone wondering who had released this fox in the henhouse.

Rikhard stood, motioning to his hird. "Knudsen, I'll leave instructions with my factor in town to pay you the money tomorrow morning. Halvorsen, it's too late to journey back home tonight. You and your party will stay at my temporary home tonight. It's small but comfortable, and it's on your way home. We will discuss what manner of service I require."

The jarl stowed away the Halvorsen treasures. "Don't forget—I see the findings of this council as binding. Halvorsen has offered compensation, and you have accepted. Therefore, I would take it as a personal affront if anything should happen to the defendant, his family, or his property. Is that understood?"

This was met with a muttered, grudging assent.

Eiric stood. "Karlsen!" he said as the jarl turned to go.

Rikhard swiveled back toward him. "Yes?"

"How would it be if I paid you back your money after a year?" he said. "I would prefer that to earning it through service."

Rikhard shook his head. "I have money. It's your service I want." With that, the jarl strode out of the hall, his guard following behind him.

19

EIMYRJA

REGINN AWOKE WITH A START, suddenly aware that she was sweating under a heap of blankets. She threw them aside, blinking against the sun that poured into the sleeping quarters she'd shared with the wyrdspinners. Now she was alone, and she could hear footfalls overhead that signified that others were up and about, and she should be, too.

The calling of seabirds and the gentle rocking of the ship told her that they must be in port.

She pulled away the underdress stuck to her skin and dug her shoes from under her sleeping bench. To her surprise, they were already dry. Her clothing was, too, though her underdress and overdress were still stiff with salt from her swim through Langvik Harbor.

How long was I asleep? As if prompted by the thought, her stomach growled, suggesting that it had been a while. The stiffness in her muscles and the fog in her head provided further evidence of time's passing. Despite sleeping for so long, she was bone weary and muddleheaded.

Her last memory was one of sailing through a cold fog so dense that she couldn't see beyond the gunwales.

And then nothing.

What awaited her at the Grove? How should she prepare? She considered removing her borrowed underdress and returning to the familiar armor of her own clothes. But she liked the feel of the fine cloth and the freedom the pantaloons gave her. Finally, she slapped the salt from her overdress and put it on over the spinner's linen. Then fastened her baldric with its amulets and pouches overtop and stowed her own dress in her carry bag.

Never own more than you can carry, Tove always said, *and don't leave anything behind that you cannot do without. You may never pass this way again.*

When she emerged on deck, she found that they were, indeed, docked in a harbor—a turquoise harbor overlooked by a seaside village so beautiful that it hurt the eyes. It was as if she'd been living in a black-and-white world all her life and had never realized that color existed.

The harbor towns Reginn had seen were gritty, run-down collections of warehouses and businesses catering to crews that came and went. Here, houses were mingled with alehouses and shops.

These houses were built of honey-colored fir, with framed wooden doors, corner posts, and upright planks forming the walls, and bark slabs protecting the roof. The corner posts were intricately carved and burned with symbols. Some she recognized, and some she did not. Many of the homes had porches and stone terraces, as if the weather was often fine enough to sit outside.

Even here, along the quay, the homes were fronted with gardens, separated from the street by low stone walls.

No sod roofs and walls in this village.

No muddy streets, either. The harbor-front street was paved not with gold but with large, flat stones cunningly fit together. As Reginn watched, a horse-drawn wagon loaded with barrels rattled down it and around a corner.

Everywhere, there were flowers, spilling from baskets and urns, lining walkways. A warm breeze carried the perfume across the water to Reginn.

"Welcome to Eimyrja, dottir," someone said.

Reginn spun around to find Modir Tyra standing forward, arms folded, watching her. She'd shed her long blue cloak in favor of a short blue jacket, more suited to this amiable climate.

"It's lovely here," Reginn said, though the word seemed wholly inadequate.

"Yes," Modir Tyra said.

"You must have a lot of trees," Reginn said, gesturing toward the elaborate wooden buildings. Another less-than-clever observation, but in most of the islands of the Archipelago, the trees had long gone for firewood. The forests that were left were gloomy and full of monsters.

In the northern reaches, it took a long time to regrow a forest.

"We have an ample supply of most everything that grows," Modir Tyra said, "including trees." She paused. "You've slept a long time. Amma Inger disembarked at our northernmost port, Sund-havn, last night, so she'll arrive at the Grove ahead of us. We've sailed on around to Vesthavn, to pick up messages and supplies from our commanders here." She gestured toward Reginn's carry bag and flute case. "Is that everything?"

"This is it," Reginn said.

"Of course. Very well, then, come." The headmistress vaulted the gunwale, landing nimbly on the makeshift plank bridge to the shore. Then turned and extended a hand to Reginn, who stood, gaping.

She did her best to follow the spinner's example, but it was only Modir Tyra's steadying hand that kept her from ending up in the wrack at the waterline. She followed behind the headmistress with two thoughts uppermost: First, she needed to get some more of these pantaloons. And second, she'd never seen a fine lady like this before.

She hadn't seen many fine ladies at all.

A nervous-looking officer in a buff-colored tunic met them onshore, accompanied by two young women wearing white overdresses over buff linen and four fresh-scrubbed children in buff-and-white-striped tunics and overdresses. The children carried small bouquets of flowers.

"Highest," the officer said with a deep bow. "I did not realize that you had been in Barbaria. Welcome home." He looked past her and, seeing only Reginn, asked, "Where are the children?"

"We were not actively recruiting this time, Birger," Tyra said. "The keeper wished to sail to the Archipelago to meet with some officials there. I went along as her guide and companion."

"Ah. I see." Birger's eyes flicked to Reginn, but Tyra did not offer an introduction, so Birger waved the women and their charges away. "Will you be staying over at the lower school?"

"Not this time," Tyra said briskly. "We'll make a quick stop, then ride straight for the temple this afternoon. What do you have for me?"

Birger held out a packet wrapped in fine leather. "These are dispatches for the garrison at Ithavoll."

Garrison? Reginn thought. Did the temple have an army?

"Thank you, Birger," Tyra said, stowing the folio in her carry bag.

As Birger walked away, Tyra turned back to Reginn. "Newly arrived candidates are called acolytes. They live here at Vesthavn and attend the lower school until their gifts are identified or they age out."

"What happens if they age out before their gifts are identified?" Reginn said.

"There's always a place for them," Tyra said. "Everyone has value. There are many ways to serve here at the Grove."

That was reassuring.

As they walked along the quay, Modir Tyra paused in front of a carved stone statue in the center of a small square. It was of a tall woman leaning on a staff, shading her eyes as she looked out to sea. Her stone cloak swirled around her as if caught in an onshore breeze, and one foot stuck out at an odd angle.

"That is our founder, Brenna Wayfinder. Hundreds of years ago, she landed here with a shipload of gifted refugees. That was the beginning of our sanctuary and our temple grove."

Reginn stood on tiptoes, studying Modir Brenna's face. The founder's expression was wistful—almost melancholy. Could it be that she missed her home in the Archipelago?

"Your first lesson at the Grove is in how we name one another," Modir Tyra said, as they climbed away from the quay. "You've met our keeper. We call her simply the keeper, or Amma Inger. As head-mistress, my title is kennari, meaning 'teacher.' Thus, you will call me Kennari or Modir Tyra. Your peers are brodir and systir, as in Systir Katia, or sistkyn for those uncommitted to a gender. I call my students dottir or son or bairn. This signifies the fact that we are a family whose relationship is one of mutual respect and love.

"You will present an interesting challenge to us, since it is rare that we accept a half-grown student to the academy. Your educa-tion will be a matter of unlearning some things so that you can learn new things."

Lady—no, Modir—Tyra turned away from the waterfront, walk-ing uphill a block until she came to a building with large double doors. As they entered, Reginn was smacked with the scent of hay and horses. A stable.

Well, she thought, manure stinks, even in Eimyrja.

A stableboy came to greet them, dressed in a buff-colored tunic and trousers. When he saw Modir Tyra, his eyes widened and he bowed low.

Tyra spoke to the stableboy, and he led out two horses.

"Horses?" Reginn blurted. "We're going to be riding *horses*?"

Tyra studied her, puzzled. "We have a long way to travel yet today."

"Oh!" Reginn said. "I thought that the upper school would be here in the village, too."

"No," Tyra said. "We seclude ourselves on the other side of the island so that we can focus on our mission."

Reginn watched with rising panic as the stableboy saddled the two horses. "I can walk," she said, shifting from foot to foot, "if you tell me the way. I'm a good walker. In fact, I like to walk."

"It's too far, even for someone who likes to walk," Modir Tyra said. Understanding kindled in her eyes. "Have you never ridden, dottir?"

"Sure I have," Reginn lied. "Lots of times. I just don't care for it, is all."

"Well," Tyra said, "hopefully you can tolerate it long enough to reach the Grove. Who knows? You may learn to love riding as much as I do."

Unlikely, Reginn thought.

When the horses were ready, Modir Tyra helped her mount up, handed her the reins, and adjusted the stirrups to fit.

"What's his name?" Reginn asked, awkwardly patting the horse's shoulder.

"*Her* name," Modir Tyra said. "Gyllir."

Tyra mounted easily, settling into the saddle as if she were born there. Reginn tried to mimic her posture, the way she pressed her knees against the horse's sides.

"Don't worry," Tyra said. "Gyllir will follow us." She urged her horse forward at a walk, and indeed, Gyllir followed with very little input from Reginn.

"What's your horse's name?" Reginn said.

"Silfrfaxi," Tyra said. "It means 'silver mane.'"

"But . . ." Reginn hesitated to point out the obvious. "His mane is black."

The headmistress laughed. "Yes," she said. "He's contrary." She paused. "*I'm* contrary."

By now, Reginn was absolutely smitten. She'd never met anyone like Modir Tyra before, who wore *contrary* like a badge of honor.

Maybe I belong here after all, Reginn thought. I'm contrary, too.

Just outside town, they stopped at the lower school, a cluster of small cottages surrounded by gardens and play yards filled with children wearing the same buff-and-white stripes as the children in town. After a brief meeting with the staff, they were on their way again.

Once out of the village, Silfrfaxi increased his pace to a gentle, ground-eating gait. Gyllir followed suit. It was nothing like the bone-shaking gallop she'd experienced on a runaway horse back in the Archipelago. The closest comparison in Reginn's experience was that of sailing through calm seas, rising and falling with the swells.

Eimyrja was stunning—green and lush, pastures dotted with fat cows, farmsteads built of wood and stone, with fields divided by stone walls. Small villages boasted markets bursting with fruits, vegetables, meat, and fish. The residents wore simple garb in drab hues of buff and brown—much like at home. Unlike at home, they all looked well fed.

Reginn recalled the struggling farms of the Archipelago, clustered together for protection, with scrawny livestock and scrawnier farmers. Some had been abandoned, the owners having gone else-where seeking better prospects. Some had been raided and burned by outlaws.

The towns weren't much better. Some residents mined coal, silver, and gold or manned the iron furnaces and smithies. Men and women worked spindles and looms, producing rough-spun yarns and scratchy fabrics. Fishermen sailed for days, returning with holds half-full of bottom-dwelling fish.

Was it better land, better weather, or the presence of magic that accounted for the difference?

When they stopped to water and rest the horses, refill their waterskins, and eat from a pouch of dried meat, fruit, and nuts, Reginn asked, "Is everyone on Eimyrja gifted?"

"Not everyone, no," Tyra said, rinsing her hands in a cold, clear stream that must join the river somewhere ahead.

"What is the role of the people who are not gifted?" Reginn said.

"We call them bondi," Modir Tyra said. "They work with us throughout the islands. We would be lost without them."

"The . . . bondi?" Reginn said, a cold quiver in her middle. "Are they . . . thralls?"

"No, of course not," Tyra said. "The bondi are free men and women. Some are descended from residents of these islands before the academy was established. Others have come because they can provide specialized skills that we lack. And some, of course, came here as children as candidates for the temple."

"So those who wash out of the temple become bondi?"

After a moment's hesitation, Tyra nodded. "Some do. But it's not a matter of 'washing out.' It's a matter of finding the right role for the individual. Everyone contributes to our success, whether gifted or not, both young and old. Everyone is important. Everyone has a role to play in New Jotunheim." Her smile was like the warm sun after a long winter.

Reginn sighed, relieved to hear it. She'd been a rootless fugitive all her life. Here was a place she could fit in, where she could find a way to succeed.

One day, I'll be just like Modir Tyra—bold, contrary, taking on the world, staff in hand, with no apologies.

Modir Tyra squinted up at the sky, then turned toward where the horses were grazing. "We'd better ride on. It will be after dark when we arrive as it is." She adjusted Silfrfaxi's gear, then swung effortlessly into the saddle.

"How did the academy get started?" Reginn said, as they walked their horses through dappled light. "What made the founder decide to come here?"

"The Grove was established as a refuge for wyrdspinners after the war that ended the reign of the gods."

"Why did you need a refuge?" Reginn said.

"I believe you already know the answer to that, from your own experience," Tyra said. "Even in good times, spinners are suspect, tolerated because of their gifts. When things go wrong, practitioners are easy targets for blame. It doesn't help that in much of the world, sorcery is seen as the province of women."

That was still true. Everyone Reginn had met in the Archipelago who claimed the gift was a woman or a girl.

But there was something about the way Tyra said it that made Reginn ask the next question. "You said sorcery is *seen* as the province of women," Reginn said. "Are you saying that it's not really?"

Tyra studied her, eyes narrowed, as if assessing what truths she was ready to receive. "Men are as likely to be gifted as women, but most don't have the courage to claim it. Odin was criticized for his use of magic, even though the other gods could see the value in it, even though they benefited from it. It wasn't considered masculine.

"That is why we usually recruit our students as babies, so they are not bound by barbarian conventions and expectations. The downside is that we often don't know what we have until they come of age."

Reginn was increasingly uncomfortable with Tyra's use of the word *barbarian* to refer to everyone back home.

"Not everyone in Muckleholm is a barbarian," Reginn blurted.

"Of course not, dottir," Tyra said, her jaw set. "Only most of them." She fell silent as Silfrfaxi picked his way across a shallow, rocky river so clear that Reginn could see small fish darting out from under Gyllir's hooves.

When they reached the other side, Tyra continued. "Like you, I was older when I came to Eimyrja. I spent my childhood in the Archipelago. I know it far too well." She heeled her horse, who lunged ahead, up the steep and rocky trail.

When the trail widened again, Tyra allowed Reginn to come alongside. "Bear in mind that after Ragnarok, the other worlds were destroyed—Alfheim, home of the elves; Asgard, stronghold of the gods; Nidavellir, the caverns of the dwarves; Muspelheim, land of elemental fire; Niflheim, land of ice and darkness; Vanaheim, original home of the Vanir gods; and Jotunheim, birthplace of magic. All that is left are the Midlands—the realm of humans—and Hel, dwelling place of the dead.

"So the Midlands have become a no-man's-land of refugees from the other worlds, including issvagr, fire demons, dark elves, frost giants, demigods, and jotun, their bloodlines commingled with often unpredictable results. It is what makes the Midlands such a dangerous place. It's difficult to tell who the monsters are."

Reginn thought of the monster Asger Eldr, who described himself as a refugee from Muspelheim.

"Eventually, the survivors in the human world began a systematic slaughter of the gifted—the children of Jotunheim—blaming us for the loss of their gods and every bad thing that befell them."

"But why would they—" Reginn broke off, recalling the many in the Archipelago who treated her as a necessary evil—useful when she served their purposes, a threat when she did not. Even though she was running a rig and so they had nothing to fear from her. "Never mind," she said.

"We are not monsters," Tyra said, "despite what you may have been told. We are wild, creative spirits, not destroyers. We are not soldiers by nature. To us, warfare seems like a pointless waste of blood and treasure. Yet, we were determined not to repeat the mistakes of the past by attempting to negotiate with our enemies. So we decided to withdraw and leave the barbarians to their own devices.

"The founder of the Grove, Brenna Wayfinder, organized a group of the most powerful spinners to create and defend a place for us. The result is Eimyrja, where we can enjoy all the benefits that magic can provide and avoid the chaos and destruction in the rest of the Midlands."

The rest of the Midlands—places like Langvik and Selvagr and all the other gritty harbor towns and crossroads Reginn had seen in her short life.

"So you just . . . abandoned the rest of the world?" Reginn instantly regretted the note of accusation in her voice. She needed to learn to watch her mouth if she wanted to succeed.

"Only in the sense that a wife abandons the husband who is beating her or a man abandons the dog that bites," Tyra said.

They were coming to the top of a ridge—a spine of mountains that seemed to divide the island in two. Mosifell, Tyra had called it. Behind them lay the picturesque port, the glistening sea, and acres of fertile farmland. Just offshore was another island, set like an emerald in the sapphire sea.

Ahead, a dense forest clothed the downslope nearly all the way to the opposite coast, which appeared to end in high, frowning cliffs. To Reginn's right, the mountains climbed even higher, with some of them cloaked in snow.

Beyond the coast, Reginn could see another island with a definite split down the middle that made it appear as if it had broken in two. Steam and cloud rose from the rift.

"What's that, over there?" Reginn said, pointing.

"The island is called Ithavoll," Modir Tyra said. "We have some facilities over there. Eimyrja is just a small part of New Jotunheim."

The official who had greeted them at Vesthavn had mentioned Ithavoll. "Birger said that there was a garrison there."

Tyra nodded. "You have a good memory, dottir. Though it's unlikely our enemies will find their way here, we keep a small force just in case."

There was something else, though. Something Tove had taught her long ago. "Wasn't that supposed to be the meeting place of the surviving gods after Ragnarok?"

"The gods won't be meeting there ever again," Tyra said grimly. "We'll make sure of that."

"Why do you return to Muckleholm, then? It sounds like you're glad to be done with it."

"It is part of our mission to find and rescue the gifted wherever they are. That is why it has been necessary for us to engage with the barbarians on a limited basis. Once or twice a year, a team of us travels through the Archipelago, offering counsel to kings and jarls. In exchange, we are given the run of the almshouses, slave markets, and orphanages, seeking babies that display the spark of magic."

That was what Gunnar had said. "So . . . you can see the gift in a person?"

"We can see potential," Tyra said. "But the nature of the gift, and the form it will take, does not become clear until the child is older."

"So . . ." Reginn hesitated, unsure whether she wanted to hear the answer. "That night at Gunnar's Hall—did you see the gift in me?"

For a heartbeat or two, Tyra seemed to debate what to say. Then, fishing her crystal pendant from inside her neckline, she displayed it to Reginn. "This is a kynstone. It is sensitive to magic. It glows blue in the presence of children who carry magical potential. As a child grows older, it changes to red or purple, reflecting the nature of the gift."

Which is better, red or purple? Reginn might have asked, but she was distracted by the glowing stone. The stone wasn't blue or red or purple. It glowed like Baltic amber or sunlight through honey, just as it had in Gunnar's Hall.

"It's not any of those colors," Reginn pointed out, as if, perhaps, Tyra hadn't noticed.

"Exactly," Modir Tyra said. "Your gift is like nothing I've ever seen. That is why I fought to have you come here."

This confirmed what Reginn had suspected. "The keeper doesn't want me here," she said. "Is it because the brown-stone gifted are not as good?"

"It's not that at all," Tyra said. "One never knows what gifts will prove critical to our survival, so I cast my net wide. It's just that the keeper treads carefully when it comes to our relationship with the Archipelago. She wants to make sure that New Jotunheim remains a sanctuary and not a target. If not for our mission to identify and save the gifted in the Midlands, we would have no contact with the Archipelago at all."

"She thinks I'm . . . some kind of a threat?"

"People are looking for you, dottir," Tyra said. "*That* is the threat."

A cold finger of fear tracked down Reginn's spine. Back in Langvik, Modir Tyra had told her that Asger would never find her at the Grove. But the keeper didn't seem so confident. Reginn recalled what she'd overheard her say when they were fleeing the jarl's ship.

Barbarians have found us before, and they will find us again if we kindle that desire in them.

20

AT RIKHARD'S TABLE

IT WAS DIFFICULT TO SAY who was most unhappy about the outcome of Eiric's hearing—the Knudsens or Eiric's systir, Liv. As soon as the jarl went out the door, Garth launched himself at Eiric, only to be intercepted by Gustav.

"No!" Gustav said. "You heard what Rikhard said. Any harm comes to Halvorsen, then—"

"You know they're working together," Garth growled. "This was planned all along, to keep us from getting our hands on the farm."

"Maybe so," Gustav said. "But there's not a lot we can do about it now."

"We can kill the coaster," Garth said, jabbing a finger at Eiric.

"Aye, we can," Finni said, "and bring the jarl down on us, and we still don't end up with Sundgard."

Liv faced off with Garth. "If you lay a hand on my brodir, you'll be committing murder yourselves. I killed Sten. Me. Nobody else. And you know what? It wasn't hard. I'd do it again in a heartbeat."

As usual, their uncles couldn't find their footing where Liv was concerned.

"You—you shouldn't even be in here," Finni said.

"None of us should be here," Eiric said. "Come on, Liv."

Liv shook him off, still facing the Knudsens. "I'll tell you one thing—come after us, and the jarl will be the least of your worries." She reinforced that by slamming the butt of her staff into the dirt floor.

Once outside, Eiric said, "That doesn't help, systir."

"Really? Then what *would* help?" She spoke so sharply that people in the market turned to look.

Eiric opened his mouth to respond, but just then Emi shouldered the door open and stepped out of the meeting hall, her arms loaded down with serving pieces. When she saw Eiric and Liv, she stopped short.

"I'm sorry, Liv," she said. "I hoped for a better outcome."

"That's the difference between you and me," Liv said. "I expected the worst, and that's exactly what we got."

"Be careful on your way home," Emi said. "They are angry enough to do something stupid."

"They don't have to be angry to do something stupid," Eiric said. He and Liv watched her walk away before they resumed their argument.

"You should have let me take the blame from the beginning," Liv said. "I might be named vargr, but they'd have no excuse to take the farm."

"It wouldn't have made a difference," Eiric said quietly. "They would never have accepted that. We knew what the outcome would be. It was always about the farm."

"I could contend with Sten and his stupid family. Now we're up against Rikhard. We've lost the farm, and there's nothing we can do about it."

"We've not lost the farm—not yet," Eiric said.

"I don't trust him," Liv said. "What kind of service is it that he wants you to provide?" She raised an eyebrow. "You know he has thralls and soldiers to spare. What does he want from you?"

"I don't know," Eiric said. "I suppose I'll find out. I'll kill him if I have to."

"Oh, brodir. Sten was a pig. This man is a snake. There's no way you can outwit him."

That stung.

"We have a year," Eiric said. "For a year, we can stay at Sundgard. Let's hear what Rikhard has to say."

Hilde was still waiting under the tree, surrounded by a handful of street urchins. Apparently, she'd been sharing the remains of their lunch with them. They scattered when Eiric and Liv approached and Hilde rose hastily to her feet, brushing the crumbs from her skirts. Ivar reached for her, and Liv handed him off.

"Let's go," Liv said, scooping up their nearly empty lunch bag. "We're staying with the jarl tonight. Whether we like it or not." She stalked away, and Hilde followed, eyes wide with wonder.

The walk back to Rikhard's compound seemed longer than it had before, but maybe it was because they were weighed down by a new set of worries.

It was already growing dark when they approached the jarl's residence, a black hulk in the gathering dusk. They were met at the gate by a brace of the jarl's guardsmen.

"We're the Halvorsens," Eiric said. "We're expected."

The guardsman nodded curtly and extended his hand. "Your weapons," he said, "for safekeeping."

Eiric rested his hand on the haft of his grandfadir's axe. "I'll keep it safe enough," he said, looking the guard in the eyes. After a bit of a stare-down, the guard said, "Come along. We'll see what the jarl says."

Of course, he said nothing about Liv's staff.

They passed through two sets of doors and two more pairs of heavily armed guards into the main room of the hall. It was bright and warm, centered by a roaring fire, augmented by soapstone oil lamps at intervals.

The guard who had challenged Eiric disappeared into private quarters at the other end of the hall. No animal stalls attached to this longhouse, Eiric thought.

His mouth watered at the scent of baking bread and roasting meat. A thrall tended to three plump chickens impaled on a spit, the flames blazing up as fat dripped into the fire. She ground spices with a mortar and pestle and sprinkled them over the browning birds.

A trestle table had been set up in the middle, with benches drawn up to either side. It had been set with wooden trenchers and bowls of dried fruit and nuts.

Eiric fixed on the fruit. Their supply of dried apples, cherries, and pears had been exhausted by the winter solstice.

Eiric noticed Liv was staring at the table, too. Alongside each trencher was a drinking cup—fashioned from glass, probably from Frankia or the east. He'd seen glass drinking cups before but never so many in one place.

Though Rikhard had described this as his temporary home, it was luxuriously furnished with fabrics and goods from the new jarl's raids and trading ventures throughout the Archipelago. Eiric was especially intrigued with the weapons displayed along the central hall—Frankish swords and helms and axes of exotic make, with engravings chased in silver and gold. Perhaps that was why Rikhard had been interested in the goods Eiric had brought to the Thing to try to compensate Sten's family.

The sleeping benches were hidden behind Persian silks. Eiric suspected that all this was meant to impress—and it did.

The thrall came and went several times, bringing more dishes to add to the groaning board. They'd always had plenty to eat at Sundgard, but Eiric had never seen such a variety of foods together in one place.

The servant lifted the chickens from the mealfire and began slicing them on a large platter.

Finally, Rikhard emerged from his chambers, followed by the usual brace of guardsmen.

He strode toward them, smiling. "Welcome," he said. "Please, sit and eat." He waved at the table. "You must be famished."

He made no mention of the forbidden axe, but Eiric noticed that his hird stayed no more than a sword's length away.

Eiric stood there awkwardly for a moment. It seemed like he should take a stand, that he shouldn't be breaking bread with the enemy. Still, his stomach was empty, and he'd need strength, after all, if it came to a fight.

Rikhard watched Eiric waver, looking amused. "What's the matter, Halvorsen, do you feel the need for a taster?" He gestured to his servant. "Faregildis, prepare me a plate."

While she filled a plate with chicken, smoked fish, barley, and bread, the jarl continued, "Of course, you *could* ask yourself if it would make sense for me to intervene to save your farm, invite you to my home, and then poison you."

"I could," Eiric said, "if I knew why you intervened and who'll end up with the farm at the end of it. I assume that you want something from me."

Surprise flickered across Rikhard's face, followed by a grudging smile. "I do want something from you. Therefore, I am unlikely to poison you before I get it."

Well, Eiric thought, that's reassuring.

When Faregildis appeared beside the jarl with a full plate,

Rikhard gestured for her to set it in front of him. He dipped the flatbread in a bowl of honey, raised it, dripping, then ate it with relish. Then started in on the chicken and barley, using the bread to convey it to his mouth.

Liv took Ivar from Hilde. "Eat," she said, and motioned for Ivar's nurse to help herself. Hilde filled her plate and sat at the far end of the table from the jarl while Liv stood, rocking from foot to foot with her brodir in her arms.

Eiric finally gave in, filling a plate and sitting across the table from Rikhard.

Faregildis poured ale for everyone. When Hilde had finished, Liv handed Ivar off and had a go at Rikhard's spread herself.

The jarl eyed Liv appraisingly. "Liv. At the hearing, you said that the farm at Sundgard belonged to—to Sylvi but that you don't carry her blood."

"That's right," Liv said. "Eiric and I shared a fadir, but Sylvi was my modir in every way except by blood."

"Who was your birth modir?" Rikhard asked. "Where was she from?"

"Why is that important?" Liv said.

"It's just that—you look very different from your brodir."

"I don't remember my birth modir," she said. "I was very young when my fadir brought me to Selvagr."

That was always the answer these days. As for reading her thoughts, one might as easily read runes at the bottom of one of the steaming mineral pools at Saxby. Eiric knew that a river of secrets ran under that impassive surface.

Eiric thought the jarl might push, but he did not. Instead, he took a different tack. "People say that the Halvorsens never marry folk from Selvagr. That they bring their wives and husbands from across the sea."

"As has been common among the peoples of the Archipelago as long as anyone can remember," Eiric said.

"Not so common these days," Rikhard said.

"Sten Knudsen was from the village," Liv said. "Marrying him was the biggest mistake our modir ever made."

With that, the jarl gave up exploring Liv's tangled ancestry and moved on to new territory. "That's an interesting staff you carry," he said to her. "May I see it?"

She passed it over.

The jarl ran his fingers over the elaborate framing at one end, the jeweled head. The shaft was made of ebony and inlaid with bone and silver.

"Where did you get this? I've never seen anything like it."

"It's a family heirloom," Liv said. "My fadir brought it from overseas."

"But how do you use it?" the jarl persisted.

"I'm sorry, my lord, I did not realize that you were interested in spinning and weaving." She took it back from him. "The raw fiber is collected on this end." She tapped the basket, spinning the staff in her hand. "I hold it in the crook of my arm like this"—she demonstrated—"with the spindle in my other hand. I would be glad to teach you, if you—"

"Never mind," Rikhard said hastily. "It sounds very . . . interesting."

"Women's work is never interesting," Liv said. "That is why it is given to women to do."

Rikhard gave her a long look, then changed the subject. "I've made some inquiries about Sundgard," he said, "since your stepfadir's family seems so keen to get hold of it. It's reputed to be the finest farm on the island. And yet—you don't seem particularly . . . prosperous."

Liv shrugged. "We get by. We've always had plenty to eat."

"No," Eiric said, growing weary of this relentless dance. "It used to be prosperous, until our fadir died and Sylvi married Sten."

Rikhard seemed to think he had ferreted out some truth. "Do you believe that it was the presence of your fadir that made the farm so prosperous?"

"No," Liv said, "I believe it was the absence of Sten."

Rikhard laughed out loud, once again ambushed by Liv's wit. It was a common problem. But it hid the very real pain and loss that Sten had caused.

"Why didn't she divorce him?" Rikhard looked from Liv to Eiric.

"She did, but he would not leave."

"She had no family to intervene?"

"Only us," Eiric said. "She didn't want me to confront him. She was worried how I would fare in a fight. She kept telling me to wait until I was older." He glared at the floor, shame heating his face. "I should have done something sooner."

To Eiric's surprise, the jarl rose and began pacing back and forth, pounding his fist into his open hand. "That's the point, isn't it? This system of outlawry and blood money, petty chieftains and sanctioned vengeance doesn't work. There is no justice and no way to enforce the laws."

Eiric and Liv looked at each other. He knew what she was thinking. *Where did that come from? And what does it have to do with us?*

"That's the way it's always been," Liv said.

"It needs to change. We need fewer, stronger nations and more powerful rulers who can afford to keep a standing army. We need a clear line of succession, not a brawl between rivals every few years. Otherwise we will be overrun."

"You're saying we need a king," Eiric said.

Again, Rikhard's eyes narrowed, as if he was surprised that Eiric could follow that logic. "I didn't say that, Halvorsen. What I'm saying is that the present system isn't working."

The jarl seemed eager to return to his original subject–Sundgard.

"Despite your experience with your stepfadir, people still seem to think that there's something special about Sundgard. They say, 'The sun always shines on Sundgard.' They speak of 'Sundgard apples' and 'Sundgard honey' with a kind of reverence."

The farm had been the focus of envious eyes for as long as Eiric could remember, especially when Leif and Bjorn were alive and there were many hands to work it.

Bjorn's deathbed words echoed in Eiric's ears. *I left Sundgard to your modir. It is blessed by the gods. It's up to you to help her keep it.*

Not doing a great job so far.

"So," Rikhard said, "what is it about Sundgard? Some might say that it is favored by the gods. Or under a benevolent spell." Once again, the jarl leaned forward, as if intent on the answer.

"It must be," Liv said, lifting her chin and looking down her nose at the jarl. "That explains why we're about to lose it."

"That remains to be seen," Rikhard said. "In fact, if you would excuse us, I will discuss this matter further with your brodir."

"My systir will stay," Eiric said. "She can hear whatever you have to say."

"No," Rikhard said. "This has to remain between us."

Eiric bristled. "Liv has a–"

"Never mind, brodir," Liv said wearily. She stood, gesturing to Hilde. "It's been a long day."

"Faregildis," Rikhard said. "Please show our guests to the privy and direct them to their sleeping benches."

He thinks he owns us now, Eiric thought.

Most would say he's right.

21

THE GROVE

IT TOOK THE REST OF the day to descend the wooded eastern slope of the mountain they'd climbed all morning. They had been following a river valley most of the way, which Reginn assumed must be the only possible path through the forest without getting lost.

The forest Modir Tyra called Myrkvid was different from any Reginn had seen before. Most of the Archipelago was either bare of trees or stippled with saplings too young to make good firewood. The few stands of old-growth forest were swarming with monsters—issvagr, the ice wolves; the draugr, the walking dead; and human outlaws. The remnants of all the broken worlds of Yggdrasil hid in the forests of the Archipelago. Those were the nights that Reginn was glad to have Asger Eldr on guard.

Here in Eimyrja, the forest was a mixture of straight, tall trees resembling ships masts and ancient trees whose gnarled branches began close to the ground, spreading out horizontally, forming a thick canopy draped with moss. Grandmodir trees, Tove would have called them, stretching out their arms so that a small child could climb up and sit straddling the branch and leaning back against the broad trunk.

Ogre trees, Asger would have said, reaching clutching fingers to grab the unwary and drag them to their underground lairs.

Asger's world was full of ogres, monsters, and the like. There-fore, so was Reginn's.

This forest floor was covered in an ankle-deep layer of leaves and mosses. Each fallen tree and branch was clothed with new growth—fungi and lichens and plants she didn't know the names of. The air was fragrant with the scent of sweet earth and wood-land flowers.

Eimyrja could be like the faery lands in Tove's stories, where beauty on the surface often hid the rot underneath. Where a person who did not keep her wits about her might lie down on the forest floor and be ensnared by vines or spiderwebs. Where a chance encounter with a riddler might lead to a lifetime of servitude.

Be observant, Tove said. *Be careful. Ask questions. Keep secrets.*

What would happen if the spinners decided that Reginn was a fraud? Would there be a place for her here as a helper or assistant when she turned out to be ordinary?

Reginn would never have believed it if someone had told her that it was possible to fall asleep in the saddle. But between the gentle gait of her horse and her weary body and worried mind, that's just what she did at some point during the long journey from the north-south spine of Eimyrja to the sea. Eventually dreams and memory mingled together

A change in the light against her lids and the scent of the sea awoke her. She straightened in the saddle, rubbed her eyes, and looked around.

They'd finally emerged from the deep forests that clothed the eastern slope of the mountains and onto the coastal plain. The dying sun painted the rugged mountains behind them in hues of red and purple, sending their long shadows across the grasslands to lap at the feet of an ash grove, centered by the largest tree Reginn had ever seen. Its canopy stretched so high, it seemed that the stars must be entangled in its branches.

It was surrounded by its children—smaller trees of the same variety that would have been landmark trees in any other company.

"I've never seen a tree that large," Reginn whispered.

"It is Vardir—the Warden Tree. It is surrounded by younger trees that spring from its roots. We call them the Guardians. Together, they comprise the sacred grove, home of the academy where we learn to honor our legacy of magic and our role in protecting the land entrusted to our care."

Even in the gathering dusk, Reginn could make out movement at the edge of the Grove and see buildings nestled under the canopy and even lodged among the branches. The plain around the Grove was quilted with farm fields, the lights from farmhouses like knots between the stitching. Sheep clustered, pale smudges against the green pastures.

As they left the shelter of Myrkvid, Reginn ducked as a large black bird took flight from a tall snag that marked the forest edge and arrowed toward the cliffs.

"Well," Tyra said, reining in, "I was hoping to delay introductions to the other dedicates until tomorrow morning, but now everyone will know we're coming."

Confused, Reginn said, "Why, did you see someone?"

"The raven. That's Kettel. He's serving as Stian's lookout." Seeing the questions in Reginn's eyes, she added, "I mentioned Stian before, who works with the horse herds. He has an affinity for animals of all kinds. Stian won't wake the keeper, but I think we can expect some curious students to welcome us."

Given what she'd already heard, Reginn preferred that the keeper stay in bed.

Tyra reached across and took hold of Gyllir's reins. "One favor, dottir. I'll want to meet with you first thing in the morning. Until then, I would ask you to say as little as possible about the Archipelago and your previous life."

"Of course," Reginn said. "Whatever you think is best."

Tyra let go and urged her horse forward. Reginn followed, her mind swimming with worry. Maybe the headmistress was afraid that the other students would shun her if they knew what her previous life was like? Or worse, pity her.

The horses must have realized that they were nearing home, because despite their long journey, Reginn was having trouble keeping Gyllir reined in.

When they drew closer to the outer ring of trees, Reginn saw what she hadn't noticed before—a wall taller than her head of twined branches and vines covered in night-blooming white flowers.

Just then, the gate opened and two figures emerged on horseback. Tyra heeled Silfrfaxi forward, and now Reginn followed suit.

Both riders were close to Reginn's age, both dressed in blue overshirts and trousers, both sliding curious looks at Reginn. One of them—the boy—had the big black bird sitting on his shoulder.

"Brodir Stian, Systir Katia," Modir Tyra said sternly, "you're out past curfew."

"Kettel said there were travelers on the way, and we were worried that they might be barbarians attacking in your absence," he said, stroking the bird's neck feathers.

"Surely Kettel knows a spinner when he sees one," Modir Tyra said.

"Maybe," Stian said, "but he's never seen a barbarian before, so how would he know the difference?" Stian fed the bird a bit of meat, and Kettel flew away.

Stian was as sleek as the bird, with straight black hair, high cheekbones, and skin the color of autumn grasses.

"Brodir Stian," Tyra said. "This is Reginn Lund, our new student."

"A new student?" Brodir Stian and Systir Katia exchanged astonished looks. "Her?" they chorused, as if she didn't look the part.

Reginn cleared her throat. "Eiklund," she said. "Not Lund. I'm Reginn Eiklund."

"Here at the Grove, we leave behind our family names," Modir Tyra said. "All of us take on the byname Lund, in honor of the first practitioners of magic and to signify that we are all a part of that family."

"But—she's as old as us!" Katia said.

"Maybe," Reginn said, tired of being talked about like she wasn't there. "I'm sixteen. How old are you?"

"Seventeen," Katia said. She was striking, with her long legs and arms and close-cropped hair. She must have been one of those the coasters called blamenn—people with blue-black skin from beyond the Grikksalt, the southern sea.

"I'm sixteen, too," Stian put in. "But we've been here since we were babies."

"Well," Reginn muttered. "Sorry I'm late."

Modir Tyra's breath hissed out in frustration. "So you're saying that Amma Inger did not even announce that we would be welcoming a new student?"

They both shook their heads. "We haven't seen the keeper since she returned," Katia said.

"I hope the domicile-masters have prepared a room for her," Tyra murmured, almost to herself.

"Maybe they did," Katia said hopefully. "We can take her back to our quad with us and see. If nothing is set aside, she can stay with me tonight, and we'll speak with the housemodir in the morning."

"Thank you," Reginn said, touched by this kindness shown to a stranger. "Right now I'm so tired I would be happy to sleep on the floor."

Katia laughed. "Don't worry. We have plenty of room."

Tyra seemed relieved to have Reginn off her hands for the moment. "Thank you, Systir Katia. I do have some matters to attend to before I sleep. Please take good care of her." She turned to Reginn. "Systir Reginn, have Katia or Stian show you to my office after the dagmal tomorrow." With that, she heeled her horse forward until they were lost in the gloom under the trees.

If Modir Tyra was glad to hand off Reginn for the moment, the feeling was mutual. While Reginn was grateful for the headmistress's support, the day had felt like one long test, and she wasn't yet sure that she'd passed. Her usually nimble mind was all used up.

"The dormitories are this way," Stian said, urging his horse toward the gate. Reginn followed, and Katia brought up the rear. Stian rode like he was part of his horse. Reginn felt like a sack of grain tied to Gyllir's back in comparison.

When they passed through the gate, the guards posted there wore the same buff livery that the wyrdspinners' servants had worn in Langvik and on the ship.

Once inside the boundary, they began to pass dwellings and buildings—stables and bakeries, smithies, alehalls, and markets. Providers of all the services needed by the wyrdspinners.

Every house was surrounded by gardens and farm plots, flowering shrubs, cherry and peach trees heavy with fruit, barley already golden in the fields, ready for harvest. It was a stunning contrast to the Archipelago, where most farmers barely scratched out a living, with little surplus to send to market.

Well, she thought, they were the ones who drove magic away.

Reginn's anxiety mingled with anticipation as they passed under the outermost branches of the Grove. It was instantly cooler, darker, the air rich with the scent of earth and flowers and the leaves of long-ago autumns.

Though her stomach still rumbled with hunger, the air itself was almost nourishing. Tiny lights rimed the tree branches and illuminated the road ahead.

If it had been difficult to control Gyllir before, now it was all but impossible. Stian noticed, turned, and murmured something to the horse, calming her.

Easy for you, Reginn thought.

The buildings of the academy were situated between the outer circle of the Guardians and Vardir, in the center. Stian reined in before a complex of four buildings that formed a quad. When Reginn dismounted, her legs were so stiff that she could scarcely stand. She held on to the saddle to steady herself until a groom in buff livery arrived to lead the horses away.

Katia reached out and gripped her elbow, tugging her toward the walkway between buildings. "This way," she said. "Let's find the housemodir in my dormitory."

Stian trailed after them until Katia turned around and gave him a look. "Your dormitory is over there." She pointed across the quad.

"But I wanted to—"

"Can't you see that she's dead on her feet?" Katia said. "You can ask your questions tomorrow."

"Fine," Stian grumbled. Leaning toward Reginn, he said, "Welcome to Eimyrja, Reginn Lund. You—we—are all so lucky to be here." With that, he turned his horse toward his own dormitory.

As soon as she entered the dormitory building, Reginn realized how different it was from the longhouses in the Archipelago. For one thing, the walls were built of stone, topped with peaked roofs made of thatch. The first floor was one large room equipped with tables and benches. Instead of a hearth in the middle of the room with a smoke hole above, this building had stone hearths at either end, with stone shafts that carried away the smoke.

"Where is everyone?" Reginn said. There was enough furniture here to serve an army.

"We have only six dedicates in the girls' dormitory," Katia said. She pointed up toward the roof. "They're in bed, where we should be." That's when Reginn noticed the ladders propped against a railing where the walls met the roofline, and heard the sounds sleeping people make coming down from above.

The housemodir's room was on the first floor. Katia knocked at the door, but there was no answer, and Reginn could hear snoring from within.

"Well then," Katia said, her cheeks pink with embarrassment, "you can stay in my room, if you don't mind sharing your bed with wights."

In her travels, Reginn had encountered vermin of all kinds, but she'd never heard of those. "Hang on," Reginn said. "With *what*?"

"With wights. Land spirits. The landvaettir." When Reginn still looked mystified, Katia said, "They are the guardians of the Grove. The wights like to stay close to me. That's my gift—and my curse." She rolled her eyes.

Reginn still didn't get it, but she was too tired to argue. At that point she would have slept with the Midgard Serpent just to get off her feet.

"Fine," Reginn said. "Let's go."

They climbed a ladder in the far corner of the room. All the way up, Reginn was conscious of a murmuring and shuffling above their heads, flickers of movement in the corners of her eyes.

"I can see them," Reginn said, "but I can't quite figure out what they look like."

"Some are as small as insects," Katia said. "Others resemble sea creatures or bulls or birds and even giants. They take the form best suited to their nature."

Too bad people don't do that, Reginn thought. It would be easier to separate the monsters from the heroes.

Katia's loft was tiny, with slanting walls and clothing hung on hooks. There were two pallets on the floor, each covered with a blanket. Katia pointed to one of them. "I don't have a roommate anymore. She was promoted to adept. So that one's yours. If the wights bother you, boot them out."

Sure, Reginn thought. I'll just boot them out. She peeked under the blanket before she flopped down on her pallet and pulled the coverlet up to her chin. It was soft and nearly weightless.

Would a runestone work on wights the way it did on vermin?

Best not to try. She didn't want to get on their bad side right away.

Katia stripped off her tunic and trousers and lay down in her chemise. "We'll ask the housemodir about getting you some more clothes tomorrow, and you can take your pick of the open lofts."

"Thank you," Reginn said. Tired as she was, she didn't drop off to sleep right away. When she looked up at the ceiling, she could see shifting shapes in the pale light from the window. They surrounded Katia like a web of protection. As she watched, two or three peeled off and settled in around Reginn.

They weren't frightening, she decided. They were comforting, in a way.

"They like you," Katia murmured sleepily.

Reginn still couldn't quite believe this was real. Just a few days ago, she'd been held captive by a demon in an endless cycle of torment.

She sent up a prayer to whatever gods might be listening: *Let it be real let it be real let it be real.*

Some part of her still expected Asger to appear and drag her back to her old life, as he had so many times before. She imagined him pacing, shedding sparks, reaching out for her and coming away with nothing at all. Shriveled. Diminished, hoarding power because he knew that this was the end.

Reginn fingered the fine coverlet, breathed in the lush night air, and fell asleep to the murmuring of leaves overhead, feeling safe for the first time since Asger Eldr had come into her life.

22

THE JARL'S ERRAND

AS SOON AS THE SERVANT led Liv and Hilde outside, Rikhard rose. "Come with me," he said. He led the way back to his private quarters. The guard who had challenged Eiric to give up his axe swept a silk drape aside to reveal a chamber with its own hearth and chairs drawn up to a small table set with two cups. To either side were what appeared to be sleeping benches.

Two members of the hird followed them in and took their places just inside the door.

"Saerda, pour us some wine," Rikhard said to one of them. To Eiric's surprise, the guardsman fetched a large leather-wrapped bottle and poured from it into the two cups on the table.

His liegemen serve him at table? Eiric thought. He couldn't imagine any of the men who had crewed under Bjorn or Leif in that role.

"Leave the bottle and go," Rikhard said, waving them out.

"But... my lord...?" Saerda said, eyes flicking to Eiric. "Wouldn't it be better for us to–"

"I am not worried, Saerda, and if I'm not worried, you should have confidence in that judgment," Rikhard said sharply.

"Yes, lord," Saerda said, bowing his head. He and his companion backed from the room, letting the drape fall into place.

Eiric watched all this with growing puzzlement. Rank and position in the Archipelago was an informal and fluid business. Any freeman could aspire to captain a ship or become jarl over a region if he fought bravely in battle and demonstrated that he was a capable leader of men. If the men who served under a ship's commander returned home as rich men, that commander would be known to have hamingja, good luck. More warriors would compete to serve under his command the next time. His power and influence would grow.

By the same token, a jarl or chieftain who mistreated the freemen in his region, or who had poor success in raids and battles, ran the risk of being replaced by someone with better skills, better fortune, more courage. In other words, someone favored by the gods.

Power was not necessarily inherited, although, as in Rikhard's case, the son of a jarl was well positioned to step into a space vacated by his fadir.

In short, warriors who fought under a jarl were not servants to that noble, but more like allies or peers—with the jarl first among equals.

Rikhard must have seen something in Eiric's expression because he said, "What is it, Halvorsen? Is something wrong?"

Eiric should have denied it, but he'd always spoken plainly, and it was hard to change that now.

"You ask the men who fight beside you to serve your wine?"

"Those who fight for me must be willing to do whatever is necessary."

They fight for *you, not* with *you.*

"And pouring your wine—is that necessary?" Eiric found himself asking.

"If I say that it is," Rikhard said with no trace of apology. He raised his cup and took a long swallow. "You should taste it. You might decide that it is very necessary."

The jarl seemed more amused by Eiric's challenge than offended by it. What kind of a man was this?

Do you ask them to wipe your ass as well? Eiric thought of saying, but knew better than to go that far.

Instead, he said, "So. These men who pour your wine—what do they get in return?"

"For one, the opportunity to drink some very good wine," Rikhard said, chuckling. Then, noticing Eiric's rising temper, he said, "You Halvorsens are a proud lot, aren't you?"

Eiric shrugged. "We know who we are," he said. "I'm told that you've collected large numbers of followers, and I'm wondering what your secret is—what you offer them."

"What do I offer?" Rikhard gazed down into his cup of wine. "Hope," he said.

Eiric didn't know what he'd expected, but it wasn't that. To cover his confusion, he finally gulped down some wine himself.

He'd never tasted anything like it.

Ale and mead were typical offerings in mead halls and long-houses in the Archipelago. Wine was rarely seen, and was served only in the wealthiest households. And wealthy households were few and far between.

Sylvi had made wine at Sundgard from fruit such as cherries and pears. It was good enough, but it was nothing like this.

"I told you that you would like it," Rikhard said, reading Eiric's expression. "It's from Frankia, and they make it from grapes. I've developed a taste for it, and now nothing else will do. An expensive habit, I'm afraid. That's why I bought Faregildis. She's from Frankia, and I'm hoping that if the grapes will grow here, one day I'll be able to make my own." The jarl refilled their glasses. "Perhaps I will grow them at Sundgard—next year," he said.

"Perhaps you won't," Eiric said, sipping at his wine this time instead of gulping. "A lot can happen in a year." *You could run into my sword, for instance.* "You said that you offer your liegemen hope. Hope of what?"

"The hope that we will find a future by restoring the best elements of the past," Rikhard said. "I want to restore magic to the world."

"I'm not following," Eiric said.

"Living in the charmed garden at Sundgard, perhaps you haven't noticed, but the Archipelago is dying. It's been a gradual thing, unnoticeable from one day to the next. It only becomes clear one year to the next, or over a decade.

"The fish in the seas are dwindling. These days a fisherman could go out every day the year round and still not salt enough away to keep a family. But he cannot sail the year round because the winter storms are worse than they've ever been.

"It's the same with farming—high effort and low yields. A freeman cannot rely on the weather anymore. There are freezes at midsummer and apple trees blooming at the equinox, when they have no chance to bear fruit."

Was it really so different at Sundgard? Or had he just not paid attention? Eiric's family had always kept to themselves, visiting the village of Selvagr only to trade for what they couldn't produce on the farm or harvest from the sea. His modir's family, especially, had always looked seaward.

He could see now, when it was probably too late, how it would have been useful to have some allies on land.

"It's never been easy being a farmer here," Eiric said. "That's why most men also fish or go coasting—"

"When we go vikingr, the takings are poor," Rikhard said. "We lose men and ships to brigands, storms, and sea monsters."

"That's not what I hear," Eiric said. "I'm told that men clamor to sail for you, that your crews come home with full pockets and tales of glory."

"Dead men have no use for silver. Those who survive find that silver loses its value when there is nothing to buy," Rikhard said. "When crops fail, a thrall is just another mouth to feed."

Eiric rolled his empty glass between his hands. This was the last thing he'd expected from this ruthless young noble. Most men exaggerated their successes and downplayed their failures.

"So what is your plan? Do you intend to seize Sundgard, fortify it, and hole up there while the rest of the Archipelago starves?"

"I could," Rikhard said, "but I'd prefer not to. For one thing, if there is magic at Sundgard, it might not be in the land at all. It might relate to some magical artifact buried on the farm. Or it might be your family that is blessed with magic."

Did the jarl take him for a fool?

"If the farm is productive, it's not because of magic," Eiric said. "It's because it's fertile ground, and my modir and systir are—have been—skilled farmers."

Rikhard laughed. "Of course. It's human nature to take credit for good fortune and to blame misfortune on the fates and the gods."

Eiric grabbed up the wine bottle and splashed more wine into his glass. "In the past three years, I've lost my fadir, my grandfadir, and my modir. Then my stepfadir tried to kill me and my systir. I've been convicted of my stepfadir's murder and declared vargr. Now we stand to lose our family's farm." Mortified, Eiric realized that his voice was shaking. He drained his glass again and slammed it down on the table. "If I am favored by the gods or blessed with magic, I don't see it."

"Ah," the jarl said. "I can understand why you are a nonbeliever."

"I'm not looking for sympathy," Eiric said. "But gods and witches and magic—it's all just stories people tell one another to explain the unexplainable, to accept the unacceptable. If magic—and the gods—once existed, they are gone now. A man has to make his way on his own."

"You and I agree, then, that magic is hard to find these days," Rikhard said. "The question is, where did it go? There are other remnants of the worlds that existed before the Last Battle. We are overrun with demons, trolls, jotun of all stripes, and, some say, dwarves and elves. In the sagas, the gods freely bred with the humans in the Midlands. Doesn't it make sense that gods and witches—or their mixed-blood offspring—have survived as well?"

Eiric thought of his argument with Liv about seidr. "Some still practice magic," he said, thinking it ironic that he was now arguing the other side.

The jarl gestured dismissively. "Fortune-tellers, hedge witches, and the like, taking money from the foolish. I'm talking about real magic, performed by the volur—witches who lived among us."

"Well then," Eiric said. "While I'm watching for wolves and fire demons in the forest, I'll keep a lookout for gods and witches as well."

Chuckling, the jarl reached into a chest beside the table and produced a scroll. He flattened it on the tabletop, pinning the corners with polished stones. It was a map. "Have a look at this."

Eiric leaned forward to have a look. He recognized several of the islands in the Archipelago. There were some others that were unfamiliar—places Rikhard must have visited that Eiric had not. To the south were sketched the coastlines of Affrika, Grikkland, Frakkland—places he had heard of but never been to. To the west, Irland and Skotland. But at least half the map was blank.

Eiric looked up at Rikhard, awaiting answers.

Rikhard sat back, lacing his fingers across his lean middle. "Recently, clues have surfaced that a magical world still exists. Have you ever heard of the Grove?"

Eiric shook his head.

"The Grove is a temple established by dedicates who fancy themselves to be modern-day volur. They call themselves wyrdspinners. Rumor has it that their temple is a palace and their realms are rich and fertile. Once or twice a year, the spinners travel through the Archipelago, offering prophesy and counseling to jarls and chieftains. In return, they are allowed to visit villages and towns, collecting orphaned babies and young children to take back with them. They want nothing else from us."

A finger of dread ran down Eiric's spine, and the hairs on the back of his neck stood up. "Children? What for?"

"No one asks many questions, since the children lack families and it means fewer mouths to feed. The spinners claim that they will be trained in sorcery, prophesy, and healing,and raised in the temple," Rikhard said. "There are, of course, other possibilities." The jarl smiled bitterly and poured more wine for both of them. "We may, in effect, be sending them into thralldom, or worse."

"What could be worse than thralldom?" Eiric said.

"Witches have been known to call forth demons through human sacrifice. That may be the source of the monsters we are plagued with now. Or they may be sacrificing them to the surviving gods." Rikhard paused to let that sink in. "Whatever the case," the jarl said briskly, "the children are never seen again."

Eiric shuddered, his natural suspicion of seidr welling up inside him. "How long has this been going on? How many children are we talking about?"

"From what I can tell, it's been going on since before I was born,"

Rikhard said. "They seem to be choosy—they only take a few a year, both boys and girls."

"It's not unusual for a temple to recruit young acolytes," Eiric said.

"Why would they recruit boys? Boys do not practice seidr."

That was a good point. Eiric had never known boys or men to claim that gift. It wasn't considered proper for a man.

Rikhard raised a hand of caution. "It may be that their motives are pure and their practice innocent. They may indeed be training healers, weather workers, seers, harvest witches, artisans, and scholars, in which case I hope to persuade them to return to the Archipelago—under proper supervision, of course."

"Where is this temple?" Eiric said.

"That's just it. We don't know where the temple is, and they won't say. We've tried to follow their ships back to their home port, but we've always lost track of them."

"What makes you think that the spinners are genuine volur when you dismiss others as hedge witches and frauds?"

"Until recently, I wasn't convinced."

"Until recently? What happened?"

"On their last visit here, the spinners kidnapped a young girl—a thrall belonging to a colleague of mine, who claimed that she was a spellsinger and healer. I sent a longboat to intercept them, but the crew went mad, abandoned ship, and drowned."

Eiric stared at him, alarmed.

"My ship was nearby, but when we raised sail to pursue them, they disappeared." He brushed his palms together.

"Disappeared?" Eiric said skeptically. "How?"

"A good question," Rikhard said. "I was there. I saw it happen. I now suspect that the so-called spinners are, indeed, volur—practitioners of magic—and that the Grove is their stronghold.

Where it is, why they've gone there, and what they are doing remains to be seen. We can only assume that their temple is somewhere out here." He pointed to the blank areas of the map. "I had no idea where to look until the council meeting this afternoon."

Rikhard opened a small chest and pulled out the items he had claimed from Eiric and Liv—the necklace, the armband, and the small gold game piece covered with runes. He set them on the table, where they glittered in the light from the oil lamps.

"In all my travels, I've never seen work like this, in the markets or on the sites of ruined temples and cities," he said. "The same goes for the weapons you cling to so tightly. I believe they come from a time before memory—from the age of the gods."

Rikhard turned the game piece in his hands so that the light caught the runic inscriptions. "This item is of particular interest to me."

Eiric was surprised. The necklace and the arm ring obviously contained more precious metal by weight than the gold tablet.

Noting his confusion, Rikhard pulled another scroll from the bin and unfurled it. "This is a volva's foretelling of life after Ragnarok." Clearing his throat, he read from the scroll.

> *Much do I know,*
> *and more can see*
> *Of the fate of the gods,*
> *the mighty in fight.*
> *The gods at Ithavoll meet together.*
> *Of the terrible girdler of earth they talk,*
> *And the mighty past they call to mind.*
> *And the runes of the Ruler of Gods,*
> *In wondrous beauty once again,*
> *There they will find once more*

The golden game pieces in the grass,
Which the gods had owned in days of old.

Then fields unsowed bear ripened fruit.
All sickness will disappear;
Baldr will come back;
Baldr and Hoth dwell in Odin's Hall
With other gods.
More fair than the sun,
a hall I see,
Roofed with gold, on Gimle it stands;
There shall the righteous rulers dwell,
And happiness ever there shall they have.

Rikhard looked up from his scroll. "Sounds like a paradise, doesn't it? According to the seeress, some of the gods survived and gathered at Ithavoll."

"So you think that is one of the golden game pieces?" Eiric said, gesturing toward the small gold tablet, eager to return to real life.

"I have no way of knowing for sure, but I think it must be. Everything taken together—the artifacts as well as the history of Sundgard and your family—these are the most important clues I've found. Maybe the Grove has nothing to do with Ithavoll and the gods, but I mean to find out."

Hammered by weariness and wine, Eiric was tired of dancing with Rikhard's gods. "I wish you good luck with that. In the meantime, what do you want from me?"

Rikhard finally decided to answer that question. "I mean to send a ship in search of the witches' temple. I want you to serve as navigator."

Eiric wrestled with himself, trying to come up with a response. He was a plain speaker—not a silver-tongued flatterer. Ordinarily, sailing away from his responsibilities and into adventure would have appealed to him very much. But this struck him as a fool's errand, destined to end in disaster for everyone involved.

"As I told you at the Thing, it was my grandfadir who brought back those pieces, some long before I was born. I wouldn't know where to start."

"I understand that," Rikhard said. "If your grandfadir or your fadir were here, I would ask them. Since they're not, I'm asking you in the hopes that you have inherited their abilities to find lost worlds."

Stalling for time, Eiric flexed the fingers on the hand Reginn had healed, something that had become a habit to keep them limber. He couldn't very well tell the truth—that he knew that if he sailed with a boatload of the jarl's men, he'd never return. There was a good likelihood that even if he found the temple, he would end up with his throat cut, leaving Rikhard with the farm and the information he sought.

Yet a choice between disaster in the present and disaster sometime in the future was no choice at all.

"I will do it," Eiric said, "if you meet my conditions."

"Your . . . conditions?" The jarl raised an eyebrow. Clearly, he thought Eiric was in no position to set conditions.

"You mentioned that you've been looking for this temple for a couple of years. Whether I navigate for you or not, if you send a longship out looking, you'll find what you've found before—nothing. Which, in my view, would be a piece of luck. If you truly believe that the spinners are volur, even if you found the temple, you would never make landfall.

"You told me what happened to the crew of your longboat. I

have no desire to go mad and drown myself in the ocean. Or die aboard a burning ship. Or be turned into a monster or a fish."

The jarl frowned, as if disappointed at Eiric's hesitation to fling himself into danger at his command. "Fair enough," Rikhard said. "What do you propose?"

"I have a boat–a small karvi. I'll go looking for your witches' temple with my boat and my crew. If I find it, I will bring back proof, information on the stronghold and its defenses, and I'll show you how to get there. Then you can return in force if you choose to." He paused, taking in Rikhard's astonished expression. "I would also ask that you keep the Knudsens–and everyone else–away from my family and my farm for a year."

"Why should I agree to that?" Rikhard said.

"Why should I agree to go vikingr with a crew I don't trust, in a ship I don't know, to find a thing that may not exist at all? I will do this thing for you if it is within my power, but I would prefer to survive it."

"What if you sail off and disappear?" Rikhard said.

What kind of man do you think I am, to sail away and leave my brodir and systir penniless and landless? Eiric thought, his irritation growing.

"I could sail away now if that was my plan," Eiric said. "I don't need your permission."

"And I could chain you to the mast of my longship and go to sea tomorrow," Rikhard said.

As usual, Eiric's temper made him reckless. "You do that, and you'll never find the temple," he said. "You'll never see land again."

The jarl surged to his feet, his hand on his fine sword. Eiric stood, too, not reaching for his axe but acutely aware of the weight of it. They glared at each other for a moment that lived like an hour.

You can do Liv and Ivar no good if you're dead, Eiric thought.

He raised his hands, palms out. "Think about it, lord," he said. "The risk is mine. If it goes wrong, I stand to lose my ship, my crew, and the farm. You can put your ships and crews to work elsewhere. At the end of the year, I deliver what you want, or Sundgard is yours."

"And if you go off on your own and are captured and tortured, the spinners will be forewarned that I am looking for the temple," the jarl said. "They may slaughter the children before they can be rescued."

Eiric got the impression that the children were always an afterthought.

"If they capture your longship, they'll have many more people to torture, many more tongues to tell tales," Eiric said. "Besides, if they are truly witches, they already know that you're coming for them. If they are not, they pose little threat to you."

By now, the fury darkening the jarl's face was leavened with a trace of respect. "If you come back claiming that you found the temple, how do I know that you're not lying?" he said.

"What sort of proof would satisfy you?" Eiric said.

Rikhard considered, then scooped up the golden tablet, displaying it on his palm. "Bring me more of these," he said. "Bring me artifacts that prove you've been to the temple, navigational charts that will enable us to return there, and tactics that will enable us to defend ourselves against the kind of magic the spinners used against my longship." He paused. "Bring back the thrall that was taken from my colleague so that we can question her." He paused. "If she's still alive."

"Do we have a bargain, then?" Eiric said.

"We do," the jarl said through gritted teeth. "But if you fail to keep your word, at the end of a year I will seize Sundgard, sell your family into the slave markets, and hunt you down with every resource at my command."

"I may not find your temple, but I will keep my word," Eiric said. He stood, inclining his head in a sort of a bow. "Thank you for the wine. We'll need to make an early start in the morning. I will let you know when we are ready to sail."

Eiric backed from the room—more an effort to protect his retreat than any show of reverence. The jarl was still furious—Eiric read the news in his hard jaw and narrowed eyes. No doubt he'd never expected this kind of obstinance from a fisherman farmer.

But by then, Eiric had figured out that Rikhard didn't want the farm at all. He wanted what only Eiric could offer—access to the Grove and the possibility of returning magic to the Archipelago. Not that Eiric believed that would really happen. But he'd bought himself and his family a year.

A lot could happen in a year.

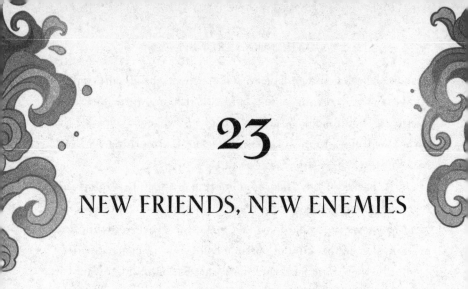

23

NEW FRIENDS, NEW ENEMIES

THE NEXT MORNING, KATIA LEFT the domicile long before sunup and returned with a stack of clothing in various sizes. Reginn tried on every garment while Katia rocked impatiently from foot to foot, vaettir flying and landing on her head and shoulders each time she moved.

In the end, Reginn settled on a tunic and trousers in the pale dedicate blue. The trousers were too long, and loose in the waist, but she rolled up the hems and tied her remedy belt around her middle, feeling the familiar weight of runestones and medicinals in their pouches. Lastly, she strapped the case with the flute in it across her back and wound her hair into a knot.

"You look fine," Katia said, rolling her eyes. "Time for breakfast."

When Katia and Reginn emerged from the systirs' domicile, several other dedicates were waiting, including Stian, who'd apparently been filling them in on their new classmate.

One was an older-looking dedicate wearing a wide-brimmed leather hat that all but obscured his face. Tufts of white-blond hair stuck out from underneath. He carried a tall, intricately carved staff made of wood. Another was a sturdy boy with hair and coloring similar to her own. And finally, there was a pale-skinned girl with cropped blue-streaked black hair who stood a little apart from the others. Her arms were heavily muscled and covered with a spiderweb of ink.

"You waited?" Katia said. "Aren't you afraid you'll be late for breakfast?"

"We wanted to welcome our new student," the blue-haired girl said. "I'm Systir Grima."

"I'm Systir Reginn," Reginn said, unsure whether she should extend her hand. In the end, she inclined her head politely.

"I'm Brodir Erland," the boy with the staff said. As he turned toward Reginn, the light reached his face. His skin was pale as chalk, his white-lashed eyes the color of sea ice.

He's blind, Reginn thought.

"Be at ease," Erland said, smiling. "Welcome to the Grove. If I can help you with anything, please ask."

"Thank you," Reginn said, still flustered. "I—I guess I have a lot to learn."

"We're all still learning every day," Erland said.

"I'm Bryn," the sturdy boy volunteered.

"Bryn is a genius of a healer," Katia said, taking his arm. "We're all lucky to have him around." She said this with fierce enthusiasm, as if daring anyone to disagree.

Bryn smiled painfully, as if sorry Katia had brought that up.

"Good to meet you, Bryn," Reginn said. "I'm interested in healing, too. I'd like to find out more about what you do here."

"Really?" Bryn said with a flicker of surprise. "You'd be welcome to come to Brenna's House and I could show you around."

"Brenna's House?"

"The healing hall," Bryn said.

With that, the conversation died.

Reginn had spent her life surrounded by people yet always alone.

Performing for a crowd was easy. Speaking to one or two people was much harder. She'd never had friends before, unless she could count Thurston, and that had not ended well. The only person she'd interacted with regularly was Asger, and he was probably not a good example to follow. How was she supposed to know what to do?

"We'd better go," Katia said. "I heard that Naima made honey cake."

Katia set off at a long-legged lope. Everyone else broke into a trot so as not to fall behind. That made conversation difficult. Reginn noticed that Erland used his staff to test the way forward, like a cat uses his whiskers.

The dining hall was built of timber and stone, the roof of cedar. Smoke rose from chimneys at either end. Reginn couldn't get used to the easy availability of trees, the many structures built of wood. What would it be like to be able to build a huge fire to keep warm whenever you wanted?

And yet here, there seemed to be little need for fires, since the weather was so mild.

As soon as they passed beyond the massive oak doors, they were met with the sound of voices. At the near end of the room, dedicates were seated at long tables, though most of the room was empty.

Cooks and servers in drab colors appeared to be clearing away dishes and leftovers.

"This way," Katia said, leading Reginn toward a table with several empty seats. "This is the table for the older dedicates."

Katia pointed her to a chair, but Reginn hesitated, staring down at a plate piled high with bread, barley porridge, eggs, and skyr. She'd never seen so much food on one plate in her life.

"This is all for me?" she said, looking to Katia for direction, just as Erland said, "Where are the honey cakes?"

"They ran out," Stian said. "That's what you get for being late to a meal."

"*You* still have some," Bryn pointed out.

"That's what I get for outrunning the rest of you," Stian said, taking a bite and savoring it.

"You could at least share some with Reginn," Katia said.

"Never mind, I'm . . . good," Reginn said. She took her first bite of porridge. It was flavored with dried cherries and honey. Dried cherries and honey together! She'd never tasted anything so fine. She considered trading everything else on her plate for more porridge. But then she took a bite of her eggs, and the sharp flavor of aged cheese exploded on her tongue.

I can die happy now, she thought, savoring it.

"Are you all right?" Katia murmured, leaning in close.

"Is breakfast always like this?" Reginn whispered.

Katia nodded. "Pretty much. Sometimes there's meat. Or griddle cakes." She paused, then added, a little anxiously, "I'm sorry. Is it not to your liking? Is there something else you'd rather have? The cooks will make whatever you'd like."

The boy on Reginn's other side had been leaning close to listen while pretending not to. Now he said, "Is it true that people in Barbaria eat only raw meat and drink flaming mead to make them fierce fighters?"

Reginn turned to look at the boy who'd spoken, but words failed her. His hair was the color of birch leaves in autumn, green and gold mingled together, and his eyes were green flecked with gold. His skin was a deep bronze overlaid with twisting vines and leaves. He looked like he could be a wood faery in one of Tove's stories.

His half smile made it hard to tell if he was serious or not.

"It's not called Barbaria, Shelby," Stian said, packed full of lofty knowledge. "It's called . . . um . . ."

"We call it the Archipelago," Reginn said. "I lived on an island called Muckleholm. We didn't eat meat very often. Most people can't afford it, even on feast days. We drink more small ale than anything else. To be honest, this is the best breakfast I've had in a long time."

Reginn had set aside a little pile of dried cherries. Now she popped them all into her mouth, closing her eyes, savoring them.

"Do you like cherries?" Shelby said, as if eager to make amends.

"Of course I love cherries," Reginn said. "They're red—like raw meat." She shoved back her plate while the others snorted in laughter.

A little humor wins over an audience, Tove always said.

"Serves you right, Shelby," Stian said. "You're going to have to work harder than that to charm your way into Reginn's . . . good graces."

"What's that you're carrying on your back?" a girl asked, having to speak loudly because she was far down the table. She raked back a fringe of stick-straight bangs. "In the case."

By now, Reginn knew they all must think it was a weapon of some kind.

"It's a flute," Reginn said.

"A *flute*?" the girl said, black eyes wide with surprise, then narrowing with eager curiosity. "Could we see it?"

"Sure."

As Reginn fumbled with the buckle, Katia leaned close and whispered, "That's Systir Eira. She makes things. Magical tools of all kinds."

When Reginn pulled the flute from its leather sleeve, there were murmurs of amazement around the table.

"Did you make that?" Eira said, her eyes feasting on the intricately carved bone.

Reginn shook her head. "It was my foster modir's. She taught me to play."

"You play?"

When I'm not slaughtering people, Reginn wanted to say. Instead, she nodded and said simply, "Yes."

She saw astonished faces all around the table, as if an ice wolf had shown an interest in playing the harp.

"Play something for us?" Eira was joined by a chorus of assent.

"Maybe some other time," Katia said. "Systir Reginn has an appointment with Modir Tyra."

"I'm curious," Grima said, speaking up for the first time since they'd sat down. "Why did Modir Tyra accept you now, when the rest of us came as babies?"

To Reginn, it seemed like the entire table fell silent, waiting for her answer.

I got in a fix in Barbaria, Reginn thought of saying. *Modir Tyra helped me out.*

Some instinct told her to say as little as possible. The same instinct that kept her out of fixes in Barbaria.

"I am lucky to be here, I know," Reginn said. "I'll do my best to convince her that she made the right decision."

"We'd better go," Stian said, standing. "Modir Tyra is expecting us."

Katia rose also, and they hustled her outside.

"It's not far," Stian said, "but you're cutting it close."

He led the way, walking fast. As soon as they emerged into the open, the raven, Kettel, swooped down and settled onto Stian's shoulder with a great flapping of wings. It was all Reginn could do not to fling herself facedown on the ground.

The grassy quad was littered with white flowers, like a galaxy of stars. Reginn could smell their fragrance as they were crushed beneath their feet. So much to look at, so much to breathe in—it made her senses tired.

They were coming up on a timber-and-stone building with a broad, roofed porch, fronted by a raised terrace. It was the largest building Reginn had seen so far. The pillars supporting the porch roof were intricately carved with images of the old gods and scenes from the old sagas. Crimson roses rioted in the beds flanking the steps up to the door.

An iron fence surrounded the building. A dozen guards were stationed at various points around the perimeter. They wore the same livery as the guards who had accompanied the keeper and Modir Tyra at Gunnar's Hall. They were the first guards Reginn had seen since she'd arrived.

When they reached the gate, Stian and Katia stopped, turned.

"This is the House of Elders," Katia said. "The academy offices for adepts and faculty are here, as well as the Founder's Hall and elders' offices. The Founder's Hall is where the Council of Elders meets to make decisions, conduct hearings, impose discipline, and . . . whatever else they do."

"The academy offices are to the left, and Modir Tyra's is all the way at the end of the hall," Stian said. "There should be someone just inside to direct you."

Seeming to sense Reginn's nervousness, Katia squeezed her hand. "Don't worry," she said. "Modir Tyra knows what she's doing. If she invited you to come here, then this is where you belong."

24

SECOND BURNING

THEY RODE AWAY FROM RIKHARD'S hall early the next morning, more than ready to leave the jarl's hospitality behind. The day had dawned clear and cold, and Eiric hunched his shoulders against the brisk wind off the sound. Still, there was a warmth in the sun that hadn't been there a month ago. Spring was coming. It always had before.

It seemed that they had all slept poorly, and nobody had much to say. Ivar's was the only cheerful face among them.

As before, Eiric rode the coastal path with his axe close to hand, searching the landscape forward and landward. He hoped that Rikhard's warning would prevent trouble along the way, but his stepfadir's family was not known for common sense.

Eiric said nothing about the jarl's demands except that he'd agreed to serve Rikhard for a year. He used the excuse of Hilde's presence and the risk of being overheard, but his systir gazed at him through narrowed eyes, and he knew that gambit wouldn't play once they were at their own hearth. He needed time to collect his thoughts, since he suspected that Liv would not be happy with the plan.

As they neared home, the wind changed, and Eiric caught a whiff of smoke. That was odd. There were no other dwellings between here and the farm and no one at home to kindle a fire. When he looked ahead, he saw a tall column of smoke spiraling up into the indigo sky.

His heart stumbled. Surely the Knudsens would not set fire to the farm they still hoped to claim. Surely not.

He heeled his horse, Dain, forward just as Liv thundered past him on her gelding.

"Liv!" he shouted, galloping after her, slitting his eyes against her dust. "Wait! Be careful!"

They hadn't quite reached the farm when Eiric heard someone screaming.

At that point, the source of the smoke came into sight. It was not their longhouse. Instead, just outside the boundary line of their farm, someone had planted a stake in the ground, piled kindling around it, and set it aflame.

At the center of the rising flames, a bound figure struggled and twisted, trying to get free, screaming for mercy.

"Emi!" Liv leaped from her horse before Eiric could rein in. Without hesitation, she waded into the flames, thrusting aside burning branches, drawing her belt dagger and desperately slicing at the ropes binding her friend.

"No! Liv!"

Eiric rolled from Dain's back and sprinted forward, using his axe to whack the burning kindling aside. Up close, the mingled scents of burning tar and woodsmoke brought tears to his eyes so that he could scarcely see.

Burning tar.

The flames had reached Emi's waist, and the skin on her face and arms was blistering. Eiric knew they were too late. Emi knew it, too. She was crying and pleading with Liv to stop, to save herself.

The scent of burning wool filled his nose as Liv's overdress began to smolder.

Emi's gaze met Eiric's. She nodded, sending a silent message. Eiric took a quick breath, then surged forward, gripping Liv's wrist and plunging the dagger into Emi's heart.

Emi released a long breath, blood bubbling from her mouth. And died.

Wrapping his arms around Liv's middle, Eiric threw himself backward, out of the reach of the flames, landing on his back with his systir on top.

Liv struggled and fought to get free, slamming her elbows into his head, cursing him as only his systir could do. It had been a long time since she'd bested him in a physical fight, but he was taking a lot of punishment.

Eiric held tight until Hilde arrived. Between the two of them, they managed to drag Liv farther from the pyre and pin her down. Hilde poured water from her waterskin over Liv's overdress to put out any remaining sparks.

Liv's hair had been burned to the scalp in places and singed elsewhere. Her skin was blistered above the overdress, her twin brooches melted to the wool. Fortunately, her heavy clothing had prevented more extensive burns.

Liv's eyes found Eiric's. "You murdered her," she said. "Emi was all I had, and you murdered her."

"Nonsense," Hilde said. "Eiric saved your life."

Liv kept her eyes fixed on Eiric. "You never approved of her," Liv said. "You begrudged every moment I spent with her."

"I'm sorry, Liv," Eiric said.

"Do you think I fear the flame, brodir?" she said. "I was destined for the flame from the time I was born."

Eiric looked back at the pyre just in time to see the stake collapse, sending sparks spiraling into the air. Emi's body was no longer visible amid the dwindling flames. The smell of burned flesh and charred bone lingered in the air.

A rattle of harness and the sound of hooves alerted Eiric that they were not alone. He scooped up his axe and swung around to see his uncles sitting their horses at the edge of the trees. They were both grinning.

Behind him, he could hear Liv gasping in pain as she struggled to her feet, propping herself up with her staff.

"Did you have a nice visit with Jarl Karlsen?" Garth spat on the ground. "You may think that he can protect you, but he's a busy man. He can't be everywhere at once."

"Why would you do this?" Liv said, licking her blistered lips. "Emi never did you any harm."

Garth cocked his head, studying Liv's face. "What did you do, jump into the flames with her? I didn't think it possible you could get any uglier, but I was wrong."

"Shut up, brodir," Finni said. "It's our right to do whatever we want with our own property. To be honest, it's too risky to have a witch in our household—especially one that's conspiring with Sten's killers."

"She was a lazy slut anyway," Garth said. "Scarcely worth her keep."

"Liar," Liv said. "You sold her services all over Muckleholm."

"She *was* a good worker," Finni said, "until she took up with you. After that, you two were always whispering, sneaking off together. Seemed unnatural to me."

"Do you really think Karlsen's blood money settles this?" Garth said, seeming eager to leave the topic of witch burning. "Do you think it makes up for the murder of our brodir?"

"Maybe not," Eiric said, "but you would've been happy to trade your brodir for the farm."

"Oh, we'll have the farm in the end," Finni said. "We'll just have to bide our time."

"Come closer, Uncles," Eiric said, his grandfadir's axe light in his hand. "It's hard to hear you from way over there. Get down from your horses and let's talk." He took a step toward them, but Liv put her hand on his arm.

"No, brodir," she said, her voice raspy from smoke. "These two belong to me." She turned and faced Finni and Garth, gripping her staff, extending her free arm toward them, her hair a sail in the wind. "I am Heidin, twice burned, twice risen. I proclaim you dra-ugr, the walking dead. Your days will pass like sand through a glass. Make the most of them because you will not see another Yule."

"Don't you curse us, witch!" Finni shouted. "Or you will follow Emi into the flame."

"I am not cursing you; I am merely foretelling your fate," Liv said. "Most would appreciate having the time to get their affairs in order."

The two Knudsens seemed to be at a loss for words. Which was a blessing, to tell the truth.

"Come on, Finni," Garth said finally. "We're done here." With that, their uncles wrenched their horses around and heeled them into a gallop. Eiric watched them until they disappeared into the trees.

A gust of wind from the sound sent ash and embers swirling. Despite the support of her staff, Liv swayed and nearly fell.

"Let's go home, Liv, and take care of those burns," Hilde said. "You may believe you're immortal, but you're not."

"Emi needs a proper sending," Liv said. "I won't leave until I've attended to her."

"Sit, systir," Eiric said. "Let me help. Tell me what to do."

Liv sat with Hilde and Ivar while Eiric did his best to separate Emi's remains from the smoldering pyre. He gathered rounded stones from the water's edge and built a small ship around her. He scooped up a handful of mingled sand and shell fragments from the beach and sprinkled it over Emi.

When he turned back toward Liv, she pried one of her brooches free from the singed wool of her dress and mutely extended it toward Eiric. He took it and set it carefully on top of Emi's ashes and bones.

"Be at peace," he whispered, knowing there would be no peace—at least, not for a long time.

25

FAMILY SECRETS

ONCE HOME, EIRIC SAW TO the horses while Hilde removed Liv's charred clothing. When she attempted to clean the broad necklace of burns that circled her neck, Liv writhed and twisted silently, beads of sweat popping out on her forehead. Eiric removed the runestick from the chain around his neck and handed it to her. As soon as she closed her hands around it, her thrashing subsided.

"Staves and stones, brodir," Liv said, releasing a long breath. "This is strong magic." Once Hilde covered her wounds, she slept most of the rest of the day, still clinging to the runestick. Eiric went out to the boat shed to see what would be required to make the karvi seaworthy.

When he returned to the longhouse, Hilde had put Ivar to bed and set out the nattmal. While they ate, Eiric looked up several times to find the blacksmith's dottir studying him.

"What is it?" he said, scrubbing his hand over his face to remove any possible dirt.

"People say that you're a ruthless, coldhearted scoundrel, but they're wrong."

"Are they?" Eiric dipped a hunk of bread into the fish stew and bolted it down. A year ago, he might have demanded to know who had slandered him, but it didn't matter now. "The council disagrees."

"They're wrong," Hilde repeated.

"You really don't know me very well," Eiric said.

"I know you well enough. You could have gone vikingr before the Thing met. Yet you stayed. You look out for your systir–"

"As she looks out for me," Eiric said.

Hilde shook her head. "You're a good man, Eiric Halvorsen, and you won't convince me otherwise."

"One thing I've noticed," Eiric said, "is that the good die young on Muckleholm."

Despite her injuries, Liv was unwilling to let Eiric's agreement with Rikhard rest unchallenged for very long. The next evening, they had a sit-down after Hilde and Ivar went to bed.

They shared the bench closest to the hearth as they had done so many times before. Eiric set out two cups between them, produced a leather flask, and poured.

Liv sniffed at her cup suspiciously. "What is this?"

"This is Rikhard's wine," Eiric said. "He sent some home with me."

She tested it with her tongue. Took a sip. "Well," she said, "his wine is good enough. What is his proposal?"

"He needs a navigator," Eiric said. "He wants me to crew for him for a year." Which was, technically, true.

"Really? Rikhard is willing to trade Sundgard for a year at sea?" She snorted, took a swallow of wine. "He's not as clever as I thought."

Eiric could tell she didn't really believe him. But it would be enough if she would only–

"Where is it that Rikhard wants to go?"

Eiric sighed. There would be no escape. "He was impressed with the items we offered as blood price for Sten. He wants to follow in the wake of our fadir and grandfadir and go vikingr along those same coasts."

The cup exploded in Liv's hand, sending shards of metal pinging against the stone hearth and pinwheeling off into the dark.

Eiric sat frozen, afraid to move.

"He wants to go to the Temple at the Grove," she said flatly.

There it was again. The Grove. A place he'd never heard of before. And now twice in as many days.

"Well," he said, "I–"

"Does he know you've never been there?"

Eiric nodded. "I told him that. But he's desperate to find it, and this is the first clue he's had. I think he's hoping that the knowledge somehow seeped into me."

"Did he say why he wants to go?" From Liv's expression, Eiric guessed that there was a lot riding on this answer.

Eiric hesitated, unsure how far to get into the restoration-of-magic story. "He believes that the wyrdspinners are vala—true magical practitioners. They've been collecting children from the Archipelago for years. He's worried about what's happening to them—if they're being used in magical rituals or sold into thralldom."

"He's worried about the children, is he?" Liv arched a skeptical eyebrow.

"He's also hoping to find a way to return magic to the Archipelago."

"On whose terms?" Liv said.

"I don't *know*," Eiric said, irritated. "I'm not on a side; I'm just telling you what he told me."

"As soon as you go crewing for Rikhard, you're on a side," Liv said. "All of this whining about the loss of seidr is rich coming from those who did everything in their power to drive it out of the world in the first place."

"Well," Eiric said, "I . . ."

"And no doubt he'll send a shipload of men who wouldn't know magic if it bit them on the ass." She slid a look at Eiric, who suspected that the comment might be directed at him, but he chose to deflect that arrow.

"Look," Eiric said, "I don't know where Bjorn's artifacts came from. I don't have any reason to believe that magic exists—at the Grove or anywhere else in the world. I don't think I'll find the graveyard of the gods, or—"

"It's not just the Grove, then," Liv said. "He's really looking for Ithavoll, isn't he?"

"Ithavoll?" Eiric said. It seemed like the jarl had mentioned that word. "Why don't you tell me, since you seem to know more about this than I do?"

"Ithavoll is the legendary meeting place of the gods, where the survivors return after Ragnarok. Rikhard is either hunting for treasure or hoping to raise the old gods." She paused, took a breath. "I'll tell you this," she said. "You cannot take Rikhard to New Jotunheim. You'll never find it, and you'll all die."

First the Grove, then Ithavoll, and now New Jotunheim? Eiric recalled the large blank areas on Rikhard's map. He'd thought of himself as well traveled, but clearly he had a lot to learn.

"What's New Jotunheim?" Eiric said.

"That's where I was born," Liv said simply.

A memory came back to Eiric—that of a girl with fisted hands and tears that would not fall. His modir saying, *If I accept this child, then you must promise me you won't return there.*

Eiric scuffled through his scanty knowledge of the Nine Worlds. "I thought Jotunheim was a howling wilderness, full of monsters."

"That's what you've been told," Liv said, as always setting herself a little apart. "That's what the Asgardians would have you believe. History is handed down by the victors."

"You can't remember much about it," Eiric said. "You were too little."

"I remember," Liv said, her face bruised by grief and longing. "Some of it's as clear in my mind as it was on the day I left. Now I know I'll never get back."

"But . . . you liked it *here*, didn't you?" Eiric found himself wanting to defend Sundgard and Selvagr even though he'd been eager to leave it just moments ago.

"Of course I liked it here . . . at least until our fadir died and Sten came and his brodirs murdered Emi." Absently, she traced the ring of blisters around her neck. "There's nothing left for me here." And then, in a rush, she added, "Except for you and Ivar, of course."

"Of course," Eiric said, glad they were no longer discussing Rikhard and his agenda.

"New Jotunheim is not a place you easily forget. I have unfinished business there."

What kind of business would an eight-year-old have? Eiric wondered. But he could tell she was grieving a serious loss.

"Well—you might get back there one day," Eiric said. "Leif and Bjorn promised not to go back there, but you never did."

Liv shook her head. "I'll never get back there, and you won't either—not without the sunstone."

"The . . . sunstone?"

"You might have been too young to remember, but on the day Fadir brought me here, Sylvi agreed to let me stay on condition that he promise never to go back there. She demanded that he give her the sunstone and my amulet to ensure that he would keep his promise." Liv swallowed hard. "I haven't seen either one since. For a while, I searched on the sly with no luck. Finally, I asked Sylvi about it. She told me to quit looking, that she'd dropped them into a crevasse. I still hoped that she was lying, that she'd kept them hidden somewhere. Since she died, I've searched high and low, but I've found nothing." She blinked back tears.

"Why are they important?" Eiric said. "What are they good for?"

"The sunstone is a navigational tool and talisman," Liv said. "It's the only reason Bjorn and Leif were able to travel to the Grove and come home again. The amulet is a figure of Heidin. It was my memory. It was my heart and my purpose."

Heidin? That was the name she used the day she came to Sundgard. The name she used when cursing their uncles.

Eiric knew exactly where they both were—in the secret compartment in the floor under Sylvi's sleeping bench. He recalled Sylvi's words on the night Ivar was born.

There's a stone set into the floor under my sleeping bench. You'll find a small chest underneath. Take my jewelry that's in there. . . . Return the rest to the barrow and never speak of it again. Do not tell Liv.

"So . . . all this time, you've wanted to go back?" Given everything that had happened, he could hardly blame her, but still—it hurt.

Liv reached out and put her hand on Eiric's shoulder. "Not all of the time," she said. "Not even most of the time. I've been happy here. I loved Fadir, and you, and Bjorn and Sylvi, even though she wasn't my modir by blood. The work's been hard, but I've felt safe here, at least, until now." She paused, shivered as if she'd taken a sudden chill. "I never felt safe in New Jotunheim."

Eiric had been pouring the rest of the wine, but now he splashed a little on the table. "Hang on," he said. "I thought it was supposed to be a paradise, a–a–sanctuary."

"A paradise, maybe," Liv said. "Enchanting, enticing, seductive even. But not a sanctuary at all. Not for me."

Eiric sat, speechless. One thought kept repeating in his head—Liv had been eight years old when she came here. Eight. How could she possibly remember what had come before so clearly? Or had she simply created what she couldn't remember out of thin air?

Liv was looking at him in that way she had, as if she were reading his thoughts. "Age is more than chronology, brodir. In that way, I am older than you think."

Eiric had always thought of his systir as an old soul, but not in any literal way. Girls grew up fast in the Archipelago. Many were married by age twelve and having children of their own. Lives were short, after all. But Liv had strenuously rejected any mention of marriage. And Sylvi needed her help on the farm.

Eiric had sworn an oath to Sylvi that he wouldn't tell Liv about the sunstone or the pendant.

Why did he believe so strongly in the power of an oath when he didn't believe in anything else?

"What would you do if you found the sunstone?" Eiric said, straddling a ridge of indecision. "Would you go back? Even though it's dangerous?"

Liv studied him, eyes narrowed, head tilted. "I don't know. Maybe I just wanted to know that I could if I wanted to." After a wistful pause, she dismissed that possibility with a wave of her hand. "Nothing to be done about it now," she said. "Don't go off chasing Rikhard's dreams. Instead, stay here and help on the farm. If we have a good harvest, we'll sell as much as we can spare for hack silver and jewelry. When Rikhard claims the farm, we can go vikingr together. There are other places to live. We'll build another Sundgard."

"I swore an oath to Modir that I would not allow the Knudsens to take the farm."

"It won't be Sten's people; it will be Rikhard," Liv said.

"If I refuse Rikhard's offer, he'll take the farm now," Eiric said. "This way, it buys us a year. If I don't find the temple, I'll be home in a year, and then we'll sail."

"If you sail with Rikhard, you won't be home in a year. He'll kill you, whether you find the Grove or not. And then I'll have no brodir, no farm, and no ship to sail in."

"I'm not sailing with Rikhard," Eiric blurted, something he hadn't meant to reveal. "I'm sailing my own karvi, with my own crew. I'm not stupid."

Liv blinked at him. "I never said you were stupid, Eiric," she said. "I'm saying that you won't get anywhere near the Grove without the sunstone. I'm saying that you will probably die in the attempt. You always think that the solution to every problem is either to fight or sail away. Your life is more important than any farm." She stood. "Think on that, brodir, before you sail."

With that, she crossed the longhouse and pushed between the hangings that hid her sleeping bench.

Eiric stared, brooding, into the flames, sipping at the last of Rikhard's wine until it was gone.

Liv was always worth listening to, but facts were facts. If he declined Rikhard's offer, the farm was forfeit now, and the jarl's hird would enforce that claim. They would be lucky to escape with the clothes on their backs. He'd have to leave the langskip behind—the ship his fadir and grandfadir had built, that he had learned to sail in. Even if they got away in the karvi, he could not go vikingr with his systir as his only crew.

Eiric had known his chances of meeting Rikhard's demands were slim to none, but he had to try. And now Liv's revelations about the sunstone had kindled a flame of hope that he could actually sail to the Grove, bring back proof, and so meet the jarl's demands.

He could save Sundgard. Maybe.

26

COURSE OF STUDY

A SERVANT GREETED REGINN JUST inside the door of the head-mistress's offices. She motioned Reginn to a seat while she went to announce Reginn's arrival. Reginn was too restless to sit, so she walked around the room, examining the framed paintings and manuscripts that lined the walls.

Many of the paintings depicted groups of students of different ages under the canopies of trees, practicing music, singing, smash-ing herbs with mortars and pestles. In one scene, students sprawled on the grass as Modir Tyra spoke to them.

Tyra appeared in many of the scenes.

The manuscripts were covered with indecipherable scribblings. Reginn knew the runes of magic—Tove had taught her—but this meant nothing to her. She followed the lines of ink with her finger, careful not to touch the symbols themselves.

"Can you read that, dottir?" Modir Tyra's voice came from be-hind, startling her, so that she spun around, cheeks hot with shame.

"No, Modir," Reginn confessed, then thought better of it. "I mean, it's a little different from the writing I've read before."

"Ah," the headmistress said, and Reginn had the sense that she could see right through that lie.

Tyra smiled. "Come to my solar, and we'll discuss your course of study." She led the way through a doorway at the rear of the entrance hall. They passed down a long corridor between more framed manuscripts, drawings, and paintings.

As they walked, Reginn wondered if she should have mentioned that she knew some runes—not the runes of writing but the runes of magic. That might help her make a good impression.

No, it was better to play her cards close until she knew what was valued around here.

What did Modir Tyra mean by "course of study"? Would she have to choose among the gifts she claimed—those of music, prophesy, and healing?

Almost immediately, she crossed prophesy off her mental list. She played at prophesy, and it brought in easy coin, but how could she claim the gift of prophesy when her own life was such a midden of misery? If she truly had the gift of predicting the future, she would have made better choices.

Then again, others had made the choices for her. Nobody had asked her opinion.

Healing brought with it a bone-deep satisfaction, the knowledge that she'd made a real difference in someone's life. She'd repaired Eiric Halvorsen's damaged arm—a gift before they parted. She hoped he'd think of her every time he raised a sail or swung an axe.

The warmth of that memory faded as she thought of Thurston. Maybe healing was like dumping a thimbleful of water on the bonefire of the world, while everybody else just kept adding fuel to it.

But music—music had been her refuge since a time beyond memory. But would music like hers be considered a gift in a place like this?

Modir Tyra called it her solar, but it was a high stone terrace overhung by a leafy green canopy so that the light had a shady, blue-green quality. Ferns and orchids spilled from niches in the stone wall of the house. Reginn could hear the sound of moving water below. When she peered over the low wall at the edge of the terrace, she saw that it overlooked a deep ravine with a series of waterfalls cascading through it.

How could anyone spend a day in this place and not want to stay here forever?

Tyra sat down on a bench and motioned for Reginn to sit opposite her. Reginn felt singled out and special to be in the presence of the headmistress in this enchanted green place, bursting with life.

Modir Tyra had the gift of making her feel valued.

"Do you have your flute with you, dottir?"

Reginn nodded, her fingers brushing the instrument case at her side.

"Good. Now. I know that you must be worried that you're behind in your studies and will never catch up. I hope that I can offer some reassurance."

"I hope so, too," Reginn said.

Tyra laughed. "As you might have guessed, each of our dedicates follows an individual course of study, because different gifts require different skills. Ordinarily, we spend their early years identifying their magical talents. Then we focus on the training that will enhance their gifts and facilitate their application." She paused. "Does that make sense?"

Reginn nodded. "I think so, but could you give me an example?"

"Of course. Shelby's gift is his ability to develop, nurture, and propagate plants. In order to make the best use of that gift, he needs a basic knowledge of existing plants and familiarity with farming techniques so that he can work with those who work in our gardens and farms."

"I see."

"The good news is that we have already identified your gift—the ability to call on the vaettir—the spirits of the dead—through song. So that much is done."

It was as if Reginn's racing thoughts had run straight into a stone wall.

"Calling the *vaettir*? No!" Reginn blurted.

"Is there a problem?" Tyra raised an eyebrow.

"Modir, I just—" Reginn licked her lips, swallowed. "About calling the spirits. It only happened that one time, with Thurston. Maybe the magic was in him, not me. I don't know if I can do it again."

"There always has to be a first time," Tyra said gently. "Like any skill, it will improve with practice."

Reginn cast about for a different niche where she knew she could succeed. "I was hoping—I already have a good knowledge of herbs and remedies and considerable experience in healing. I met Bryn today, and he offered to show me around the healing halls. Maybe I could help out there."

"We'll see," Tyra said. "I'm not sure there will be time for that."

That didn't sound like a yes. The headmistress had made the choice for her. That was familiar. And not in a good way. Modir Tyra had chosen a gift that Reginn was reluctant to claim, a vocation that might lead straight to failure.

As Reginn fumbled for a response, the headmistress leaned forward, taking her hands. "I know you don't want to hear this, but, dottir, you must focus on the gift that is unique to you. The gift that may save us all."

"Wh—what do you mean?"

"For some time, Jarl Karlsen has been actively seeking information about the Grove. His men have tailed me on my last few recruitment visits to the Archipelago. He's been visiting my partners at the foundling homes, asking questions. His agents have been prowling every port in Muckleholm, inquiring for a pilot who can lead him here.

"Finally, as you know, he attempted to intercept our ship at Langvik. I worry that soon, our access to the gifted in the Archipelago will be a thing of the past. That would be disastrous."

Tyra squeezed her hands, then let go. "Mind, that may not happen, but it would be foolish to ignore the threat. Especially after Karlsen attempted to kidnap you."

"Well, he didn't exactly—" Reginn stopped, thought about it. What had Asger said about Karlsen?

Let's just say that Karlsen and I share some common interests, and he can provide resources that I haven't had before now.

"Remember, it was only through the use of magic that we made our escape," Tyra said. "Karlsen witnessed that. He'll be more convinced than ever that we're worth pursuing. We believe that the barbar— the rulers of the Archipelago may be planning an invasion or attack on New Jotunheim."

Reginn's mouth went dry. "But—I thought you said that no one would find us here."

"It is unlikely," the kennari said, lifting her chin. "Even if they somehow found their way here, they would never make it through the barrier. But preparation is the best defense. And we need to be able to continue our mission in the Archipelago."

"Why would they come here?" Reginn said. "I thought they were anxious to get rid of us."

"In the Archipelago, it is rumored that our streets are paved with gold and our temples overflowing with riches," Tyra said. "That would be tempting to any coaster."

Reginn recalled Gunnar gushing over the wyrdspinners. *It's said the temple is like a palace, with floors inlaid with gems and fixtures of gold and silver.*

He'd mentioned other riches, though. *Their tables groan with cheese, butter, skyr, fish and game, and berries of all sorts.* So many people at home were starving.

As if reading her thoughts, Tyra said, "Perhaps they are beginning to realize the price they've paid for driving us from their shores. Whatever the reason, we must stand ready to defend ourselves. So much past knowledge has been lost. Your ability to speak to the dead will allow us to mine the wisdom of the ancients, providing us with weapons, tactics, and defenses that have long since passed from our knowledge."

Reginn recalled those lean seasons, long nights she and Tove had spent huddled in the cold woods with empty bellies. Fleeing villages with howling dogs at their heels, pelted with sticks and stones and frozen dung. Tove confronting men who wondered what it would be like to lie with a witchling.

And, worst of all, Asger Eldr.

She would not go back to that. Ever.

Reginn squared her shoulders. "I will do whatever it takes to protect the Grove from those who would do us harm."

Tyra smiled. "I saw the strength in you the first time we met. And if I am not mistaken, it is growing." The headmistress's approval was like the warm sun on Reginn's face.

"So I would like you to continue to work on your music. Both the flute and vardlokkur—the spells of summoning." She sighed, fingering the hem of her sleeve. "We have no teacher of spellsongs here at present. It is a lost art. That was one reason that I was so eager to have you join us. I hope that you can teach others to join in.

"I've asked some of the other dedicates to spend time with you, so that you can see how they are employing their gifts in support of New Jotunheim."

"I look forward to that, Modir," Reginn said.

"Your other task in the near term will be to learn to read and write. That way, you'll be able to read the sagas, histories, spell-songs, and stories from those who came before us. Those are all a part of our collection. So we'll focus on reading and writing first, so that you can benefit from the learning of others."

Reading and writing? Reginn struggled to hide her dismay.

She could read the runes of magic already, which was more than most people in the Archipelago could do. She could read the mind of a crowd and know when it was growing bored or restless or skeptical. She could read the stories in the bones and the face of a client, in order to know how much to reveal of what the bones were telling her.

She could read Asger's moods, which had long been the key to survival.

Surely that was enough reading to get along.

Writing, Reginn hadn't done so much of. She could carve the runes of magic into bone or stone or flesh, or paint them in oak gall ink. Why should she spend time on bookwork when Modir Tyra was asking her to hone the skills that would protect New Jotunheim—that would make Modir Tyra glad she'd taken a chance on her?

"Is that really necessary, Modir?" Reginn blurted. "I mean, it seems like that would take too much time."

"Once you can read and write, you'll be able to benefit from the wisdom of past generations and record your own for the future. Imagine the progress we can make when we can build on the past rather than starting over with every generation."

"I already know the sagas," Reginn said. "Most of them, anyway. And the old songs."

"Songs and sagas and verses are useful in the transmission of knowledge," Tyra said. "But as time passes, they become corrupted.

People shape them to serve their own ends. Soon the magic leaks out of them, and they are discarded because they are no longer effective. People who leave no written history eventually disappear."

Reginn could see the need for some kind of a record. She'd learned remedies and runes and spellsongs from Tove, but already some rarely used charms had been washed from her mind by the relentless surf of time and trouble. How many more would be forgotten? How much of what Tove had taught her would die with her?

"The rest of the world has fallen into darkness," Modir Tyra said. "Only New Jotunheim shines, like a beacon in the night, because we have magic and because we can read and write."

Reginn could tell there was no point in arguing. "When do we begin?" she said.

Before the headmistress could answer, the bells sounded in the clock tower overhead.

"We have one more hurdle to overcome. The Council of Elders is meeting this morning, and you and I are on the agenda. Come with me to Founder's Hall. I'll introduce you to the elders, and they will vote on whether to accept you as a dedicate."

27

CREW

IN THE DAYS FOLLOWING THEIR return to Sundgard, Eiric readied the karvi to go to sea. It had been a long time since she'd sailed farther than the herring banks off the surrounding islands. He'd done the routine repair work over the long winter, retarring the joints and filling them with hemp, replacing missing rivets, and stitching up rips in the sail where the long strips had come apart. He filled storage chests with smoked fish, dried fruit, and casks of ale, rechecked the tent frame and strapped it in along the gunwale.

Liv watched these proceedings in grim silence.

Despite the risks of traveling to town, it was a relief to trade the oppressive mood at Sundgard for the stares and whispers of Selvagr. Eiric had insisted on using his own crew. That might be easier said than done, given that he had none.

When Eiric put the word out in the village that he was looking for crew, nobody rushed to answer. When he approached one or two men directly, they shook their heads, avoiding his gaze.

Sylvi's line was known to be rich in hamingja—in other words, lucky. Favored by the gods or the fates or whoever made such decisions. Even her name meant "from the house of strength."

In the past, most men in the village would have been eager to sign on to an Eiricsen venture.

True, that was when his grandfadir was still alive, but Eiric had a good reputation as a navigator and a strong pitch to make. They would be sailing in search of the Grove—the stronghold of the wyrdspinners. Churches and temples could be rich targets, and legend had it that the streets of this temple were paved in gold.

In these hard times, there should have been men desperate enough to be willing to undertake a long journey to an uncertain destination guarded by dangerous magic—if the payoff was rich enough.

Eiric told himself that it was late to recruit for the summer, that the best crews were already on the water. Most of those remaining were layabouts, cutthroats, drinkers, or scrubs.

That could be it. Or it could be that after a time during which Leif died, Bjorn died, and Sylvi died; Eiric came under threat of exile; and they stood to lose their farm—it might be that people thought that the Eiricsen luck had finally run out.

It was beginning to look like he might have to resign himself to a solo voyage.

One afternoon, Eiric made a final visit to Stevenson's to collect some iron rivets he'd ordered for spares. The blacksmith was a man of few words, but Eiric could tell from his narrow-eyed glances and the way he chewed his lower lip that the big man had something to say.

"Out with it, Stevenson," Eiric said, wrapping the rivets in a square of leather and stuffing them into his carry bag. "What's on your mind?"

Stevenson scanned the street outside his open door, as if looking for listening ears; then the words tumbled out in a rush. "I just want to say that what happened at the Thing was shameful. I'm sorry about your fadir and grandfadir, and especially your modir. I begged her not to marry Sten."

Eiric looked into the blacksmith's weathered face, his faded blue eyes. "Me too," he said. "She didn't listen to either one of us."

Stevenson laughed. "Sylvi was never one to seek a safe harbor. She always sailed howling into the storm." He cleared his throat. "So. What I wanted to say was, you'd better be on your way as soon as you can. It's not safe for you here. The Knudsens might not come after you themselves, but they've put a pretty price on your head."

"I'll be ready to sail soon," Eiric said. "But—" He hesitated, then chose honesty over pride. "I've been having trouble finding a crew."

"Aye," Stevenson said. "They're afraid of Gustav and the rest."

"If they're afraid of the Knudsens, then I don't want them crewing for me," Eiric said.

"Please understand," the smith said. "Your family has always been standoffish. People in the village know nothing about you save what they hear around the longfire. It's not their fight, and they see nothing to be gained by getting involved in it. Most expect you'll be ash in the wind by the bonefires of autumn. After you're dead, they'll still have the Knudsens to contend with."

Seeing Eiric's scowl, he added, "Like I said, they don't know you."

"I'll sail alone if I have to," Eiric said.

"If I were a younger man, I'd offer to go with you." Stevenson rubbed his chin. "As it is, I'd be willing to stay at Sundgard and help Liv and Hilde on the farm while you're gone. I'd make sure that everyone knew I was there. I'm on the council, so it might discourage trespassers."

"You would do that? But what about—all of this?" Eiric gestured toward the forge, the racks of finished products and items to be repaired.

"There's a small forge at Sundgard," Stevenson said. "I used it years ago, when I stayed over doing work for the farm. I spent a lot of time there, before Sylvi married Leif."

The truth struck like a bolt from the heavens. "You loved her."

Stevenson nodded. "Aye," he said, "but once she met Leif, my hopes were crushed. People say, 'There's something about Sundgard.' There's something about the Halvorsens, too."

Eiric didn't know what to say.

Stevenson smiled. "If I stay at Sundgard, I can watch over Hilde, who is the only family I have left. What I would ask in return is that you not overlook her good qualities."

"I don't understand," Eiric said, though he did.

"She's always been sweet on you," Stevenson said, "though wary of taking up with a coaster. My point is, you might be good for each other. Whatever happens with the farm, I'm still hoping that, at the end of these troubles, you'd be interested in coming and working with me at the forge and learning the trade. You do have the build for it, though maybe not the temperament."

What makes you think these troubles will be ending? Eiric thought.

The blacksmith must have read something of that in Eiric's face, because he said, "Just keep it in mind. I would like to see Hilde settled again before I cross to Helgafjell. Liv would be welcome to share our hearth as well."

Liv will never live in Selvagr, Eiric thought.

It was all but impossible for Eiric to ask anyone for anything, but the more he thought about it, the better he liked the idea of Stevenson and Hilde staying at Sundgard while he was gone, watching over Liv, Ivar, and the farm. It took a bit of the edge off the guilt he was feeling.

"I can make no promises about Hilde," Eiric said. "I don't know when I'll be back, and who knows? She may find someone else in the meantime."

And so it was agreed. Eiric was already out the door when he realized that he had invited Stevenson to come and stay at Sundgard without consulting Liv.

He'd left his horse, Dain, in a corral at an abandoned farm just outside the village and had walked the rest of the way in the hope that he could come and go from Stevenson's without being seen. Now, as he walked down the street, he couldn't shake the feeling that he was being followed. The village wasn't that big, and the main street not so busy, that it would be easy to do so unobserved, but each time Eiric spun round, he saw no one.

Finally, he straightened his back and walked on. Everyone knew where he lived. If someone wanted to find him, they would.

It's good that you're leaving, crew or no crew, he thought. You're as jumpy as a skogkatt.

When he arrived at the old farmstead, he circled around behind the ruins of the longhouse and stopped short. Someone stood waiting between him and the corral.

It was a young man—a stranger, with short, ragged red hair and blue eyes. When he got a look at Eiric's face, he turned a shade paler than he already was and took a step back.

"Who *are* you?" the boy said.

"My name is Halvorsen," Eiric said.

"Oh!" the stranger said, recovering his footing. "You're the one I'm looking for."

"Is that so?" Eiric rested his hand on the haft of his axe. "Well, then speak."

The stranger read his expression and was quick to say, "I'm looking for a job, and I hear you're looking for a crew."

"Who told you that?" Eiric said.

"Everyone," the boy said. "They say you're sailing for the witches' temple."

"Who told you that?" Eiric said.

"Everyone. I want to crew with you."

Really? Eiric thought. Then you're the only one in Selvagr.

"Who are you?" Eiric said, looking the boy over. He was tall and well made, muscled from hard work.

"My name is . . . Thurston," the boy said.

Sure it is, Eiric thought.

"Until recently, I was a thrall in Langvik."

"Until recently?" Eiric eyed him skeptically. "Did you run away?"

"I was freed," Thurston said, opening the neck of his tunic to show that he wore no thrall's collar.

"Have you crewed on a longship?" Eiric said.

Here, the boy's eyes shifted away. "Langvik is a port town," he said. "I know my way around ships."

Eiric snorted. He'd heard that before. If you've ever sailed, he thought, you've sailed as cargo, not as crew. Shaking his head, he turned away, toward the corral. To his surprise, Dain stood on the far side, ears pinned, snorting and stomping.

"Dain!" Eiric called. "Come on. Let's go home."

Dain advanced a few steps toward him, then shied back, eyes rolling.

"Halvorsen!"

He spun around to find Thurston startlingly close, glaring at him, jaw clenched. His eyes had gone dark and turbulent as the winter sea, his hair flickering around his head like flames in the onshore winds.

"Look," he said. "I will admit that I'm not a skilled sailor. But I'm strong and willing, and I think I could be useful as part of an experienced crew."

Eiric sighed and rocked back on his heels. "Are you any good at fighting?"

Thurston drew himself up. "As you know, thralls are not allowed to handle weapons," he said. "Still, I don't think you'll be disappointed in me."

"I'm not worrying about being disappointed; I'm worried about being dead."

"The fates will dictate when you die," Thurston said. "It's not up to me."

"Why do you want to go to the temple?"

"I never said I wanted to—" Thurston began, then changed his mind mid-sentence. "There's a girl I'm looking for. I'm told she was carried off by the wyrdspinners." He paused, then rushed on. "She was the one who freed me. I want to help her."

That's when Eiric recalled something Rikhard had said—that a thrall belonging to a colleague had been kidnapped by the spinners. Could Thurston be talking about the same person?

"This girl you mentioned—that freed you. Was she a thrall like you?"

"Yes," Thurston said.

Maybe I should take *her* on as crew, Eiric thought.

"How many men have you recruited so far?" Thurston said.

There was no reason Eiric should answer this honestly, but he had no particular reason to lie. Besides, he was too tired and discouraged to care. "At this point, none."

Thurston blinked at him. "None? How many will you need?"

"Three would make a good crew, two good hands would do in a pinch," Eiric said. "So, as you can see, every man counts. I can't bring on anyone who can't pull his weight."

"Tell me this," Thurston said, lifting his chin. "Can you sail your ship alone?"

Eiric didn't want to answer that question, so instead he whistled, then shouted, "Dain!" hoping his horse would suddenly recall that he had a warm stall and grain to go home to. His horse edged a little closer but remained out of reach.

"Could you sail alone?" Thurston persisted. The aspiring sailor burned with a fervor that was off-putting. That kind of intensity would get under Eiric's skin within the confines of a sea voyage. Or anywhere.

Yet there was a saying that Sylvi favored—beggars cannot be choosers.

"Sailing that far alone wouldn't be easy," Eiric admitted. "What's your point?"

"So a second crewman—even inexperienced—might be useful," Thurston said.

"Not if that crewman talks me to death," Eiric said, vaulting the fence. He walked toward his horse, hand extended, and Dain snuffled at it, hoping for apples, maybe, his whiskers tickling Eiric's palm. Eiric gripped the sidepiece of the bridle.

He led Dain through the gate and tied his reins to the railing, since the horse still seemed jumpy. Blessedly, Thurston had finally stopped talking. He'd moved back from the corral and was leaning against the ruins of the longhouse, waiting.

The day was fading. It was time for Eiric to be on his way. But first, he walked back to where Thurston still waited.

"If you're serious about wanting to crew with me and are willing to take orders without question or complaint, I'll take you on. But you need to know what you're getting into. You'll need to listen close and learn fast. There's no telling what kind of weather we'll meet, and there's no shelter on a karvi. I've got a tent we can raise if the winds are calm, but when the weather is at its worst, we'll be out in it."

Thurston nodded, said nothing, stared at him with furious eyes.

"I've never been to the temple, though my grandfadir may have been. I don't know how long it will take to get where we're going or if we'll get there at all." He paused, thinking that maybe he shouldn't be honeying it up so much. "We don't know what we'll find when we get there. We may be struck dead the instant we set foot on shore. Your friend may be long dead or bewitched beyond recognition."

"She's alive," Thurston said flatly.

Eiric could tell he was making no impression on his new crewman. That in itself was worrisome. "Fine. I hope you're right."

"I agree to all of your terms," Thurston said, as if none of it mattered to him. "When do we sail?"

Eiric thought a moment. Chances were slim to none that a delay would bring more crew his way. What it would do was cost him time in the good weather and give the Knudsens another opportunity to finish him. It would mean more carnage, more dead men on the ground.

"Do you know where Sundgard is?" he said abruptly.

Thurston nodded. "That's where I was heading when I came across—" He waved his arm, indicating the corral.

"Be there an hour before sunrise, two days from now. You bring a weapon—and a better coat. I'll handle the rest."

Eiric returned to his horse, untied Dain's reins from the railing, slid his foot into the stirrup, and swung up into the saddle. The gelding danced and crow-hopped a bit before he settled, his head turned toward home.

Eiric dug in his heels, and Dain responded, leaping forward as if eager to leave this place. Eiric looked back, once, to see that Thurston still stood, watching him, a light-rimmed shadow against the bulk of the longhouse.

28

COUNCIL OF ELDERS

MODIR TYRA STRODE DOWN THE hallway with Reginn trailing behind her, complaining like a wagon with squeaking wheels.

"Do we have to go to the council *now*?" Reginn said. "I wish you had told me earlier so that I could have prepared."

"This is not something that you can prepare for."

"But . . . I won't know what to say, how to act, what they want. What if they ask me to play for them? I should practice first."

"Reginn," Modir Tyra said, surprising her by using her given name. "You play beautifully; you sing beautifully. You have been performing in alehouses for most of your life before drunken crowds of barbarians. You'll be fine."

"Kennari—"

Modir Tyra spun around to face her. "Do you want to stay here at the Grove or not?"

"More than anything," Reginn said.

"Then you have nothing to worry about." Her expression softened. She reached out and put her hand on Reginn's shoulder. "I believe in you," she said. "I hope you can learn to believe in yourself."

They passed through a gallery bordering a central courtyard and into the other building.

"All of the council offices are over here," Tyra said. "The separation from academy and temple staff is more than symbolic. You will find that the council's focus is commerce, while the academy and the temple focus on our mission of educating the gifted and honoring our jotun ancestors."

"Why would they be involved in choosing dedicates for the temple, then?" Reginn said.

"Why, indeed?" She paused, and then added, "The council is most interested in your ability to contribute to the realm once your training is complete. If you can convince them that you can help protect New Jotunheim from coasters and other external threats, you'll do well."

When they reached the end of the corridor, they came to a pair of large, elaborately carved double doors. Once again, guards in crosshatched blue livery were posted in front, along with a servant.

"Let Elder Skarde know that we are here," Modir Tyra told the servant.

"Who's Elder Skarde?" Reginn whispered after the servant had gone.

"He's the chair of the council," Tyra murmured. "Fond of flattery."

"Isn't the keeper the head of the council?" Reginn said.

"No. The keeper attends council meetings, but she is not a voting member. She is on the academy side."

Reginn was surprised that the kennari was being so frank with her. She remembered what Tyra had said as they began their journey through the mountains.

I'm contrary.

I'm contrary, too, Reginn thought. So maybe the council wouldn't be so bad.

Moments later the servant returned. "They will see you now."

Like nearly everything else at the Grove, the Founder's Hall was constructed mostly of wood, from the rich oak paneling on the walls to the soaring roof overhead. Heavily carved arches opened to alcoves on either side. All told, the hall could hold hundreds of people.

Just seven people sat around a massive oak table in an alcove at the far end of the room. Servants in drab colors came and went, refilling glasses, offering trays of food, and clearing away used plates. Clerks sat at desks along the wall, taking notes and drawing up documents. Reginn noticed that there were more servants than there were council members.

The keeper sat a little to one side, her chin resting on her laced fingers, her gaze following Reginn and Modir Tyra as they walked forward.

The Council of Elders was diverse in all but age and appearance—they were all remarkably young, and they shared a radiant, unblemished beauty.

"I thought that they would be older," Reginn murmured to Modir Tyra.

"Appearances can be deceiving," Tyra said with a wry smile. "They are older than you think."

There were four women and three men, and all kept staffs close to hand—even the men. Reginn eyed the staffs enviously. That was one piece of paraphernalia she'd never acquired during her years in the alehouses. These were elaborate—richly decorated, wrought of a variety of materials including iron and wood, studded with precious metals and stones.

She'd never seen a man with a distaff in the Archipelago. Shepherding and spinning—and magic—were seen as women's work.

Not for the council were the blue cloaks of the faculty and dedicates. Their clothing varied as widely as only fancy clothes can—furs and velvets and satins in brilliant colors despite the temperate weather. All in all, they were a flock of very pretty birds—except for the keeper, who wore her usual sober blue overdress. Had any of them walked into an alehouse where Reginn was working, she'd have looked to them for the big money.

"Good day, Tyra," the man at the head of the table said. He was striking—tall, broad, and glittering, his blue eyes outlined with black so that they stood out against his pale skin. His long raven's-wing hair was laced with colored braids pulled into a knot on the back of his head. He had heavy rings on his fingers, gold bands on his arms, and a crystalline pendant at his neck like the one Modir Tyra wore. "What have we here?"

"Elder Skarde," Tyra said, inclining her head. "I am pleased to present our newest candidate, Reginn Lund."

Reginn inclined her head exactly the same distance as the head-mistress had.

"Well now," Skarde said. "She is a pretty creature, though she seems a bit . . . rough."

Rough? What's that supposed to mean? It took considerable effort for Reginn to maintain her stage face.

Skarde crooked a finger at her. "Come closer, child, so I can have a look at you."

Reginn took one step forward. Then another. The pendant at Skarde's neck began to glow that familiar amber like sunlight through comb honey. He stared down at it, transfixed, so that his face became a monstrous landscape of light and shadow. Every member of the council turned to look at him.

Reginn stopped and held her ground. Instinct told her that he was not the sort of man a girl wanted to come close to.

"She's hardly a child," a woman said. She wore loose red velvet robes over a slender frame, and her tightly curled hair was cropped short over warm brown skin. Her only ornament was a pair of gold brooches securing her cloak. "I'm Elder Scarlet," she said to Reginn. "How old are you, dottir?"

Reginn fought the temptation to claim to be younger than she was. "I'm sixteen, Highest," she said. Then couldn't resist adding, "Just turned."

"Goddess of the blessed grove," Scarlet said, shaking her head. "And you have just come to us? I cannot begin to imagine what you must have gone through in that dreadful place."

A murmur of agreement ran down the table.

"That said," Scarlet continued, turning to Tyra, "does it make sense to admit someone whose upbringing is so alien to what we have here on Eimyrja?"

"Some children find a way to thrive against all odds," Tyra said. "Reginn is one of those children. That strength is one of the qualities that will make her such a valuable contributor to Eimyrja."

"Survival is one thing," another councillor said. He was clad in yellow silk with a lavender waistcoat over top. "But a temperament and skill set that enable a child to survive in a cesspit of violence and vulgarity may not promote success within a society such as ours. It's just a shame that she could not have come to us sooner, when she was, perhaps, more *malleable*."

"I can understand your apprehension, Elder Gisli," Modir Tyra said, "but you've seen what I can do. I will hone her into an adept that will be a credit to us all."

A fragile-looking woman next to Gisli looked Reginn up and down with bright black eyes. She resembled a wren wearing a peacock-feather coat. "All of our other candidates have come as babies. I think what Elder Gisli is saying is that she might be a . . . negative influence on her fellow students, who have led sheltered lives."

Scarlet looked horrified. "You aren't suggesting that we send her back to Barbaria, are you, Margareta?"

"No, of course not," Margareta said. "But perhaps she would be better suited for one of the undeveloped out islands, where society is more . . . primitive. We are always in need of help out there."

Reginn stood, fists clenched, her temperature rising. What right did they have to talk about her like this when they knew nothing about her?

"Let me take her to Ithavoll," Skarde said, looking from Reginn to the pendant and back again. "I'm there often, and I could provide the supervision she needs."

And I could provide a blade in your gut, Reginn thought.

"No!" Modir Tyra said. "That would be a waste of your time and talent. We need her here."

"The kennari is right, Elder Skarde," the one called Margareta said, fingering her own pendant. "A woman's touch is what's needed. I'll be glad to take this young one under my wing and give her the training she needs to succeed."

"She could come back here, eventually," Skarde said, "if I determine that she is a suitable candidate for the academy. If not, the temple at the rift will welcome her."

"With all due respect, Elder Skarde, the evaluation of students is not your area of expertise," Tyra said. "Elder Margareta, your offer to mentor Systir Reginn is generous, but I fear it would take time away from more important responsibilities."

Reginn looked from elder to elder, wondering what was up. They were squabbling like heirs over a silver cup that wasn't good enough for the main hall.

"What do you think, Elder Frodi?" Tyra said, directing this to a gaunt young man who hadn't spoken up thus far. He twitched, as if startled to be singled out.

His shock of red hair resembled a poorly made haystack, as if he'd come straight from bed to table. He'd put a shine on, though. His coat and trousers were tailored of emerald-green silk, his hands studded with jewels, his staff among the finest in the room, embedded with blue stones, the distaff end a web of spun gold. His face was fine boned and full lipped, his blue eyes bright. He might have been mistaken for one of the dedicates but for his staff, his fine blue cloak, and the arrogance that burned within him like a torch. To Reginn's eyes, he might be the dissolute youngest son of a rich merchant who should have stayed in bed a little longer.

"What do I think?" His bruised eyes fixed on Reginn for a long moment, then flicked to Skarde. "I think we should allow our kennari to work her magic with this candidate before we make our decision. Everyone has a role to play in New Jotunheim"—these words came out thick with irony—"but we are not so rich in talent that we can afford to squander potential. There is always room for new blood and new magic."

This opinion was met with glares and glowers all around. Was that why Modir Tyra had asked his opinion? Because she knew what he would say?

It's as if the others don't want to give me a chance, Reginn thought. Why?

Now the keeper spoke up for the first time. "We do not send our dottirs and sons to the out islands without the support, training, and discipline the academy provides. This child must be given the opportunity to prove herself." She paused, her gaze resting on Reginn. "My point is, we are in need of every gifted hand that we can find. A diamond in the rough is still a diamond, after all."

Reginn's growing rage was tempered by surprise. She would never have expected Amma Inger to speak up for her.

Maybe she should be speaking up for herself.

"Begging your pardon, lords and ladies," Reginn said, "but shouldn't you make your decision based on who I am and what I can do rather than where I come from and what I look like? I've come a long way, after all."

Modir Tyra's breath hissed out. Otherwise, the room fell deadly silent—so silent that Reginn imagined she could hear the mice scurrying behind the walls. If there were mice in Eimyrja.

"Very well," Skarde said, shifting in his chair and gesturing to the servant for more wine. "Tell us about yourself."

Ignoring the fear squirming in her middle, Reginn pretended that she was facing an unruly tavern crowd. "I am Reginn Eiklund of the Oak Grove, Tove's adopted dottir. Honed by flame and trouble. I was raised by a spinner who taught me the elements of magic, along with the difference between right and wrong. The Archipelago may be a desperate place, but there are good people there."

Reginn could read an audience. The notion that there were good people in Barbaria did not go over well.

"Interesting," Elder Gisli said. His expression said that he wasn't interested at all. "Here on Eimyrja, we believe that the gift is inborn, not taught. What is your gift, and how will it support our mission here?"

Reginn's instinct told her to go all in. "I am a spellsinger, laeknir, and spakona." Spellsinger, healer, and seer.

"So versatile," Margareta said, arching an eyebrow. "And modest and self-effacing as well. Is there anything you cannot do?"

Reginn put her hand on her flute. "Shall I play for you?"

"That would be helpful," Gisli said, "if we were hiring talent for an alehall. Unnecessary in this case."

Reginn's cheeks heated in embarrassment. She opened her mouth to respond, but Tyra leaned close and whispered, "He's just trying to get a rise out of you in order to prove you're a savage. Don't fall for it."

Reginn swallowed what she was about to say, though it remained as a lump in her throat. She bowed her head. "As you wish, Highest."

"I have witnessed Systir Reginn in action," Modir Tyra said. "She can sing the vardlokkur and call the vaettir. It is like nothing I have ever seen."

Reginn was glad that she didn't bring up the raising-the-dead part. That was not a claim that she wanted to make in front of this crowd.

"That is old magic," Skarde said. "These days, we put a much higher value on practical gifts, such as the ability to ensure large harvests, defeat our enemies, or find precious metals in the ground."

"And yet we know that in the past, the vala wielded far greater power than we do now," Tyra said. "They shaped magic with runes and so bent it to their needs. Even Odin Allfadir feared us and took extraordinary measures to steal our secrets. What if we could mine the knowledge of the past and achieve a level of practice unseen in centuries? Wouldn't that be more valuable than gold?"

"Where is the evidence that such a thing could happen?" Fadir Gisli said.

I know the runes of magic, Reginn might have said. But thought better of it. She kept it in reserve, like the gold sewn into the hem of her skirts. It would likely be seen as just another brag.

"I cannot guarantee that Systir Reginn will be successful in this any more than I can guarantee that any child brought here as an infant will manifest a gift that you deem to be useful. You can see that the light of magic is strong in her, though different from what we have seen before. Given that the original mission of the Grove was the support and preservation of the wyrdspinners, I hope that you will give her the opportunity to demonstrate her abilities before you make your decision."

The council members looked at each other. Reginn saw *no* in nearly every face. Everyone but Frodi. He was staring at her intently, but she could not read his expression.

Finally Skarde said, "Thank you, Systir Reginn. Now please leave us, so that we may discuss your candidacy."

Tyra squeezed Reginn's shoulder. It felt like a squeeze of reassurance or approval. "Wait for me in my office," she said.

29

BURIED SECRETS

IT WAS PITCH-DARK BY THE time Eiric arrived back at Sundgard. He led Dain to the summer barn so that he could see to him without waking Liv, Hilde, or Ivar. He wanted to clean up and polish his story before he told his systir he was leaving in two days' time.

It wasn't until he walked up the track toward the house that he noticed the light leaking between the timbers in the walls. Somebody was up.

Swearing softly, Eiric entered the house through the winter barn, soft-footing it until he could see into the main hall. Maybe he could still make it to his bed without being seen.

In the light from a small oil lamp, he saw Liv on her knees next to their modir's sleeping bench. She'd pushed the bench aside and lifted the stone that hid the compartment beneath. Sylvi's small chest sat open. Liv sat back on her heels, eyes closed, clutching with both hands something that shone brilliantly through her fingers. That must have been the source of the light that had alerted him.

The sunstone, he thought, heart sinking. How had she found it? More importantly, how could he get it back?

He was in no mood for a confrontation, but he couldn't risk

losing his only hope of finding the Grove and saving Sundgard. If Liv hid it away, he might never find it again.

He walked forward, into the light. She didn't notice him until he knelt by her side and spoke.

"Hello, systir," he said. "What have you found?"

She blinked at him as if awakening from a trance.

"This is my past and my future, brodir," she said, opening her hands.

It wasn't the sunstone. It was the gold-and-silver pendant set with amber, the one she'd been wearing when she arrived at Sundgard. The figure of the goddess.

"I don't understand," Eiric said.

Liv made no attempt to explain, only gazed at him, smiling, her eyes lit like flames in amber.

"Isn't that the pendant Modir took from you when you arrived here?"

She nodded. "It's been calling to me. I was beginning to think that I was losing my mind."

When Eiric looked around, he saw other places where the stone floor had been disturbed. It appeared that she had been searching for some time.

"I'm glad you found it, then," Eiric said. His eyes kept straying to the open chest. Clearly, she'd found the secret compartment. Was it possible she—

"And look what else," she said, handing Eiric the leather bag. "It's the sunstone. Now there'll be a real chance of reaching the Grove alive."

Eiric pulled the sunstone from the pouch, weighing it in his hand. "This is the sunstone?" he said, feigning surprise.

Liv rolled her eyes, unimpressed with his efforts. "As you well know."

Eiric eyed Liv suspiciously. This was the last reaction Eiric had expected from his systir. If she knew he'd hidden their modir's chest from her, then why wasn't she angry? Why hadn't she searched it out earlier? Why would she so easily give up the sunstone? Had she made her peace with his plans to travel to the Grove?

Taking no chances, he slid the chain around his neck so that the sunstone rested on his bare chest next to the chain bearing Reginn's runestick and Leif's amulet.

His skin heated and prickled, his head swam, and he heard that voice again.

Come back to me.

"Are you all right?" Liv's voice roused him. She was gazing at him through narrowed eyes.

"I'm all right," Eiric said hoarsely. "It's—it's been a long day."

All she said was "I am so sick and tired of this place."

This seemed like a good time to raise other sensitive topics, such as the fact that he'd invited Ulff Stevenson to stay at the farm while he was gone.

"I picked up my rivets from Stevenson today," Eiric said. "He apologized for what happened at the Thing. He offered to stay at the farm while I'm gone."

"That seems like a good idea," Liv said, still distracted by the business in her own head. It was as if, now that she had the pendant, these were all petty concerns.

"It might discourage mischief from the Knudsens," Eiric pointed out, ready with arguments that now seemed unnecessary.

Liv nodded.

"There's more news," Eiric said. "I've found a crewman."

Now she showed a spark of interest. "Really? Who?"

"His name is Thurston, and he's a former thrall from Langvik," Eiric said.

"How do you know him?"

"I don't," Eiric admitted. "He approached me, saying that he'd heard I was looking for crew and he wanted to sign on."

"Why?" Liv said, back to her usual blunt self. "Nobody else wants to."

"There's a girl he's interested in," Eiric said. "He believes that she was carried off to the Grove. He wants to find her and help her."

"Does she want help?" Liv said.

"I don't know!" Eiric exploded. "It's not like I chose him from a crowd. He's the only one who's expressed any interest, other than Rikhard's men. He's fit, and he seems motivated. Maybe it's better that he's not from here, so he's not worried about offending the Knudsens."

"You may be right," Liv said.

"I need to leave soon, or I'll lose some good weather. I don't see anyone else volunteering in the next week." He paused, took a breath, then said, "I plan to sail the day after tomorrow."

He'd expected resistance, but it didn't come. Instead, she thought a moment. "Can you bring in the first cutting of hay tomorrow? Rain is coming."

"I'll do that," Eiric said, though he knew he'd have a thousand other things to do.

"The sails are repaired and ready to go," Liv said. "I'm finishing up new coats for both of us. Could Stevenson be here the day before we sail? The cows will need milking that morning, and I hate to leave that to Hilde along with everything else."

Eiric was nodding before she finished speaking, eager to have everything settled before her personal weather changed. "He's coming tomorrow to have a look at the old forge and see if it's usable. It might be that—" He stopped, his brain finally catching up with what his systir had said.

"Wait," he said, staring at her. "What do you mean, the day 'we' sail?"

"It's one thing to find Eimyrja," Liv said, fingering her pendant. "It's another to survive once you get there."

"What's Eimyrja?" Eiric said.

"That's an island in New Jotunheim, where the temple grove is. With this amulet, the sunstone, and me, you'll have a chance. It will be a safer voyage with three crew, and I'd venture a guess I'm a better sailor than this Thurston. So it's decided. I'm coming with you."

30

A CLEAN SLATE

REGINN COULDN'T SAY HOW LONG she waited in Modir Tyra's office for the council's verdict. It seemed like an eternity.

Is it good that they're taking a long time? Or is it a bad sign?

At least they hadn't rejected her out of hand. Maybe they were arguing about whether to send her back to the Archipelago or to one of the out islands. Or maybe they couldn't decide which of the out islands.

Finally, Reginn heard the headmistress's brisk footsteps in the corridor.

Just inside the doorway, Modir Tyra stopped, gazing at Reginn, her face unreadable.

"So? What did they say?" Reginn laced her fingers together to stop them from trembling.

Modir Tyra closed the door, crossed the room, and sat down beside her. Then laughed a little.

"Kennari?" Reginn said, mystified. "What is it? What happened?"

"No worries, dottir," Tyra said. "We've bought some time, at least. And they've dropped the idea of sending you directly to the out islands. You have been accepted under certain conditions."

"What conditions?"

"First, there will be a six-month probationary period. I'll update the council quarterly. During that time, they'll want to see evidence that the benefits of having you here outweigh the risks."

"What are they so *worried* about?" Reginn said, frustration sharpening her tongue.

"You must understand. The founders of the Grove were fleeing a slaughter in the Archipelago. If the founding modir had not taken this step, the spark of magic would have been extinguished. It's no wonder that they're cautious."

"But—wasn't that hundreds of years ago?"

Tyra's lips tightened. "Some wounds run deep. Despite the barrier, they constantly worry about a barbarian invasion. Instead of a possible solution to their problems, they suspect that you may be a threat."

"Me? A threat?" That was preposterous, but Reginn knew that Tyra was not joking.

Tyra extended her crystal pendant toward Reginn. It seethed with a color like molten gold. "It is because your megin—your magic—is not something they've seen before. They can tell how very powerful you are."

"And yet—it was almost as if they were fighting over me," Reginn said.

"Trust me, dottir, one day the council will learn to leave the temple and our students alone," Tyra said grimly. Reginn waited for an explanation, but it didn't come.

"I know you're worried about Jarl Karlsen and the rest," Reginn said. "Maybe it's time to make a clean break."

Tyra laughed. "You keep saying that. Like I told you, it is part of our mission to identify and give sanctuary to the gifted," Tyra said. "You more than most know how important a refuge can be. It would be a mistake to cower behind the barricades. A defense is important, but so is engagement."

"Elder Frodi seems different from the others," Reginn said. "It seemed like he wanted me to succeed."

"Yes," Modir Tyra said thoughtfully. "Perhaps."

"You said there was more than one condition. What else?"

Modir Tyra sighed. "Secondly, they would like me to assist you with mind magic."

"What do you mean?"

"I gather that you have had a hard life up to now. That can produce habits, attitudes, and survival skills that might have served you well in the Archipelago but that will impede your success here. That is what the council is worried about. So. I have the gift of teaching through mind magic. I shape minds to make them receptive to new ideas and new skills, clear away biases, preconceived notions, guilt, and trauma, so that new knowledge takes root more quickly. And then I give you a start with the basic skills every student needs—reading, writing, cyphering, and so on."

Reginn wasn't sure that she followed everything the headmistress had said. "So, you'll use magic that will help me learn more quickly so I can catch up with the others?"

Modir Tyra nodded. "Most of your age-mates are already contributing to New Jotunheim. The council is concerned that it will take years before you can support our mission. I think we can prove them wrong."

Reginn poked at this from all sides. She could see no harm in it, and yet a voice deep inside was whispering a warning. Asger's voice.

Don't trust anyone who says he wants to help you.

No, Reginn thought. Asger, get out of my head.

Tyra eyed her thoughtfully. "Now. There is a risk—I've never done this for someone as old as you. Someone with so much history. I don't know if it will be as effective as it has been in others."

"I won't forget my music or my spellsongs or remedies?"

Tyra laughed. "That would defeat the purpose, wouldn't it? The intent is not to make you start over, but to clear away the elements that will not serve you here and replace them with those that will. Most of us have pain and loss that we would like to forget."

"The other dedicates—how many of them—"

"All of them," Tyra said. "Of course, they were quite young, so they had considerably less . . . clutter . . . to clear than you do. But I give them a start on basic skills so that they can focus on their magical vocations."

That was exactly what Reginn wanted to do—focus on her magical vocation without bothering with the rest.

One of Tove's favorite sayings popped into her head. *When you're weighing out silver, use your own scale.*

Reginn rubbed her temples. "I don't know," she said. "And if I don't agree?"

Tyra put her hand on Reginn's shoulder. "If you do not meet these conditions, the council will send you back home."

That made it an easy decision. She had to succeed here—she just had to. She could not return to the Archipelago and wait for Asger to hunt her down. This was her one chance. "All right," she said. "Let's do it."

Tyra raised an eyebrow. "You're sure?"

"Yes." Reginn looked her in the eye.

"All right," Tyra said. She retrieved her staff from where it leaned against the wall in the corner. The distaff's cage was made of silver and gold set with gemstones and topped with a large, unpolished almandine garnet.

Wrapping the fingers of both hands around the staff, Tyra said, "Now focus on the gemstone and drop the barriers that contain thought and memory. Let them go."

Reginn stared at the garnet, which seemed to expand until

it filled her entire field of vision. Modir Tyra rolled the distaff between her palms. Reginn felt a faint tugging as it twirled, as if the fibers of her mind were being pulled into a roving that wrapped around the head of the distaff. Spinner of thought, spinner of emotion, spinner of memory.

The thread of her life spooled out. Hunger like a wolf in her middle. Digging through sodden, half-frozen leaves, searching out a green shoot to gnaw on. Picking through windfall apples under a tree, shaking off angry bees. Heaving all night after eating fermented fruit.

Clinging to the lower branches of a tree while ice wolves circled below. Fleeing gravewights through a frozen swamp, her feet crashing through skins of ice and landing knee-deep in black and poisonous water.

Finding sanctuary within the oak grove, calling silently for help until *she* came, lifting her out of her burrow of leaves. Reginn could no longer recall her face.

Ah, little one, she said. *Your magic is older than the gods.*

Racing, hand in hand, as the risen dead—the draugr—howled on their heels. Squeezing back into a crevice in the rocks overlooking a sulfur spring where the fumes would confuse the outlaws' hounds and make them lose their scent.

In better days, tucked close to a hearth fire in an alehouse, waking now and then to hear Tove's voice as she worked the crowd. The clatter of coins and hack silver as they fell into her cup. The thrill of the first sweet notes she drew from the flute.

Meetups at the edge of the forest, where women came to buy the remedies they could get nowhere else, along with Tove's whispered counsel.

A jeering crowd whose words stung almost as much as the stones they threw.

"Don't they know we're trying to help them?" Reginn had said the fourth or fifth time they'd been run out of town.

"They are frightened of us because we are powerful," Tove had said.

Reginn fingered a lump on the back of her head. "If we're so powerful, then why can't we make them stop?"

"One day, perhaps we will," Tove said.

And then, finally, Asger Eldr, the devourer of magic. The one force of nature that Tove couldn't counter. Whose power grew as theirs dwindled.

Gradually, Reginn calmed, her breaths slowed, and the anxiety that continually dogged her dwindled to one small strand in the web of the world.

New threads were added to the batt. The unfamiliar runes she'd seen on the wall in the outer office, now woven into words that had meanings. Pages of books–books!–flying by. Sagas and stories she'd never heard before. Memories that belonged to someone else.

A young woman, leaning on her staff because part of her foot was missing, stepping off a ship onto a desolate island. She motioned to her companions to stay on board while she laboriously climbed from the beach to a place where she could survey the land. She looked down on an ancient burying ground, where the earth had weathered away to reveal the outlines of the ships of the dead, along with bones, weapons, and other artifacts. Her eyes followed the bleak contours of the land to the horizon.

Nodding approval, she smacked the butt of her staff into the ground. A carpet of green spread in all directions as long-dormant seeds sprouted and the land bloomed.

A beautiful child with copper eyes and wavy hair huddled in a corner, her arms wrapped around her knees. Wetting herself whenever the door opened to men who stank of ale and sweat. Until the spinners came and took her away.

A ship beaten to pieces on an unfamiliar beach. A fair-haired coaster clambering over the bones, pulling iron rivets and wooden dowels from the remains. Later, he worked shirtless in the sun, muscles rippling under his sunburned skin as he cut down tall pines and oaks, then split and shaped them. There was something familiar about his frame and the way he moved.

A much-younger Modir Tyra, on her knees at the edge of the sea, clawing frantically at the sand, tears streaming down her face.

"Dottir." And then, louder: "Dottir!"

Reginn awoke with a start to find Modir Tyra looking down at her, her face pale under the gold. The headmistress watched her as if she were an egg about to hatch and she didn't know what kind of creature would emerge.

"Modir?" Reginn whispered.

Tyra touched the pendant at her neck and murmured, "Thank you, Highest." Turning to Reginn, she murmured, "I feared we'd lost you."

Somehow, she'd ended up on a cushioned sleeping bench next to the terrace wall, with Modir Tyra sitting beside her, holding her hand. Reginn's thoughts were a tangled skein of confusion, with patches of color from half-forgotten scenes.

"What happened, Modir?" Reginn whispered. "Did something go wrong?"

"I am so sorry, dottir," Modir Tyra said, stroking damp hair away from Reginn's forehead. "No one has ever had this kind of reaction before. I should have been more cautious. There was so much to unpack, so much history, so many walls and barriers, so much darkness and pain and raw power. It came to the point that I had to let go or be pulled under myself. You fainted, then. You've been out for two hours. I was beginning to fear the worst."

Reginn wasn't sure what to make of this. It sounded as if the headmistress had seen something inside her that was so dark and dreadful that she posed a danger to the sheltered students at the Grove. But now, when Reginn looked back, it was as if she were peering into a valley full of mist, with only a few memories, like the tallest trees, poking through.

The memories were still there, though. Every once in a while, the mists would part, and a scene, a conversation, or some other memory would prick through. A woman with a kind heart and welcoming arms. A demon with ember eyes. A boy with sun-bleached hair whose kisses were as intoxicating as the bee-stung meads of the warglund.

There were bad people there—barbarians. They had shackled her. They had tried to burn her, and she'd barely escaped with her life.

She had no desire to descend into the mist and see what was hidden underneath. Let it stay buried. None of it mattered, because she was never going back there. Unless—

"Are you saying that it didn't work? Does it mean that I'm—that I'm not suited for the academy after all?"

"Oh, no, no, no, dottir," Tyra said. "I don't mean that at all. The fault is mine. I was, perhaps, too eager to relieve you of the burdens you've been carrying."

The elders had demanded that Modir Tyra cleanse her mind of memories from her past life. It was in Reginn's best interest that she succeed.

Modir Tyra had rescued her, had saved her, and for that she would always be grateful. "I think you have," Reginn said, swallowing doubt. "I think it worked brilliantly."

31

VIKINGR

EIRIC ROSE LONG BEFORE DAWN on the day before sailing. He wasn't sleeping anyway. With the sunstone resting against his skin, he was seized with an overwhelming urgency, the conviction that it was time to go, that he was already late—but for what? His head swam with dreams of a journey to paradise. He dreamed that he ran down to the beach and launched his boat, raised his sail, and followed the glittering path of the moon on dark waters until he passed beyond the horizon.

Which raised a question. Had Bjorn and Leif returned to Liv's birthplace by choice or because of the power of the stone? Perhaps it wasn't just that the sunstone made the journey *possible*. It might be that the sunstone made the journey *necessary*.

The day was cloudy and cold, with a misting rain. Eiric released Dain into the pasture, over the cows' strenuous objections, then returned to the barn and retrieved his fadir's sword.

He carefully cleaned the blade and restored the edge, his fadir's dying words echoing in his ears.

This sword is Gramr—given by Odin, won by Sigurth, mended by Regin of the dwarves, and used by Sigurd to slay the dragon Fafnir. Now it is yours. It brings good fortune to those who honor the gods.

What about those who don't? Eiric thought. Well, it had worked for him so far.

The weapon was rather plain but made of a lustrous steel unlike any Eiric had ever seen. The grip was wrapped in leather, and the crosspiece inlaid with silver. Just below the crosspiece, on both sides, the blade was engraved with the image of a snarling wolf and a rune.

It seemed fitting, somehow, to carry Leif's sword back to the Grove.

Eiric had already loaded the karvi with spare lines, fittings, tar, and other marine supplies. Now he and Liv dragged their ship down to the beach in order to finish loading all but the last few items. Small is better, Eiric told himself, knowing there was no way that he and Liv could have dragged the longboat from the boat-house to the water's edge by themselves.

They stowed away barrels of smoked fish; salted meat; dried apples and cherries; ship's biscuits that would take a man's tooth if he wasn't careful; crocks of butter, cheese, and honey; and skin bags of skyr. Finally, casks of water and ale. Though Liv had a knack for fitting supplies into tight spaces, by the time they were finished, all that was left was a narrow corridor and seat on a chest for the navigator with space to maneuver the tiller, and two seats forward for the other crew members.

Stevenson arrived at the farm before the midday, cheerful as always. Liv went back inside to put the last stitches into the storm coats she was making and to finish one last pair of socks, leaving Eiric and Hilde to show Ulff around the farmstead, the pastures, and the forge.

It was all very awkward, ever since the blacksmith had raised the possibility of a match between Eiric and Hilde. Ulff kept trying to include Hilde in the conversation, while she kept her peace. They were all soaked to the skin by the time they went in for the midday.

After the meal, Eiric slipped away and walked out onto the headland to experiment with the sunstone.

Bjorn had demonstrated how navigators used blocks of clear crystal to find the sun on cloudy days. He'd even left a bucket of quartzite pieces in the boathouse. But Eiric had never really seen him use them for wayfinding at sea. When he'd sailed with his fadir and grandfadir, they'd kept to waters they knew, navigating through memorized chants and landmarks.

They'd never sailed off the charts they carried in their heads. Not with Eiric on board, at least.

Layers of cloud and rain obscured the horizon and dispersed the light, bringing with it the taste of salt and the scent of faraway places.

By now, the rain had slowed, but the fog had thickened to a cold mist, plastering down Eiric's hair and sending rivulets of water running into his collar. A good day to test the stone's capabilities.

Since he was standing on his own land, looking out at the sound he'd sailed since he was three, Eiric knew exactly where the sun should be.

Still, he brought the stone to his eye, sighting through it toward the open sea.

A trick of the light caused the ruby to appear as two images. He pivoted, keeping the stone in line with the horizon, until the two images merged into one.

The voice went through him like a bolt of lightning.

Come back to me.

With that, it was as if someone gripped him by his neck and yanked him forward so he all but flew off the headland and into the sea. As it was, he fell to his knees at the edge of the cliff, gasping, pressing his hands to his head. When he gazed out into the fog, he saw an image of himself, hanging from a massive tree.

"Halvorsen!"

The voice startled him so that the vision dissolved into ragged strands of mist.

Eiric stuffed the sunstone under his shirt, stood, and turned in one movement, reaching for a sword that wasn't there.

It was Rikhard. Had he seen the sunstone? Hopefully not. His hird was standing a distance away, between Eiric and the long-house, out of hearing range.

"Are you well?" The jarl studied him, eyes narrowed.

"Perfectly well," Eiric said, raking his sopping hair back from his face. For his part, the jarl seemed untouched by the weather, shedding the rain like a seal.

"Are you praying to Njord for a successful voyage?" the jarl said, his expression a mixture of perplexity and amusement.

"Yes," Eiric said, "but he's unwilling to commit at this time." He planted his hands on his hips. "What brings you to Sundgard?"

"I understand that you're sailing tomorrow morning," Rikhard said.

Word gets around, Eiric thought. He nodded.

"I wanted to make certain that the goals of the enterprise are clear."

"It's a mission of mercy," Eiric said, unable to keep the sarcasm from his voice. "I'm to discover the location of the temple grove so that you can save the stolen children of the Archipelago."

Rikhard's eyes narrowed, but being unable to find anything to quarrel with in that, he said, "I also wanted to make sure that you have everything you need."

Eiric gestured toward the beach, where *Dreki* rested, the incoming tide swirling around her keel. "Most everything is already loaded," he said.

Rikhard stared at the little karvi, rendered temporarily mute by surprise. "*That's* your ship?"

Rikhard might be a deadly snake of a man, but something in Eiric made him want to poke him. A death wish, perhaps.

"Aye," Eiric said. "Isn't she a beauty?"

"There's scarcely room for a pilot," Rikhard said, "let alone a crew. I beg you to accept my help and my ship. *Fossegrim* is the fastest ship in the Archipelago. Or if you want to go smaller–"

"How many times have you gone vikingr?" Eiric said.

The jarl's jaw tightened. "I have three warships, two knarr class, and–"

"I didn't ask how many ships you have," Eiric said. "Owning a fine horse doesn't make you a horseman. I asked how many times you've gone coasting yourself. By that, I mean gone raiding for months at a time, carrying most everything you need aboard ship and foraging the rest along the way?" He paused and, when Rikhard didn't answer, said, "I've sailed with my fadir and grandfadir every summer since I was five years old. Most seasons, we'd be gone from the time the ice broke up in the harbor until the bonefires of autumn."

During this, Rikhard had been shifting from foot to foot impatiently. Obviously, he preferred lecturing to being lectured. "I don't dispute your experience," he said. "That's the reason I asked you to undertake this task. But sometimes experience blinds us to–"

"One thing I've learned is that more is not necessarily better when it comes to crew. More mouths to feed, more egos to stroke, more fights to break up. I've sailed on big and small ships, and I can tell you that a bigger ship is not necessarily a safer ship. I don't plan to start a fight, so I don't need an army. I'd rather crew on a karvi built by me and my grandfadir with a crew that I trust than a dragon ship built by somebody I don't know."

"Assuming that you don't know how long this trip will take, shouldn't you lay in more supplies rather than less, to make sure that you don't run out? Shouldn't you leave room for any cargo you might bring back?"

"I've never tried to bring enough provisions to feed a crew from spring to fall, even on a larger ship," Eiric said. "I'm a coaster—I'm used to foraging what I need onshore. I catch fish along the way, and smoke it, dry it, or salt it. So I'm mainly bringing barley, water, salt, and dried fruit. Since this is a spy mission, I'll be carrying the most important cargo in my head." He tapped his temple. "I expect our supplies to be nearly exhausted on the journey to the Grove, so there should be ample room for any artifacts I bring back as proof."

"How many crew have you hired?" Rikhard said.

"My ship, my crew, my plan, my business," Eiric said, folding his arms, lifting his chin. "Isn't that what we agreed upon?"

Rikhard blew his breath out his nose. "Your stubbornness may be the end of you," he said. "I only hope it doesn't result in the failure of this venture."

"Stubbornness cuts both ways," Eiric said. "I gave you my word that I would see this through. A less stubborn man might have second thoughts about taking on a task where so many others have failed."

They stood looking at each other for a long moment.

And then, unexpectedly, Rikhard laughed. "I like you, Halvorsen," he said. "If I don't kill you, we might eventually be friends." He took another look at the beached ship and seemed to reconcile himself to Eiric's plan. "Just so you know, I will have members of my guard posted at a distance up and down the headland to intercept anyone who comes prowling around."

Eiric knew the jarl expected Eiric to thank him for that extra layer of security, but he guessed the gesture served Rikhard's agenda more than his own. "I have no objection, assuming they are out of sight of the house. After everything that's happened, my people may shoot first and ask questions later."

He had no people, but Rikhard couldn't be sure of that.

"Very well, then," Rikhard said. "I wish you good fortune and a speedy return."

With that, he turned and strode back to where his hird waited.

32

DANCING TO THE MUSIC THAT NO ONE ELSE HEARS

IN THE WEEKS FOLLOWING THE Council of Elders meeting and Modir Tyra's use of mind magic, Reginn struggled to read the books the kennari had given her.

They were histories and sagas and stories about Brenna Way-finder, founder of the Grove, and Jotunheim, the homeland that had been destroyed during the Great War. That's what Modir Tyra had said. They might have been tales from the Caliphate, for all Reginn could glean from them. She would barely get beyond the first page before her mind wandered off down less resistant paths.

Gradually, old memories poked through the fog of Tyra's magic, like weeds through a furrow. People, mostly. Tove, who'd rescued her, raised her, and sold her off to Asger Eldr, thus teaching her the meaning of love and the pain of betrayal. Asger, whose desperate need all but made her disappear. Eiric Halvorsen, who mingled violence, kindness, and rough courage.

Reginn's mind was still a tangle of old and new threads with lots of broken ends. Every night she lay sleepless, trying to spin them into something strong enough to withstand the pressure of everything she had to learn. Everything she had to do.

Learn to read. Learn to write. Summon the dead. Protect New Jotunheim.

She would find a way. She would not allow the ugly world she'd left behind to reach out and destroy this sanctuary.

As promised, the kennari arranged for Reginn to spend time with the other dedicates. That was a welcome break. With Katia, she rode horses along the eastern coast of the island, from the Langa River in the north to the village of Austhavn to the south. There was no question that she now preferred riding to reading. Along the way, Katia pointed out the barrows and burrows and nests of the wights and described their role in protecting the sanctuary.

They dismounted atop the high cliffs where the Langa roared down to the sea. The onshore breeze drove spray from the falls into their faces. On the far side of the river, the forests were just as thick as in the Grove itself.

"That's the Modirlund," Katia said. "The founder's forest. Further north is Sundhavn, the closest port to the temple."

Reginn gazed out to sea, to their systir island of Ithavoll. Yellow fumes rose from the rift that split it in two. North of the rift, Reginn could see clusters of buildings, horse corrals, and the like. On the south side, a barren plateau peppered with ruins.

"Have you been to Ithavoll?" Reginn said.

"Oh yes," Katia said. "Many times."

"What's it like?" Reginn said.

Katia shrugged. "It's not as beautiful as Eimyrja, but then, nothing is. Our largest production facilities are over there, so it's critical to the future of New Jotunheim. For that reason, there is also a strong security presence."

"Production facilities? What do they produce?"

"Everything we need that we cannot grow," Katia said. "I expect that magical fabricators like Systir Eira and those like me with security assignments will be posted there permanently once we are raised to adept. There's also a lovely temple overlooking the riftwall."

Elder Skarde mentioned a temple, didn't he?

From the dispute between Tyra and the elders about Ithavoll, Reginn had assumed it was the last place a person would want to go. Through Katia's eyes, it didn't sound so bad.

A day or so later, Reginn was scheduled to work with the seer Erland Lund.

Erland was waiting outside the dining hall after the dagmal, a leather bag slung over his shoulder, his staff in his left hand.

"Where to?" Reginn said.

"I like to work in the woods," he said. He nodded toward the perimeter of mammoth trees and began to walk. As she'd noticed before, he walked briskly, confidently, as if his memory and his staff were enough to ensure a clear path ahead.

As they walked, Reginn resolved not to ask rude questions, such as what happened to his eyes or why he wore that broad-brimmed hat.

"You're probably wondering what happened to my eyes," Erland said.

"Oh! Well. Yes," she said, flustered. Had the seer read her mind?

He laughed. "Don't worry. That's usually the first question people ask. And the answer is, I don't know, exactly. I must have been born this way, because my fadir left me in the forest."

"Why would he do that?" Reginn blurted.

"I think he viewed it as returning an imperfect child to the gods. I imagine that siring a demon child like me would be a bit . . . off-putting."

"You are not a demon child," Reginn said with a conviction so deep that she could not find the root of it. "What happened?" she said. "How did you survive?"

"I was found by a woman gathering wood. She took me to a foundling home. That's where Modir Tyra found me."

Strands of memory brushed Reginn, like spiderwebs in the dark. Someone had once plucked her from a nest of oak leaves. *Tove.*

Then, a fragment of conversation with an angry blue-eyed coaster. *My stepfadir left my baby brodir in the forest to die.*

Of course. Parents abandoned children all the time in the Archipelago.

They'd walked a short distance into the forest when Erland turned off the path and plopped down under a tree. "Here, I think," he said. "This one runs deep."

Reginn soon found out that Erland didn't perform any fancy ceremonies, throw down the sheep bones, finger the entrails of rabbits—none of that. Instead, they sat cradled in the roots of this massive tree, leaning back against the trunk. Erland propped his staff in the crook of his elbow and stared, unblinking, into the distance.

Reginn could entertain a crowd for hours, but it wasn't often that she was one-on-one with anyone other than Asger Eldr.

She shifted and squirmed, startling at every sound. When she heard a rustling, she was halfway to her feet before she realized it was a pair of red squirrels, chasing each other.

"Are you all right?" Erland said, brow furrowed.

"I'm fine," Reginn said, settling back into her spot. "Everything's fine."

After a stretch of time, neither one speaking, Reginn felt the damp seep through her pale blue breeches, and wondered if they'd have to go back to the laundry again. Finally, she said, "What's going on?"

He startled, blinked. "I'm meditating," he said.

"Oh," she said, and fell silent again.

After another space of time, she said, "Is it working? Are there any messages or visions?"

He surfaced, as if from a deep pool. "It takes time," he said.

After another few minutes, she brought out her flute, fitted her fingers to the holes, put it to her lips, then lowered it again, afraid it would be distracting.

"Go ahead and play," he said. "I don't mind."

"You say you're blind," Reginn snapped, "and yet you always know what's going on?"

"There are many ways of seeing. I may be blind in one way, and yet I see what others don't."

Reginn buried her face in her hands, mortified. "I'm sorry," she said. "I'm just–I'm afraid I'm not very good at this."

"You're not very good at what?" Erland looked perplexed.

Never admit to a weakness. Your enemies will exploit it.

Everyone is your enemy.

Why do I keep hearing voices in my head?

Whose voices are they?

Why didn't Modir Tyra take away the voices along with the memories?

"Reginn."

She looked up, startled, to see that Erland had taken hold of her hands.

"Please. Be kind to yourself."

Reginn was momentarily speechless in the face of such empathy.

"Ever since Modir Tyra used her mind magic, I've felt lost," she said. "Some of what I knew before, I've forgotten. What I do remember won't do me any good. As far as I know, I've never had friends, never gone to school, never stayed in one place for longer than a week. I don't know how to be human. I always say and do the wrong thing."

"Maybe you were just in the wrong place," Erland suggested. "Or maybe you just don't remember."

"I don't know that there is a place for me," Reginn said. "All I have to go on is a half-remembered nightmare." *And I seem to be failing at learning to read.*

Erland sat thinking for a long moment. "What I am trying to say is that we all have strengths and weaknesses. I prefer to focus on my strengths. You should, too. If you are a child of chaos, then no doubt you have developed a certain agility, an ability to survive uncertainty and change. You have unique skills. Right?"

Reginn stared at him, unable to come up with a response.

"You have learned to dance to the music that no one else hears. You are a survivor, and so you will do well here."

That struck a chord of truth in her.

Abruptly, Erland stood, collecting his bag and staff. "Speaking of music, come with me. I want you to meet someone."

He led the way toward the dining hall. Instead of entering by the front doors, he walked around to the back, to the kitchen building.

The kitchen doors stood open, allowing the breeze to flow through.

"Naima!" Erland shouted. "Are you in there?"

"I'm on the side porch," somebody called back.

Erland and Reginn circled around the kitchen to a roofed porch. A girl in bondi drab sat on the steps, snapping beans. When she spotted Erland, her face lit up like a midsummer dawn. "Erland!" she said, setting her bowl of beans aside and adjusting the scarf that bound her blond hair. "You're here early. I still have some–"

Then she spotted Reginn, and the smile faded from her face, leaving no expression at all. "Highest," she said, getting off a shallow bow. "I am sorry. I did not see you at first."

"Reginn, this is Naima," Erland said. "Naima, this is Reginn, a new dedicate."

"Welcome, Highest," Naima said in a manner that didn't sound welcoming at all.

"Just call me Reginn," Reginn said.

"Naima's the head cook here," Erland said. "She's responsible for all of that delicious food you've been eating."

"Oh!" Reginn said, as awestruck as if she were being introduced to royalty. "But—you're no older than we are."

Naima shrugged. "It's just cooking," she said, returning to her seat and picking up her bowl of beans again.

"But . . . I've never tasted food so good. And there's so *much* of it."

"One thing you should know about Reginn," Erland said. "She's *really* into eating."

"There's nothing like starvation to give a person a real appreciation of food," Reginn said.

Naima stopped snapping and studied Reginn through narrowed eyes. "Starvation?"

"Reginn is newly come from the Archipelago," Erland said. "She's not had an easy life."

"This was probably a good move for you, then." Naima stood, parking the bowl on one hip. "Well, I'd better get back to—"

"Naima works magic in the kitchen," Erland said, "but cooking is the least of her skills. She plays the talharpa."

Reginn gaped at the cook. "Really? A talharpa? I've heard of those, but I've never actually seen one. Let alone heard one."

"Naima and I meet up and play most evenings," Erland said.

"Erland . . ." Naima said, shooting a wary look at Reginn.

Erland took Naima's free hand. "Reginn is a good person, Naima. We can trust her."

"How do you know?" Naima hissed. "You just met her, right?"

Erland jabbed his thumb into his chest. "Spakona?" He cocked his head and raised an eyebrow. "Remember—I see what others do not."

All this while, Reginn had been edging away, unsure how to gracefully take her leave. "Listen, this seems like something you two should discuss on your own. If it helps, I don't remember anything anybody said. Except the part about the talharpa. Someday, I'd like to hear it."

"Stop right there," Erland commanded. Reginn stopped edging. Then he turned back to Naima. "You're a little late if you're meaning to keep our friendship a secret," he said. "Nearly everyone on the island knows about us."

"Every *bondi*," Naima repeated. "They're not the ones who make the rules around here. And enforce them."

"Look, Reginn is my friend, and I hope you two can be friends."

A warmth kindled under Reginn's breastbone. *I'm his friend?*

"Besides," Erland went on, "she plays a wicked flute. I thought you might like to hear her play."

"The flute?" Naima looked from Reginn to Erland, her expression softened with longing. "It's been a long time since I heard a flute."

"I know you're busy," Erland said. "If this isn't a good time, we can come back."

"I would like to hear your flute, Highest," Naima said, not making eye contact. "But I have to get these beans snapped before the nattmal."

"Why don't we help you with the beans?" Reginn said.

Naima looked at her like she'd grown a second head.

"*I* can help you with the beans," Erland said, "and Reginn can play while we work."

"Only if I get to hear you play the talharpa," Reginn said. "Fair is fair."

Stools were fetched, and soon Erland and Naima were seated side by side, companionably snapping. Reginn unpacked her flute and cradled it in her hands. "Is there anything in particular you'd like to hear?"

"Play something lively, so we'll work faster," Erland suggested.

"I'm from Muckleholm," Reginn said. "I only know sad songs."

But there were songs from the Westlands that stirred the blood, so Reginn played "Take Up Your Sword, Calum" and "By Liffey's Banks" and "Lady of the Bogland," which wasn't lively, but struck deep.

By then, the beans were snapped. Naima took them inside and returned. In one hand she carried a stringed instrument resembling a lyre; in the other, a bow. She sat, leaning the instrument against her shoulder and resting it on one knee.

Erland opened his carry bag. He pulled out a lyre and began sounding the strings with his fingers and adjusting the tuning. When he was satisfied, he balanced it on his knee, fingering the strings, playing music that only he could hear.

After testing the tuning against Erland's lyre, Naima began to play. Three beats later, Erland joined in, the sounds interweaving, the notes coming together and then splitting away again.

Reginn just listened, enthralled, through the first two songs. They were familiar, but she'd never heard them played this way.

In fact, since in her past life she'd worked every night, she'd had little opportunity to hear music other than her own. How had these songs made it all the way across the sea? *It's songs and stories that we carry with us when all else is lost.*

At the end of the second song, Erland cocked his head. "It's good," he said, "but it could definitely use a bit of flute." He looked at Reginn. "Could you join in?"

Reginn froze like a mouse pinned by an owl. "I don't . . . I've never played with anyone else," she said. "I wouldn't know how."

"Play something you know," Erland said, "and *we'll* join in."

"This is called 'Alfhild's Lament,'" Reginn said, taking a breath and raising the flute to her lips.

To Reginn's ears, the flute sounded weak and thready after the web of sound the strings produced. She played a few bars, and then Naima's bow slid across the strings, crooning an underlayment to the flute, supporting it, but not overwhelming it. Then Erland caressed the strings of the lyre so that the notes sounded like raindrops. Together, they told the story of star-crossed love between elves from warring clans.

With the last notes sounding in her ears, Reginn knew she wanted more. More of this music that entangled the heart.

"Do you know 'Solstice Fires'?" Naima said.

"I do know it, though not well," Reginn said. And then, echoing Erland, said, "Just play, and I'll join in."

Maybe, she thought, hope rising within her, I've finally found the place where I belong. Where I can truly join in.

33

MUSA

MODIR TYRA HAD PROMISED THAT mind magic would give Reginn a head start on the reading and writing skills that were valued in New Jotunheim. In that regard, it was disappointing. When she looked at a page in a book, she recognized a few words that floated up from the page like bits of meat in a thin broth. Other times, the letters just seemed to scramble, leaving a murky stew.

It still took her forever to read books of any length, and even longer to write anything. Her hands were used to shaping one rune at a time—not pages and pages. Her mind was used to embracing one symbol at a time—savoring it. Exploring its power, not skating over the surface like a water strider.

Reginn quickly lost interest in pages of watered-down runes. But she did her best to hide how bad it was from Modir Tyra. She could not afford to admit that even Tyra's mind magic had failed her. She asked Katia and Stian for suggestions, but they were bewildered by her thickheadedness. They'd never really had to learn to read. The kennari's intervention had done it for them.

Reginn had a long list of readings and assignments to complete before her six-month review, the one that would decide her future. So in one of their regular meetings, she finally admitted to Tyra that she was torturously slow.

"I love reading," she lied, "but it still takes me forever. Do you think another session of mind magic would–"

"I'm hesitant to try that again, given your reaction the first time," Tyra said, raising both hands, looking a little panicked. "I don't want to put you at risk over this. You have the skills. I know that you'll gain speed with practice."

As always, Tyra was upbeat, trying to reassure her, but Reginn didn't share her optimism.

I am not going back to the Archipelago just because I can't read, she thought.

"I know you're frustrated," Tyra said. She frowned, thinking. "It may be that Elder Frodi would be willing to help you."

"Elder Frodi? Why him?"

"He was once a gifted teacher–the best we had, I believe."

"Frodi?"

Tyra laughed. "It was a long time ago. People change over time."

How long ago could it have been? Reginn thought. He didn't seem that old.

"Now he's the archivist for the academy–the expert on our manuscript collection. Just be forewarned–he doesn't work with students these days. But he might be willing to work with you."

So now Reginn was on her way to see Elder Frodi.

The library at the Grove was another timber-and-stone building, nestled in the border of Guardian trees surrounding the Warden Tree. The living trees that served as corner posts gave the impression that the building had been planted rather than built or assembled. The trees stood high on tall roots, so the first floor was nearly a story off the ground. Underneath was a shady garden walled in by arbors covered in fragrant white flowers, centered around a clear spring that sang over moss-covered stones.

This place is pushy, Reginn thought, always in your face, making a claim on your senses, demanding that you listen, smell, taste, touch—whether you want to or not.

Tyra had said that the archivist's office was behind the library, so she circled around to a walkway that led from the back door of the library to a cottage that must be the office. It had an abandoned air. The shutters were closed, and the few potted plants on the porch were dead. Spiderwebs glistened with dew in the morning sunlight.

In the rear of the cottage, she saw some signs of life, namely a stack of empty ale and wine casks, a pile of dirty dishes, and a used chamber pot.

She pounded on the back door. "Elder Frodi!" she called. "It's Reginn Lund, the new dedicate."

There was no response. She pounded again, harder. Still no answer, but she heard a scuffling sound that said the cottage was occupied.

"I wanted to thank you for what you said at the council," she shouted.

A raspy voice came through the door. "You can thank me by leaving me in peace."

"Please, Elder Frodi, a moment of your time."

"People say 'a moment,' but it's always more than that." He fumbled with the latch, then wrenched the door open. She staggered back, all but overcome by the stench of stale air, sweat, old vomit, and rotting food.

It was fortunate that after years in the healing trade, she had a strong stomach.

She almost didn't recognize the man in the doorway. It was Frodi—of course it was—but he seemed a shadow of the man she'd seen a few short weeks ago. Maybe the fine clothes he'd worn to the council meeting had disguised his gaunt frame. The blue eyes were bloodshot, purple shadowed. He was clad in a long linen shirt, wrinkled and stained, his thin legs poking out underneath, and he smelled strongly of ale.

Reading her expression, Frodi raked back his hair with a trembling hand and said, "As you can see, I'm not well."

"Can I—can I get you anything?"

"I have enough ale to last through tomorrow if I am prudent," Frodi said. "If I am not prudent, my servant will fetch more."

"Perhaps I can help," Reginn said, her hand on her remedy bag. "I have some skill as a healer, and—"

His lip curled in disdain. "Do you really believe that I would submit to the care of an unschooled barbarian?"

"I am not unschooled, Highest," Reginn said, unable to blunt her sharp tongue. "There are many ways to learn in this world. Some would say that experience under a skilled mentor is the best teacher."

"Perhaps," he said, "but I have no need of your skills." He squinted at her. "I assume that you did not come here to tend my many wounds."

"Modir Tyra said that you might be willing to help me," Reginn said.

"Did she?" Frodi laughed bitterly. "It seems to me that I already have."

"Yes, Highest," Reginn said hastily, "but we were hoping that you might also help me improve my reading skills."

"Your reading skills?" He rubbed his bristled chin. "Isn't that the kennari's job?"

"Well, yes, but I'm still having difficulty with—"

"That's the thing with Tyra," Frodi said. "One favor begets another." He fisted his hand and pressed it against his forehead.

"Tell Tyra that I'm tired of cleaning up her messes."

With that, he turned away and slammed the door.

For several seconds, Reginn just stared at the closed door.

Skita. She walked back to the library building, scuffing her feet along the path like a pouting child. Slowly, she trudged up the stairs to the second-floor entrance, dragging her feet, putting off the inevitable as long as she could. She knew how to read and write the runes of magic. That was more than most people did. When there was so much else to learn, why should she spend time with musty old books?

The scent hit her as soon as she reached the top of the stairs. Like dead leaves or dust. No, not exactly. Like sun-dried herbs or the packets of flower petals people tucked into trunks and the backs of drawers to keep wights from nesting there.

It was like the scent of the forest in springtime, when the snow melted and the sun heated the earth beneath. The bones of the past making promises about the future.

Reginn blinked, shook her head, as if to fling away the memories. Those weren't her memories—were they? When had she ever stayed in one place long enough to have need of drawers? When had she ever been in a forest like that? The Archipelago was a howling wilderness overrun by monsters.

That was the downside of Modir Tyra's magic—Reginn was never sure which memories were her own and which might have been put there by the headmistress. She'd always trusted in herself, at least, but now—was she going mad?

She stepped from the staircase onto the landing and looked up.

She was standing in the base of a tower lined with shelves and staircases that spiraled up and up. Every so often the ascent was broken by a landing that led off into a side corridor. The staircases and railings were entwined with flowering vines.

The interior was flooded with light—a green, leafy light like the kind that penetrates a canopy of trees.

The shelves were filled with leather-bound volumes inscribed with gold that extended as far as she could see. Books that would take a lifetime to read. Three lifetimes. She'd end up with her head packed with stories about the adventures of others without ever having had any of her own.

"Quit whining," somebody said. "It's not like you have to read them *all*."

Cheeks flaming, Reginn spun around to see that a girl sat on one of the landings just overhead, her legs dangling, close enough that she might have stretched out a bare toe and tickled Reginn's ear.

"Oh!" Reginn said. "I'm sorry. I didn't see you there. And I wasn't whining." *Not out loud, anyway.*

The girl seemed flustered, as if she hadn't thought Reginn would overhear her. But she recovered quickly. "Yes, you were," she said. "I could tell."

She wore loose trousers and a tunic of a rough-spun gray cloth that might have been sewn from grain sacks. They seemed to be intended to hide any shape she had. Her features were as distinctive as her clothing was nondescript. She had narrow eyes and a sharply sculpted face, framed by stick-straight black hair that had been chopped to chin length.

The girl swung down from the staircase like an acrobat, landing right next to Reginn.

"What are you doing here?" she asked. "Nobody comes here. It's like a tomb, these days." She laughed then, as if she'd told the best joke ever.

Reginn hated when people laughed at their own jokes.

"I was hoping to work with—with Elder Frodi. But he refused, so

I guess that's not going to happen."

The girl scowled. "*Elder* Frodi? Since when?"

"I–I don't know," Reginn said.

"What made you think he'd work with you?" the girl demanded, eyes narrowed.

"Modir Tyra sent me," Reginn said, startled by the change in demeanor.

"She did?" the girl said. "Who are you? I haven't seen you . . . around here before."

"I'm Systir Reginn. I'm a new student."

"*You* . . . are a new student?"

Reginn was growing weary of this reaction. Very weary. "Right."

The girl planted her hands on her hips. "First off, you should know that Frodi never works with students anymore. Dedicates and adepts don't really use the archives much, and Frodi seems to have lost his taste for research. I'm surprised that Tyra would send you here."

"Well . . ." Reginn didn't especially want to share her shortcomings with this girl. "I need a little help with reading."

"You need a *little* help?" The girl raised her eyebrow, cocked her head sideways.

"A lot of help," Reginn confessed.

It seemed to be impossible to lie to this girl.

To be honest, it saved time.

"It doesn't matter, anyway," Reginn said. "He slammed the door in my face."

The girl seemed to be debating what to say next. "I'm not sure how much help Frodi would be," she said finally. "He has a bit of a drinking problem."

Recalling the elder's haggard appearance, Reginn took a chance. "A *bit* of a drinking problem?"

The girl laughed. "A *big* drinking problem." She ran a finger over a shelf, sending dust floating to the floor. "He hasn't been here in . . . a long time." A shadow passed across her face.

Reginn laughed, too. A little. It was good to get what sounded like an honest answer, but that didn't solve *her* problem.

Skita, she thought.

"What's the matter?" the girl said, her smile fading.

"I have to learn to read in order to move on," Reginn said. "At least I need to be able to fake it."

"Didn't Modir Tyra do her mind-magic thing with you?" The girl mimicked spinning a staff between her hands.

"Yes," Reginn said.

The girl rolled her eyes. "You should be all set, then. Why would you need Frodi's help?"

Reginn shrugged. "It didn't take very well. I'm still not very good at reading, and I'm hopeless at writing. Maybe it's because I'm older. My head is already filled up."

"Age shouldn't make a difference," the girl said. "But why did they bring you here now? Is it because your gift is so spectacular that Tyra made an exception?"

"Modir Tyra and Amma Inger saw me perform in an alehall. I don't know about *spectacular*, but Tyra said that I had a rare gift."

"A rare gift that you displayed in an alehall?"

Reginn's hackles rose. "I'd rather spend my time in an alehall than in a dusty old archive," she snapped.

"So sorry," the girl murmured. "What was your act?"

"I'm a musician and—and a spakona and a laeknir."

After an expectant pause, the girl said, "That's *it*? They brought you here for that?"

"She saw me call the spirits—the vaettir," Reginn said, on the defensive.

"Katia calls the vaettir," the girl said, unimpressed. "Why are you special?"

"Not landvaettir," Reginn said, proud that she'd at least picked up that term already. "Tyra believes that I can speak to the spirits of the dead."

"I see," the girl said, eyes narrowed. "Can you?"

"Can I what?"

"Speak to the dead?"

"Maybe."

"And Tyra sent you to Frodi?"

"She thought he might work with me."

The girl frowned, chewing her lower lip.

"But if I can't learn to read, none of it matters." Reginn stared down at her toes, and when the girl didn't offer any comment, said, "I guess I'd better go back to Modir Tyra and tell her Frodi said no."

"Don't blame Frodi," the girl said quickly.

"Why not?"

"He has his reasons for drinking. It's not his fault."

Reginn rolled her eyes. "That may be, but that doesn't help me. I have to find a way to catch up."

"Mm-hm," the girl said, still distracted by her own thoughts. Or maybe it was Reginn's thoughts—who knew?

Reginn cleared her throat and gave her a sideways look. "You spend a lot of time here, right? Maybe . . . could *you* teach me?"

"Teach you to read?"

"Yes," Reginn said.

She paused, but the girl said nothing, only stared at her. Reginn forged on, desperately. "I'm a fast learner; everybody says so. I already knew the runes of magic when I came here, so it shouldn't take much to—"

"*You* . . . know the runes of magic?" the girl said skeptically.

"Yes," Reginn said. "So—"

"Prove it," the girl said.

Reginn's hackles rose. "I don't have to—"

"You're the one asking for a favor, right?"

She had a point. Reginn rolled up her sleeve, exposing the scars on her forearm. She traced them with her fingertips. "This is Uruz, for strength and courage," she said, "and Sowilo, for success."

The girl stared, eyes wide. She reached out her hand, as if she might touch them, then drew it back. "How many do you know?"

Reginn shrugged. "Maybe . . . four or five?"

"What do you use them for?"

"I use them for divination, curses, blessings, healing, protection." Reginn shrugged. "The usual."

"Do they work?"

Reginn thought about it. In addition to Svefnthorn, the thorn of sleep, she'd used Limrunar carved into sticks for healing; Alrunar, to protect against poisons; Brimrunar, sought by sailors to protect them at sea; runes to stanch the flow of blood, to assist in childbirth.

"Usually, yes," Reginn said.

"Who taught you?"

Reginn thought hard. That part of her past had been shredded. "I can't remember," she said finally. "Maybe I've always known them."

"Did Modir Tyra or the keeper see you use the runes?"

"Why do you want to know?" Reginn was getting exasperated with the interrogation.

"It's important," the girl said. "Did you tell them you know the runes of magic?"

Reginn shook her head. "I haven't mentioned it, no."

"Well then. Let me give you a word of advice. Don't ever tell anyone here that you know those runes," the girl said.

"Why not?" Reginn said, trying to recall whether she'd told anyone already. Self-consciously, she folded her arms, hiding the fading marks.

"Just don't. Also, don't ever tell anyone you saw me, talked to me, or mention that I was here."

"How could I?" Reginn said crossly. "I don't even know who you are."

"Good," the girl said. She stood fluidly, ending with one foot braced against her other knee, like a dancer. "Good luck with everything. You'll have to find another tutor." She turned as if to climb the stairs.

"I could pay you," Reginn said. "I have a little money, and I can get more."

"What use would I have for money?" the girl said, lips quirking in amusement. She swung to the platform above, landing as lightly as a silkseed.

"Wait!" Reginn shouted.

The girl frowned down at her, putting her finger to her lips. "Be quiet. You don't want anyone to hear you."

"Why not?" Reginn demanded. "*I'm* supposed to be here. Apparently, you're not. If you don't help me, I'll tell everyone you were lurking here in the library. I'll tell them what you look like. I'll tell them everything you said." Reginn cast about for the kind of crime that could be committed in a library. "I'll tell them you were stealing books."

The girl reared back, eyes wide, as if she was shocked at this display of spine. "If you do, you'll be sorry in ways you've never dreamed of," she said.

"Don't threaten me," Reginn said. "You have no idea what life is like on the outside. I'm from the Archipelago. I am not afraid of you, and I am not going to wash out of this place, because you are going to help me." She said this with all the force and confidence she could muster.

Survival skills, Modir Tyra had called them. Maybe they hadn't been completely stripped away.

The girl's lips curved into a smile. She didn't seem frightened at all. "You're not like the other sleepwalkers around here," she said, easing herself down until she was sitting again and wrapping her arms around her knees. "Clearly, you need help. Therefore, I will commit to meet with you. But first, I need a commitment from you."

Reginn put her hand on her purse. "I told you I would—"

"I need something else," she said. She extended her arm, pulling back the sleeve to expose a rune on her upper arm—one Reginn had never seen. "You must add this rune to your collection."

"What is that?" Reginn said.

"It signifies that we are blodkyn," the girl said.

Reginn shook her head. "I don't want to be your systir or your best friend," she said. "I just want to learn to—get better at reading and writing."

"That is the price for my help," the girl said.

"Why would I accept an unknown rune on a stranger's say-so?"

"Why would I put myself at risk to teach a barbarian to read? By accepting this rune, you protect me and take on a little risk yourself.

"And that's not all. You're going to have to apply yourself. At our first meeting, we'll go over the language runes, sound out words, and read together. I'll show you which books are important. You can read others if you like, but only after you've read the ones I recommend."

Right, Reginn thought. Like I'll be reading extra books.

"So. Do we have a bargain or not?" The girl lay back on the landing, her arm covering her eyes. "I find this conversation exhausting."

Reginn had to admit, this girl looked worn out after only a few minutes' conversation. How much help could she be?

I can do this, Reginn thought. I've been taking up the runes for years with no harm done.

If you have to talk yourself into something, it's probably a mistake.

Reginn resisted the temptation to put her hands over her ears. It wouldn't help when the voice was inside her own head.

"Does it matter where I put it?"

"I suggest that you put it somewhere nobody will see it," the girl said. "Not your lover, not the kraken in the salt sea, not the–"

"Can I make a drawing of the rune so I can apply it in private?"

"It must be done in my presence," the girl said. "But, if you like, you can wait until we meet again."

"I'll do that," Reginn said. That would give her time to think about it and look for ways around it.

"We'll meet again three days from now, early morning. After that, I'll expect you to come here at least once a week. I'll leave selections on the table for you. If you don't come for them, I will stop. If you don't return them, I will stop. Don't tell anyone you know the runes of magic. Don't tell anyone about me."

She said all this in a rush, as if she'd had this list prepared for a long time.

She stood and ran her fingers across some niches in the wall. "You can leave me notes under"–she peered closely at the wall–"under *Wool Production Year Two.*"

"How can I leave you a note if I don't know how to write?" Reginn muttered.

"Better study up," the girl said. Climbing to the next landing, she brushed her hand over a set of larger niches, biting her lip. "I'll leave you books and materials under . . . *Bovine Lineages at the Founding.*"

"I don't get it," Reginn said. "Are you a dedicate here, or one of the faculty, or a librarian?"

"I washed out as a dedicate a few years ago," the stranger said. "Not dedicated enough, I suppose." She paused. "Or too dedicated."

"But they let you stay on?" Reginn said eagerly. That would ease her mind, to know that if she failed to meet the council's standard, they would not send her back to the Archipelago.

The girl looked around, tilting her head back, surveying the shelves and shelves of books. "The truth of the matter is, I could not bear to go," she said.

Well, at least that supported what Modir Tyra had said.

"What's your name?" Reginn said.

"It's better if you don't know," the girl said.

"What should I call you?" Reginn persisted.

The girl thought a moment. "You can call me Musa," she said. "I'm the library mouse." She swung up to the next level, making it clear this meeting was over.

"I have a question," Reginn blurted, eager to keep her a little longer. "Why *Bovine Lineages*?"

Musa laughed. "I've used that hidey-hole for a long time. If you want to stash things where nobody will look, that's the spot."

Why is everything such a big secret? Reginn thought, irritated. She wondered if she could find out more by asking some of the other students. Maybe she should go to Modir Tyra after all.

"Reginn," Musa said as Reginn made for the door.

"*What?*"

"Everything is such a big secret because if they find out you've been talking to me, they will torture you, and when they have what they want, they will kill you," Musa said.

34

THREE'S A CROWD

THE MORNING AFTER RIKHARD'S VISIT, Eiric and Liv rose before sunup. Liv kindled the mealfire, and they shared a dagmal of porridge, smoked ham, and flatbread with cloudberry jam.

"Enjoy it," Liv said. "This is likely the best meal that you will have for a while." Clearly, she meant to lower expectations early on.

After, Eiric laid out their weapons. His grandfadir's axe and shield. Leif's sword, Gramr. A plain, razor-edged dagger that had belonged to Sylvi.

"You should have a sword of your own," Eiric said, wishing he'd thought of it sooner.

"I'll take the dagger," Liv said. "Beyond that, I'll have this"—she touched her pendant—"and my staff. That will do."

Then they went to say goodbye to Ivar, who now slept on a pallet next to Hilde's sleeping bench. To Eiric's surprise, their brodir was awake. He lay calmly, eyes wide open, as if waiting for them.

"Farewell, Ivar," Eiric said, extending his forefinger so that Ivar could grab on. His brodir had a strong grip. "If your uncles come onto our property, run them off."

"Jarl Karlsen, too," Liv added. "Only offer hospitality to the best sorts of people."

In response, Ivar smiled and kicked his legs and arms like a crab lying on its back. Eiric was a little amazed at how attached he'd become to this small person with his modir's eyes.

"Grow quickly," Eiric said. And in his head added, *Survive*.

With that, they picked up the last of their belongings and made their way down to the beach. The fog still hung thick over the water, muffling the sound of the lapping waves. It was just past high tide, and *Dreki* was all but floating at her mooring.

Eiric stowed away their weapons and handed Liv one of two bags of chop silver. "Keep this with you," he said, tucking the other one into his coat. "Hopefully at least one of us will survive and have need of money."

She nodded and stowed it. Then leaned on her staff, waiting.

"One other thing," Eiric said. "The other crew member–Thurston. I don't want him to know about the sunstone or the pendant, or much of anything beyond what he already knows."

Liv rolled her eyes. "So you don't trust him? Good choice."

Eiric splayed his fingers. "At this point, I don't trust anyone except you–and I'm not sure about you."

"That's wise, brodir," Liv said, giving him a peculiar look. "Where is this Thurston? Shouldn't he be here by now?" She looked down the shoreline toward town. "Is that him?"

Eiric followed her gaze. A dark figure was making his way along the headland toward them, silent as smoke.

"That's him," Eiric said.

Liv watched, transfixed, as Thurston came closer, knuckles whitening as she gripped her staff. "What's this?" she murmured, eyes narrowed. "Where did you find this person?"

"I met him between Selvagr and Sundgard," Eiric said. Something in his systir's face made the hairs on the back of his neck stand up. "Why? Do you know him?"

Liv closed her eyes, concentrating, her staff clenched in one hand and her amulet in the other. "I don't know him in particular, but I know that he is not what he seems."

Eiric fought down his frustration. He'd always respected Liv's instincts, but now all her insights were couched in magical, mysterious language. Couldn't anything be straightforward anymore?

He leaned toward Liv, speaking quietly. "If you don't want him along, tell me now," he said. "I'll make some excuse and send him on his way." He and Liv had sailed the karvi together in the past, so he knew it could be done. And it wasn't as if he would be turning away an experienced hand.

"Let's see what he has to say, and then I'll decide."

"Halvorsen," Thurston said with as close to a smile as Eiric had seen on him. He was wearing a better coat, as instructed, leather gloves, and a woolen cap, and he had a stuffed carry bag slung over his shoulder. "I hope I'm not late." Then his eyes went to Liv, and the smile faded. "Who might this be?"

"This is my systir, Liv," Eiric said. "She'll be our third crew member."

"This is your systir?" Thurston's eyes shifted from Eiric to Liv and back again. "She's coming with us?" He turned to Eiric, speaking low and fast, as if that way, Liv couldn't hear. "Do you think it's a good idea to bring your systir on such a dangerous voyage?"

"Liv is skilled with oars and sail," Eiric said. "She can take care of herself."

"Actually, we're still debating whether you'll pull your weight," Liv said. "My brodir tells me you lack skills as a seaman. We have enough ballast on board as is." She sniffed the air and fixed a hard eye on Thurston. "Do I smell something burning?" Clearly, she saw something in him that Eiric had missed.

"Liv is a part of this crew," Eiric said. "If that doesn't suit you, find another ship."

Thurston inclined his head, scouring all vestiges of doubt from his face. "Forgive me," he said. "I look forward to being schooled by this very capable woman."

Liv gazed at him coolly, hands on hips. "Fair enough. Just keep your distance, leech."

Leech?

Thurston stowed his carry bag, and it was time to shove off. Eiric looked back at the longhouse, where he had been born, where Liv had killed Sten; at the woodlot where his modir had died; at the boat shed, the scene of so much learning and lore. He found himself wondering if he would ever see them again.

But the pull of the island called Eimyrja was stronger than the pull of home. Eiric untied *Dreki*'s mooring line and flipped it into the stern. All three of them waded into the water, pushing her free of the sand. Eiric held the ship steady while the other two climbed aboard—Liv claiming a pair of oars midships, where she could also help with the sail, and Thurston assigned to a pair of oars up front. Eiric took his position in the stern, handling the tiller.

Aided by the outgoing tide, it wasn't long until they were a good distance down the sound toward the open sea. A few lights were burning in the village of Selvagr, and Eiric imagined that he felt the pressure of unfriendly eyes.

He and Liv joined together on the halyards to hoist the red-and-white woolen sail. The winds were now freshening and shifting to offshore, and the karvi picked up speed, spray flying as her sail filled and bellied out.

That was another advantage to a small crew—there was little time for thinking.

In a few moments, Eiric would sit down at the tiller and recheck their course. But for now, he stood in the stern, legs braced, head thrown back, eating the wind.

They might be on their way to disaster, but the prospect of new and different disasters was somehow more appealing than the disasters he'd left behind.

35

BRENNA'S HOUSE

BRENNA'S HOUSE WAS LOCATED IN a secluded glade at the far edge of the Grove, overlooking a river that ran from the Mosifell Mountains to the sea. The complex centered on a hot spring that boiled up from deep beneath the earth into a grotto lined with stones, covered in the strange mosses and plants that could thrive in such a place. Reginn wrinkled her nose at the sulfur smell, but it was quickly dissipated by the sea air.

The main building, like the other buildings at the temple, was built of timber and stone. Broad galleries on all sides opened to the sea breeze, something that could never work in the Archipelago, where cold winds howled for much of the year.

Bryn had promised to meet her on the porch of the central building, where the sickest patients were housed. He wore the standard-issue dedicate blues, except that his tunic was blue, striped with white.

"Sure you want to do this?" he said with a grin. "This place will ensnare you if you let it."

Reginn fingered the remedy pouches at her waist, which for her had always been a kind of talisman. "I'm in," she said.

"I'll show you around the wards, and then we'll walk the grounds and see the cottages," he said. "The cottages are for convalescents still under care of the healers. I'll be interested to hear how the setup compares to what you're used to."

"I don't remember much," Reginn said.

Bryn laughed. "We'll see."

In fact, Reginn could say with complete confidence that Brenna's House was nothing like what she was used to. Not even close.

Once inside, Reginn was struck first by how clean everything was. The walls were whitewashed, so blood spatter and other waste would be easy to spot. The floors were of soothing gray stone covered in woven rugs and thick sheepskins.

Most of the wards had four to six patients each. Some looked to be gravely ill, but there was none of the stench of urine and skita and infection and death that Reginn associated with sick people. There were attendants in all the rooms, wearing bondi colors.

When Reginn and Bryn passed through, the attendants greeted them, joking with Bryn or pulling him aside to have a look at this patient or that. The patients, too, received him warmly, calling out to him if he didn't stop to say hello. One of the wards housed mostly children, and they swarmed around him like bees on a honeycomb, all trying to get his attention.

The last room they visited was devoted to the preparation of medicines and nourishing foods. Reginn recognized some of the herbs and botanicals that went into their remedies.

"This is amazing," Reginn said over and over. "You are so fortunate to have a place like this."

Which was true. If there were dedicated healing halls in the Archipelago, she'd never seen one. She did her work in alehouses and private homes. She preferred alehouses, which were usually roomier and cleaner, and had fewer problems with vermin and interfering family members. Plus, alcohol was always available.

Wounds, broken bones, and the like were easiest to treat. At least the problems were readily identifiable, and she knew how to clean out infections, straighten bones, and offer runes to relieve the pain. She tried to avoid tending birthing modirs, since there were better, more experienced midwives to be found.

Many of the sick were on the streets, having been turned out by landlords and family members afraid of contagion or unable to cope with people who were not right in the head. Whenever she and Asger stayed in one place for very long, word got out that she was a healer. She would be mobbed on the street by modirs with sick babies in their arms and thin, ragged souls with the wasting disease. They would try to catch her when Asger wasn't around to drive them off.

Most people tried to hide the fact that they were sick for as long as possible. That meant that those who sought treatment were often beyond saving.

The worst cases were those whose lungs had been ruined in the mines or who had developed bloody rashes and growths from exposure to unknown poisons.

Many who could have recovered were left in the forest. People in the Archipelago could not afford to tend unproductive people who took a long time to either heal or die.

When they'd visited all the wards, Bryn led Reginn back outside, turning down one of the stone paths that snaked through the complex. They passed a garden where a handful of patients were sunning themselves. One woman was navigating a stone labyrinth, head down, concentrating. Another patient walked along a wall, one hand running along the top for support, his leg encased in splints.

"Brodir Bryn," the boy said when he spotted them. "I did six rounds today."

"Good," Bryn said, nodding. "How do you feel?"

"Like I can do three more," he said, and moved on.

The boy with the splints wore spinner blue, but the rest appeared to be bondi.

Bryn turned down a walkway toward a group of cottages set off by themselves. "There's someone in here that I want to look in on," he said. "Her name is Alva Bondi, and she's ten years old. Two weeks ago, there was an incident on Ithavoll. Her fadir was killed and she was injured.

"Alva's physical injuries seem to have healed, but she's not the same. She doesn't speak; she doesn't move. She eats next to nothing. I don't know what to do for her. I thought maybe a little music would help."

The door of the cottage was locked. Bryn knocked and murmured, "It's me."

An attendant opened the door and stood aside so they could enter, eyeing Reginn warily.

"Any change?" Bryn murmured.

The attendant shook her head. "She's the same."

Reginn followed Bryn across the room to where a young girl was sitting in a chair by the window. It appeared that someone had placed her there and she hadn't moved since. Her red-brown hair had been shorn into a rough mop.

"Hello, Alva," Bryn said. "I'd like you to meet my friend Reginn."

Alva showed no sign that she'd heard.

"Reginn is new here," Bryn said. "She is a spinner, like me, and she also plays the flute."

Reginn pulled a chair closer to Alva and began to unfasten her instrument case. "I'd like to play something for you. What would you like to hear?" she said.

Alva expressed no preference.

"Is there a song your fadir liked that I could play for you?"

Alva said nothing.

"I'll choose, then," Reginn said. "Your name means 'female elf,' and this is a song about the elves."

While she played, Bryn tapped his foot to the music and smiled. Alva did not respond at all. It was very much like singing to the dead.

When Reginn finished, Bryn whistled and clapped, as if hoping that his enthusiasm would be contagious.

A single tear spilled from Alva's eye and rolled down her face.

Reginn returned the flute to its case and took one of Alva's hands. Pain and guilt and grief torrented through that connection.

She traced a rune on Alva's palm with her forefinger.

Alva flinched, as if startled. Then, for the first time, she met Reginn's gaze directly, a question in her eyes.

"This is Ul," Reginn murmured so softly that Bryn couldn't hear. "It signifies a turning point. A decision that only you can make. You cannot stay where you are—it's too painful. You must go forward or back. Which way will you go?"

She kissed Alva on the forehead and stood.

Just outside the cottage, Reginn said, "What exactly happened to her?"

"I don't know," Bryn said, and it didn't take a spakona to know that he was lying.

Why would he lie about that? Whose secrets was he keeping? Alva's or his own?

"Let's go this way." He turned off the main path toward one of the larger cottages. "This is the bathhouse, one of my favorite places. I don't think anyone will be in here this time of day."

The sign over the door said Brenna's Springhouse. Bryn opened the door and led the way inside.

The inside of the bathhouse was warm and steamy—again, with that sulfur scent, but Reginn was getting used to it.

"The water comes from the hot spring," Bryn said. "It's said to be healing. There are large common pools and some private bathing areas. The springs are why Modir Brenna chose this site."

"She was interested in healing?"

Bryn nodded. "Maybe it was because of her disability, but she seemed to have a strong interest in treating the sick. I think that she intended for Eimyrja to be more of a resource and sanctuary for others than it has been. It's fair to say that the temple mission has . . . evolved since the founding."

Reginn waited for him to explain further, but instead he opened a door and said, "This is one of the private bathing rooms." He stood aside to allow Reginn to enter.

It was set up to resemble the grotto outside, with steaming water pouring over an artificial waterfall, skylights overhead, ferns and flowers all around.

"They add cold water to adjust the temperature so that it's tolerable," Bryn said. He slid a sheepish look at Reginn. "Sometimes, after a hard day, I just come here and soak."

Bryn moved to the door and closed it, then motioned to a stone bench next to the pool. "Do you have a minute? I'd rather talk in here than outside, where we might be overheard."

Reginn hesitated, then sat. Maybe she shouldn't be alone with this boy she'd just met. Maybe she shouldn't be sharing secrets, but they were his secrets, after all, not hers.

She could feel the heat of the steam rising from the water. On impulse, she kicked off her shoes and cautiously dipped her feet into the pool.

"Ohhh," she said, looking up at Bryn with a broad grin. "This is fine. So fine." Paying the wet bank no mind, she dropped onto the edge of the pool, rolled up her trousers, and slid her legs in up to her knees. Leaning her head back, she closed her eyes and all but purred.

Bryn laughed. "I love the way you meet the world. You take such honest pleasure in everyday things."

She lifted her head and looked at him narrow-eyed. "What do you mean?"

"Whether it's Naima's pies or a fistful of blueberries or rolling down a grassy hill and landing in the creek—you never hold back." He raised both hands to forestall any objections. "That's a good thing," he said. "Most of us don't appreciate what we have because we've never known anything else."

"You're right," Reginn said. "You have no idea how lucky you are."

"One day," Bryn said, "we'll go to the Archipelago and help the people there."

"Really?" Reginn said. "You plan to go and help the people who drove us out?"

Bryn nodded. "That was always the founder's plan. Modir Tyra is determined to carry it through."

"But won't that be dangerous?"

He shrugged. "We will go in strength, prepared to defend ourselves. And once they see that we are there to help, we believe they will welcome us."

"Maybe," Reginn said skeptically. Still, she had to admire Tyra's good intentions. "Is that what you wanted to tell me?"

He shook his head. "From what I've seen, you have many gifts—many options to choose from when it comes to a vocation. Though you have considerable experience and talent in healing, healing is no longer a priority these days at the Grove."

"It's not? But—why would they put so much effort into something they didn't care about?" She gestured, taking in their surroundings.

"Most of this was built during the lifetime of the founder," Bryn said. "It's been well taken care of, but they haven't added to it in

more than a hundred years. As you can see, it's staffed mostly by
bondi." Bryn paused, chewing his lower lip. "The council would
prefer that I devote all of my time to investigating the decline of
the gifted bloodline and ensuring its survival."

"The . . . decline of the bloodline?" This was new. "What do you
mean?"

"I'm told there were many gifted born here in the years immediately following the migration, but the numbers have declined
considerably since the founding modir crossed over. We don't
know why. The keeper and the council have been keen to solve that
ever since. That's been my primary assignment once I was identified as a healer. I'm following in the footsteps of two other failures."
He sighed. "I feel like I'm beating my head against the wall."

"Where would you even begin?" Reginn said.

"They've already put rules in place regarding"—he blushed—
"regarding fraternization with the bondi, not wanting to dilute the
bloodlines. On the other hand, they encourage—ah—"

"Fraternization?" Reginn guessed, thinking that for a healer,
Bryn was easily embarrassed.

"Fraternization among the gifted," Bryn said. "Especially those
whose gifts are particularly rare and useful. Any resulting children
are welcomed into the nursery at Vesthavn in the hope that they
will be strong in megin."

"How's that working out?" Reginn said.

Bryn rocked his hand. "Not especially well. Some are blessed
with the gift of magic, but not many. Most of our new candidates
still come from the Archipelago."

If there is such a shortage, you'd think they'd be less picky about
who they accept, Reginn thought, recalling her ordeal at the Council of Elders.

"Is anyone helping you with that research?"

He shook his head. "We're spread thin. Everyone is pretty much on their own these days. All of the dedicates are specialized. Katia wrangles landvaettir, who provide reliable security. Shelby makes sure we have a generous food supply. Eira makes weapons and devices. Stian is in charge of nonhuman allies."

Nonhuman allies? Since Bryn seemed to be finished, Reginn said, "What about Grima?"

"What about her?"

"What is her vocation?"

Bryn thought a minute. "I don't know."

Reginn waited for clarification and, when that didn't come, said, "What do you mean you don't know?"

He shrugged. "She's never said."

"You've never asked?"

"It's her business," Bryn said as if baffled that Reginn would raise the topic.

That's weird, Reginn thought.

"My point is," Bryn said, "that if you're given a choice, you might want to–"

"I wasn't given a choice," Reginn said bluntly. "I've been asked to focus on summoning the spirits of the dead."

He looked at Reginn, wide-eyed. "Oh! Well, that's settled, then. Good for you. It sounds as if you'll be doing important work."

"Maybe," Reginn said. "Like you, I'm a lot more confident in my skills as a healer."

"I'm not complaining," he said in a rush. "Please don't think that I'm complaining."

"Everybody complains sometimes," Reginn said with a shrug.

"No," he said. "It's not right to complain, especially to someone who has lived most of her life in Barbaria. The council has a responsibility to see that Eimyrja has all of the magical resources it needs. So I hope you'll never repeat what I said to anyone else."

"Why would I?" Reginn said. She pulled her knees to her chest and wrapped her arms around them. "You know, right now, I don't have a work assignment. I'm just learning about the Grove, reading books, and spending time with the other dedicates. I haven't been given a big assignment because I'm not ready.

"One thing I have done before is work as a healer. At least working here, I'd feel like I was contributing, that I was good at something. I could learn from you, and maybe that would free you up to work on the things the council wants."

"I'm not sure that more time is the answer," Bryn said, "but I'd love to have some help if it's something you want to do."

And so it was agreed. One day a week, Reginn would come and help at the healing center.

Before she returned to the domicile, Reginn walked deep into the trees, seeking a rarely trafficked place. When she was confident she was out of sight of everyone, she pulled her carving tools from her carry bag. Painstakingly, she carved a rune into the bark of a birch tree. Limrunar. Meant to transfer injury from a person to a tree.

"Heal, Alva," she whispered. "Heal and thrive."

36

LIBRARY MOUSE

THREE DAYS OF THINKING SURFACED no alternative to submitting to the library mouse's demands. So on the day of their next meeting, Reginn came prepared with her medical blade and clean linen in her remedy bag. The sun had not yet penetrated the canopy of trees when she crossed the quad to the library. It was empty of people, as usual, and quiet as a tomb. While she waited, she began leafing through one of several books that had been left out on the table, trying to remember the runes and sound out words.

The book was beautiful, with hand-colored illustrations and a binding stamped in gold. It was a history of the Grove, complete with a portrait of Brenna Wayfinder on the title page.

Following the lines of runes with her finger, Reginn mouthed the words. Sometimes the illustrations held clues to what was in the text, but they were so brilliant as to hurt the eyes. Eimyrja might be beautiful in real life, but it was exhausting on these pages. Dedicates, adepts, and elders had a glow about them, with beatific smiles and robes that swam around their limbs like schools of brightly colored fish.

The bondi attended the gifted, their rapturous faces suggesting that laboring at skita jobs at the Grove was the stuff of dreams.

If I'm going to go to the trouble of reading, Reginn thought, I want to read books that tell the truth.

"You're right," Musa said, and Reginn jumped. "Those are all a waste of time." She swung down from the staircase and landed next to Reginn.

Reginn gaped at her, still trying to come to grips with the library mouse's ability to come up on her without making a sound and slide into her head. Musa wore the same cloud-gray clothes that she had before. Maybe she had several sets of them, though why a person would have more than one set of ugly clothes, Reginn didn't know.

"These are the books that are required reading. They should already be familiar to you from Tyra's schooling." Musa tapped her head with her forefinger.

Reginn picked up another of the books and flipped through it. It was vaguely familiar. Maybe.

The library mouse perched on the edge of the table. "So. Are you in?"

"I'm in." Reginn pushed the book aside and unwrapped her blade.

"Now, remember, it's important that nobody–"

"I know," Reginn said brusquely. She rolled her right pant leg as far as it would go and chose a place on her inner thigh. It was an awkward position, and it was hard to see what she was doing. "Show me again."

Musa pushed up the sleeve on her left arm to display the traces of the symbol carved there.

Sweat blossomed on Reginn's forehead as she made the first cut. But years of experience had given her a sure hand, and with a few quick strokes, it was done.

"Excellent," Musa murmured.

At first, Reginn felt only the bite of the blade, and then the blood trickling down from the shallow cuts. She scooped up the rag she'd brought and went to blot it, but Musa said, "Let it bleed. It will stop on its own."

Now Reginn could feel the burn of magic in the wound. She took several slow, deep breaths, then looked up at the library mouse. Musa sat, eyes closed, her expression as blissful as that of the opium eaters in the south islands.

It was an eerie reminder of Asger's demeanor when he leeched power from her.

Gradually, the burn of magic faded. When Reginn looked down at the cuts on her leg, she saw that they had healed into bright red ridges.

"How do you feel?" She looked up to find Musa eyeing her anxiously. The blood rune on Musa's arm glowed through the thin fabric of her sleeve, as if aflame.

"I'll live," Reginn said curtly. "Shall we begin?"

Musa rested her hand on one of the books on the table. "Let's begin with this one. Read the first page."

The ancient leather cover cracked and flaked as she opened it. This was all text, no pictures. Slowly, painfully, Reginn worked her way through the first paragraph.

Musa was frowning. "You're sure Modir Tyra did her thing with you?"

"Well, she *did*," Reginn said, "but I had a bad reaction. Unusual, anyway. I passed out for a couple of hours."

"*What?*"

"But some of it came through," Reginn said, struggling to be hopeful but honest. "I'm sure of it. I mean, I have ideas in my head that I didn't have before."

"I'm sure you do," Musa murmured. "What do you remember

about your life before you came here?"

"Some. Fragments. Bits and pieces. It's . . . it seems to be coming back to me." She paused, then added in a rush, "Maybe I should go back to Modir Tyra and ask her to try again." Even though Tyra had said no to that already.

"No!" Musa said.

Reginn stared at her. "Why not? If it didn't take the first time, then maybe it will this time." *No offense, but it would be a lot easier than spending hours in a dark library sounding out words.*

"If you let her know that her magic didn't work on you, then she will begin to realize how powerful you are."

Reginn had never felt powerful. She'd always felt that she was skating along the edge of fraud, selling services that she might not be able to perform. Except that one night at Gunnar's, with Thurston, when she had surprised herself.

"What makes you think I'm powerful?" Reginn said.

"Can't you feel it?" When Reginn shrugged, Musa said, "You spend too much time worrying about what's going on around you and not enough time looking inside yourself."

"Where I come from, if you sit around daydreaming, you won't last very long," Reginn said.

"If you're powerful enough, no one would dare touch you," Musa said.

Fair enough, Reginn thought. This much was true. Since leaving the Archipelago, Reginn had felt more and more capable, more and more confident, despite being behind all the others. It was as if some malleable core inside her had hardened into steel. Modir Tyra herself had said that Reginn seemed to be growing more powerful by the day.

Was it the Grove that nourished her? Was it the Archipelago that drained her?

Was it the absence of Asger Eldr, who sucked her dry?

"All right," Reginn said. "Suppose I'm powerful. Isn't that a good thing? I mean, I want to do well here."

Musa sighed, as if Reginn was hopelessly naive. "Power *is* a good thing—if it's something that the council can take control of and use. Unrestrained power is a threat." The mouse studied Reginn through narrowed eyes, as if deciding whether to say more. Finally, she said, "Let's start with the basics, then, and see how you do."

She began by going over the bookish runes and the sounds they represented. Musa claimed that runes could be combined to make all the words a person would ever need. Maybe because of Tyra's spellwork, Reginn found that they were already familiar.

Even if they were words Reginn had been using all her life, how could a person look at a clump of unfamiliar symbols and figure out what word they stood for? Especially when the runes seemed to run together. Especially when letters sounded like one thing and sometimes another. It seemed random, impossible to predict.

"Knowing the sounds helps you figure out the words when reading," Musa said. "And reading makes you better at spotting the whole words you've seen before. You'll know more and more words, and then you can go faster."

Soon, Reginn could sound them out, and she could read some of the words. But not very many, and not very fast.

"You're a quick learner," Musa said, and Reginn clung to that bit of rare praise as if it were a raft in a dangerous current.

As it turned out, she needed it. They worked through the day, as the angle of the sun coming through the windows shifted, signaling the passing of hours. When Musa showed no signs of stopping for the midday meal, Reginn pulled out a couple of muffins and some cheese that she had scavenged from the kitchen the night before. She offered half to Musa, but the library mouse declined.

When Reginn persisted, she said, "I don't eat in the archives."

Reginn felt guilty, but that didn't stop her from eating. Nothing stopped her from eating, other than a lack of food. Once she cleared the crumbs away, they shifted to writing. That actually went a little better, though the vellum she wrote on was unfamiliar. She was used to the hand control required to craft the runes of magic. She just needed to get used to the new shapes she was learning.

As the day wore on, though, Musa seemed to fade, her voice growing softer, even her snark dampened by fatigue. Though Reginn was eager to keep working as long as she could, she finally said, "Are you all right, Musa? I appreciate everything you've done, but maybe it's time to quit."

The library mouse nodded, closing her eyes. "I find it . . . taxing . . . to be with people," she said. The fact that she didn't argue spoke volumes.

"I'm a healer, too," Reginn said. "Maybe I could help."

Musa smiled as if she found this amusing. "Ah no," she said. "I believe I am beyond your skills. But,before you go, I want to give you this." She slid a drawing across the table. It was a detailed map of the library that showed what collections were where. "In case you go foraging on your own."

"Thank you," Reginn said simply.

"Now," Musa whispered, "what you need to do is practice. Don't bother reading the assigned histories, they're not accurate anyway, and to be honest, nobody cares whether you read them or not. If you look in the bovine niche, you will see that I've left three other books for you. Two are earlier, more factual histories, and the third is a biography of Modir Brenna. I expect you to have read them by this time next week. Return then, and I will have more reading for you.

"You can practice writing by writing a summary of each book and leaving notes for me in the wool niche with questions and concerns. I'll respond as quickly as I can. All right?"

Reginn nodded, feeling strangely bereft. "Is there anything I can do for you?"

"Read. Ask questions. Be careful what you say and who you say it to. Don't tell anyone you've spoken to me and keep quiet about the runes. It's all right to make friends with the other students, but never forget—they are Tyra's, body and soul." She huffed a little laugh. "I'm guessing you are, too."

Reginn just stared at her, unable to summon a response. So few people had ever stood up for her, been kind to her, encouraged her. Tove. Eiric Halvorsen. And now, Modir Tyra, who had stood up to the keeper, to the council, had done whatever it took to make a place for her here.

Then again, Tove's love had been fragile as spun glass.

Musa sat silently, as if watching the river of thoughts flow through Reginn's head. Finally, she whispered, "Stay alive."

37

SHELBY

THE DAY AFTER HER VISIT to the library, Reginn shifted on a hard stone bench at the edge of a garden, squinting to keep the early morning sun out of her eyes. To either side of her, cherry trees hung heavy with fruit, tantalizingly out of reach.

Today was her day to follow Shelby around. Shelby's gift was the conjuring of growing things—plants, shrubs, and trees. Reginn couldn't fathom how observing dedicates whose gifts were so different from her own would help her in her own studies.

Still, she was looking forward to it. How hard could farming be compared to reading? And surely it would be relaxing after her conversation with Musa. Shelby was charming and funny and easy on the eyes.

At home, farms weren't even a reliable place to get a handout. They offered only shriveled fields, skinny cows, and barking, biting dogs. If something did grow, like as not a swarm of beetles would appear and eat it up, or a herd of wild boars would root it up. Many of the herbs and remedies she used grew wild, plants that most farmers considered weeds.

She was glad to be outside on a beautiful day, away from the spooky secrets in the archives.

If they find out you've been talking to me, they will torture you, and when they have what they want, they will kill you.

It's all right to make friends with the other students, but never forget—they are Tyra's, body and soul.

Why wouldn't they be? She's their teacher. She's the only one who cares about them. Us.

Just because Musa was a recluse didn't mean Reginn had to be.

She yawned, wishing she hadn't stayed up so late. She'd met Erland and Naima at an amphitheater in the woods, flute in hand. At first it was just the three of them, but soon a few bondi arrived. Most came to sit and listen, but a few brought instruments of different kinds. Apparently these gatherings were a poorly kept secret.

It had been a long time since she'd had so much fun.

To be honest, she'd never had that much fun.

Her stomach growled loudly. She should have grabbed something for breakfast before coming here. She couldn't seem to manage to rise early enough to walk to the dining hall and then get somewhere else on time.

Reginn's stomach growled again, interrupting her plots and plans and focusing her attention once more on the cherries high above her head. She climbed onto the stone bench, stretching up to reach the sprays of fruit.

"Let me help with that," somebody said, startling her so that she lost her balance and fell. Instead of landing flat on her face on the stone walk, she hit something more yielding, somebody who grunted in surprise, then crushed her against him to keep her from falling.

She breathed in the scent of warm earth, ripe fruit, and flowers.

Shelby.

A memory elbowed in, bringing the scent of char and images of ember eyes.

You are mine, meyla, and mine alone. If anyone comes between us, I will kill them.

In a panic, she wrenched free, planting both hands on Shelby's chest and pushing him so that he stumbled back, just barely keeping his feet.

He stared at her, brow furrowed in confusion. "Reginn? Are you all right?"

It took her a moment to gather enough breath to speak. "I'm sorry I fell on you," she said, heart thumping, cheeks burning. "I . . . um . . . I was trying to get at the cherries."

"So I guessed," Shelby said. "Don't apologize. Feel free to land on me anytime." His smile would have charmed the skin off a hazelnut. "Now lift up your overdress."

"What?" Reginn glared at him, clutching her skirts to either side.

"To catch the cherries," Shelby said. "Based on what I've seen in the dining hall, I assume you'll want more than a handful."

"What's that supposed to mean?" Reginn said, hackles rising. "You think I'm greedy, a glutton?"

"No," he said, raising both hands, palms out. "I mean you're really thin and it looks like you've not had enough to eat for a long time." He reached out and tucked a tendril of her hair behind her ear, raising gooseflesh on her neck and shoulders. "And you said you liked cherries."

Shame washed over her. *You've got to stop thinking the worst of people, even if it's true most of the time.*

"I'm sorry," she said.

Never say you're sorry.

Who were these voices in her head, and why wouldn't they shut up?

She looked up into Shelby's face. "What if it gets stained?" She fingered the fabric of her overdress.

"They don't have laundries in Barbaria?" Shelby grinned. "Don't worry about it. If it gets stained, ask the housemodir for a new overdress."

That simple.

Cautiously, Reginn lifted her skirt so it made a little hammock. Shelby gestured, and the branches of the cherry trees bent low, dropping fruit until her lap was heavy with it.

Reginn sagged back onto the bench, scooped up a handful of cherries, and somehow resisted stuffing them into her mouth, stems and all. Carefully, she bit off each plump fruit, dropping the stems onto the ground, then spitting out the pits.

Shelby sat next to her, waiting until she'd finished the lot and her fingers were stained red.

"Thank you," she said. "I'll probably be sorry I ate those so fast. I guess we should get to work."

"Great," Shelby said. "What should we do?"

Reginn blinked at him. "I thought you would tell me."

He shrugged. "I've not had anyone shadow me before," he said. "All of us–"

"I know," Reginn said. "You all came as babies."

"If it were up to me," Shelby said, "we would go to a secluded cove I know of. I could feed you cherries and you could show me the fine points of barbarian lovemaking." He grinned, pretending that he wasn't really serious, but there was an element of challenge in there, too.

Curiosity quivered through her. What would it be like to feel Shelby's lips on hers? Maybe Asger's hold on her was fading, just a bit. A dark suspicion surfaced as Reginn recalled what Bryn had said. Had Shelby been encouraged to "couple" with her?

"Such a tempting offer," Reginn said, "but you should know up front that it is the custom in Barbaria for the woman to cut out the heart of any man she's coupled with and wear it on a thong around her neck."

Shelby stared at her for a long, horrified moment, then burst out laughing. "That's out, then," he said, blotting tears from his eyes. "I'll keep my heart to myself, thank you." Sobering, he added, "It's easy to forget that you're new here. If I offended you by coming on too strong, I'm sorry. We're pretty casual about coupling in Eimyrja, as long as we, you know, use common sense."

"No worries," Reginn said. "Keep in mind that I'm used to fending off drunks in an alehouse."

"So. What would you rather do?" Shelby said.

"Could you show me around the temple gardens? I'd like to . . . I'd like to see where all the food comes from."

"I should have known." Shelby stood, mopping his brow as if he'd made a narrow escape. "It doesn't all come from here. We have farms on Vestholm as well."

"Vestholm?"

"It's one of our out islands, just off our west coast. Eventually, we expect that it will feed all of our residents."

Reginn recalled the lush green island she'd seen while traveling with Modir Tyra. Vestholm, she repeated to herself.

"Most of what we grow on Eimyrja is for local use," Shelby said. "Let's go to the vegetable gardens first." They walked down a narrow lane between two rows of laden cherry trees, through a gate, and into a warren of garden plots. Reginn recognized peas, celery, cabbage, ground elder, and horse beans. Two mid-age people in loose, moss-colored tunics and trousers were hoeing between the rows. They stopped working and leaned on their tools, watching silently as Reginn and Shelby passed by.

Reginn took a quick look over her shoulder. The two gardeners noticed and hastily went back to work.

"Who are they?" Reginn said, gesturing toward the gardeners.

"Who are who?" Shelby said, as if he hadn't noticed them.

"The people working in the garden."

Shelby's confusion cleared. "They are bondi."

"But do you *know* them?" Reginn said. "Do you know their names? Anything about them?"

"Should I?"

"They work for you," Reginn said.

Shelby shrugged. "There are a lot more bondi than there are dedicates and adepts. And that's not even counting the ones on the out islands. It's hard to keep track."

They crossed over from the vegetable gardens to an area of blueberry bushes, grapevines, elderberries, and raspberry canes. Even with a belly full of cherries, it was hard for Reginn to resist tasting every kind of fruit, even the kinds that weren't ripe yet.

Shelby cradled a handful of elderberries in his hand. "These will be ripe before long," he said. "Naima makes the best elderberry pie."

"So you know *her* name?"

"Of course," Shelby said, eyeing her warily. "She's the one who makes the pies."

Reginn took a deep breath. *You need to calm down.* Having been a thrall herself, it was as if she was looking for evidence that this wasn't the paradise it promised to be.

They'd moved on to the herb gardens by now, where Reginn felt more sure of herself. Here was henbane, poppy, chicory, marsh mallow, angelica, and garlic. She brushed her fingers over the aromatic leaves and stored away their location for future use.

"Where are all the graduates of the temple school? I haven't even seen that many teachers besides Modir Tyra."

"Those who have left the temple grove are called adepts. They are working all over New Jotunheim."

"What do the adepts do?"

"They support the temple by teaching students at the lower school at Vesthavn, supervising on the farms in Langadale, making needed tools, building structures, and so on. The council also has a large group of adepts and bondi working on the out islands—on Vesthavn and Ithavoll. I'm hoping to be named adept soon, so I can move on from the Grove for good. Some in our year have already gone. I'll probably be sent to Vestholm, where we're building out more farms."

Reginn was struck by a sudden fear that all the other dedicates would be completing their studies and moving on to new territories while she remained behind at the Grove. Learning to read.

"Have you ever heard of a dedicate being assigned to the library?"

He lifted an eyebrow. "Why would they do that? Nobody goes there these days. Why do you ask?"

"I really like it," Reginn said. "I'm thinking I might want to be sent there if I wash out."

"Not much chance of that," Shelby said. "Washing out, I mean. Modir Tyra seems to think that you are the answer to our prayers."

What will happen if she finds out that I'm not?

38

QUARTERLY

REGINN CLIMBED THE STEPS TO the House of Elders. When she looked over her shoulder, she saw Stian and Katia blowing kisses from the door of the dining hall. Wishing her good luck.

After three months at the Grove, she was cautiously optimistic that her quarterly meeting with Modir Tyra would go well. More importantly, that her progress would satisfy the council.

Reginn carried with her a portfolio of her work to share—the spellsongs she'd written down in the runic alphabet she'd learned from Musa and summaries of some of her assigned reading. She felt prepared to read from most any book the headmistress handed her, even if she'd not seen it before.

Reginn still spent considerable time in the library, gaining confidence as she mastered the increasingly more complex manuscripts Musa sent her way.

By now, she'd shadowed every dedicate in her class except for Grima. They'd scheduled meetups several times, but they always ended up canceled for one reason or another. The dedicate walked the campus in a kind of bubble, a mystery yet to be solved.

"Don't worry," Katia said. "Grima will meet with you when it suits her. Tyra keeps her pretty busy. If it's important to the kennari, she will make it happen."

Otherwise, Reginn's life had settled into a reassuring cadence. She spent one day a week at Brenna's House, allowing Bryn more time to chart the lineages of children born on Eimyrja and identify what factors predicted the birth of a gifted child. Or, as he put it, to beat his head against the wall in a focused kind of way. When she inquired about Alva, Bryn told her that she'd been moved to a more secure, less traveled part of the healing campus.

At least once a week, she sat in with Naima and Erland and played until the wee hours. So many people had begun dropping by to listen that they eventually had to move it to a new location—a clearing in one of the nearby groves, where they were less likely to be seen. The day and time changed week to week in an attempt to keep the gatherings secret. Often there was ale lifted from the council house.

Gradually, Naima's reserve toward Reginn dissipated, like mist on a calm day, as their shared love of music drew them together. Sometimes Reginn felt like she had more in common with the sharp-tongued musician than she did with her fellow dedicates.

Instead of bringing Reginn to Modir Tyra's office as before, the bondi in the reception hall led Reginn into a room with a larger table. Tyra stood at the head of it, smiling. "Please," she said, gesturing to a chair. "Sit down. I've asked Elder Frodi to join us as well so that he can speak to your progress over these past months."

Reginn's knees went weak, and she nearly collapsed into the chair. It was all she could do not to vomit all over her portfolio. It was just her luck that Frodi would dry out enough to attend this meeting. There was no telling what he would say.

"Are you well, dottir?" Modir Tyra asked, brow furrowed in concern.

"I—I'm a—the thing is . . ."

Tyra smiled sympathetically. "There is no need to be nervous. Elder Frodi has had nothing but good things to say about your progress."

"He—he has?" Reginn croaked.

"Here," Tyra said. "Have some water." She poured water into a cup from a pitcher on the sideboard and set it in front of Reginn. Reginn gulped some down, practically choking on the lemon slices floating in it.

She took one deep breath, then another, pressing her hands against the tabletop to keep them from trembling. Gradually, her pulse slowed.

If you tell the truth, Tove always said, *then you don't have to keep track of your lies.*

"I'm sorry," Reginn said. "It's just that I don't want to disappoint you."

"I see very little chance of that," Tyra said.

Oh, I see a lot of chances, Reginn thought. Lots and lots of chances.

Slowly, methodically, Reginn unbuckled her flute case and set the instrument out on the table alongside the pages.

Tyra looked up, toward the doorway. "Ah. Here he is."

Frodi stalked in like the cock of the yard, his cool gaze brushing over Reginn and then sliding away.

Reginn stood and greeted him, smiling. "Elder Frodi! It's so good to see you! I did not know you would be here."

He blinked at her, found his footing, and said, "Dottir! Of course I would be here." He circled around to the farthest seat at the table and sat, still clinging to his staff with one hand.

"I brought some of the projects we've worked on," Reginn said brightly, spreading the sheets of vellum on the table. "Modir Tyra, these are my notes on the assigned readings."

Tyra pulled them toward her and scanned them. She looked up. "Good summaries," she said. She looked up at Frodi. "Did she do this on her own?"

Frodi cleared his throat. "Entirely," he said dryly.

"I also wrote down some of the spellsongs that I already knew," Reginn said, passing Tyra sheets covered with the jagged, up-and-down runework. "Elder Frodi helped me with some of the words I wasn't sure of. If there are any mistakes, it's my fault."

Tyra traced the lines with her forefinger. "I'm not noticing any on a first read," she said.

Reginn turned to Frodi. "Elder Frodi, did you bring any books that you want me to read from?" She was finding it difficult to think of this bookish young man as "Elder."

"No, dottir," Frodi said, his eyes narrowed as if he was trying to ferret out her game. "My thought was that Modir Tyra would choose to give you something fresh to read."

"That's a good idea," Tyra said. "I'll fetch something from my personal library. I'll be right back."

As soon as the door closed behind her, Frodi leaned toward Reginn until she could smell the liquor on him. "Why didn't you say anything to Tyra?" Frodi said. "She clearly believes that we've been meeting regularly."

"Look," Reginn said. "I'm a new student here. The last thing I needed was to be complaining about a council member. What good would it do? It's not like she could make you meet with me."

"It appears that you didn't suffer from my absence," Frodi said with cool disinterest.

"I could read and write a little when I came," Reginn lied. "Some of the other dedicates helped me out, and I've improved with practice." Reginn was acutely conscious of the blood rune cut into her thigh. Would Frodi recognize it if he saw it?

"Well then," Frodi said briskly. "It's all worked out."

Reginn thought about what Musa had said. "Why don't you come to the library anymore?"

Frodi flinched a little. "Who says I don't?"

"I've never seen you there," Reginn said.

"Unless you're sleeping in the stacks, you know nothing about my comings and goings. That said, I do prefer to work in my office, where it's quieter."

Quieter than an empty library? Reginn thought.

Just then, the door banged open, and Modir Tyra entered with an armload of leather-bound books.

"I'm sorry for the delay," she said. "It took me a while to locate some of these." She set them on the table in front of Reginn. "I thought you could choose from these now and read the rest at your leisure."

Reginn spread them out so that she could read the titles. "I've already read these two," she said. "They were in the library." She unearthed a small volume that looked to have been rebound several times. When she opened it, the pages appeared too fragile to touch, so thin that she could read the page underneath right through it, muddling the text.

"Good choice, dottir," Tyra said, smiling her approval.

"It's so faint that I can barely read it, though," Reginn said, squinting.

"Here. This may help." Flipping over one of Reginn's written pages, she slid it between two pages in the ancient book so that the top page was easier to decipher.

Reginn scanned the page, then looked up. "I've never heard this poem before."

Tyra snorted. "You would be unlikely to hear it in the Archipelago. That's one reason I chose it. It's from the Lost Texts of the Jotun."

Reginn read, transitioning into the lilting chant she used for sagas in verse.

> Heidin brought many gifts to Odin's seat:
> Garments woven of dew and dreams.
> Spellsongs to ensnare the stars.
> Spellwork to charm wolves and all of the beasts
> On the land and under the sea.
> Soft rains to quench the flames of Muspell and
> The warm sun to wake the flowers
> And trees and every good growing thing.
> She turned the barren worlds into a garden.
> These things she gave the gods.
> She offered good counsel, prophesy, and healing
> And brought the wisdom of the dead to serve them.
> The gods of Asgard were frightened.
> They shaded their eyes against her brilliance.
> Called her witch and sorceress.
> Feared her power.
> Repaid her largesse with treachery.
> Three times they slew her in Odin's Hall.
> They stabbed her and burned her, and yet
> Still she lived and took their bloody answer back to the Utangard.
> This was the beginning of the end of the world.

Reginn looked up from the manuscript. To her surprise, tears glittered in Modir Tyra's eyes and even Elder Frodi wore a look of awe.

"That was beautiful, dottir," Tyra said. "Your voice brings that story to life."

"It's not just the reading," Frodi said, "but the singing of it. I've only ever seen this on the page. Those lines were meant to be sung."

"Reginn summons the dead," Modir Tyra said. "That is why I guessed that you might be willing to work with her. Elder Frodi, thank you for coming and for helping Reginn grow and thrive. Now I should like to speak with Reginn in private."

Frodi rose, nodded to the two of them, his gaze lingering on Reginn for a long moment before he left.

"Dottir, I cannot tell you how proud I am," Modir Tyra said. "I thought that it would take much longer for you to master reading and writing. When the keeper and the council hear of this, they will have to agree that we made the right decision in rescuing you from the Archipelago."

"I hope so, Modir," Reginn murmured.

"I understand that you've been working at Brenna's House on a regular basis," Tyra said.

Skita, Reginn thought. I should have said something sooner. It is always better to tell your own story than to let somebody else tell it for you.

"Yes, Modir. That's something I wanted to discuss with you today. I've been helping at Brenna's House one day a week."

"Did Brodir Bryn ask for your help?"

"No, Modir," Reginn said. "As you know, I was a practicing healer in the Archipelago. I've always had an interest in helping others, so I asked Brodir Bryn if it would be all right to give him a hand, so that I don't lose the knowledge of it."

"That is generous of you, dottir, but it is unlikely you will have need of that skill here in New Jotunheim. We want you to continue to sharpen your skills in reading, writing, and music. But now it's time to put your knowledge of vardlokkur into practice. Healing the living is admirable, but speaking to the dead is a higher calling."

Reginn had known all along that this was coming, but still—some part of her must have hoped that it would disappear, like mist on the beach after sunrise. She honored the dead, but she was much more interested in the living.

"I understand," Reginn said. "I would still ask the favor of continuing to work at Brenna's. It—it makes me feel close to our founder, and it builds on the knowledge I have." She stopped, hoping she hadn't said too much, but she was determined to speak up for Bryn and secure permission to continue to work with him.

"Very well," Tyra said, "but we will need to revisit this if you are falling short of your benchmarks as we go forward. Tomorrow, we will begin our work in the temple catacombs."

"What are the catacombs?"

"They are caves and tunnels located among the roots of the Memory Tree. They are the resting place of those who came before us, including those who died in the Last Battle."

"All right," Reginn said.

"Meet me outside your dormitory tomorrow after the dagmal. Wear clothes that you don't mind getting dirty." Tyra smiled. "Now go and celebrate your first-quarter accomplishments."

39

WAYFINDING IN THE DARK

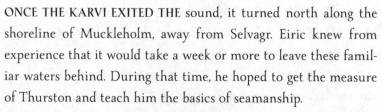

ONCE THE KARVI EXITED THE sound, it turned north along the shoreline of Muckleholm, away from Selvagr. Eiric knew from experience that it would take a week or more to leave these familiar waters behind. During that time, he hoped to get the measure of Thurston and teach him the basics of seamanship.

Liv appeared to have taken Thurston's measure from the moment they met, and yet they seemed to have entered into a tense armistice. It helped that Eiric had assigned them fixed stations in order to balance their craft. Thurston never said another word against her, but his eyes followed her constantly, as if he needed to know where she was at all times in order to prevent an ambush. Eiric found it immensely irritating, but Liv seemed to take it in stride.

Was Thurston smitten with her? Afraid of her? In awe of her? Did he have a problem with women in general or Liv in particular?

Thurston never seemed to sleep. Anytime of day or night, Eiric could look forward and see the former thrall's eyes glowing like embers through the darkness. That made it difficult to consult the sunstone in secret or have private conversations with Liv. As Rikhard had pointed out, it was a very small ship.

To say that Thurston was a hard worker was an understatement. He was tireless on the oars, willing to take whatever watch Eiric assigned to him, and seemed interested in learning more about navigation and managing the sails.

Almost too interested. Because of his lack of skills, he sometimes got in the way of the shrouds when they reefed the sails or tangled himself in the lines at critical times. But Eiric only had to correct him once.

He was a tireless bailer, too. No matter how tightly caulked and tarred, a clinker-built ship took on water, especially in heavy seas. With Thurston on the job, Eiric wouldn't describe it as bone dry, but as close to it as could be achieved in a small boat in the open sea. At least there wasn't water sloshing back and forth over their feet with every swell.

The first week, they enjoyed good weather and a fair wind as they sailed with their home island of Muckleholm visible to the left and seemingly endless ocean to the right. Despite the drama caused by his peculiar crew, Eiric felt the tensions of home draining from him.

It was always like this when he set sail in the spring.

Once, winters had been a cozy time of storytelling, boatbuilding and repairs, rope making, toolmaking, and wood carving. Liv and Sylvi would take up positions on either side of the massive upright loom, passing the stick shuttle and weaving sword back and forth between them, winding the new-made fabric onto the roller at the top, their voices lacing together, too.

For the past three years, he'd come home in the autumn to Sten's insults and brutal fists, Liv's fierce resistance and bursts of rebellion, and Sylvi's attempts to mediate among people who had no interest in compromise.

There followed a long winter of avoiding each other, punctuated by brief outbreaks of violence. As soon as the ice broke up in spring, Eiric made a quick exit to another season at sea.

Would you have been less eager to go to sea if things had been better at home?

Probably not. He'd always been eager to go to sea.

Would Sylvi have married Sten if you'd been a more dutiful son?

For all her life, Sylvi had been cursed with disappointing men.

To take his mind off his shortcomings, Eiric pulled a fishing line from his seabag and baited the hooks with bits of a baitfish he'd netted earlier in the day.

When he looked forward, he saw to his surprise that Thurston was finally sleeping, propped against a sea chest.

"Liv," Eiric said, gesturing toward the sail. Together they gripped the halyards, leaning back with their feet propped against a beam, gradually lowering the yard until the sail was low on the mast and so capturing very little wind. The ship gradually slowed.

After tying off the rigging, Eiric played the baited line out from the stern, wrapped it loosely around his hand, and waited. Before long he had ten large cod flopping around in a net.

When Eiric saw the channel opening that meant they'd reached the northern end of the island, he angled into shore in a sheltered harbor on the western side, where a freshwater stream descended to the bay in a series of pools and waterfalls. He and Liv knew the area from previous visits. It was a good place to beach a karvi with a limited crew. Since the northern end of Muckleholm was relatively unsettled, and the turbulent waters ahead limited an approach by sea, it was unlikely they would encounter any outlaws seeking a quick taking by land or sea. It was a good place to replenish their water supply and camp overnight.

"Why are we stopping?" Thurston said, awakening and sitting up with a jerk. "We're not there yet, are we?"

"Hardly," Liv said, hiking up her skirts and belting them around her waist. "This is a good stopping point." Picking up her staff, she vaulted over the side, landing in knee-deep water. "I would like to eat some fresh fish and greens before we leave land behind for a while. And from the growing stench, I can assure you that everyone on board can use a bath."

With that, she waded onto the beach and began collecting driftwood for a fire.

Eiric followed with the fish, smacking them soundly against a stone until they lay still. He laid them out on a flat rock, gutted them and prepared them for cooking by threading them onto sharpened sticks.

When the fire was burning well, Liv announced that she was hiking upstream to bathe. She would collect forest greens on her way back.

That left Eiric and Thurston. Eiric sent Thurston to fetch the empty water barrels from the ship. They refilled them from the stream, then rolled them down to the water so they could wrestle them over the gunwales and back into the boat. It was hard work, and soon Eiric was sweating, despite the cool onshore breeze. By the time all the barrels were back on board, Liv still hadn't returned, so Eiric and Thurston sat down by the fire.

Long moments passed, with neither one of them speaking. Thurston might be a hard worker, but a conversationalist he was not. By turns, he sounded arrogant as any lord and then twitchy as a rat in a room full of cats.

Liv seemed to know everything she needed to know about him, but Eiric had been asking casual questions, trying to ferret out more information about him. Even when pressed, he had little to say.

Today, Thurston was jumpier than usual, his fingers beating a tattoo on his knee. He'd look up the path Liv had taken, then toward the ship on the beach, back to Eiric, and then quickly away.

It was almost as if he finally had something to say but couldn't bring himself to spit it out.

Eiric poked at the fire, wondering whether to start grilling the fish or wait until Liv came back. Or recaulk the seam below the gunwales on the starboard side that always seemed to take in water. Or reinforce the shroud on the port side that appeared to be fraying. He could do any of those things, but what he wanted to do was sit and stare into the flames.

"Were you born here, Halvorsen?" Thurston said abruptly. "Have you ever lived anywhere else?" It was the first time he'd expressed any interest in Eiric beyond his usefulness as a means of transportation.

"I was born at Sundgard, and I've lived there all my life," Eiric said. "Why do you ask?"

"I wondered if you have ever had the experience of feeling out of place. Of being a stranger."

"A man doesn't have to leave home to feel like a stranger," Eiric said. Then, recalling that people often ask a question that they want to answer themselves, said, "Where are you from originally? Were you born into thralldom, or were you taken in a raid?"

Thurston looked at him straight on for a moment, then seemed to choose one question to answer. "I come from a place called Muspelheim," he said. "Have you heard of it?"

Eiric *had* heard the word, in some of Bjorn's tales about the old gods. It was the land of fire, home of fire demons and other such. But he was unaware of any contemporary place by that name. "In the old stories, that's the land of fire," he said. "One of several worlds that I cannot remember the names of."

"Correct," Thurston said. "There were nine altogether. Muspelheim played a role in both the creation and destruction of the worlds. Now it no longer exists."

Eiric squinted at him, surprised that Thurston would feel the need to tutor him on the myths of the past. That was probably more words than Thurston had said during their entire time at sea. And it was on a completely unexpected topic. "It seems odd that anyone would name a town after Muspelheim," he said. "It never sounded like a place I'd want to live."

"I suppose that is why there were nine worlds," Thurston said. "I'm not terribly fond of this one."

"Everyone feels that way, at one time or another," Eiric said, confused by this unexpected heart-to-heart.

"You cannot begin to imagine how I feel," Thurston said with a withering look. Arrogant Thurston was back.

"Where is Muspelheim?" Eiric said.

"As I told you," Thurston said, his face a mask of impatience. "It is nowhere, it is gone, and I am here now, against my will."

"You volunteered for this trip," Eiric said, irritated, "for reasons of your own. You practically begged to sign on as crew."

Thurston stood and paced back and forth. "I don't mean that I am here with *you* against my will. I mean that I am here in the Midlands, where I have to contend with Midlanders like you."

Eiric was beginning to think that his new crew member was seriously afflicted. Possibly delusional. His axe was within easy reach, but he still couldn't tell whether he was in danger or not. "Why are you telling me this now?"

"Because your systir is a volva—a witch—and she sees through my illusion. She knows exactly what I am, and she is going to tell you sooner or later."

"Your . . . illusion?" Eiric couldn't help looking up the hill where Liv had gone. If Liv had recognized Thurston for what he was, then why hadn't she said anything?

In fact, she had. She'd told him that Thurston was not what he seemed but did not object to bringing him along.

Speaking of Liv, she should be back by now.

"I am a son of Muspell," Thurston said. "Some call us eldrjotun–fire giants, or thursen–fire demons." He extended his arms and gave a little shake, as if discarding a cloak. To Eiric's astonishment, he transformed before his eyes, shedding his red hair, blue eyes, and bulky body until someone entirely different stood before him. He had sooty black hair and black eyes, and his lean body was clad entirely in black, down to his black leather gloves. His only decoration was the silver buckle at his waist and the pendants at his throat.

Most importantly, he was no stranger. He was Asger Eldr, the fire demon who had been Reginn's master. Who had tortured her in front of him. Who Eiric suspected had set fire to the alehouse in an attempt to murder them both.

Reginn's parting words came back to him. *Just know that this is the first time a man has touched me and it hasn't caused me pain.*

Eiric gripped his axe and stood. "Tell me why I shouldn't cut your heart out right now."

"That would be a mistake."

"Really?" Eiric said. "I don't see a downside."

"Because you need my help."

"When I weigh whatever help you can give me against the pleasure of killing you, it's not a hard choice."

"Think it through, coaster. Our interests coincide, at least temporarily."

"I don't see that our interests coincide at all," Eiric said. "As far as I know, I have nothing in common with fire demons."

Asger sighed. "We both want to reach the Grove, for different reasons. You are sailing on behalf of Jarl Rikhard in an effort to save your farm. I am going in search of my property. The witches set fire to the alehouse and kidnapped my thrall from Langvik the night we met."

Eiric rolled his eyes. "You expect me to believe that *spinners* set fire to the alehouse?"

Asger nodded. "Perhaps you saw their ship in the harbor—the one flying the blue rune banner? It seems they'd had their eye on my meyla for some time."

Eiric *did* remember seeing such a ship in the harbor that night, not far from Rikhard's longship.

"When I saw that the alehouse had caught fire, I raced back there and searched for Reginn, but could not find her. Not long after, she was seen being forced aboard the spinners' ship."

"So you're claiming that Reginn is at the Grove?" Hope welled up in Eiric—hope that Reginn was alive, that she'd not burned to death in an alehouse the night they'd met. That maybe their story wasn't over.

Hero.

Another memory was coming back to Eiric, a scrap of conversation, something Rikhard had said when explaining why he'd decided to send an expedition to find Eimyrja.

On their last visit here, the spinners kidnapped a young girl—a thrall belonging to a colleague of mine.

Who would have been in a better position to see this alleged kidnapping than Rikhard, whose ship was anchored nearby?

The last piece of the puzzle clunked into place, revealing a clear picture—that Eiric had been a fool. *You could have been sailing on Fossegrim in a comfortable cabin with a full crew, but you were determined to go it alone in order to maintain control. So Rikhard simply planted a spy within your skeleton crew.*

"How long have you been working for Rikhard Karlsen?" Eiric demanded.

"I do not work *for* the jarl," Asger said stiffly. "I work *with* him, temporarily, because we have common goals. Just as you and I do."

There was some logic to what the demon said, but it didn't matter. This voyage was dangerous enough without having to watch his back the entire time. "Explain to me now why my systir and I shouldn't sail away and leave you here to find your way back to Selvagr or wherever it is that you den up," Eiric said, testing the edge of his axe with his finger. Another stupid move—it drew blood.

This last threat seemed to gain Asger's attention. "Look, Halvorsen, before you make a hasty decision, I suggest we—"

Eiric never heard whatever it was he was going to suggest, because just then, somewhere above them on the hillside, Liv screamed, piercing him all the way to the bone.

40

THE CATACOMBS

"WHY ARE YOU DRESSED LIKE that?" Shelby said when Reginn sat down at the upper-school table for the dagmal the next morning.

"I'm going to be working with Modir Tyra today," Reginn said. "She told me to wear old clothes. I don't really have any old clothes, so I got these from the ragbag in the laundry." She wore battered old breeches that she'd hacked off at the knee and a loose-fitting bondi tunic. She'd wrapped her hair in a scarf.

"Are they finally letting you out of the library?" Grima said.

"Why don't I ever see any of *you* in the library?" Reginn said.

Katia, Bryn, Stian, and Erland were also sharing the upper-school table, but nobody spoke up right away.

"I used to go, and library staff would read to me," Erland said. "There's never anybody there these days."

"If you come while I'm there, I'll read to you," Reginn said. "I need the practice. What about the rest of you?"

They looked at each other. "What's the point?" Shelby said. "I know the basics—history, science, and all. We've gone beyond all that in our specialized vocations. I can learn more out in the forests and gardens than I can in a dismal library. The only thing growing in the library is mold. Anyway, I have work to do."

"You know how I've been spending my time," Bryn said, shrugging. "Can't do that work in the library."

"Like most house spirits, the vaettir in the library are cranky," Katia said, wrinkling her nose. "I would be, too, if I had to stay inside all the time."

"Isn't that what house spirits do?" Reginn said.

"That doesn't mean they're happy," Katia said.

"It's not house spirits," Grima said. "I hear the library is haunted. A dedicate died there years ago."

"She probably read herself to death," Shelby said. "Crawled into a book and never came out."

"Stian?"

"The same. Look, there aren't many of us these days, and the next class is even smaller. The bondi help as much as they can, but there are some tasks that require magic. That is why Modir Tyra uses her gift to give us a head start—to teach us what we need to know so that we can go forward. That way we can be productive in our vocations earlier. We've all been working since we were ten. Some of us spend our days on the out islands."

The out islands. The council had wanted to send her there right away, but Amma Inger had objected.

"But there are so many books," Reginn said. "So much history. So many stories. So much to learn. Aren't you afraid you're missing out?"

Katia laughed. "Listen to you! You sound like a new convert to the religion we all grew up with. Now you're preaching to the faithful."

"Maybe when we're older there'll be time to read books," Shelby said. Which brought to mind Reginn's own reaction when Modir Tyra told her that she needed to learn to read. So much had changed in just a few months.

"Speaking of haunted," Reginn said. "Today we're going to the catacombs."

Bryn looked astonished. Everyone else looked blank.

"What is that?" Katia said. "I've never heard of it."

"It's a complex of tunnels under the Memory Tree," Bryn said. "Higher-ups at the Grove have been buried there for centuries. I went there once to examine remains, to try to figure out if there was evidence of a change that would explain why the founders produced lineages of gifted children and we do not."

"What did you find?" Grima said.

"I found out that I don't know what I'm doing when it comes to mining secrets from bones," Bryn said. "I'm better with people who are alive."

"I don't know what I'm doing, either," Reginn said. She stood. "Wish me luck."

Modir Tyra was standing outside the dining hall when Reginn walked through the doors. "Well, dottir," she said, looking her up and down with raised eyebrows, "it seems you took me at my word."

Reginn's cheeks burned. "Well, yes, Modir, I generally do unless I have reason not to."

She laughed. "I deserved that." Tyra looked as polished as always. The only difference was that she was wearing tall boots and a heavy canvas coat over her tunic and trousers. "In honor of your efforts, I'll see how much of a mess we can get into. Follow me."

Reginn followed the headmistress along one of the main walkways through the temple campus, eventually turning onto a narrower path that threaded through several groves of trees until it reached a massive, many-branched tree that stood on the cliff overlooking the sea, lording it over a circle of smaller trees.

The tree bristled with ribbons rippling in the winds from the sea, some tattered and so faded it was difficult to tell what colors they had been in the first place.

"This has been known as the Memory Tree since the founding of the temple," Modir Tyra said. "When members of the faculty died, dedicates tied ribbons to the branches, each inscribed with a memory of that person—something he or she had taught them, or accomplished to the benefit of the temple. We've continued doing that to this day. Sweethearts add ribbons swearing undying love to each other and take them down when things go sour."

A cluster of seemingly new, bright red ribbons caught Reginn's eye. She pulled one down and read the message.

Freedom for the bondi

She pulled down another.

Death to the council

Wordlessly, she handed them to Modir Tyra, who read them, lips tight, and stuffed them into her pocket. "It seems that all kinds of messages are posted here."

Between two of the massive root knees, a stone entryway had been built. Tyra unlocked the sturdy wooden door with a large key hanging at her belt.

"Watch your head," she said. "And be careful. These steps are steep."

Indeed they were. Reginn had to turn around and descend the steps like a ladder down a stone shaft.

When she reached the floor of the chamber, she stepped away from the foot of the staircase and looked around.

"Wyrd of the founder!" she said. They were standing in the anteroom of what resembled an underground palace. Marble formations extended like pillars from ceiling to floor, glistening with the damp, faintly illuminated from within. Massive roots lined the walls and descended into the earth beneath. Reginn could hear water running somewhere nearby. Pale stems formed a tangled canopy overhead, resembling the interlaced fingers of the dead, clutching bright red berries. The scent of old stone and decay filled her nose.

"Strangely beautiful, isn't it?" Modir Tyra said.

"I've never seen anything like it," Reginn said. Kneeling, she reached for a berry that had fallen to the floor.

"Don't touch that," Tyra said sharply.

Reginn jerked her hand away. "What is it?" she said, still on her knees, studying it.

"It's called mourner's tears," Tyra said. "Or death berries. It's a fungus that grows only in the presence of the dead. Every part of the plant is toxic, the berries most of all."

Reginn leaned in close, so she could sniff at it. It had a sweet scent, like a berry might. It seemed familiar, but she couldn't recall where she might have come across it before.

"It smells like it's good to eat," she said.

Tyra laughed. "That guarantees that there will be plenty more hosts," she said.

"I wouldn't think you would allow poisonous plants in Eimyrja," Reginn said.

"Sometimes," Tyra said, "poisons are useful. Come."

Reginn followed the headmistress through a doorway into a smaller room. This room was lined with niches containing caskets made of gold and silver. Each was easily worth a fortune, to Reginn's practiced eye.

"The earliest founders are buried closest to the tree, in these first two rooms," Tyra said. She pointed toward a passageway that led deeper into the cavern. "More recent tombs are that way.

"I would ask you to stay in this room for now. In particular, focus on this one." She led the way to the far end of the room. The entire wall was occupied by a tomb, striking in its simplicity.

Lamps burned on either side. Fresh flowers were scattered over the altar in front, along with a vase of elder orchids.

Stone benches were arranged in a semicircle around the tomb.

Engraved into the stone was a name.

Brenna Wayfinder, Founding Modir

"*Oh!*" Reginn said. "It's the grave of the founder." She brushed her fingers over the stone. "Who tends this?"

"It is among the duties of Amma Inger," Tyra said. "She has watched over this grave ever since the death of the founding modir."

For a moment, Reginn thought she must have misunderstood. "How is that possible?"

"The founder bequeathed to the amma an unusually long life," Tyra said.

"Oh. I see," Reginn said, though she didn't really. "How should I begin?"

"For now, dottir, I want you to sing vardlokkur to Modir Brenna and see if she will answer," Tyra said.

Reginn couldn't help but think that the founder would not be pleased to be disturbed for no good reason. It seemed as if, even now, she could feel a presence behind the stone. A disapproving presence. A spirit that wanted to be left alone.

"Could I maybe start with someone less important?" Reginn said, her voice quavering.

"I don't want to make you uncomfortable, dottir," Modir Tyra said. "It's just that I believe that the founder may have the answers we need in these critical times. One of our students was able to reach Modir Brenna many years ago. I'm hoping it can happen again. I'm afraid that if we don't act quickly, the line of gifted may die out completely."

"I'm sorry, Modir," Reginn said. "Of course, I'll do the best I can."

The headmistress settled onto one of the benches, her staff in the crook of her arm, as if awaiting immediate results.

"If she should answer," Reginn said, "is there anything in particular you would like me to ask?"

"Should she answer, take it slowly," Modir Tyra said. "I do, however, have a special interest in the runes of magic."

41

KEEPER

WHEN REGINN LEFT THE FOUNDER'S tomb, hoarse and discouraged after three hours of fruitless singing, she felt the need to talk to somebody. She considered returning to the dining hall, in the hopes of finding some of the other dedicates there. But those who worked in the out islands often didn't return for the midday meal.

Besides, she was afraid that she would sound like she was complaining. They never complained—Bryn had come closest—and every one of them had made a point of telling her how lucky she was to be here. She *was* lucky—she knew it—to be in this garden of a place with plenty to eat and no Asger Eldr to worry about.

Musa was the only one she could speak her mind to. If anything, the library mouse was more cynical than she was.

What did it say about her that she had more in common with a library hermit than her fellow dedicates?

As always, the library appeared to be deserted. Reginn squinted against the sunlight streaming in through dusty windows. "Musa?" she said, just in case the mouse might want to make an appearance. There was no answer.

Reginn sighed, then climbed the steps to the bovine niche. She found three books, their covers battered and darkened with age.

The top one had a title emblazoned on the leather cover: *Vardlokkur–Call and Response*.

These must have been the volumes of ancient spellsongs Musa had mentioned.

Reginn carried them down and set them on the table.

Next, she climbed to the wool niche. Reaching inside, her groping fingers found a roll of vellum, crackling with age. As she withdrew the bundle, flakes of dried leather powdered the landing.

A smaller scrap of vellum was bound around it.

Carefully, she carried the roll back to the table and flattened the note so that she could read it.

> *R– There is a magical lock on these to keep anyone without the key from reading them. That tells me that they might be important. I thought you, of all people, might have the tools to unlock them. –M*
>
> *P.S. Don't let anyone see you reading these. Destroy this note after you read it.*

Musa was being cautious, as usual. Reginn pushed the note into a lantern and watched while it burned to ash.

She untied the string binding the pages together and slipped off the vellum wrapping. The pages inside were old–very old, it seemed.

They also appeared to be totally blank.

Reginn brushed her fingers over the blank pages, mystified. She'd heard of invisible inks that became visible when run over a flame, but Musa had mentioned a key.

Why would Musa think Reginn, of all people, could unlock them?

Then something the library mouse had said came back to her.

Don't ever tell anyone here that you know those runes.

The kennari had said that she had a special interest in the magical runes.

Maybe Musa thought that the runes were the key to unlocking these pages.

But which one?

Reginn set out the jar of ink and boar-bristle brushes she'd been using to practice her writing. Pulling one of the blank sheets toward her, she brushed a symbol onto a corner of the vellum. Thurisaz—useful for breaking bonds and fetters.

Nothing happened.

Only a dozen more to go.

Reginn wondered if she was wasting her time. For all she knew, the runes had nothing to do with it. But her other choice was to dig into the volumes of spellsongs.

What she really wanted to do was talk to Musa.

So she soldiered on. What else? Dagaz, rune of awakening and enlightenment? She brushed the ink onto the vellum, enjoying her mastery of these familiar strokes compared with her struggles with the mundane.

The page was as blank as before.

Now she tried Kenaz—a rune of learning and teaching, known for bringing light into darkness.

She stared, wide-eyed, as letters began to surface on the page, like bubbles from a deep pool. Reginn waited until they organized themselves into lines of text. It appeared to be a journal entry. There was a date at the top.

Laboriously, she read the text, tracing each line with her finger.

New Jotunheim, year 1, month 6, day 23
Negotiations have broken down again. Most on Eimyrja are happy we are here and are pleased with the changes we have made already. They are

excited about the prospect of the healing halls and the ability of spinner magic to make a positive difference in their lives.

What the residents won't agree to are the changes we deem necessary to protect us from enemies in the Archipelago and elsewhere. They are seafaring folk, accustomed to sailing wherever they like and trading with whomever they want. We've explained the risk of alerting coasters from the Archipelago to our presence. We've assured them that there is no longer a reason to leave the islands, that we will provide everything they need, but they continue to resist. I have asked the Council of Elders to have patience, that the people will come to understand why we need to remain cloaked in secrecy until we are stronger. Some on the council are openly advocating for coercive measures. I have told them that I want no part of that. –B.H.

That was all. Who was B.H.?

When Reginn unlocked the next page, she found that it was dated several years later.

N.J., year 6, month 5, day 18
While I continue to express my concerns about the measures implemented by the council to manage the people of Eimyrja, there is some reason for optimism. The healing halls are finally open, and our first class of dedicates has begun to treat patients. At first, they will be tending their fellow students and faculty only, but soon we will open our doors to everyone in New Jotunheim. My goal, of course, is for Eimyrja to become a center for healing and scholarship for the Midlands, including the Archipelago. Those of us who have been gifted with magic have the right to protect ourselves, but also the obligation to use our gifts to benefit all of humankind. –B.H.

So, Reginn thought. It seemed that, at least at the founding of the Grove, healing was a priority. To someone whose initials were B.H. Reginn shuffled that page to the bottom of the stack. She was reaching for her brush again when someone spoke.

"Systir Reginn. What are you doing?"

Reginn was so startled that she dropped her brush, spattering ink across the next blank page. When she looked up to see who had spoken, her heart froze in her chest.

It was the keeper.

"Amma Inger!" Reginn yelped. Desperately, she blotted at the spilled ink with her sleeve.

The keeper cocked her head, frowning. "Leave it be, dottir. Our servants in the laundry will not thank you for using your sleeve as a washrag."

"I'm sorry, Highest," Reginn said, still flustered. "I didn't realize anyone else was here."

"I was looking for Elder Frodi," the keeper said, scanning the aisles between the shelves and peering up at the iron staircase.

"Elder Fr— He's not here," Reginn said, leaning forward over the stack of pages, resting her arms on top to hide them.

"I can see that," the keeper said. To Reginn's alarm, she pulled up a chair and sat across the table from her, as if she planned to stay awhile.

This was the first time Reginn had seen her up close—the first time she realized how very old she was. Her hair was a white cloud around her face, her face cobwebbed with lines, the skin on her hands loose over bone. Her eyes, though—her eyes were like sapphires set on either side of her beak of a nose. A small cluster of purple elderflower orchids was pinned over her right ear.

She wore two amulets—one a figure of a woman, carved from bone, worn to a sheen from constant fingering. The other was a kynstone pendant similar to those worn by Tyra and Elder Skarde. On her right hand, she wore a massive ring set with a garnet that sparkled in the light from the windows.

"Highest," Reginn began.

"You may call me Amma, if you like," the keeper said.

"Amma. I—I've been spending a lot of time in the library since I arrived, and I know my way around. Is there something I could help you with?"

"You could begin by answering my question," the keeper said. "What are you working on?"

"Oh. I'm—ah—practicing my writing," Reginn said, flattening her sweating hands on the vellum, hoping that none of the unlocked pages were showing. "I've been writing down some of the songs I already know."

"Could I see?" Amma reached for the top sheet.

"There's nothing to see yet," Reginn said, holding the pages in place. "I was just beginning. Before that, I was reading." She picked up one of the books Musa had set out for her and leafed through it. "It's a book of vardlokkur—songs I haven't seen before. Modir Tyra thought that I would be interested in them, being a musician myself."

"I remember," Amma Inger said a little wistfully. "You played the flute so beautifully in Langvik—and now at the concerts in the Grove."

At the concerts in the— Reginn stared at the keeper, mouth open but empty of words.

"Don't look so panicked, dottir," Amma Inger said, laughing. "I know more than people think I do. The bondi know that I am very fond of music. And your voice is magic in itself."

"It is kind of you to say that," Reginn croaked. Ordinarily, she might have enjoyed basking in the keeper's praise, but right now she just wanted her to leave so that she could gather her thoughts. Did Naima know that the keeper knew about the concerts?

"Music was my gift," the keeper said. Then pressed her lips

together as if she hadn't meant to reveal that.

"Really?" Reginn said, puzzled as she recalled the storm the matriarch had raised against Rikhard's longship. She opened her mouth to ask the question, but Amma Inger spoke first.

"I am also a weatherspinner," she said, "as you may have noticed when we escaped the jarl's longship. I conjure boundaries and barriers of energy." She paused. "Most of the gifted have more than one way to express their power. It's a difficult choice sometimes."

"But . . . you don't make music anymore?"

"No," she said. "Music is a luxury that I can no longer indulge. I am stretched too thin."

"Really?" Reginn persisted, since it was obvious the keeper regretted the loss. "If you love music, it still seems like you–"

"You offer too many opinions, dottir, about matters that are beyond your understanding," the keeper said.

Reginn knew when to back off. "I'm sorry," she said. "That's what Modir Tyra says, too. It's just that I am trying to learn. Back in the– the Archipelago, I did a little of everything. I sang; I told stories; I was a healer; I did foretelling." She shrugged. She couldn't help thinking of Bryn and his struggles to meet the council's expectations and still do his heart's work.

"I'm surprised that you remember so much about your life before," Modir Inger said, her eyes narrowing. "Tyra's treatments are generally very thorough. I would have expected her to leave you a bit more . . . focused on the future."

"I asked her to spare my music and my–my other skills. I wanted to make sure that they would not be affected."

Amma Inger fingered her kynstone amulet, which ignited, resembling molten gold flowing through her closed hand.

"Where did the kynstones come from?" Reginn said into the awkward silence.

"They were given to us by Brenna Half-Foot, the founder of the Temple at the Grove, so that we could identify the gifted at a young age."

"*Half-Foot?* I thought her byname was Wayfinder," Reginn said.

"She always went by Half-Foot," the keeper said. "It was only after she died that the council decided to polish her memory by calling her Wayfinder. Brenna would have hated that. She always told me that her disability brought her closer to the people she intended to serve."

"What was she like?" Reginn said. "The founder, I mean."

The keeper considered this. "Her lineage mingled Vanir and jotun bloodlines. She was . . . so very powerful and wise. And yet she was someone who believed that there was good in everyone."

"She was a goddess?" Reginn said.

Modir Inger shrugged. "The Midlands are full of mixed-blood refugees from the destruction of the Nine Worlds. Brenna always felt guilt for the gods' repeated attacks on Jotunheim."

"What do you mean?" Reginn said. "I know the gods and the jotnar were always fighting with each other, but–"

"It was the jotnar who taught the elements of magic to the Vanir gods, who betrayed them to their Aesir enemies," Modir Inger said bluntly.

Reginn frowned. Tove had schooled her in the legends as they had once been passed down to her. None of this fit with what she knew. "But didn't the Vanir god Gullveig bring the gods the secrets of magic?"

"Gullveig was the name the Aesir gods gave her," Amma Inger said. "Her real name was Heidin. She was a jotun volva, who came to Odin's Hall seeking peace at the behest of the Vanir gods. The Aesir gods responded by burning and stabbing her three times. That started the war among the gods. Eventually they made their peace and joined forces against Jotunheim. They knew that the jotnar were the only ones who could compete with them for power."

"But wasn't it Odin who hung from the world tree and so found the secrets of the runes of magic?" Reginn persisted.

Amma Inger snorted. "How does that even make sense? Their skalds didn't put much effort into that story." She cleared her throat. "No. Odin stole the runes from the Norns, who were jotun. The world was built from the flesh of Ymir, a jotun. Magic is rooted in our tradition. It was Brenna's intention to create a sanctuary for the gifted, for those with jotun blood. It was her hope that we could prosper here and eventually become a resource to the world. However, her choice of location was strategic."

"What do you mean?" Reginn's head spun as she tried to reconcile the stories she knew with what the amma was telling her.

"New Jotunheim includes Vigrid, the site of the last battle of Ragnarok, and Ithavoll, the traditional gathering place of the gods. The Asgardian texts predict that after Ragnarok, the surviving gods will return to Ithavoll. Our presence here ensures that the return of the gods to Ithavoll would not go unchallenged."

"But—the gods are dead," Reginn said.

"Maybe not," Amma Inger said. "That is why it is so important to be able to read the old texts."

Her seasoned face settled into lines of sorrow. "Brenna did her best to save us, but she always allowed us free will. And so we disappointed her, at the end. I will always regret that."

"How did you disappoint her?"

"She had no wish to take revenge on the barbarians, or the descendants of the Asgardians, nor did she wish to create a new race of gods herself. Some of the jotnar had other ideas. After all we'd been through, they wanted to punish those responsible. Some saw no reason why we should deny power to ourselves. A deep evil took root here, fueled by greed and a lust for power. It continues to this day. If something isn't done, we'll have a repeat of the final battle right here."

Reginn found herself wishing that she'd never gotten into this conversation with this old woman, with her dire warnings and gloomy words. Reginn had come to the Grove to escape the dangers of Muckleholm. Now Amma Inger was shoveling onto her shoulders a load of worry that she wasn't strong enough to bear. It made her want to put her hands over her ears and sing tavern songs until the keeper left.

Abruptly, the keeper said, "Has the kennari mentioned raising the dead?"

Reginn licked her lips. "Not in so many words," she said.

Amma Inger released a long breath. "She will," she said. "Be very careful when she does, dottir. The dead are best left in peace."

Reginn opened her mouth, and the words flooded out. "Amma— I'm a new dedicate, just trying to catch up with everyone else. I'm not confident in my gift. Why are you telling me this? You should tell someone with the power to make things right."

"Systir Reginn, forgive me," the keeper said. "I thought you understood. That is exactly what I'm doing." She stood amid a rustle of cloth, pulled free her pendant, and extended it toward Reginn.

It glowed—like light through comb honey. Or water rich with oak tannins. The finest, clearest amber from the east.

"I've never seen anything like this."

"What does it mean?" Reginn said.

"It means that if anyone can save the world, it is you."

She tucked away the amulet and smiled sadly. "I hope that before I die, I can hear you play the flute again."

42

NEVER DO A DEAL
WITH A DEMON

THE SOUND OF LIV'S SCREAM was still reverberating in Eiric's ears as he charged up the hillside, axe in hand. His systir was not a screamer by nature, and he could tell from the mix of anger, fear, and desperation in the sound that he might already be too late.

He'd never had trouble here before, but it had been a year since his last visit. A lot could happen in a year. Possible disasters streamed through his mind—wolves, giant serpents, trolls, human monsters of all kinds.

Liv screamed again as he leaped over fallen trees and scrambled over boulders, sometimes running in the streambed itself. As long as she was screaming, he knew that she was alive. He thought he knew where she would be.

Why hadn't he gone looking for her sooner?

Because Liv bridled at any kind of nannying by her little brodir.

Finally, he broke into a clearing where a small pool had been created by a rockfall years ago.

"Look out, brodir," Liv cried. He heard a sound behind him and instinctively dodged aside. Something massive struck him a glancing blow, still all but knocking him off his feet. He breathed in the rank predator scent, caught a glimpse of matted fur, and heard growling and the snapping of teeth as the animal bit down on air instead of flesh.

He swung around to face the beast, putting his back to the rocky outcropping that framed the trail. Issvagr. Ice wolves. There were two of them—wolves the size of ponies with silvery coats and black ears and muzzles. It was said that they were descended from Fenrir, the wolf who terrorized the gods. There were several packs on Muckleholm Island, but he'd never seen any in this area before.

"How do you like our puppies, boy?" somebody said with a coarse laugh.

Eiric looked beyond the circling wolves to see a pack of men gathered around the spring. Liv stood among them in her underdress, hair still wet from washing, her arms pinioned by men on either side, one of them holding a knife to her throat. One of her eyes was purpling, and blood was streaming from her nose. Her pendant and staff were missing.

She'd done some damage, too. One of the men was sitting on a fallen tree, pressing his hands against a gut wound, contemplating the blood flowing over his fingers with mournful confusion.

Eiric had heard that the ice wolves could be semi-domesticated—until they weren't. Many who thought to use them to protect a herd of sheep from other predators had learned that lesson the hard way.

Maybe they'd be sorry in the end, but that didn't help his current situation.

"We're glad you showed up," the man with the knife said. "We wanted to save the bitch for later, but we promised the pups some supper."

Maybe it was the word *supper*, or maybe the man gave some sort of signal, but one of the wolves sprang at Eiric, silent as smoke. He raised his axe to distract the beast, waited till the last second, then shoved his dagger between the wolf's ribs as he sprang. He would have gone down under the wolf's weight but for the wall of stone behind him.

They ended in an unhappy embrace, the wolf's massive paws on his shoulders, Eiric ducking his head away and raising his arm to prevent his face from being chewed off. The wolf's teeth ripped open the skin on his arm, then grazed the top of his head, and he could feel blood running down his neck and under his collar.

He twisted the blade in order to do as much damage as possible, until he lost his hold on the blood-slippery hilt.

Desperately, he whacked away at the wolf's back with his axe, slicing at it over and over. At first, the wolf scarcely seemed to notice until it finally rolled backward and retreated, limping badly, taking the dagger with it. That left Eiric with only the axe in his hand and at least one more wolf to contend with.

If only I had my sword and my shield, Eiric thought.

If wishes were fishes . . .

He scooped up a large branch and swung just as the other wolf attacked. It struck the wolf in mid-leap and sent it flying in the other direction. The wolf got up, seemingly unhurt, and began to creep forward again, ears back, teeth bared, hackles raised.

"Halvorsen," a soft voice said behind him. Asger Eldr came up beside him and stood, arms crossed, surveying the scene. "Who are these men?"

"Vargr," Eiric said. "Outlaws. They've been exiled from their home villages for committing a serious crime." It did not escape him that he would have been in the same situation had Rikhard not intervened to pay the blood price.

As the wolf came closer, Eiric raised his axe again. But the wolf stopped in its tracks, sniffing the air, its yellow eyes fixed on Asger.

It stood frozen for a long moment, then arched its back, tucked its tail, and fled.

"Where are you going, you coward?" a man with a red beard shouted, flinging a rock after the animal.

"It seems my systir is right, eldrjotun," Eiric said. "You do need a shower."

"I have this effect even when freshly bathed," Asger said, shrugging. "Most animals are rightly afraid of fire."

The wounded wolf limped away, too, following his companion, but collapsed in a heap before it made it to the woods. The bearded man knelt next to the downed wolf. "She's dead!" he cried, glaring at Eiric and Asger.

The dispatch of the wolves resulted in a shouting match among the outlaws regarding what to do next.

The blademan had an idea. "Drop your weapons," he said to Eiric, "or I'll cut the bitch's throat."

"Don't you do it, brodir," Liv said. "Kill these vermin, and I will sing your praises in Helgafjell. Surrender, and I will haunt you the rest of your days."

"Shut up," the blademan said, grabbing a fistful of her hair and yanking her head back, brandishing the knife before her eyes. "You're ugly now, but you could be uglier."

"Here's your problem," Eiric said, wiping his bloody axe against his sleeve. "If we give up our weapons, you'll murder us and sell my systir into slavery when you're done with her. On the other hand, if you cut her throat, then we will kill you all and leave you for the ravens to feast on."

"*You* . . . will kill all of *us*," one of them sneered, leaning on his spear. He was missing an eye, an ear, and most of his teeth. "Who? You and your scrawny friend?"

"It looks to me like you're not very good at fighting," Eiric said, tugging at his ear. "You should take up another trade before you lose a piece that you can't do without."

For a moment, the outlaw was speechless before the explosion came. "I'll cut you in pieces so small the ravens won't bother."

"As a peacemaker, you leave a lot to be desired," Asger said.

"I never pretended to be a peacemaker," Eiric retorted.

"If we work together, we can save your systir," Asger murmured.

Eiric glanced back at him. "Is that so?"

"I will take the knife away, and you'll kill the blademan. Then we'll finish the rest."

"Sounds easy enough," Eiric said, making no effort to hide his skepticism. "How do you propose to take the knife before he murders Liv?" He looked the demon up and down. "And why would you come to a fight without weapons?"

"I left the flaming sword at home," Asger said. "It draws far too much attention. But I have weapons, and I won't fail. But first I must have your word that if we survive, you will take me the rest of the way to Eimyrja."

"And then what?"

"Your obligation to me ends there, if that's what you want."

"What are you two muttering about?" the blademan said. "This shouldn't be a hard decision."

"We're laying a small bet on final body count," Eiric said. "I say I should be able to count the wolf, but he disagrees." He shrugged. "If you're impatient, you can always attack."

"Or I could break the girl's arm," the blademan said, demonstrating by twisting it up behind Liv's back. Eiric could tell from her expression that it hurt, but she scarcely flinched. She had endured a lot of pain in her three years with Sten.

He also knew from the look on her face that if she had anything to do with it, the vargr would pay. She was not the forgiving sort.

"If you break her arm, she'll bring less at the market," Eiric said. "Not a good business decision. Just a moment more while we sort this out."

"You are positively incendiary," Asger said with a note of admiration in his voice.

"Says the fire demon," Eiric said.

"So? Do I have your word?" Asger said.

This was not a promise that Eiric wanted to make, but he saw no other option.

He nodded. "You have my word."

Asger smiled. "Stay where you are until I've disarmed him. Then move quickly." With that, he unwound his lash from around his waist. Coiling it around his hand, he walked briskly forward.

"I apologize for the delay, gentlemen, but let me share what we've decided."

The outlaws watched him come, perplexed, but saw little danger in this strange emissary. Liv watched him, also, but more warily than the others.

When Asger was still a good six feet from the blademan, his hand flashed forward, and what appeared to be a flaming snake encircled the blademan's wrist, jerking it forward. Howling, he dropped the knife, shaking his hand, trying to free himself.

As Eiric charged in, Liv threw an elbow to the outlaw's face, a knee to his crotch. She wrenched free of her captors and ran. With a two-handed swing of his axe, Eiric swept the man's head from his shoulders.

Eiric embraced the anger that had been building in him since he'd run up the hill. The fight became a melee of spattering blood and flying bodies, the stench of burning flesh, the clatter of blades, roars of pain, and the wet, sucking sound of men taking their last breaths.

Asger was a blur of soot black and flame. He seemed to be everywhere at once, nimbly avoiding those who lunged at him.

Eventually, it came down to four against two, but the four who remained fought like furies, and they couldn't seem to finish it.

Eiric's problem was an outlaw wielding a long spear and a short blade that kept him from getting close enough to use his axe. He would dart in, swinging, only to be forced back before he could do any damage.

There came an ear-shattering boom, like a clap of thunder, and a blinding flash of light exploded against the spearman's chest, all but cutting him in two, sending blood and burned bits of flesh raining down on Eiric.

Eiric swept up the man's spear in his free hand and turned, expecting to see Asger smirking at him.

Instead, he saw Liv standing on the far side of the pool, staff in hand, gown swirling around her, illuminated like a Valkyrie from the old stories. Her pendant glowed at her neck.

Everyone, including Eiric and Asger, stood and gaped at her, weapons dangling forgotten in their hands.

"I *told* you she was a sorceress," one of the outlaws bellowed. "I told you not to trifle with her." As one man, the three survivors turned and raced for the woods.

Liv took aim with her staff once more, sending torrents of flame after the fleeing men. One by one, she found her targets and each exploded into ash and bone and smoldering flesh.

A hush fell over the clearing, still littered with scattered weapons, articles of clothing, the bodies of the other outlaws, and the dead wolf. After the clamor of battle, now the only sound was the thrashing of water going over the falls, the rattle of branches overhead, and the moans of dying men.

43

NAIMA

AS REGINN LEFT THE LIBRARY one midday, her stomach made it known that it was empty, and it was hours before the nattmal. She knew that she could find something in the kitchen that would tide her over in the meantime.

As she had before, she circled around to the rear of the dining hall, hoping to slip in the back door.

But as she approached the porch steps, she heard voices. Two people on the porch.

"Look, I don't know of any way to get her out of these islands," somebody said.

"I didn't ask you to do anything. I shouldn't have brought it up. I'll handle it myself."

"Naima, don't try and intervene. It's too risky."

Naima laughed, low and bitter. "First you tell me there's nothing to worry about, and then you tell me it's too risky to intervene. How does that make sense?"

That's when Reginn realized that she was eavesdropping on Naima and Erland.

She could see the backs of their heads over the porch railing. All they would have to do was turn around and they would spot her. What she really needed to do was creep away and pretend she hadn't overheard anything.

But by now her curiosity was pricked. So she hunkered down where she was, like a rabbit that hopes it can blend in with its surroundings.

A really stupid rabbit.

When Naima didn't respond, Erland spoke again. "Bryn says that she isn't getting any better anyway."

"That won't stop him," Naima said.

"He has to find her first."

"He'll find her."

"Listen. We'll go together to Modir Tyra and explain what's happened. She'll know what to do."

Naima sighed. "I've told you before, *Highest,* you may be a seer, but you have a real blind spot when it comes to Tyra, the council, and the Grove. You keep forgetting that my secrets are not yours to give away."

"I don't know why you won't give her a chance to—"

"If you make the wrong choice, you'll be reeducated. I'll be dead."

"All right," Erland said. "I'm sorry."

"You'd better get back."

They both stood, and then Erland drew Naima in for a lingering kiss. When he stepped back, Naima looked over his shoulder and saw Reginn crouching in the grass.

Not that she said anything. But the slight stiffening of her body and the tightening of her lips told the truth of it.

"We're meeting Reginn tomorrow night, right?" Erland said. "She said that she has something new she wants us to hear."

"Sure. Fine. If that's what you want."

Naima watched Erland walk away. When he rounded the corner

of the dining hall, she strode toward Reginn with an expression that made Reginn reach for her dagger.

Naima noticed that, too. She stopped, rocking back on her heels. "I don't know what you heard, but if you breathe a word about this to anyone, you'll be eating ground glass in your delicious porridge," she said.

"I know you don't have any reason to trust me, but I'm not your enemy," Reginn said.

"Good to know," Naima said.

"I mean, I thought we were friends."

"Of course, Highest," Naima said, dipping into a curtsy. "Now I need to get back to work."

"You always play the 'Highest' card with me, and it's getting annoying," Reginn said. "You were talking about Alva—weren't you?"

Naima stopped in her tracks. "Who's Alva?" she said, without turning around.

"I saw her at Brenna's House," Reginn said. "I'm helping Bryn one day a week."

"Good for you," Naima said. "I still don't know what you're talking about."

"You can tell Erland not to trust Modir Tyra, but he doesn't really believe that she could do anyone any harm."

Naima finally turned to look at her. "Don't *you* trust Modir Tyra?"

"I want to. She stuck her neck out for me and literally saved my life. She stood up for me at the council. She really seems to want me to succeed."

"But—"

"But it's hard for me to trust anyone. People have a lot of reasons for doing things." Reginn's affection for and belief in Tyra was like a shim of ice layered over a deep well of mistrust.

Naima took a deep breath. "I still don't understand who you are and what you're doing here."

"I was a thrall in the Archipelago," Reginn said. "Or Barbaria, as people around here like to call it."

"You were a . . . thrall," Naima said, folding her arms, cocking her head. "A slave?"

Reginn nodded. "Still am back home. My master is a thursen—a fire demon. So when Modir Tyra offered me the chance to escape and come here, I took it."

"Why did Modir Tyra bring you here? What is your vocation?"

Reginn shook her head. "I've told you a lot already. Now you. I want to know what happened to Alva. Bryn told me there'd been an incident on Ithavoll." She waited, knowing that there's nothing like silence to encourage people to talk.

"What possible good could it do if I told you?"

"I don't know yet," Reginn said. "That depends on what I hear. But if you don't tell me, I'll ask Bryn. Or Erland."

Naima rolled her eyes, as if she knew she was making a mistake but couldn't figure out a way around it. "The first thing that you should know is that your paradise of New Jotunheim is not a safe place for children."

"What do you mean?"

"They keep disappearing."

What? Reginn felt as if she'd come upon a snake pit in the middle of a garden.

"I don't mean the dedicates," Naima hurried to say, as if that might be Reginn's chief worry. "Anyone under the eye of the temple staff is left alone, but acolytes in the lower school and bondi here in Eimyrja and especially on Ithavoll are fair game."

"What do you mean, they're 'left alone'? Who leaves them alone? Who's doing this?"

"Council guards haul them away, and they're never seen again."

You knew it was too good to be true.

"On whose orders?"

Naima shrugged. "The council's, I suppose. Who else?"

"For what? Are they selling them as thralls, or—"

"I'm a lowly bondi cook," Naima said. "You'll need to ask some-one who knows."

"So . . . is that what happened with Alva?"

"Almost. Two guards dragged Alva away when she was out pick-ing berries, but her fadir intercepted them. In the struggle, all four of them went over the sea cliff at Ithavoll. Alva was the only one who survived. She thinks it was all her fault."

That's always the way, Reginn thought. The innocents feel guilty, and the guilty sleep soundly at night.

"Hopefully, the council doesn't know she's alive, but it's only a matter of time before they find out. We managed to smuggle her to Eimyrja, but she can't stay at Brenna's House, especially if Bryn is spreading the word."

"He was *not* spreading the word," Reginn said, compelled to defend her friend. "Since I'm working over there, he thought I should have information about the patients I'll be seeing. He didn't tell me what happened to her."

Naima waved that off, as if it didn't matter either way. "So, Highest," she said. "Now you know. What are you going to do about it?"

Reginn bit her lip, casting about for ideas. "Isn't there someplace she could be hidden, until she recovers?"

Naima shrugged. "Not that I know of. It's not like I'm free to travel around the islands, looking for options. As long as she's here, she's in danger. It would help if she cooperated with us, but if she's not locked up, she wanders. I think she's looking for ways to join her fadir in Helgafjell." She smiled sadly. "I'm not sure that we did her any favors by saving her life."

In the Archipelago, such dilemmas were common. Reginn hadn't expected to face them in paradise.

"Modir Tyra told me that some of the bondi were the original people of the islands, here before the spinners came, and others have been brought here since. Which are you?"

"I was born here," Naima said.

"And so, your parents were . . . ?"

"My parents were adepts," Naima said.

Reginn stared at her. "And so—"

"How did I end up as cook for the academy?" Naima laughed. "I did not inherit a gift deemed suitable for dedicate training. And somebody has to do the cooking."

"But—"

"We all serve the temple in our own way. You'll hear that, over and over. Only no one is saying exactly how these missing children are serving the temple."

Reginn felt like her insides had been pulled out through her nose. "Why has this been tolerated all this time?"

Naima removed her scarf and shook out her hair. "Perhaps you've noticed that the weather is fine here, and everyone has enough to eat."

Modir Tyra had said much the same thing when Reginn had questioned her about the bondi. Who would want to leave?

"By far, the most valued—and dangerous—gift of all in New Jotunheim is the gift of mind magic," Naima said. "Spinners who have it exert control over others. We all go through a process of education, whether you're a dedicate or a bondi. At the end of it, nearly everyone is eager to serve and satisfied with their assigned roles."

"Not everyone," Reginn murmured, thinking of Naima, and maybe even herself.

Naima shrugged. "Some have the gift of mind magic," she said. "And some have the gift of resistance." She looked Reginn straight in the eyes. "Those who are found to have that gift generally don't live very long."

Reginn shivered, recalling what Musa had said. *If you let her know that her magic didn't work on you, then she will begin to realize how powerful you are.*

If what Naima said was true, it meant that Reginn had better do everything in her power to appear totally compliant.

"Does Modir Tyra know about the children?" Reginn said.

"I don't know," Naima said. "The temple has always been a little separate from the council. Maybe you should ask her yourself." She tied up her hair again. "Well, I need to go back to work. You don't want to be seen fraternizing with the bondi. There are rules, you know."

"Thank you, Naima, for being as frank as you have been," Reginn said.

Naima snorted. "You seem to have the power of making me say too much."

"I'm used to keeping secrets," Reginn said. "Maybe there's a way I can help."

"Such as?"

Reginn cast about for ideas. "I can try to find out what's happening to those who are taken. I can try to find out why."

"I'm not so concerned with the what and the why," Naima said. "But I *will* find a way to put a stop to it." Her voice trembled a bit, but her expression said that it was with rage and not fear.

"Just . . . be careful," Reginn said.

"*You* be careful," Naima said. "You may believe your status protects you, but trust me—it doesn't. You have a lot more to lose than I do."

Reginn rolled her shoulders, trying to ease the tension in them. "This is more like home than I expected," she said. "Depending on whether you're viewed as gifted or not."

"Make no mistake, Highness," Naima said. "We're all bondi. Some of us are more aware of it than others."

44

STORMY WEATHER

WITH THE BATTLE WITH THE outlaws over, Eiric had nothing to say. He'd set sail with his systir and a freed thrall from the Westlands. Somehow, he'd ended up at sea with a witch and a demon. He'd thought he was in command of this adventure, but now he wasn't sure.

To be honest, his ego was bruised. This was the second time in a few months that Liv had stepped in to save his ass.

Based on what you've seen today, Eiric thought, you'd better get used to it.

He knelt beside the wolf's body, retrieved his dagger, and rinsed it off in the pool. Then walked around the clearing, collecting weapons.

As he did so, the witch and the demon faced off.

"So, eldrjotun," Liv said, cocking her head, arms folded. "Or would you prefer fire demon, devourer, elemental, risi, thursen, troll . . . ?"

Asger pretended to study on this. "They all have somewhat different meanings," he said. "Perhaps you've heard the saying, 'As handsome as a risi, strong as a jotun, ugly as a troll, stupid as a thursen'?"

Liv rolled her eyes. "No," she said. "I have not heard that."

"So while risi brings with it a certain appeal, my walking-around name is Asger Eldr. That is what I prefer."

"Thank you for your help, Asger," she said. "I will not forget it."

"I will not forget it, either," Asger said. "One day I will ask you for a favor in return."

"And I will grant it, if it is within my power." She sounded like a queen with her courtier.

Don't do a deal with a demon, Eiric wanted to say, but he'd already made his own.

"So, spinner," Asger said. "Am I–"

"Call me Liv," Liv interrupted.

"So, Liv–am I right in believing that you are more than a sorceress?"

Liv studied him, eyes narrowed. "Why would you think that?"

"I've met my share of vala," he said, "but never anyone like you."

"That's because there *is* no one like me," Liv snapped.

Eiric knew from experience that this was all she meant to say on the matter.

"Why don't you make yourself useful, *Asger Eldr*?" Eiric said. "The vargr most likely have a permanent camp somewhere close. Go see if you can find it. There might be something there that we can use. Liv and I will go back to the beach and get the boat ready to sail tomorrow."

"And if the camp is occupied?"

"Kill them," Eiric said.

Asger hesitated, as if worried that Eiric would break his promise and sail away without him, then disappeared into the woods.

Once he was gone, Liv put her hand on Eiric's shoulder. "Thank you, brodir," she said. "You saved my life. I was foolish to allow myself to be surprised like that."

"I'm the bigger fool," Eiric said. "I thought we'd be safe here because we always have been before. Obviously, I was wrong." He paused. "Thank you for stepping in to finish it. I guess you were right when you said that I would never make it to the Grove without your help."

"This is not the kind of help that I was thinking of," Liv said.

"It was welcome, just the same," Eiric said, not meeting her eyes. "I am sorry that I discounted your magic at home. I didn't know better."

"I didn't know better, either," Liv said. "If I had, I would have buried Sten under the back pasture a long time ago."

"That would have changed all of our lives for the better," Eiric said with a rueful smile.

"Listen, Eiric," Liv said. "I know you are wondering how I did—what I did. I don't know the answer. It wasn't something that I planned or practiced. I am changing, and I believe it has to do with this." She held up her amulet, the movement setting it swinging. "Some days, I don't feel like myself anymore."

Eiric recalled what she'd said about it back at Sundgard.

This is my past and my future, brodir.

Were these changes a good thing? Was there a new distance between them? Was she withdrawing, or was it his own discomfort with her growing power?

"If you are what Rikhard calls a wyrdspinner, or one of the vala—what happens when we reach Eimyrja?"

Liv shrugged. "I don't know that, either. But I would have to think that it is better that we face it together."

Liv returned to their ship while Eiric stripped off his clothes and washed away the blood and dirt and sweat that had accumulated during their week at sea and their day on shore. He rinsed his clothes as well, hoping they would have time to dry before nightfall. Once dressed, he followed his systir down to the beach.

He had planned to stay a week or longer at their camp here, smoking fish, foraging food, and doing the repairs necessary for the next leg of their journey.

After the attack at the clearing, any illusion of safety had dissipated like morning mists. If the vargr had made it this far north, there was no safety to be had anywhere in Muckleholm. That gave their preparations an air of urgency.

Asger returned from the forest, also freshly scrubbed, with leather bags slung over his shoulders containing dried fruit, nuts, and smoked meat he'd scavenged from the outlaws' camp. Aside from that and a large iron pot, he reported that there had been nothing else of use.

After a hurried meal of roasted fish, Liv prepared to smoke the rest. The fire had burned down to coals, so she wet some chips of applewood and dropped them on top of the coals. She butterflied the remaining fish, salted them thoroughly, and laid them over the fire on skewers. She upended the iron pot over top to keep the smoke in.

While the fish was smoking, they set about repairing their boat, working as long as the light lasted. Eiric stuffed caulk in the spaces between the strakes, while Asger smeared it with tar he melted between his hands. Liv inspected the sail and the lines, replacing any that showed the slightest signs of wear, since they did not know when they would make landfall again, or where.

Or if.

Despite his exhaustion, Eiric slept fitfully that night under his tarp in the stern of the ship. He was plagued with fevered dreams in which ice wolves sprang out of the ocean and swarmed over his ship, dripping salt water and blood.

In one dream, he returned to the farm at Sundgard and found the livestock spavined, the crops withered and brown, the winds blowing through the open doors of the longhouse.

The others—even Asger—were still sleeping like the dead when Eiric climbed over the gunwales, landing barefoot in the wet sand. The sky was brightening over the eastern hills, signaling the coming dawn. Low clouds to the northwest and a shift in the wind predicted a change in the weather. He could smell it in the air.

Never set sail into a storm, Bjorn always said. *Wait for fair weather. You'll find trouble enough without tempting the gods.*

Eiric walked down the beach and around the bay to the northernmost point of land. When Eiric had sailed with his fadir and grandfadir, it was Bjorn's custom to offer a sacrifice to Njord, the god of the seas, whenever they entered unknown waters. Eiric had always made fun of that ritual. But now, on this day, he pulled out a leaf-wrapped bundle containing one of the fish Liv had smoked the night before.

"Fadir Njord, we commend to you this ship and this crew and petition you for a safe journey as we leave land behind." With that, he threw his offering toward the horizon. It sailed so far that he didn't even see it land.

Can't hurt, he thought. Might help.

Now he drew the sunstone from beneath his shirt and sighted through it toward the horizon. The twin images of the inset ruby converged like two drops of blood pooling together.

The effect was immediate. A charge like a bolt of lightning ran through him and raced to fix on a spot in the northwest where the sky met the sea.

He looked to the right, and to the left, but there were no landmarks to thread his course between. Only endless seas, and the seductive whisper of the stone between his hands.

Come back to me.

When he returned to their camp, he found Liv and Asger eating dried fruit and smoked meat from the vargr's stores. Eiric helped himself to some, since everything else had already been stowed. Nobody had much to say.

"Let's go," Eiric said.

The water was still fairly calm in their little bay, but as soon as they cleared the north end of the island, they encountered rising winds and heavier seas. Even in fair weather, it was a challenge to sail against the prevailing westerlies. After another hour on a northwest course, Eiric could tell they were in for it.

When sailing the karvi, he and Bjorn had always kept to semiprotected coastal waters. Now, it seemed, he was going to find out just how seaworthy she was.

Eiric lashed the tiller in a fixed position to offer some course correction so that he and his systir could take charge of the sail. Liv helped him reef the sail to reduce the force on the mast and rigging. The two of them handled the sheets, adjusting the angle so they could sail off the wind. *Dreki* flew forward like the dragon she was, swooping and climbing as water poured over the forward gunwales. She might be seaworthy, she might be light as a thistle, but she wasn't built to keep out storm swells.

Eiric set Asger to bailing, but it was like trying to empty the ocean with a ladle. There were times when he felt like he was swimming more than sailing as *Dreki* took on water. The clothes he had worked so hard to dry out were soaked through with sweat and salt water. The water was cold, though not as cold as those times he'd set sail as soon as the harbor was freed of ice.

Liv shouted, "Heil, brodir, wherever we're going, we're making good time."

"Heil, systir, at least there's plenty of wind!" Eiric shouted back.

Too bad it was blowing from the wrong direction.

Asger had nothing to say because he was spewing over the side. In fact, they all took their turns, fortunately not all at the same time.

Liv and Asger were better sailors than they had been at the beginning of their journey, but they'd not encountered rough weather until now. Eiric was constantly shouting orders to Liv as they managed the angle of sail. There were times when they had to come around, that the ship stalled in the water, the standing rig straining as she tried to find the wind.

He wanted to get out of the path of the storm, because he had no desire to keep company with it all the way to Eimyrja, but he had no idea how broad it was, and he didn't want to sail too far off course. If he was even on course. Most likely they were not.

With the weather as thick as it was, there was no hope of sighting against the polar star or anything else.

Again and again, Eiric rechecked their bearing with the sunstone. It should have told him nothing since he had no horizon to sight against, but still, the light rolled out ahead of them like a path to the gods, and the voice whispered, *Come back to me.*

He had bet their survival on the reliability of the sunstone that had taken his fadir and grandfadir to Eimyrja and back again.

So they said.

What if it was a sorceress's trick, meant to send them sailing in endless circles, enchanted by the witch's whisper until they starved to death?

As time passed, he was too weary to worry. Hour after hour, the rain slashed down, *Dreki* dove into the canyons between the waves, rode up the mountains on the other side, shivered and shook like she might fly apart. Eiric's fingers were raw from clutching the ropes, his voice hoarse from shouting orders. At one point, he startled awake, realizing that he had dozed off.

That wouldn't do. He dunked his head into the seawater sloshing between the ribs, then shook like a dog, sending water splattering all around.

Dreki was climbing again, up, up, up the face of a wave until she stood all but vertical in the water. Whatever gear wasn't lashed down slid the length of the ship, joining him in the stern.

Come back to me.

The voice of the sunstone filled his ears, stuffed his heart full, clouded his mind.

Then he heard the sound of cracking wood. Liv, at midships, swore on all the gods. Eiric rolled sideways just in time to avoid being pinned under the falling mast, but it still struck him in the head. He fought himself free of the sodden sail and lunged for the tiller, but the little boat had already turned abeam. A massive wave crashed over the deck, filling his eyes and mouth with salt water. He struggled upright again in time to see Liv swept over the gunwales and into the sea. That was all he knew for a very long time.

45

THE PRICE OF KNOWLEDGE

WHEN SHE'D FINISHED THE NEWLY unlocked pages of Brenna's journal she'd set out to read, Reginn rerolled them and climbed the steps to the bovine niche. She'd taken to stowing the unlocked pages in the larger, less accessible niche.

She hadn't heard anything from Musa in weeks, and she was nearing the end of the journal pages.

Maybe she'd missed something. She reached into the niche, groping deep, past the rolled vellum. Her fingertips brushed leather. She grasped, pulled, and came away with fragments that crumbled in her hands.

Now she reached in with both hands, taking a better hold and pulling it toward her.

It was a fragile leather packet, darkened with age. At one time, it had been tied with cord, but that had long since rotted away, leaving only traces on the leather.

Too old to have been left by Musa. Probably actual bovine lineages.

Some instinct made her want to take a closer look. Cradling the packet in her hands, she navigated the staircase to the first floor and set it on the worktable. Gently, she unfolded it, the leather cracking despite her care.

Rolled inside were sheets of vellum, similar to those Reginn had been using to practice rune writing. She flattened them on the table.

They were covered with writing, drawings, and symbols done in an unfamiliar ink. Some of the pages were dated.

N.J., year 400, month 11, day 7

Reginn did the numbers in her head. If the Grove was six hundred years old, then this would have been written about two hundred years ago.

Some of it appeared to be practice writing, the copying out of lines. On another page, the scribe had written different versions of a name, large and small, bold and faint, some flowing, some in runes as stark as winter trees.

Gertrud

Gertrude

Trude

And then, in a different hand:

Frodi

Frodi

Frodi

Frodi? Reginn frowned. It didn't make sense. Elder Frodi might be a bit weather-beaten, but he couldn't be that much older than

Reginn herself. All the gifted in Jotunheim were young, with the exception of Amma Inger. The only old people she'd seen were among the bondi.

On the day Reginn went before the council, the kennari had said that the council members were older than they looked.

Not two hundred years old.

Maybe Frodi was the name of some famous founder of the Grove and so had become a common name on Eimyrja. She'd have to ask Frodi what he knew if she ever saw him again.

Other pages were covered with runelike symbols. Crudely drawn and unfamiliar. Reginn traced them with her finger. It was almost as if Trude, whoever she was, was practicing runes Reginn had never heard of. Or making up her own.

There were two she thought she recognized. Kenaz, the spark of knowledge and learning, the one that had turned out to be the key to the founder's pages.

And Naudhiz, related to need or unfulfilled desire.

Trude

†

Frodi

It was something that sweethearts might carve into the bark of a tree.

Sweethearts who knew the runes of magic.

Reginn rewrapped the sheets of vellum and restored them to their hiding place deep in the niche.

Then, on impulse, she wrote a note of her own.

MUSA

Who was TRUDE?

She rolled the note and left it in the correspondence niche.

Time to trade one tomb for another.

She left the library and trotted across the quad toward the Memory Tree, though there was no need for punctuality. Whenever she arrived, the dead would be waiting. After the first few sessions, Modir Tyra had grown tired of sitting for hours while Reginn sang herself hoarse, pleading for somebody—anybody—to answer. The kennari returned to her office, leaving instructions to send for her if Reginn got a response. She offered to provide a bondi servant to tend to Reginn's needs while she was in the catacombs, but Reginn declined. The presence of others just made her conscious of repeated failures.

Besides, Reginn had come to enjoy being alone in the tombs. The dead were a lot less demanding than the living. It gave her a chance to practice her music and write her own undisturbed.

Outside the door to the catacombs, she always stopped to read any new messages that had sprouted on the tree. For days, there would be nothing new. Then would come a fresh crop of memorials, blistering with anger.

Dor, 6 years old, disappeared at Jarnfen while searching for bog iron. Be at peace, little one.

Grif, 48 years old, died in granary explosion, Ithavoll. Prepare a place for us.

Grette, 33 years old, died at the tar pits in Brennaby.

First reaping: Revne, age 10; Signe, age 18; Kare, age 54; Troels, age 27. Taken, not given.

What did that even mean?

Reginn noticed that, with or without her intervention, the ribbons came down after a few days. Maybe I should stop reading these, Reginn thought. But now she felt obligated to hear the voices that no one else heard.

That does them no good, she thought. Even working at Brenna's was frustrating because she was afraid to use runes to help the sick. Could she really believe Musa's warning not to tell anyone? Maybe the mouse had her own reasons for wanting to keep them secret.

On impulse, Reginn pulled down the newest memory ribbons and stuffed them into her carry bag.

Inside, she quickly made her way to the founder's tomb. She set her instrument case down on one of the benches and unbuckled the straps.

"Modir Brenna, I am Reginn Lund, your dottir, seeking your wise counsel," she said, as she always did. She sat cross-legged on the bench and began to play. She had been working her way through the songs that Tove had taught her, hoping she would find one that would catch the ear of the founder.

She had developed a routine, similar to what she might use for an alehouse set. An hour on the flute, followed by a half hour of singing. A mixture of old songs and new. She'd begun by focusing on vardlokkur only, but that grew tedious in a hurry.

An hour later, all Reginn had to show for it was a sore backside and cramping fingers. Maybe she should throw in some drinking songs to liven things up.

She took a break to eat her midday meal of bread, cheese, and an apple, thinking that maybe she wasn't the right messenger. Maybe it was the wrong message. She felt crushed, weighed down by a cartload of doubt.

There was an offering bowl on the altar fronting Brenna's tomb.

On impulse, Reginn pulled the ribbons from the Memory Tree out of her bag and used them to bind a bundle of sage and sticks of fossil resin. It took several tries with her strike-steel and stone to set it to smoldering. She placed it in the offering bowl and then, on impulse, added a runestone. Raidho. The pathfinder.

> Modir Brenna Half-Foot, I am your dottir, Reginn Eiklund, Dedicate.
> Here to sing the summoning.
> Here to seek your counsel and protection.
> I am lost, Modir.
> I do not know who to trust.
> I do not know the way.

Then something brushed her, like a butterfly wing or a spider-web in the dark. Like that moment when the wind shifts, foretelling a change in the weather.

"My journey is done, dottir," a voice whispered. "Let me rest."

A geysir of hope rose within her. It was a response, at least, even if it was a no.

> Your journey is done, but mine is just beginning.
> I would put on the volva's cloak,
> I would carve the runes of magic into my flesh,
> And so leave my mark on the world.
> I would pick up the staff of the gifted,
> I would set my feet upon the righteous path,
> If you will help me find my way.

The skin on Reginn's forearm prickled and burned, and she slapped her hand over the runes etched there. And then the founder spoke.

"You have Uruz, Sowilo, and Raidho," the founder said. "That is more than most. It should suffice."

"It takes more than runes and courage to find the right path," Reginn said. "It requires knowledge."

"There is a price to be paid for knowledge, dottir. Are you willing to pay it?"

Yes! Reginn wanted to say. But she knew better.

Instead, she said, "That depends on the price."

"You would bargain with me?"

"I would know the price before I agree to pay it."

"In that, you are wise, child. The one who came before you paid with her life. Now go, and trouble me no more."

46

VIGRID

EIRIC AWOKE TO THE SOUND of gulls and ospreys. He struggled to sit up, his sodden clothes weighing him down. He was lying half in and half out of the midships hold, waist deep in water. Gripping the gunwale, he came up on his knees and peered over the side.

The karvi was rocking gently with the lapping waves, her keel scraping over black sand, all but beached in a small cove.

He looked forward, to where Liv should be, then all the way to the bow, for Asger. He saw no one. He scanned the beach and saw only the bleached bones of sea creatures and the salt-encrusted carcasses of trees. There were no footprints leading away from the wrack line. Dread coursed through him, coming to rest like a dead-weight under his heart.

"Liv?" he said. No answer. "Liv!" he shouted. Nothing. Then he tried "Asger!"

That's when it occurred to him that he was ashore in a strange land, and there was no telling who might come to answer his call. He groped beneath the gunwale next to the tiller and found to his relief that his sword and axe, wrapped in oilcloth, were still lashed across the beams, and his shield was locked into the rack on the outside. He cut them free and laid the bundle across his sea chest close to hand.

He planted his hands on the gunwales, hissing with the pain, and vaulted over the side, landing knee-deep in warm water. He'd raised blisters over the calluses on his hands, and they left smears of blood on the sun-bleached wood.

Unwrapping his weapons, he faced the beach, his sword in his right hand, his axe in his left. Something in him hoped that enemies would come boiling out of the trees so that he would have somebody to kill.

Or so that he could go down fighting.

Deep in his bones, he knew what must have happened. His inexperienced crew had been swept overboard. That often happened in heavy seas. He should have told them to lash themselves to the mast, but that was always a hard sell. If they did that, they knew they would pay the vikingr price if the boat overturned.

Rage and regret boiled up in him as he tallied up his losses over these past few years. His fadir. His grandfadir. His modir. And now, most likely, his systir.

Memories pounded through him, leaving him bruised and aching.

Liv on the shore that first day, clutching her amulet with two hands, her face like fissured stone.

I am not frightened, she'd said. *You detain me at your peril.*

Liv confronting Sten, then running him through with their fadir's sword and saving Eiric's life. Liv at the Thing council, talking rings around the Knudsens, revealing them for the fools they were. Liv deploying her wit against Rikhard.

Liv sending flame screaming across the clearing.

It struck him like a fist in the gut that the only one left of his family was Ivar.

Let the Knudsens have Sundgard if they wanted it so much. He was no farmer, as his modir had told him the week before she died.

He should have listened to Liv when she'd begged him not to do a deal with Rikhard and to let the farm go. He should have agreed when she suggested that they go vikingr together and start over elsewhere. Ivar could have joined them when he was weaned. But Eiric's pride would not allow it. He could not stand to see the Knudsens win.

Eiric understood that life was hard, that people died young in the Archipelago every day. Raiders might attack, slaughter those who resisted, and carry the rest off as thralls. Women died in childbirth, leaving orphans behind. The very old walked into the forest and never came back. Families with too many mouths to feed would return a newborn to the gods before it took hold of anyone's heart.

Bjorn's line had long been known as being strong in hamingja—the kind of luck that drove a man's success and brought good fortune to those who followed him. Had that trait been extinguished? Was Eiric doomed to an unrelenting siege of bad luck to balance the scales?

He'd never put much faith in Bjorn's stories about Valhalla—a paradise for warriors who died in battle. But he did believe that there was such a thing as a good death.

Once again, he scanned the shoreline all the way to the points on either side. There was no one there to kill. Nobody available to do him the service. Wavelets kissed the beach, and wading birds hunted in the shallow waters, unperturbed by his presence. Beyond the sand, the shoreline was overgrown with thistle, crowberry, and heather. Mottled green hills rose into the distance.

Sweat trickled down Eiric's back. He was cooking in his heavy storm coat, even though it was sopping wet. He stripped it off and hung it over the side of his ship to dry and pulled his linen shirt away from his skin.

His fingers found the sunstone. *Welcome to Vigrid, son of Asgard*, it whispered. *Welcome to the last battlefield.*

Vigrid. The name was vaguely familiar, but it was not Eimyrja. Not the island of the spinner witches. After all his losses, the sunstone had landed him in the wrong place. It had betrayed him.

He gripped the pendant hard, as if he could crush it in his fist. Then slid the sunstone free of its chain, meaning to throw it far out to sea. He cocked his arm and closed his eyes so that he wouldn't see it fly.

He couldn't let go of it. Swearing, he restored the amulet to its usual place next to Leif's pendant and the runestick Reginn had given him.

The wise man looks after his ship first, Bjorn whispered.

Stop listening to the voices in your head, Eiric told himself. *When have they ever been helpful?*

Yet still, he did as he was told. Keeping a wary eye shoreward, Eiric waded all the way around the little dragon, checking for damage. The mast had cracked in two just above the kerling. He pried free the splintered base of the mast and trimmed the remainder. Once reseated, the mast would be shorter, but functional.

The sheets had snapped when the mast went down, and the yard was splintered. Eiric unstrapped the spare from under the gunwale and slid it through the lashing alongside the broken yard to reinforce it—a quick fix in case he had to depart in a hurry. Then he rolled the sail and stowed it in the racks along the port side.

The tiller was still lashed in position. He cut it loose and raised the rudder, relieved to see that it had not broken in the shallows.

His sea chest that doubled as a rower's bench was still locked in place. Liv's was still at midships. Most of their other provisions and gear were gone, though they had been well stowed and lashed down. He lifted the corner of the sail, half-afraid that he would find his systir's body underneath. At least then he would know for sure.

It was not there. There was no sign of her staff, either.

Liv *could* still be alive. Unlikely, but she was a survivor—not the sort to go quietly, and she could swim like a fish. It all depended on their location when she went overboard.

Eiric chose to cling to that hope, even though he might never know for sure. It was the not knowing that gnawed at him.

Wading next to his ship, he pushed her through the shallows and into the mouth of a creek that flowed into the cove, towing her far enough upstream that she couldn't be seen from the shoreline. All he could do was hope that she would be there when he returned. If he returned.

The entire time, he kept waiting to be challenged.

He had to admit, this place looked nothing like the Archipelago. He dipped his hands into the stream and allowed the water to trickle through his fingers. He'd never seen water so clean anywhere close to human habitation.

Maybe it was an uninhabited island.

Eiric still carried the weight of Muckleholm with him in his salt- and dirt- and blood-encrusted clothes. He stripped, rinsed his clothing in the clear water, and pounded them against rocks to dislodge the history in them. When they were as clean as he could get them, he hung them from tree branches in the sun. Then scrubbed himself, sluicing the sand and salt and grit from his hair, combing through it with his fingers and tying the top lock back with a thong.

For a brief time, he held on to a root on the bank and allowed the creek to roll over his naked body. When he finally climbed out of the water, he dried quickly in a sun that beat down like midsummer. He dressed in dry breeches and a loose linen shirt and pulled his mail shirt over top, hiding the sunstone and his pendants underneath.

Maybe it was the much-needed bath, or maybe it was this place, but energy coursed through him like the mead of the gods. Despite his grief, he felt stronger, more alive than he had in a long time. What kind of a man was he turning into, who sheds grief and loss like water off sealskin?

Still standing on the creek bank, Eiric downed a pouch of the outlaws' dried meat and berries. The entire time, he listened and watched for any sign he'd been spotted as an intruder. All he heard was birdsong and the movement of water over rock. There were no answers as he debated what to do next.

A man cannot choose the life the Norns weave for him, Bjorn said. *What he can do is control how he responds to what the fates hand him.*

Eiric couldn't get back what he'd lost. He could bemoan his bad luck, blame Sten and the rest of the Knudsens and Jarl Rikhard for ruining his life.

He still had options. For instance, he could become a hermit. This appeared to be good land, and he had a ship and fishing gear. He could survive, though clothes would be a problem before long.

Ivar might be better off with Hilde. Maybe he could be the blacksmith Stevenson hoped for.

Or Eiric could choose another path. If this wasn't Eimyrja, he might be close. If he could find his way there, he could find out what was happening to the children carried off from the Archipelago. He could sieve out exactly what these spinners were up to and bring back the proof. If he succeeded at the task Rikhard had given him, he would be aligning with a winner. He stood to gain power in the Archipelago, where the jarl seemed to be ascendant.

If he died in the attempt, then that, apparently, was what the fates decreed.

Bjorn's voice came back to him. *Eiricsens don't align with others. Other men align with us.*

Get out of my head, Grandfadir, Eiric wanted to shout.

Instead, he strapped on a baldric and belt so that he could carry his sword, axe, and bow. With a coil of precious ship's rope slung over his shoulder, he felt ready to begin exploring.

Eiric decided to follow the stream. The trees that had grown up along the watercourse provided good cover, so he couldn't be seen from farther up the hill. He had questions that needed answering. For that, he needed one person, not an army. He also wanted to get to high ground so he could take a better look around.

The way was steep and rocky, and in places it had been obliterated by rockfalls and volunteer saplings. At times he had to wade in the water to get around some obstacle or another. Eiric was sweating under his mail before he'd gone very far.

Doggedly, he climbed on. Every time he rounded an outcropping or crested a rise, he'd be confronted by a new, heartbreakingly beautiful glen or pool or waterfall. It engaged all his senses—the scent of flowers, the sounds of moving water and the buzz of bees, the warmth of the sun on the back of his neck.

If Eimyrja was like this, he could understand why his fadir and grandfadir were drawn back there over and over. What he couldn't understand was why no one was there to defend it.

By the time he crested the final rise, the sun was past the midday point and the shadows lengthening. His empty stomach was complaining more and more. But the view was worth the climb.

He'd reached the edge of a broad plateau that extended to the horizon on the north and south. The plain was riven by a fault line that had left a broad crevasse between the two parts. This side had been pushed much higher than the other, forming a cliff. Even at this distance, Eiric could hear the sound of moving water.

Scattered over the flatland on the near side of the rift were the ruins of what appeared to be ancient fortifications.

The grass covering the field was lush and green, spangled with white and yellow poppies. The terrain underneath was oddly lumpy and pocked with holes, as if older ruins lay deeper. A long spine of stone ran nearly all the way across the plateau, clear of vegetation, bleaching in the sun.

The scene on the other side of the rift was strikingly different. He could see that it had once been a large city, with temples, halls, and houses, now fallen into ruins.

Amid all this ancient rubble stood a complex of buildings that were considerably newer—meaning they had been built within the last two centuries.

It appeared to be an army encampment—a fortified building surrounded by stables, paddocks, latrines, and barracks.

If it was an army camp, then why wouldn't they have taken the high ground, on this side?

At the edge of the rift stood one of the newer buildings—this one more ornate than the others, with a soaring roof and towers at each end. Was this the Temple at the Grove Liv mentioned?

Eiric eyed the paddocks greedily, but there was no way to cross that distance in daylight without being spotted and run down, and that would be a stupid way to die.

Not the loftiest of goals: Don't die in a stupid way.

What would spinners sequestered on an island protected by magic need with an army? Once again, he wondered if the sunstone had led him to the wrong place.

The only way to find out was to do more exploring, and for that he needed the cover of darkness and, if the fates decreed it, a horse.

So he settled in to wait.

47

BRENNA'S JOURNAL

N.J., year 310, month 12, day 21

As we celebrate the Yule in the time of short days, the elders have a new dilemma—their own mortality. Unlike me, they are greedy for more time in which to grow their power and extend their scope beyond these islands. They have begun to see themselves as gods who deserve fealty from everyone in the Midlands. They see each new class of dedicates as rivals instead of colleagues and seem convinced that any day might bring an invasion from the Archipelago or a rebellion of the people who welcomed us here in the first place.

More than three hundred years have passed since the founding of New Jotunheim, and the Archipelago has left us in peace. Inger and I travel there and back twice a year, collecting the jotnar wherever we find them and bringing them home. Conditions there have gone from bad to worse—they could use our help.

These days, I split my time between the healing halls, the new library, and the temple classroom. Those are the places that soothe my soul as I prepare to cross into the borderlands. I am so very tired of the Midlands.

I visited the halls of memory yesterday. My tomb is nearly finished. Despite my pleas for simplicity, the stonemasons have built a stunning monument that few people will see. They know, my trusted friends, that I am more concerned about protecting the vault behind it and the secrets it keeps.

Despite their entreaties, that knowledge will die with me.

Inger does not like the stone barrow the masons are building for me. If she thought she could get away with it, I believe she would creep in at night and undo the day's work.

When I tell Inger that I must go, she doesn't want to hear it. "You could stay if you wanted to," she says.

I suppose that expectation is my fault.

I fear that some of the kennari, too, will feel abandoned. Betrayed, even. They want me to name a successor, to establish a structure that will outlive me. They don't understand that I did not come here to be worshipped, nor do I intend to found a church to come between me and the people of the Midlands. To me, a temple is a reservoir of knowledge—a sanctuary that nurtures learning. Not a road to power, but a response to and refuge from it.

I will stay a little longer, but the temple and the academy must prepare for a time when I am gone.

—B.H.

48

DEAD RECKONING

REGINN REROLLED THE PAGE, THEN returned it to the niche with the rest. There were just a few pages left, but she'd lost her appetite for whatever the founder had to say. She had not been to the catacombs in two days.

What was the point? Brenna Half-Foot had demanded that Reginn commit to paying whatever price the founder required, which could very well be her life. Reginn's old insecurities resurfaced. It was as if Brenna thought that Reginn's magic was the sort that could earn a girl hack silver in an alehall—and that was all. She had no desire to go back to the catacombs only to be stiff-armed again.

And yet . . . Reginn could not stifle her natural curiosity.

> *I am more concerned about protecting the vault behind it and the secrets it keeps.*

What was in the vault? Was it the riches Gunnar had raved about? Not much chance she would ever find out.

The keeper had warned her about the dangers of the borderlands. Modir Tyra had warned her about the keeper. Musa had warned her about the risks of using the runes.

Stalling, she pulled out Trude's packet again. She had just spread it out on the table when someone said, "Reginn."

Startled, Reginn looked up to see Musa sitting cross-legged on one of the upper landings of the staircase. At the same time, she noticed that the blodkyn rune on her thigh was tingling and burning.

"Oh!" Reginn said, resisting the temptation to brush at the spot. "I didn't expect to see you."

"I got your note," Musa said, serious as a plague. "I need to talk to you."

"Now?"

"The sooner the better."

Reginn shrugged. "All right." She sat back down at the table, Trude's pages spread out before her.

"Why did you ask about Trude?" Musa said. "Where did you hear her name?" Her gaze fell on the packet on the table. "Where did you get that?"

"I found it in one of the niches," Reginn said, tapping it with a forefinger. "It looked as if Trude—whoever she was—was trying to work out some of the runes of magic. I wondered if you knew who she was."

"Why were you poking around? I thought you had work to do."

Reginn blinked at her, blindsided. "I'm sorry—"

"Have you shown that to anyone? Told anyone what you found?"

"No!" Reginn growled, irritated at being put on the defensive. "If it's a problem, maybe you should have explained the rules. You were the one who told me to explore the library and which niches to use."

"I thought they were empty," Musa said. "Anyway." She waved toward the packet. "Burn that and don't speak to anyone else about it."

Musa had been—well, not kind, exactly—but helpful to Reginn. Still, Reginn had had about enough of her unexplained warnings and manufactured mysteries.

"If you're going to tell me what to do, you're going to have to explain to me why somebody's two-hundred-year-old scrawlings are a threat to anyone."

Musa scowled. "Don't exaggerate," she said. "They're not that old."

Reginn ran her finger over the top page. "This is dated four hundred years since the founding. So. Two hundred years ago."

It was Musa's turn to be at a loss for words. "You can't be serious," she said finally. She swung down from the staircase, landing lightly by Reginn's side. "Let me see that." She thrust out her hand.

Reginn was loath to give up Trude's pages after Musa had told her to burn them, but she handed them over.

Musa scanned the contents of the packet, nodding as if they were familiar. Then looked up at Reginn. "What day is it today?"

"The fourth month, twelfth day," Reginn said. "The six hundred and third year since the founding."

Musa stared at her with the stricken look of a person who has stepped off a cliff into thin air.

"So," Reginn said after what seemed like a long time, "have you heard of Trude? Was she a dedicate here? A member of the faculty?"

Musa raised her hand, palm out, to stop the cascade of questions from interfering with whatever she was thinking. "And yet… Frodi still lives?" she said, her voice cracking.

"Well, yes," Reginn said cautiously. "If you're talking about the archivist."

"How old is he?"

"I'm guessing he's seen no more than twenty winters, though he does look older when he's been drinking."

"You didn't tell him about me?"

Reginn shook her head. "You said not to tell anyone."

"Tell me—who else? Who's on the Council of Elders?"

Reginn sighed, trying to remember the high-ups she'd met the one time.

"Elder Skarde. Elder Gisli. Elder Scarlet. Um. Elder Margareta. Elder Frodi. There are two more. I don't remember their names."

"What about adepts?" Musa said, when Reginn ran out of elders.

"I really haven't met any adepts," Reginn said. "They're working on the out islands, I guess."

"Modir Tyra? Amma Inger? They still live?"

"Of course," Reginn said, her impatience growing. Nobody could dance around a subject without really saying anything like the library mouse. "What does this have to do with Trude?"

"I believe that it means that Trude was a fool," Musa muttered. "That maybe she trusted the wrong person."

Reginn began gathering up Trude's pages, restoring them to the packet. "If you're going to talk in riddles, I can make better use of my time."

"Wait," Musa said. "Stay. I'm sorry. You deserve an answer."

Reginn tucked the packet into her carry bag and stood next to the table, waiting.

"The dead have all the time in the world," Musa said. "The living are impatient because their days are numbered. At least . . . that's the way it's always been. The good news is that you don't need to go back to the founder. I can tell you some of what you need to know if you decide that you want to hear it."

That was enough to persuade Reginn to settle into her chair.

Musa stood, hunched over, her fisted hands gripping her tunic on either side. "Gertrude Lund, called Trude, was a dedicate at the Temple at the Grove until she was murdered here in the library. I thought it was just recently, but if what you say is true, it happened more than two hundred years ago."

"Murdered?" Now Reginn was riveted. "How?"

"Watch," Musa said, "I'll demonstrate." Soundlessly, she ascended the staircase, barely touching each landing until she had climbed to the highest level—higher than Reginn had ever been before. "She was up here, searching the oldest volumes in the archives, when somebody grabbed her from behind, lifted her over the rail, and dropped her." She flipped onto the railing and balanced there, like an acrobat from a traveling show, her clothes rippling around her.

"Musa!" Reginn cried, vaulting over the table and standing at the foot of the stairs. "Get down from there before you fall."

Musa stepped from the railing and hurtled downward. Seeing nothing she could use to break her fall, Reginn stepped forward and extended her arms in a foolish attempt to catch her. Somehow, Musa slipped right through her grasp and lighted like a feather right in front of her.

"I landed a lot harder the first time," Musa said.

Reginn took two steps back, raising both hands, palms out. Her heart thudded painfully in her chest. "What are you?" she whispered. "Some sort of—of—"

"If you had any doubts about whether you can speak to the dead, dismiss them."

"You're saying that—that *you're* Trude?"

"What's left of her." Musa sat cross-legged on the first landing. "If you take a closer look, you'll see the spot." She pointed.

Reginn knelt next to the staircase and ran her fingers over the battered wood plank floor. Though it appeared to have been scrubbed many times, it was stained brown with blood shed long ago.

"You've heard of landvaettir. A vaettir is a spirit tied to a particular place. You could call me a library vaettir—a spirit that is tied to the library."

Reginn sat back on her heels, remembering that the other dedicates claimed that the library was haunted.

"Who would have murdered you?"

"A very good question," Musa–no, Trude said. "I thought I knew,
but now I'm not so sure. I'll tell you what I know, and maybe then
you can tell me what you think."

"Fair enough," Reginn said, already breaking her new rule
against making bargains with the dead.

"I told you that I was a dedicate, and that is true. At that time,
the academy served many more students. It was easier for one person to hide out among many. I was awkward and shy–I preferred
the company of books and dusty old manuscripts. Modir Tyra was
the director of the academy–"

"You're saying that Modir Tyra is more than two hundred years
old?" Reginn interrupted, though after everything else, she couldn't
say why that surprised her.

"That's what I'm saying."

"But–"

"Just listen," Trude said.

A memory surfaced, of something Kennari had said when
Reginn remarked on how young the council members were.

Appearances can be deceiving, Tyra had said. *They are older than you think.*

Tyra never mentioned that it might apply to herself.

"Tyra wasn't as powerful then. Nobody was," Trude said. "Dedicates had to study, and read, and sit through lectures in order to
learn. There were many more faculty as well. Tyra was fascinated
with the age of the gods, especially the final battle between the
gods and the jotun. When she learned that I had the gift of speaking to the dead, she kept after me to try and connect with those
who died at Ragnarok, even though I'd never heard as much as a
peep from any of them."

"How would you even go about that?" Reginn said.

"She wanted me to reach out to the founder," Trude said. "She believed that Brenna had the key."

"Well," Reginn said, "that hasn't changed."

"She was right," Trude said.

"You spoke with Modir Brenna?" Reginn said. Jealousy flickered through her, though being jealous of a dead person for speaking with a dead person was petty at best. "I didn't get very far."

"I did," Trude said. "We became close. I believe that's why I was murdered."

Reginn recalled what the founder had said.

The one who came before you paid with her life.

"She blames herself," Reginn whispered.

"It was my fault, not hers," Trude said. "She warned me what would happen if I told anyone. I didn't listen."

"Who did you tell?"

"I told one person," Trude said. "There was an adept by the name of Frodi who taught ancient symbols and dead languages." The words spilled out, as if she'd been waiting more than two centuries to tell this story. "You wouldn't call him handsome, but he was striking, with his red hair and eyes the color of the sea. He had this raw, kinetic intellect and intense curiosity. In those days, this was more like a real academy, with classes and lectures. I could have listened to Frodi lecture all day. He would stride back and forth, that red hair flaring around his head when he turned, punctuating his words by slamming the butt of his staff into the floor. He did not tolerate laziness or lack of preparation. I admired that, but some dedicates made fun of him from the safety of the dormitory. We all feared his withering gaze and lashing tongue.

"Everyone used the library in those days, but I practically lived here when I wasn't in class or in the catacombs. I was so eager to succeed for Modir Tyra. I'd pore over old manuscripts, looking for spellsongs I hadn't tried. Frodi was the only person who spent as much time here as I did. At first, he never raised his eyes from his work or acknowledged my presence. Finally, late one night, I asked him for help with a translation, and one thing led to another. Eventually, he began making suggestions and offering resources that might be helpful.

"It was an odd partnership. I was a misfit. He was a misfit, too. We both mistrusted the council and the high-up faculty. The first time Brenna Half-Foot responded to me, it felt like a shared success. Frodi warned me not to say anything to Modir Tyra until I had some hard evidence to offer. So we kept it just between us.

"I never mentioned Frodi to Brenna, and I was selective in what I shared with him. Brenna wanted me to read her journal and know the truth about the history of the temple, but I couldn't because I had no knowledge of the runes. The founder didn't want to open her tomb to me—she said it was too dangerous. Frodi kept pushing for access, saying the artifacts and history locked inside could occupy us both for the rest of our lives.

"I envisioned the two of us working together forever. Eventually, I persuaded Brenna that the only way I could know the true history of New Jotunheim and protect her legacy was to enter the tomb and find the runes that would unlock the journal. So she gave me the key."

"You've been inside the tomb," Reginn said.

Trude nodded.

Reginn cleared her throat. "Was it—was it everything you hoped it would be?"

Trude shrugged. "I focused on the runes, so I could figure out how to read Brenna's journal. I shared a few of them with Frodi, but I never told him where they came from. Maybe I knew, in my heart of hearts, that all he really wanted was to get at what was inside the tomb. I never worked out which runes would open the pages because I was murdered before then."

Reginn was lost. "So . . . what are you thinking?"

"When I was a dedicate here, it was uncommon to live one hundred years, two hundred years, and the like. Nobody seemed to be as powerful as they are today. Now, it seems, the people in power—the elders and the faculty—are all but immortal. Why is that?" Trude paused. "It must have begun soon after my death because the same people are here now as then. But very few students, and very few teachers."

"There are more students—younger students, called acolytes—in the lower school on the west side of Eimyrja," Reginn said.

"Really?" Trude said. "That wasn't the case before. We used to be all together, here at the Grove. Strange that they would split us up when there are fewer students."

"Tell me," Reginn said, "when you were here as a dedicate, were there bondi?"

Trude seemed lost for a moment, and then her confusion cleared. "Oh—you mean the original residents of these islands? Of course. They worked for us, and we provided schooling for the children and treatment in our clinics."

That sounded much like the arrangement that the founder had intended.

"Did they . . . disappear? The children in particular?"

"No," Trude said. "Nothing like that." She paused. "I mean, it could have been happening and I didn't know about it. That's happening now?"

"Yes." Reginn waited as time trickled on, like sand through a glass, sensing that Trude was working things out in her head.

"There's something I need to tell you about the blodkyn rune," Trude said finally.

As if in answer, the emblem on Reginn's thigh prickled and burned.

"It is a means of transferring strength and power from one person to another," Trude said. "That is why I insisted that you apply it before we began working together. It gave me the strength to move physical objects and carry on extended conversations." It was as if the mouse was shrinking, until she was nearly lost in her ashy clothes.

"I see," Reginn said, her voice hard as a flake of flint. "So you can just . . . steal power whenever you want?"

"I couldn't have helped you without it," Trude said, a plaintive note in her voice. "And trust me, you have power to spare."

"What are the limits?"

"I don't know," Trude said.

"You don't know," Reginn echoed. "You should have told me. You should have given me a real choice." First Asger. Now Trude. She was tired of being sucked dry by magical parasites.

"And if I had, what would you have done?" Trude said. "If that was the price for my help?"

Reginn knew the truth of it, even though she didn't want to admit it. "I would have said yes. But that doesn't excuse–"

"Listen to me," Trude said. "I can't help you if you don't listen. I shared the blodkyn rune with Frodi."

"So you were taking power from him, too?" Reginn growled.

"No," Trude said. "It was the other way around. Frodi's gift was that he was brilliant, but he wasn't satisfied with that. He wanted to be more than a scholar, but he couldn't match the megin of the faculty or of the other adepts. She paused. "You know what that is, right?"

Reginn nodded. "It's raw power, the vital essence, different from a particular gift or talent. Every living thing has some . . . except, maybe, demons," she added, thinking of Asger and his hunger.

Trude nodded. "And you have more than most gifted. Children are born with a lifetime supply that dwindles as they grow older. The gifted have more than most. I felt bad for Frodi, so I gave him the rune so that he could draw power from me. I thought it would bind us more closely together."

Reginn's thoughts had been floundering like a beached fish, but now they coalesced around a dark suspicion. "You're thinking that Frodi got greedy and decided to go for broke," she said. "Like the story of the goose that laid the golden eggs."

"Or the cow that gave mead instead of milk. He must have thought he could have his fill without humoring me. Or he wanted me out of the picture so that he could take all the credit and the glory."

"Listen, you don't know that—"

"Don't worry," Trude said wryly. "Infatuation wears thin after two hundred years."

"Whatever happened, it must have worked out for him, since he's an elder now," Reginn said. But the grim look on Trude's face said there was more to the story. "What is it?" she said. "What are you thinking?"

"I think it goes beyond the betrayal of a smitten dedicate," Trude said. "When I was here, we had lots of students with a range of gifts and faculty to match, and we partnered with the bondi. Now we have few students and faculty, and bondi are disappearing. On the other hand, the place is blooming and is ruled by very powerful elders who live forever."

"So it seems that the mission has changed," Reginn said. "You think it has to do with the blodkyn rune?"

"I don't know for sure," Trude said, "but Frodi knows, and we're going to make him tell us."

49

GRAVEYARD OF THE GODS

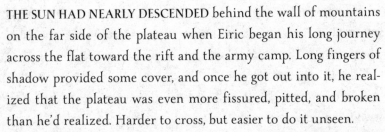

THE SUN HAD NEARLY DESCENDED behind the wall of mountains on the far side of the plateau when Eiric began his long journey across the flat toward the rift and the army camp. Long fingers of shadow provided some cover, and once he got out into it, he realized that the plateau was even more fissured, pitted, and broken than he'd realized. Harder to cross, but easier to do it unseen.

The farther he went, the clearer it became that he was navigating the ruins of a once-great city. The stone foundations and half walls told him that the buildings were more elaborate than anything he'd seen in his coasting with his fadir and grandfadir.

Definitely finer than anything he'd seen in the Archipelago.

This place called to him in a way that Muckleholm never had. It was as if he was being welcomed home after a long time away.

Come back to me.

Evidently, it had also been the site of a great battle that had gone unplundered all this time. The outlines of swords, axe-heads, and other weapons could be seen under centuries of accumulated dirt and undergrowth. In some cases, large trees had grown over top half-exposed skeletons of horses and men in a vain attempt to obscure the history that had happened here. A tarnished, silver-chased hilt protruded from one side of a massive oak, the point sticking out the other side.

Eventually, Eiric reached the near end of the long spine of stones. He kicked one of the smaller bits, and it rolled away. A chill seized him, and the scent of ancient death and decay filled his nose. The scent of things best left undisturbed.

Not stones. Bones.

He leaped back from the array, one hand on his axe, the other on Leif's amulet, heart pounding. He studied the scene through new eyes. It appeared that some massive creature from before the memory of man had died here, on this plain. Some sort of massive serpent.

Had it been during this last battle or long before? What kind of hero would fight a creature like this?

Steeling himself, he bent and picked up one of the smaller bones and stowed it in his carry bag before he walked on.

Once, a stone vault collapsed under his feet, and he had to fling himself back to avoid falling into the pit below. Crawling forward to the edge, he peered in. In the dwindling light, he could make out the shapes of bones and other objects at the bottom. It appeared to be a rich hoard. It was tempting to climb down and investigate further, but climbing out would be treacherous, especially if he was loaded down with grave goods.

But he could tell already that there was enough treasure here to buy the farm three times over, if Rikhard would take that in payment.

His mission was to collect information, though. Still, he was encouraged by these finds as he soldiered on. By now, it was getting to be dead dark, and the moon had not yet risen. That slowed him some. His worst fear was that he would trip or fall and break a leg, which would put a humiliating end to this adventure.

There were so many stupid ways to die.

So many questions needed answering before then. What had happened to the victors? Why had they let the spoils be? Why hadn't anyone ever returned to this place?

Across the rift, the land was crawling with soldiers. Why had they not come over here and helped themselves? Soldiers plunder. Were they soldiers or not?

The moon rose, and now, after two hours of slow progress, Eiric was able to move more quickly. At one point, he saw something glittering in the moonlight. When he knelt to have a look, he recognized it as one of the gold game pieces Rikhard had been so interested in. His pulse quickened. Had his fadir and grandfadir walked over these grounds before him? He tucked the piece in his carry bag and forged on.

As he drew closer, he realized something else. There were no bridges across the rift. Why not? Did these men have no desire to explore what was on the other side?

Which meant that if he managed to get across, there would be no easy way to return.

That made the back of his neck itch and prickle. He was a coaster. He never liked to roam too far from his ship.

Eiric finally reached a point where he could look over the edge of the cliff to what lay below.

A river roared through the rift, white as milk and seething against stone walls stained from the icy spray and fumes boiling up from below. Remnants of dead ferns and mosses covered the far side, studded with poisonous-looking flowers the color of bruises. It resembled the Elivagar—one of the frozen, venomous rivers in Bjorn's stories.

Across the way, a low wall lined the cliff top. It wasn't tall enough to keep anyone out, so he assumed it was to prevent anyone from wandering off the edge when they were in their cups. Helpfully, torches blazed on the wall at intervals, presenting a lighted target.

The temple he'd noticed earlier was lit as well, with torchlight leaking through the windows. It appeared to be anchored firmly to the cliff top but extended out over the boil below.

Below the temple, Eiric could make out what appeared to be caves and tunnels leading into the cliff. That could be a safe way to cross the army camp undetected. It could also be a trap if those tunnels didn't go anywhere.

Steam and gas burst up from the river below, and Eiric nearly took a direct hit. All but overcome by waves of dizziness and nausea, he threw himself back from the edge, landing flat on his back, sucking in fresh air again. He'd nearly fallen into the gorge.

Well then. That explained the lack of bridges.

Why would anyone build a temple so close to such a hazard? The ceremonies would have to end early if the wind blew the wrong way.

So he faced a choice. He could explore this side of the rift, safe from the army across the way. Plenty to do and see, and treasure to harvest over here. He could map the terrain and collect grave goods—hopefully enough to satisfy Rikhard and save Sundgard.

And then what? He had no desire to return to Sundgard without Liv, so he and Ivar could live out their days as farmers with a sad story to tell. If his systir was still alive, she might have landed on the other side of the island. He'd never know if he didn't find a way across.

He crept forward again, covering his mouth and nose with his sleeve. That made it marginally better. Most of the time, the high winds through the rift carried the poisons away. But when geysirs of steam and gases erupted from below, they carried the fumes all the way up the walls of the chasm. If he could time it right, he might be able to swing to the other side between blasts. If he timed it wrong, he'd end up as one more withered vine on the wall.

At least it would be easier swinging from high to low. Getting back would be another story. A rudimentary plan was taking shape in his mind.

Dropping his belongings at the edge of the rift, Eiric drew his axe and cut a green limb from a nearby tree. It was thick yet limber enough for his purposes (he hoped). He secured one end of his precious rope to the center of the branch and scanned the far edge for a suitable tree, well rooted with a divided trunk. Taking careful aim, he threw.

The limb spun end over end across the gorge. Any doubts that he could throw that far were quickly dispelled. The stick flew between the two trunks of the tree.

He waited again to see if there was any outcry on the other side, but there was none. Gently, and then more forcefully, he tugged the rope toward him until the branch was anchored crosswise against the crotch of the tree.

He looped the rope around a tree on his own side, drawing it taut and anchoring it with another stick. He put his weight on it several times to test it. That fastening needed to last until he was safely across and then be breakable so that he could retrieve the rope.

He did not plan on leaving his rope strung across the river like a signpost.

Ropes were precious.

He looped a shorter walrus-hide line over the rope and attached it to his belt for safety. He hoped that gravity would do some of the work for him.

He tied one of his leg wrappings across his nose and mouth and pulled on the leather gloves that Liv had made him.

Meanwhile, he'd been timing the blasts of steam and gases. Leaning forward, he waited until one eruption had just ended, then cast off from the edge of the cliff. What followed was a blur of a headlong ride. His eyes were tearing and burning so that he just got his feet up in time to deflect the blow as he smashed into the cliff on the far side. The rope had sagged so that he was hanging two body lengths below the rim.

He kicked his feet forward, aiming for a small ledge, finding footing on the second try, grabbing on to a dead tree just in time to huddle against the stone as another blast of steam and gas erupted from below. When it receded, he looked up, toward the rim. It seemed impossibly far away. Propping his feet against the side of the cliff, he climbed toward the top.

The last few feet were the hardest, clearing a slight overhang in order to get his hands on the top of the low wall. Every muscle straining, Eiric pulled up until he could peer over the wall. In time to see a squad of guardsmen jogging toward him.

Well, he wasn't going to climb back down again. So he swung his body up and over the wall, landing hard on the other side. He came to his feet and detached himself from his rope just as the soldiers closed in.

Maybe he could talk his way out. Though that had never gone well in the past, he was always hopeful. So he drew his sword and his axe and stood waiting.

The column slowed as they neared him, coming to a stop outside his reach. They looked him up and down, eyes wide, as if he were a draugr out of a barrow. The soldiers included some who resembled any citizen of the Archipelago, with pale to tawny skin and hair that ranged from brown to fair. Others were outlanders, a mingle of races.

The soldiers gave way as a rider approached on one of the

finest-looking horses Eiric had ever seen. The rider was a young woman with long limbs, amber eyes, and blue-black skin. Unlike the others, who wore dusty dun-colored uniforms, she wore blues of a different style.

She was so striking that it took him a moment to notice the beasts swarming around her horse.

He blinked. Blinked again. No. Not beasts. Maidens, with pointed teeth and bloody claws, who eyed him as if they'd like to take a bite.

Then they were back to beasts again, resembling compact griffins with long, spiked tails.

Eiric looked around. Nobody else seemed to notice them; either that or they were used to them. Even the horses didn't seem to care.

Maybe they weren't really dangerous, just—

"They don't like your weapons," the girl said, gesturing toward his sword and axe. "They have a distaste for bloodshed that they don't inflict themselves."

Me too, Eiric thought. Which meant he wasn't letting go of his weapons anytime soon.

"Who are you?" the girl said. "Are you a barbarian?" She looked him up and down as if barbarians might be appealing, once you got to know them. Or even before.

From the soldiers' expressions, it seemed that opinion was not widely shared.

"I'm Eiric Halvorsen," he said. "I'm from Muckleholm, in the Archipelago."

"Muckleholm," she repeated, eyes narrowing, as if the word was familiar. "Really?"

"Really," Eiric said. Since she didn't offer, he asked. "Who are you?"

"I'm Katia Lund," she said. "Temple dedicate."

Now I'm getting somewhere, he thought. "That's what I'm looking for–the Temple at the Grove." He gestured toward the building cantilevered over the rift. "Is that it?"

Just then, another rider in buff came up alongside Katia. An officer, based on the extra badges she wore and a tight-assed expression that said she wasn't impressed with him at all.

"Who is this, Highest?" the officer asked the dedicate.

"This is Eiric Halvorsen from the Archipelago, Captain Yrsa," Katia said. "He wishes to go to the temple."

Captain Yrsa focused on Eiric. "How did you get here?"

"My ship ran aground across the way there." He waved vaguely toward the opposite side of the rift.

"That's impossible," Yrsa said. "That is Vigrid, site of the Last Battle. Those are the deadlands. Nothing and nobody survives over there."

Eiric was at a loss for what to say next. He'd lied often enough in his life, but it was his custom to lie first and then tell the truth if the lie didn't work out. He wasn't sure where to go from the truth.

"There *are* a lot of ruins over there," he said. "I didn't see anyone else. That's why I came over here."

"You've made a mistake, then," she said. "No one comes here unless it's by permission of the elders and with proper notice."

Well, you see, Eiric thought of saying, *when you come without notice, that's what we call coasting.*

If he said half the things he thought of saying, he'd be in more trouble than he already was.

"I'm looking for my systir," he said. "She was washed overboard in the storm that blew me aground. I was hoping someone had seen her." He paused, and when nobody said anything, added, "You can't miss her. She looks nothing like me."

If he thought his attempt at humor would be disarming, he was wrong. While they'd been talking, more and more armed and armored soldiers had boiled out of the buildings and collected behind Yrsa and Katia.

He'd never seen so much fine weaponry in one place. Most bands of soldiers and raiders in the Archipelago carried a motley assortment of found and scavenged weapons down to farm axes and makeshift spears.

Many of these men carried swords as well as axes and wore finely crafted armor.

If this was the temple, it had to be the best protected one he'd ever seen. That would make sense if the streets were paved with gold, like Rikhard had said.

If this was the Grove, it had been oversold.

"Could you at least tell me where I am?" he said.

"This is Ithavoll," the officer said, "a province of New Jotunheim." New Jotunheim. Liv had told him that she was born in New Jotunheim.

Ithavoll. That name sounded familiar, too.. Had Rikhard mentioned it?

"Eimyrja is where I want to be," Eiric said, trying to recall what Rikhard had told him. "I'm here to speak with whoever is in charge of the temple."

If he thought that would win him friends, he was mistaken.

"What's your business?"

"That's between me and her."

"I'll send a message to the Council of Elders. They'll decide what to do. In the meantime, you'll need to hand over your weapons." Yrsa stepped forward, arms out to receive them.

"No," Eiric said. "These weapons are precious to me."

"Then you should not have brought them here."

Eiric considered fighting his way through, but that would leave him on the run, no wiser than before. Katia's beasts stirred and circled and showed their teeth, as if they'd read that impulse in him.

He looked at Katia, and she shook her head. "Dead men have no need of weapons," she said. "Give them up."

Eiric handed over Leif's sword, Gramr, Bjorn's axe, and the smaller of his two daggers, wondering if he would ever see them again. The sunstone lay heavy on his chest, alongside Leif's talisman and Reginn's runestick. To his surprise, they didn't bother to search him.

Then again, from the looks of things, they didn't get many visitors—invited or not.

"Lock the barbarian in the guardhouse," Yrsa said, turning away.

"Captain!" Eiric called after her. "Is this how Ithavoll treats its guests?"

She swiveled back. "You are a barbarian, not a guest. And guests come with notice."

50

REAPING

REGINN WRAPPED A SHAWL AROUND her shoulders before she left the library. Lately, she'd taken to covering her arms to prevent anyone noticing traces of runes.

Musa was getting to her. No. Trude. Trude had a plan that required Reginn's cooperation, but Reginn wasn't ready to say yes. Maybe she shouldn't have accepted the blodkyn rune from the library mouse. She had a lot more to lose than did the vengeful spirit who haunted the library.

Reginn didn't know who to believe or who to trust. A part of her longed for the simple brutality of the Archipelago.

Not really. She needed to keep her head down and find a way to succeed.

The quad was all but deserted. It seemed she saw less and less of her age-mates. No doubt they had been sent to work on assignments elsewhere in the islands. Often, even at night, the dormitory was nearly empty.

The only dedicates who still did much of their work on campus were Bryn and Erland. Her concerts with Erland and Naima were the high points of her days.

And yet—she wasn't sure that being surrounded by the other

dedicates would dispel her sense of isolation. Reginn had no peers here. Her classmates were naive, incurious, and serenely comfortable with their privilege. All the experiences she'd had before coming to New Jotunheim set her apart, despite Tyra's efforts to wipe them away. She had more in common with Trude and Naima than with any of the other dedicates.

Everyone has a role to play in New Jotunheim.

Speaking of Naima. Reginn wondered if she might answer some questions about what was happening with the bondi that would help her figure out whether Trude's theories could be true.

Maybe Reginn was just eager to talk to someone who wasn't dead.

This time of day, the kitchen was always bustling with activity, with Naima and her assistants hard at work on preparations for the nattmal. They'd be chopping vegetables and fruits, stirring cauldrons of soup, proofing bread for baking, and turning meat on the spits. It was always a feast of mouth watering smells. Naima and the other bondi would be calling out to each other, trading stories and jibes. It was a great time to find something good to eat when she couldn't wait for the nattmal.

Reginn circled around to the back door of the kitchen, as was her practice for visits between meals. To her surprise, the kitchen was eerily quiet. She heard only the chop of knives and the clatter of dishes.

Inside, the cook's helpers were ranged around the room at their usual stations, working, but there was none of the usual chatter or gossip. It was as if Reginn had wandered into the tombs by mistake.

"What's going on?" Reginn said, her voice loud amid the unaccustomed silence. "Where's Naima?"

There was no answer. Everyone continued to work. Nobody made eye contact.

From the funereal atmosphere Reginn knew there was some kind of bad news. "Is she sick? Did she get hurt?" she persisted.

Still, no one spoke. Reginn knew most of them, had joked with them, played music with them and for them.

They still don't trust me, she thought. Why should they?

Finally, Kelby, one of the cook's helpers, looked up at her. "They took her," he said, then returned to his work.

"Who? Who took her? And why?"

"They were guards. Soldiers," Kari, the baker, said. He pounded out the dough with unusual force. "As to why, you would know better than we do, *Highest*."

Kari's use of the title stung.

"I'll see what I can find out, Kari," Reginn said. She raced through the front doors, heading for the council house.

Just outside, she all but ran into Modir Tyra crossing the quad. Tyra gripped Reginn's shoulders to keep her from toppling over. "What's on fire, Dottir Reginn?" she said.

For a moment, Reginn was too breathless to reply. When she could speak, she said, "Kennari. I . . . was just in the kitchen . . . looking for Naima Bondi, the head cook . . . and she wasn't there."

Tyra laughed. "I know you're always hungry, but surely one of the other pantry workers could have helped you."

Reginn was beginning to recover her wits, beginning to realize that she needed to play her cards close until she found out what had happened.

"Everyone in the kitchen seemed upset, as if they thought she was in some kind of trouble," Reginn said, swallowing hard. "They said that soldiers took her away. I told them I would try to find out what's going on."

"Really," Tyra said, frowning. "Don't worry, dottir. Be at ease. I'll look into it." Reaching down, she tucked Reginn's wayward hair behind her ears. "How goes your work at the founder's tomb?"

"It—it goes well, Modir, I believe," Reginn said haltingly.

"Good," Tyra said. "I look forward to hearing more about it." The headmistress studied her for another long moment, then strode on, toward the council house.

But Reginn did not turn back toward the catacombs or walk on to the council house. Instead, she went looking for Erland. The only places she knew to look for him were the dining halls and the groves. She knew he wasn't at the dining halls, so she headed for the groves.

When she was deeply in, and confident of not being overheard, she began calling his name. The only answer was the murmuring voices of trees in the wind. Even the birdsong was hushed.

"Erland!" she said. "Erland—it's me. Reginn."

At first, there was no answer. And then, like a rivulet of blood running from an open wound, she heard the sound of his lyre. She followed the thread of it, realizing that this section of the woods was familiar.

She found Erland sitting on a blanket, leaning back against the broad trunk of a tree, his long legs splayed out in front. His hat was tilted forward so that his face was all but hidden. His lyre was cradled in his lap.

"Erland?" Reginn whispered, but he didn't seem to hear. He only played on, desperately.

As she came closer, under the canopy of the tree, she recognized it as the tree she'd carved Alva's rune into.

Hanging from the tree like a discarded rag doll was Alva. Her head hung forward, a curtain of hair obscuring her face. Her body was covered in dirt and bruises, and she was barefoot.

Reginn reached out and touched one bare toe. It was icy cold.

Erland still hadn't seemed to notice Reginn's presence. He

continued to play, ripping notes from his instrument, tears streaming down his face.

Reginn took a running start and scrambled up the trunk, finding a perch in a crotch where the trunk split. From there, she could
reach the rope above Alva's head. It looked to have been braided
from split linen. A great deal of care had gone into it.

Reginn could picture how it had gone down. Though much
younger, Alva had been nearly as tall as Reginn. She imagined her
crouching in the tree, looping a strip of linen over the branch, tying
it into a snug knot.

Reginn drew her dagger and gripped the rope.

"Erland!" she said sharply. "I'm going to cut her down. Catch her
when she falls."

That stirred him. Setting aside his instrument, he stood beneath
the tree and extended his arms. Reginn sliced through the linen
and Alva fell and he caught her. He cradled her a moment, then set
her carefully on the ground.

Reginn jumped from the tree, landing hard, feeling the impact
into her hips.

Erland was kneeling next to Alva, desperately straightening her
clothing, untangling her hair, as if he could fix this with a bit of
tidying.

Reginn knelt on the opposite side. "What happened, Erland?"
she said.

For a moment longer, he continued to fuss. Then sat back on his
heels. "Naima went to see Alva," he said. "She must have been followed. Or maybe somebody said something. While she was there,
Skarde showed up with a pair of guards as backup. He tried to take
Alva. Naima stood up to him, and in the struggle, Naima killed
him. Alva ran. The guards took Naima. When I heard what happened, I went looking for Alva, and found her here."

"How?" Reginn said. "How did she kill him?"

Erland shrugged. "I don't know. I don't–I don't think he was expecting resistance." He threw up his hands, tears running down his face. "I don't know what to do."

Well, that's no help to them, Reginn thought, before she could stop herself. At least she didn't say it out loud.

She collected herself. "Erland, I–I'm so sorry," she said finally. "Do you know where the guards would have taken Naima?"

Erland shook his head. "There is a prison under the council house," he said. "It's not big. Most prisoners are quickly redeemed or executed. If she's still alive, I imagine she's there." He gripped her hand, as if eager for reassurance. "She'll be redeemed, don't you think? They'll see how much she has to offer and take that into account. Everybody makes mistakes."

"Killing the chair of the Council of Elders is a big mistake," Reginn said, thinking Naima was probably already dead. "They may find that hard to forgive."

"I should have done something," Erland said. "I should have gone to Modir Tyra before now and told her what was going on. She could have intervened before things got this far."

"Can you look ahead, Erland?" Reginn said. "Can you see what would have happened if you'd taken that path?"

Erland closed his eyes, breathed deeply, and tried to go to that haven inside him. But it seemed that there was no refuge to be found. He opened his eyes and said, "All I see is death and fire and grief everywhere I look."

Reginn had called the other dedicates naive. When she looked back at her friendship with Naima and Erland, their subversive little concerts in the forest–who was naive, really? Naima was the only one who saw what was coming, this person who wasn't considered gifted enough, or gifted in the right way.

"Reginn?" Erland said, breaking into her roiling thoughts. "Did you hear me? We could go to Modir Tyra now. Once she understands, she might be able to do something."

For a moment, Reginn allowed herself to imagine that they could deliver this situation into more capable hands and take the responsibility off their shoulders.

But she also knew that talking to Modir Tyra about it would be like pulling on the loose end of a ball of yarn. Everything would come unraveled.

She knew, deep inside, that Modir Tyra would betray her trust, just like Tove did.

"I already asked Modir Tyra about Naima," Reginn said. "I'll see what she says before we decide."

Erland seemed relieved to be handing it off to Reginn.

"All right," he said, blotting his eyes with his sleeve. He stood and slid his lyre into its cover. "I'll carry Alva back to Brenna's House." Slinging his instrument over his shoulder, he scooped up the small body and took the path back toward the healing grove.

Reginn took a moment to finger the rune carved into the tree, recalling what she'd said to Alva.

This is Ul. It signifies a turning point. A decision that only you can make. You cannot stay where you are—it's too painful. You must go forward or back. Which way will you go?

Alva had made her decision.

51

BRENNA'S JOURNAL

N.J., year 350, month 8, day 8

Today, representatives from the Council of Elders came to see me in my self-imposed exile and demanded the following:

1. The amulets that representatives of the academy use to detect the presence of magic in those we bring back to New Jotunheim.

2. A geas that will protect all members of the council and the faculty of the academy from violence and rebellion.

3. The gift of immortality.

4. Finally, they want me to teach them the secrets of the runes and how to use them.

These demands are, of course, impossible, since the members of the council have proven themselves unworthy of wielding that much power.

I listened politely (I have grown considerably more patient in my old age). I told them that I would consider their requests overnight and give them my answer in the morning. This was met with all manner of threats and considerable bluster, which I weathered like one of the twisted old junipers on the rocky coast of the northern sea. Eventually, they left.

I spent the next hours building a wall of weather and illusion around New Jotunheim that could be penetrated only with the guidance of one of three sunstones I devised. The wall would protect us from our enemies and remove any excuse for building an army for "self-defense," something I know they have been discussing.

It would also protect the peoples of the Midlands from us.

I called in Inger, of course, my dear friend, my rock, my heart. I did not tell her everything, but I believe she guessed most of it.

First, I asked her to maintain the boundary I'd built—a life sentence that would limit her ability to do the things that she loved. She did not flinch but accepted that burden gracefully.

Second, I gave her the sunstones I had made that would allow her to pass through the barrier without taking it down. "This will allow you to continue your mission to the Archipelago, seeking the gifted and bringing them here for training. I wish I could say that you are bringing them to a safe place, but that is no longer true."

Finally, I gifted her my garnet ring, and with it, immortality. She tried to refuse it, knowing that it meant I was leaving.

"This ring does not offer protection against the gods, should they return here," I told her. "But that is no longer my greatest concern. In carrying out my wishes, you will be in grave danger from members of the council."

"Please," Inger said. "Stay, and fight alongside me."

"I have walked the Midlands for far too long already," I said.

"You warned me that love between a human and a god can only lead to heartbreak," Inger said. "Whatever the future holds, it has been worth it. I will keep your tomb and keep the truth every day of my life."

Next, I called in Modir Tyra, recently named kennari of the academy. She is a brilliant teacher—the dedicates all love her, and she is devoted to them. I know that she will do everything she can to protect them.

She seemed both nervous and flattered to be called into my presence. I charged her with the protection of the dedicates, the academy, and its mission, and the continued study of our history. Along with a sunstone, I gifted her with a pendant, carved from Heidin's anklebone, to remind her of the gods' treachery and give her unusually long life.

Unlike Inger, she did not beg me to stay, but accepted her charge gravely. "If you are intent on leaving, Highest," she said, "could you teach me the runes of magic before you go? That would seem to be the best protection against our enemies."

I denied her request. Her gift of mind magic makes it difficult for me to read her and predict what she will and will not do. Tyra carries with her a deep bitterness toward the Archipelago, rooted in her experiences before she came to us. She has a fierce desire for justice–to avenge the wrongs of the past, in the Midlands and elsewhere, and raise the jotnar–the spinners–to their rightful place in the world.

But hers is the one gift among the many at the Grove that can prevail against the council. If she chooses, she can keep the academy and the temple safe.

That work accomplished, I ate my usual nattmal of grains and fresh fruit from our orchards and bathed in the hot spring until the blood rushed through my veins. I dressed in a simple linen shift and sandals as I prepared to meet my peers in the borderlands. It is time. I am more than three hundred years old.

I poured a thimbleful of mourner's tears into my cup, then filled it with wine, knowing I would have to be careful not to drink too much before I finished my business in the Midlands.

I took out my brushes and ink and wrote the council a letter. I am copying it here because I doubt that the original will survive me for long. I leave this in the hopes that a practitioner of the old magic will unlock the text and read this journal long after I am gone. Perhaps others will learn from my errors.

Elders, adepts, dedicates, and faculty,

At the end of life, it is appropriate to review one's accomplishments, acknowledge mistakes, and do whatever is necessary to preserve a legacy.

Despite our trials in the Archipelago, I have always believed in the essential goodness of humankind. When I gathered my beleaguered flock and *brought them to New Jotunheim, my intent was, first, to build a sanctuary in which the gifted could heal and thrive and practice and learn without fear of imprisonment, enslavement, or death.*

Second, I hoped to establish a paradise on this island that would demonstrate what could be accomplished by partnering spinner magic with respect for the natural world.

In those things, I have mostly succeeded.

My third goal was to establish a sense of mission within the academy and the temple that values every person, gifted or not, and seeks to make this flawed world we now share a better place for everyone.

In that, it seems, I have failed.

You have given me your demands. Here is my answer.

1. I must deny your demand for knowledge of the runes, as I am not convinced that you will use this knowledge for the good of everyone in the Midlands. I will take them with me to Helgafjell, the world of the dead.

2. You have said that you need the protection of the runes because of the risk of attack from the Archipelago. In my frequent visits to Muckleholm, I have seen no evidence that such a thing is planned. Nevertheless, I have erected a magical boundary that will protect New Jotunheim from those outsiders who would do us harm. I have given sunstones to the faithful who tend the Temple at the Grove. They can be used by temple staff to pass through the barrier to the Archipelago in order to recruit the gifted and for humanitarian purposes. I charged them to guard the stones well and use them wisely because the boundary works both ways—it keeps intruders out, and keeps us in.

3. This boundary should free you to relax the restrictions on the bondi and allow them to follow their traditional way of life without interference. Their role in these islands should be as partners, and not as servants.

Together, you can continue to build the paradise that is the goal of us all.

4. The jarls in the Archipelago are learning the cost of living in a world without magic. That knowledge does them no good if we do not present them

*with an alternative. Now that we have a safe haven, we must continue to
identify the gifted and bring them here for training. Those dedicates can then
return to the Archipelago under our protection and use their gifts for the
benefit of all.*

*To that end, I will provide four amulets that will enable you to see the
spark of magic in the people of the Archipelago. It will not, however, identify
the kind of gift straightaway. Only as the children mature will it become clear
whether the magic has roots within the boundary or outside it. We must
learn to nurture all the gifted, whether they be the children of Asgard or of
Jotunheim.*

Reginn read that passage again. What did that mean? She
searched back through the stories Tove had told. The worlds of
gods and humans were considered innangard—inside the boundary.
All else was utangard—outside. In fact, Utgard was another name
for Jotunheim. So the crystals could eventually distinguish wyrdspinner magic from the magic of the gods.

There was one more paragraph in Brenna's entry.

*The gifts of magic do not pass reliably from one generation to the next
like a farm or a set of carving tools. They are meant to be shared by all of
humankind. I promise you this—if they are tampered with or turned to an evil
purpose, this will be the last generation of the gifted in New Jotunheim. —B.H.*

That was the last entry.

52

DANCING ON THE EDGE

BEING LOCKED IN A GUARDHOUSE gives a man time to second-guess his past choices and worry about his future.

Eiric's cell was more spacious than he'd expected and finer than most houses in the Archipelago. They'd fed him twice now, both meals better than any he'd had in a long time. They'd chained his hands together and his feet together, but they'd allowed enough length so he could shuffle around if he wanted or make himself uncomfortable on the floor in several different ways.

His cell had one small window that faced the rift, so he could hear the thunder of the falls and see the deadly mists boiling up. Every once in a while, the wind would bring a whiff of poison that set his eyes to watering. At least it seemed likely to discourage anyone from exploring the far side in search of his ship.

It was too quiet in this place. There were no other prisoners and very few guards. Any lockup in an army camp this size ought to have more business. Soldiers were not that well behaved.

What did the wyrdspinners need with an army? Armies were expensive to outfit and maintain. Was it for offense or defense?

Why would they need an army for defense with the weather wall in the way?

He'd nurtured a faint hope that Katia would somehow intervene on his behalf. Unbidden, he heard Liv's voice in his head.

Really, Brodir? Isn't it possible that here, in New Jotunheim, there exists a girl who isn't susceptible to your charms?

He found himself longing to feel the lash of Liv's wit again.

That reminder of his losses brought Reginn Eiklund to mind. Was she really here somewhere? Should he ask about her? Or would that put her at risk?

Finally, he heard a commotion outside the guardhouse, the tread of many feet and loud voices. Obviously, something was happening, which was maybe better than nothing.

Maybe.

Captain Yrsa marched in with a quartet of burly soldiers. Eiric stood to await the news.

"Let's go, Halvorsen," she said, unlocking the door to his cell. "A representative of the council has come to evaluate you."

Eiric hesitated, expecting the captain to elaborate, but she brusquely waved him forward. "Elder Scarlet is waiting. We don't have all day."

He shuffled a few feet toward the door at the center of a buzzing hive of guards, exaggerating his stumbling gait. "Could you at least free my feet so that I can walk?" he said. "Do you really think I'm going to run away?"

Grudgingly, Yrsa unlocked the chains on his ankles and removed them.

Outside, more armed soldiers waited, so that in the end, his escort numbered more than thirty, with others lined up in case they were needed. Eiric scanned the area, looking for horses, or a wagon, or some other means of transporting him to the Temple at the Grove. A fancy carriage with six fine horses stood in the stable yard, surrounded by servants in dun-colored uniforms.

The only spot of color was a tall woman in crimson robes with an elaborate staff. This, then, must be Elder Scarlet, one of the wyrdspinners Rikhard spoke of. She stared at him as the guard hustled Eiric forward until he stood close to the low wall that ran around the edge of the cliff.

The soldiers clustered around him, bristling with steel.

Yrsa crossed the yard to speak to the newcomer. The lady in red handed the captain a small bag. Some kind of payment? Then the two of them came and stood in front of Eiric.

Scarlet was quite pretty, with unlined brown skin and coppery hair cut close to her head. She's an elder? Eiric thought. She wasn't much older than him.

"He looks like one of the gods from the old stories," the spinner blurted, staring at him with a mixture of fear and fascination, all the while keeping a white-knuckled grip on her staff. She fingered the crystal amulet at her neck. It also glowed bright red. "He appears to have Asgardian blood."

"He's just big is all, Highest," Yrsa said. "Maybe he's part troll."

"He claims that he came from the deadlands?" The spinner pointed across the river with her staff.

Yrsa nodded. Eiric's rope was still coiled next to the wall. She nudged it with her foot. "He used this rope to cross over. He claims to be from the Archipelago, here to see Amma Inger."

"Amma Inger." The spinner heaved a sigh. "As if we don't have enough problems. I can't believe this is happening now."

Eiric's presence seemed to be a major inconvenience. Or at least poorly timed.

"Does she know he's here?" Yrsa said.

"Not yet," the spinner said. "We need to handle this quickly. The fewer people who know about this, the better, especially when we are so close to sailing."

Sailing? Sailing where?

Eiric might have been a cow that had wandered into the wrong pasture for all his contributions to this conversation so far. He knew he should just keep quiet and listen, but he was running out of patience, and he had questions of his own.

"I'm Eiric Halvorsen," he said. "I don't believe we've met."

At the sound of his voice, the spinner pivoted and pointed her staff at him. The tip glowed a sullen red, and Eiric raised his manacled hands as if he could ward off a magical attack.

"Highest," Yrsa said in a low voice. "Remember—steel trumps sorcery on Ithavoll."

The spinner tipped her staff vertical again and tried to act as if nothing had happened.

Good to know, Eiric thought. Now if he only had his weapons back.

But now, at least the spinner was ready to speak. "I am Elder Scarlet Lund, acting chairperson of the Council of Elders, the governing body for New Jotunheim," she said. "How did you get here?"

Eiric tried to recall the lies he'd already told. "My systir and I were fishing the north banks, and there was a storm. We were blown off course. My ship was pounded to pieces, and I swam to shore. I was hoping to find my systir had survived as well."

"No," Scarlet said. "You could not have made it through the boundary without help."

"And yet I am here," Eiric said, resisting the temptation to strike a pose. These people seemed to be good at denying the evidence of their eyes.

"How did you survive in the deadlands?" she demanded.

Eiric looked over his shoulder, across the fuming rift. "It didn't seem particularly . . . dangerous," he said. "Maybe I was lucky."

"You say you came by accident, and yet you asked to see the

keeper, who is the director of the Temple at the Grove," Scarlet said, raising an eyebrow.

Eiric considered claiming to be the director's long-lost chance child but he was beginning to realize that he needed more information before he threw in with anyone in particular.

As Bjorn always said, don't take sides until you know who is winning.

Actually, he never said that.

"Halvorsen!" Scarlet snapped. "How do you know the keeper?"

"I heard of her because she sometimes visited the Archipelago, seeking, ah, new recruits," Eiric said.

"Is it possible that she dropped the boundary in order to allow you to come in?"

"I don't know why she would do that," Eiric said. "We've never met."

"It has happened before," Scarlet said.

Was she referring to his fadir and grandfadir?

Eiric was growing weary of this verbal sparring. It seemed like a waste of time, because whatever he said, she didn't believe it. "If there's someone besides the keeper that I should be speaking to, please tell me," he said. "I don't mean to cause trouble. All I want to do is find my systir, if she still lives, and return home."

"First, you must go before our council."

"All right," Eiric said. "Where do I find them?"

"They will be on our systir island of Eimyrja," she said. With her staff, she pointed toward the temple at the edge of the rift. "Before we travel to Eimyrja, you must be purified in our temple here."

Eiric shrugged. "The sooner the better, then."

Elder Scarlet smiled at him, and the back of his neck prickled. He'd had hungry looks from women before, but never quite like this. Like she was heading to a feast and he was the main course.

She nodded to Yrsa, then took a step back as soldiers filled in around him. Staff in hand, head held high, she led the way down the cliff's edge to the temple.

Eiric eyed the soldiers to either side of him. That's peculiar, he thought. There was none of the usual rough handling, taunts, or insults he was used to seeing among soldiers with a prisoner in hand. Except for the heavy chains around his wrists, they escorted him like a valued guest.

Eiric and his escorts followed Elder Scarlet up a few stone steps to the doorway of the temple. As soon as he stepped inside, he could smell the fumes from the rift.

The interior of this temple had been constructed from blocks of gray granite. The effect was severe and somber—not ornate as he'd been led to believe. Despite what Rikhard had said, he saw no marble statues, gold vessels, or silver fittings. Neither the windows high on the walls nor the flickering light from torches placed in sconces all around the sanctuary dispelled the long shadows that extended like fingers from the corners. Unlike some temples he'd seen in his travels, there was no place for worshippers to sit. He hoped that meant the rituals and services were brief.

Eiric followed Elder Scarlet up the center aisle until she stopped at the base of a raised platform. The fumes were even stronger here, the air thick with gases, and Eiric blotted at his streaming eyes with his sleeve.

"Come." Gripping her cloak to either side, Scarlet climbed the remaining steps to the top of the platform.

Eiric and his escort followed after. Atop the dais, Eiric was so enveloped by the vapors from the river that he could scarcely breathe. The fumes seemed to be coming up through the platform itself. He bunched up his shirtfront and pressed it against his nose and mouth.

When he reached the elder's side, she shed her elaborate coat and handed it off to Yrsa, who seemed to be playing dual roles of army captain and servant. Underneath, Scarlet wore a simple shift, a wide leather belt around her waist carrying a narrow sheath. She did not seem as bothered by the fumes, but maybe she was used to them.

When he heard the sound of the river below, he realized that they must be in the part of the temple that overhung the rift.

"Prepare him," Scarlet said.

Yrsa gripped the front of his shirt, pulling it away from his body. Before Eiric realized her intent, she sliced it all the way down the front with her seax. A few more strokes, and it fell away entirely.

"Blood and iron!" Eiric growled. "This is my only shirt. I would have removed it if you'd asked." Though it would have been hard to do with his hands chained together.

"Be at ease, coaster," Elder Scarlet said. "You won't have need of it for the ceremony." She studied him, running her eyes over his chest, his arms, down to his toes, as if he were a pig she might buy at the market.

She slid the strap of her shift down, exposing one shoulder, displaying an emblem inscribed into her skin. It was a symbol Eiric hadn't seen before. It reminded him of the runes Reginn Eiklund had painted onto his skin a lifetime ago.

"We welcome you, Eiric Halvorsen, with our symbol of blood kinship. Although you are a barbarian, we believe that someone with your . . . extraordinary strength . . . can make a major contribution to our success. Everyone has a place—a role to play—in New Jotunheim."

It sounded as if the acting chairperson of the Council of Elders expected him to stay on permanently.

"While I am eager to learn more about Eimyrja, I have obligations in Muckleholm. Once I fulfill my oath to my patron, it might be that—"

Scarlet shoved an incense burner into his face. The fumes were cloyingly sweet—in a good way because it covered up the stench of the river. His head spun, his hands and feet tingled and burned. Gradually, he seemed to detach from his body, his essence light as goose down. If he spread his arms, he knew that he could fly.

He scarcely felt it as the spinner cut the rune into the flesh of his chest.

Scarlet took a step back to admire her work, and Eiric could feel the connection between them, a cord going taut.

"Beautiful," she whispered. "We will do great deeds together, you and I."

She scooped up the incense burner again, gave him another dose of vapor, then set it aside.

"Free him," Scarlet said.

"Highest," Yrsa said, frowning. "That might not be the wisest—"

"I would see him fly, Captain!" Scarlet snapped.

Eiric floated there, dreaming, while Captain Yrsa removed the chains on his hands.

Scarlet closed her hands over his, stood on tiptoes, and kissed him hard on the mouth.

When she stepped back, the front of her gown was smeared with his blood. "Now," she said, taking his elbow and turning him so that he faced the river, "fly."

It was then that Eiric realized that he stood on the edge of a platform with the venomous river churning below. Here there was no wall to get in his way.

Elivagar, he thought, swaying. He looked across to the opposite bank, to the deadlands. To Vigrid, the site of the Last Battle. The blood and bones there called to him. He inched his toes over the

edge (where had his shoes gone?) and drew himself up. Now the
pendants that he wore kindled, sending light out across the rift,
scorching his chest.

"Wait," Scarlet said, gripping his elbow.

To either side, Eiric was aware of soldiers shifting nervously.

Scarlet reached out and fingered Leif's pendant with its twin
runes, the sunstone next to it. Then poked at the runestick with
her jeweled forefinger. "What's all this?"

"Keepsakes," Eiric said. "Pendants left me by my fadir and grandfadir, and a token given me by a girl in an alehouse."

"Give them to me before you fly," Scarlet commanded, "for safekeeping." The spinner held out her hand.

Eiric closed his hand over Leif's amulet and held on tight. Light
channeled into him, clearing his head. "No," he said.

"Come, don't be silly," Scarlet said, her breath hissing out
between her teeth. "Hand them over and then you fly."

Eiric closed his other hand over the sunstone. "You've taken my
weapons, you've ruined my shirt," he said stubbornly. "These stay
with me."

Scarlet glared at him with mingled impatience and disgust, as
if her favorite child had gone rogue. She took a step away. Then
another.

"Take them," she said to the armed guard.

Some of the soldiers gripped his arms, and others grabbed for
the pendants, and what was left of the spell shattered. Eiric twisted
free of the soldiers on either side of him and drew his dagger from
the sheath inside his breeches. He pushed the man to his left away
from him, and he fell, screaming, out of sight. Seizing the man to
his right in an awkward embrace, Eiric cut his throat, stripped him
of his fine sword and axe, and sent him after his comrade, arms
and legs pinwheeling in panic.

"Fly," he said. Two more waded into the fray, and he tossed both in the river. His newly acquired sword cut the next man nearly in half. It wasn't as fine as Gramr, but it would do in a pinch.

And this was a pinch.

The fumes from the river made his eyes burn and his head pound. Blood and sweat ran down Eiric's face and tasted salty on his tongue. Positioned as he was, they could come at him only one or two at a time. Every man that tried ended dead at his feet or in the river. Strange. It seemed he grew stronger with every man that flew.

He needed that strength. These soldiers were not at all discouraged by the fate of their comrades. They trampled over their brodirs to get to him. He resorted to simply pitching them over the side to save time.

Leave off, he wanted to say. *This isn't working for you.*

Truth be told, it wasn't working for him, either. He was still trapped at the edge of the poisonous river with scores of soldiers between him and any reasonable exit. Though he would take many of the temple soldiers with him, it wouldn't change the outcome. He was going to end the day as a corpse floating down the river.

Scarlet had drawn back and stood clutching her staff, her little knife in her other fist. Her face was slack with astonishment and dismay. She might have been one of the Valkyries in Bjorn's stories who came to claim a hero who refused to fall.

That gave him an idea. If Scarlet was acting chair of the Council of Elders, she must be a high-up. High-ups made good hostages. Howling, he lunged forward, cutting down the soldiers who stood between him and the elder. Blades cut into his bare shoulders, but he forged on.

Too late, the spinner realized the danger. Scarlet staggered backward, slashing at him with her blade, but Eiric hooked an arm around her neck and pulled her tightly against his bloody chest, his own blade against the spinner's throat.

"Stand down," he shouted, "or the elder dies!"

"Stand down!" Yrsa echoed, actually shoving her own soldiers away from him, nearly getting herself gutted in the process.

Eiric dragged the elder back to the edge, wrenched the staff from her hand, and pitched it into the river. That prompted a keening wail that could likely be heard in the Archipelago.

"Shut *up*," Eiric hissed. "I'm in no mood to put up with that. Keep at it and we'll see if *you* can fly."

To his surprise, the elder fell silent. She stood, trembling. She was young, spectacularly beautiful, but oddly, her scent was that of an old woman—sage, mint, and stale mead.

This was yet another standoff. Nobody was going anywhere. He was still surrounded by soldiers bent on killing him. But at least it brought the fighting to a stop so he could catch his breath and mop the blood and sweat from his eyes.

Now he heard something else over the sound of the boiling river. The thunder of hooves, as if a stampede was heading their way. It changed to the clatter of hooves on stone.

Four horses charged through the open door at the front of the temple and galloped straight up the aisle toward the dais. There were three riders leading a fourth riderless horse.

The riders reined in, horses rearing, just in front of the platform, where all three dismounted. Two of them were clad in the blues that Katia had worn. In fact, one of the three *was* Katia. Another was a boy of similar age, pretty as a wood elf, with green-gold hair and eyes. The third was a woman, older than the other two, wearing a deep blue cloak and carrying a tall staff.

She strode forward, followed by the younglings. As if by magic, the soldiers parted to let them through. When they reached the front of the crowd, they stopped abruptly, staring at the bodies and weapons all around, at Eiric, covered in blood, with his knife at Scarlet's throat.

Captain Yrsa came up beside the newcomers. "You'd better not come any closer, Modir Tyra," she said to the woman in the blue cloak. "This barbarian fights like a berserker."

"Help me, Tyra," Scarlet whispered, as if she thought Eiric couldn't hear. "Make him let me go."

Modir Tyra didn't answer. She stood frozen, seemingly transfixed by the scene before her, her fingers closed around a large pendant that glowed such a brilliant red that her entire front appeared to be spattered with blood. Finally, Katia leaned close and murmured something in her ear, breaking the spell.

"Who can tell me what's happened here?" Tyra said.

"This barbarian crossed over from the deadlands yesterday," Yrsa said. "We locked him up and sent word to the council. Elder Scarlet arrived this morning to announce their verdict." Yrsa looked to Scarlet, who seemed reluctant to speak up in her current situation.

"But she didn't announce any verdict," Eiric said. "She told me I needed to be purified in the temple before going before the council. She brought me up here, cut off my shirt, cut a rune into my skin, and tried to throw me in the rift. I cooperated until we got to that last part."

Now Scarlet's words tumbled over one other. "It was the sense of the council at this particular time that the presence of this barbarian constituted an unnecessary risk when so much is riding on—"

"Enough!" Tyra said.

Scarlet seemed blindsided by this pushback. "Modir Tyra, with all due respect, it is not your place to—"

"Systir Katia told me about this stranger at Ithavoll," Tyra said. "I spoke with the council this morning, and they said that was the first they'd heard about it."

Scarlet shifted in Eiric's grip. "But–but that's not true," she whispered. "We discussed it and determined that the safest course was to . . ." Her voice trailed off when it became clear that she wasn't convincing anyone.

"The council has requested that my dedicates and I escort him back to the temple at Eimyrja, where the council will render a final judgment."

Yrsa stared at Tyra as if she'd lost her mind. "Highest, that isn't safe. He's a monster, a beast, an animal who–"

"He's a boy, Captain," Tyra said. "A castaway on our shores. This is not how we treat our guests in New Jotunheim."

"A *guest*?" Yrsa said, looking horrified.

Eiric did his best to look harmless, but that was hard to do covered in blood with a blade in each hand and a hostage.

Scarlet tried again. "Surely, Tyra, you remember what happened the last time we–"

"Rest assured, Elder Scarlet, I haven't forgotten." Tyra paused, as if to let that sink in. "What is your name?" Tyra said to Eiric.

"Eiric Halvorsen."

Modir Tyra's eyes narrowed. She's heard that name before, he thought.

He was aware of a strange sensation, as if mice were nibbling at the edges of his mind. He shook his head to clear it.

"Eiric, you don't want to hurt Elder Scarlet, do you?"

"No," he said.

"If I disperse these soldiers and promise they won't kill you, would you let her go?"

"Yes," he said.

"Elder Scarlet, if he releases you, will you promise not to take revenge on him?"

"Of course," she said so quickly that Eiric knew she was lying.

Modir Tyra gazed at her for a long moment before she turned to Yrsa. "Captain, I'll need your word that he will not be harmed if he surrenders. Otherwise, the council will have serious questions about why news of this barbarian's arrival was not communicated through regular channels."

The captain did not want to say yes, Eiric could tell. Which suggested that she would keep her word if she did.

"Yes," she muttered finally. "You have my word." She turned to the waiting soldiers. "Tend to the wounded and dead," she said. "Then you are dismissed."

Remarkably, they did as they were told, silently carrying the wounded into the garrison house and collecting the dead.

Eiric couldn't believe his eyes. What kind of soldiers were these, who could see their comrades cut down and then disperse like sheep when ordered to?

Now it was time to keep his end of the bargain. He withdrew his blade from the elder's throat, let go his grip, and stepped away.

Elder Scarlet retreated to a safe distance, joining Captain Yrsa, Modir Tyra, and the dedicates. She gripped Tyra's arm and leaned in, but Eiric could still hear every word she said.

"This cannot be allowed to stand, Tyra, and you know it. That barbarian laid his hands on me in full view of these soldiers. He threw my staff in the river and threatened my life. How can we expect the bondi to remain compliant if he gets away with this?"

"He is no bondi, and clearly he is no average soldier. He is something more than human, which is why we should walk a careful path. Can you imagine having such a soldier on our side? *Look* at him."

Scarlet stole a look, saw that Eiric was watching them, and looked away, cheeks flaming. "We cannot take that risk."

"It is the council's decision, and I have no standing to go against it."

"Modir," the wood sprite boy said. "We need to leave now if

we're to make the crossing before the tide comes in." He and Katia were standing by the horses, and he motioned to Eiric to join them there.

"Wait," Eiric said. He turned to Yrsa. "I'll need my sword and my axe back."

"Absolutely not," Yrsa said, folding her arms. "If you think we're going to send you armed into the heart of the temple grove, you're—"

"Give them to me for safekeeping," Tyra said. "When the council has made its final decision, we can decide what to do with them."

Grudgingly, Yrsa motioned to one of her soldiers, who delivered Eiric's weapons into Tyra's hands. Once the handoff was made, they mounted up. Eiric's gelding rolled his eyes and snorted at the half-naked, bloody creature attempting to mount him, but eventually submitted.

"This is Shelby," Katia said, motioning to the boy. "And that's Modir Tyra, headmistress at the academy." She pointed at the headmistress, who rode a little way ahead.

"Good to meet you," Eiric said. "Thank you for intervening."

"Oh, we had to," Katia said, laughing. "You're the first barbarian we've met who actually looks the part."

Eiric looked down at himself. "I can't argue with that."

"Wait till he washes the blood off before you rush to judgment," Shelby said, looking Eiric up and down. "I'll bet he cleans up well."

"Elder Scarlet's half in love with him by now," Katia said, pretending to swoon.

She has a strange way of showing it, Eiric thought. As they rode away, he felt the pressure of the elder's glare between his shoulder blades.

53

BLOOD SACRIFICE

"REMEMBER," TRUDE SAID. "YOU'VE GOT to lure Frodi to the library. Don't share too much until you get him in here."

"Right," Reginn said. "What if he won't come? I've never seen him here."

"You're a resourceful person," Trude said, waving away Reginn's doubts. "Make something up."

"What happens to me if it turns out we're wrong about Frodi?" Reginn said.

"Well," Trude said, "I trusted Frodi, and now I'm dead." When Reginn still hesitated, Trude said, "Help me with this and I will give you the key to the founder's tomb."

And that was an offer she couldn't refuse.

Reginn pondered this as she left the main library building through the rear door, following the covered walkway to Elder Frodi's cottage. Fueled by anger over what had happened to Alva and Naima, she'd agreed to help Trude prize the truth out of Frodi. But now she couldn't help wondering what had happened to her resolve to keep her head down and her options open.

Unlike Eiric Halvorsen, I don't see myself as a hero.

The building had been tidied up a bit since her last visit. The dead plants were gone, as was the stinking chamber pot. She pounded on the back door. "Elder Frodi!" she called. "It's Reginn Lund."

There was no response. She pounded again, harder, and heard movement inside.

"What do you want?" The archivist's voice was rough with disuse.

"I found something in the library, and I hoped that you could help me with it."

A mouse.

"You should have figured out by now that I don't tutor students anymore."

"This isn't about tutoring," Reginn said. "It's about research. I found a manuscript." As she said this, the hairs on the back of her neck prickled. This mirrored too closely Trude's first interaction with Frodi.

"You found—a *manuscript*—in the library," Frodi said through the door. "How very unusual." And then, savagely: "Go away."

"Of course," Reginn said. "It's just that—Modir Tyra said you were the expert on runes and symbols. We're meeting in a little while, and I was hoping I would have more information for her when I do."

With that, the door slammed open. Reginn had to leap back to avoid being knocked over.

Frodi's eyes were bloodshot, and it appeared the day's drinking was well underway. Still, he looked better than he had the last time she'd surprised him in his hermit hole. He was wearing breeches, for one thing, and a black wool coat over a clean linen shirt. Perhaps he'd decided that he'd better keep his breeches on during the day.

"Let me see it," he said, thrusting out his hand.

"It's in the library," Reginn said.

"You didn't bring it?" Frodi scowled. "Why in the world would you—"

"The pages are really fragile," Reginn said. "They must be very old. I didn't want to risk handling them any more than I had to."

"They've lasted this long," Frodi snapped. "Surely they could weather the distance between there and here. I don't have time to—"

"You say that, but I'll be the one in trouble if it's ruined."

Frodi looked past her, down the walkway to the library. Licked his lips and shook his head. "Sorry." He turned away.

He's scared, Reginn thought, stunned. The archivist is scared of the library. No wonder he's never there.

"All right," Reginn said. "I am sorry to have bothered you." She took a few steps back down the walkway, then swung around. "The thing is—your name was on one of the pages."

"*My* name?"

Reginn nodded. "Which didn't make sense because the pages were so old. It made me wonder whether Frodi is a family name that—"

"No," he said, studying her through narrowed eyes. "I am the first of my name—and likely the last."

"There were pages of runes and scribblings," she said. "And another name—Trude. Any idea who that could be?"

Apparently he did because he turned white as sea-foam. "Trude. I—ah—I may have heard that name." He hesitated, shifting his weight from foot to foot, his fingers tightening around his staff, then gestured to her. "Come in, where we can speak in private."

He took a step toward her, reaching for her arm, but she evaded his grasp. "I have to get back," she said. "I shouldn't have waited until the last minute. I need to put things in order before I go see the kennari."

"Wait," he said. "I want to—"

"I need to go," Reginn said. "I don't want to be late for my meeting." As she jogged down the walkway to the library, she heard him calling after her. Then swearing. Then footsteps hurrying behind her, the thud of his staff against the wooden walkway.

Reginn jogged back toward the library, resisting the temptation to break into a dead run. Fortunately, she had a head start. When she burst through the doors, Trude said, "Is he coming?"

"Yes," Reginn said breathlessly. She'd already made a partial copy of Trude's pages and stowed them in a folio. She had just enough time to scoop it from the table before the back door slammed open.

"Dottir?" Frodi said, pausing just inside the door, allowing time for his eyes to adjust to the dim light. "Systir Reginn?"

"I'm here, Highest," Reginn said. "I've decided to take your advice and ask Modir Tyra first."

"Wait," Frodi said, moving toward her, the head of his staff kindling to light the way. "Before you do, show me what you have. I believe I can tell you what you want to know if you allow me to have a look at the manuscript."

"There's no time," Reginn said. "I'm afraid of being late as it is. Anyway, I thought you weren't interested."

Frodi blocked the doorway. "I need to see it before you show it to anyone," he said flatly. "Give it to me."

"I know what this is about," Reginn said, scowling. "You want to take credit for finding it."

"Don't be stupid," Frodi said. "I am in no need of credit from Tyra or anyone else, least of all at the expense of a half-civilized barbarian who can barely write her own name." He came forward, and Reginn backed away, toward the staircase. He lunged at her. She sidestepped him, well served by years of practice in the alehalls of the Archipelago. Frodi tripped and fell headlong into a bookshelf, his staff clattering to the floor. Reginn turned and ran back up the stairs.

Guess Frodi won't be speaking up for me at council anymore.

The archivist rose to his feet, blotting at a cut on his forehead with his sleeve. "What is the *matter* with you?" he said irritably, scooping up his staff. "Have you gone mad?"

Reginn's stomach clenched as a terrible thought flickered through her mind. What if Musa/Trude was some sort of trickster spirit and had set her up to ruin whatever chance she had to stay at the academy?

"Highest, forgive me," Reginn said. "I have to go, or I'll be late for my meeting."

Frodi stood at the foot of the stairs, the head of his staff uplighting his face. "Go ahead," he said, "if that's what you are determined to do. Only leave the folio with me. I will review it and return it to you later."

Reginn climbed the stairs to the third level. Then to the fourth.

"You're wasting your time," Frodi said. "You cannot get out that way."

Higher and higher she climbed until she reached the top landing. The archivist looked very small from here.

Frodi peered up at her. "Don't be ridiculous. Come down now, and I'll be willing to forget this ever happened."

"I don't want to get in trouble," Reginn said. "It's just—it's the first thing I've found that might impress Modir Tyra. I really want to stay here at the Grove."

"I can make that happen, dottir," Frodi said.

Trude whispered, "Don't trust him."

Reginn said nothing.

"Perhaps . . . perhaps you could let me have a look at just one of the pages," Frodi said, "so I can assess how valuable it might be."

Reginn pulled out one of her carefully crafted pages—one with Trude's and Frodi's names and a mixture of real and made-up runes. She let go of it. It spiraled down like a leaf in autumn, until it fell into Frodi's waiting hand.

Greedily, he scanned it, tracing the lines with his forefinger. Then carefully slid it under his coat. "There, now. That wasn't so hard. Are the others like this?"

Reginn shook her head. "The rest of them are mostly runes. I don't know what they mean."

Frodi climbed up to the first platform. "Let's have a look, then."

"No," Reginn said. "Get out of my way. I'm going to meet with Modir Tyra." When he didn't budge, she made herself at home, leaning against the railing. "I'll wait here. I'm sure she'll come looking when I don't show up."

Reginn could sense the fury rising in Elder Frodi, threatening to incinerate her future at the Grove.

"Do you really think Modir Tyra will take your side against a member of the council?" Frodi spat. "Do you?" With that, he began to climb.

Reginn watched as Frodi climbed the steep metal staircases below. Second level. Third level.

Reginn moved an oil lamp to the edge of the platform and dangled one of the pages above it. "That's far enough," she said. "I'll burn these before I let you take them from me."

Frodi's eyes were fixed on the vellum page. "Do not do something rash that cannot be undone."

"You know all about that," Reginn said, "don't you?"

Frodi's gaze shifted from the page to Reginn's face and back again. "I don't know what you're talking about." And then, in a rush: "Dottir, be careful! The corner is smoldering."

Reginn lifted it out of danger and batted away some sparks. "Careless of me," she said.

"Perhaps we can make a trade," Frodi said. "I've noticed that you've admired my staff. I could have something similar made for you." He spun it, so that the light reflected off the glittering top, sending stars scrambling along the walls.

"Tell him he has a puny staff," Trude whispered.

"You expect to buy me off with baubles?" Reginn said. "You must think that barbarians are attracted to shiny things."

Apparently, that was exactly what he thought because he seemed taken aback by this response.

"I am more interested in power than pretty things," Reginn said.

"Fine," Frodi said. "Give me the pages, and I will make sure that you are elevated to adept."

"Promises are cheap," Reginn said, "and easily forgotten. And unruly dedicates are easily disposed of."

Now he looked truly unsettled. He hunched his shoulders as if he felt a cold hand on the back of his neck, the first prick of a blade.

"So what, exactly, do you want?"

"I'm aiming a little higher than adept," Reginn said. "In fact, I think we should be partners."

"Partners." Frodi struggled—unsuccessfully—to keep the astonishment off his face. "In what possible enterprise?"

"Perhaps you've been told that I can speak to the dead," Reginn said. "It's true. That is how I found these pages. That gives me access to secrets that have been hidden for thousands of years, including the use of the runes of magic. Knowledge is power, wouldn't you agree?"

He nodded, eyes fixed on the scrap of vellum in Reginn's hand, and she knew that he wasn't really listening.

"Look at me!" she commanded.

And so he did.

"By the goddess, Reginn," Trude whispered, a note of admiration in her voice.

"I need a partner with the rank and influence that will enable me to make the best use of what I've learned. But that requires that you be straight with me."

"Of course," Frodi said, his eyes straying to the folio.

"Liar," Trude whispered.

"I'm going to ask you some questions," Reginn said. "Every time you lie to me, I'll burn a page." Again, she dangled the vellum close to the flame.

"Why would you do that?" he said. "You're only hurting yourself."

"This is just a fraction of what I have," Reginn said. "I can go to the well again and again."

"To be fair," Frodi said, "you ought to give me a page for each honest answer."

"Very well," Reginn said, "but I will be the judge of which answers are honest."

With that, Reginn shoved the blade all the way in. "Tell me about Trude."

Frodi went very still, the landscape of his face in shadow against the light from his staff. "Who is Trude?"

"You used to work together here in the library."

"I believe that you have me confused with someone else."

"Not true," Reginn said, setting the page aflame. The vellum blistered, then crumbled into ash. Embers spiraled down toward the archivist on the stairs.

Frodi reached up, as if he could catch the burned remains in his hands, then apparently thought better of it.

"As I told you," Reginn said. "I speak to the dead. Sometimes the dead have plenty to say, especially when they hold a grudge."

Frodi hunched his shoulders again and looked around.

"You're getting to him," Trude said.

Reginn pulled out another page. "Don't waste any more of my time by denying that you knew her. Both of your names are all over these pages."

"All right," Frodi said. "I knew her. She was a dedicate here who had something of an obsession with me."

"Liar," Trude muttered. "I considered him a mentor and friend, that's all."

"I understand that she provided megin to you via the blodkyn rune."

Frodi gazed up at her, his blue eyes narrowed as if he was seeing her clearly for the first time. "You *have* been busy digging, haven't you?" he said with a faint smile.

"What happened?" Reginn said to Frodi. "How did she die?"

"Apparently, she fell from the top of this staircase," Frodi said, shrugging. "Apparently, she'd been drinking."

"Why should I believe you?"

"Why ask questions if you don't believe the answers?" Frodi said. "Believe whatever you want."

"It's your job to convince me," Reginn said, setting another page aflame.

"Stop!" Frodi shouted. "Please. Ask me another question."

"Was it disappointing when you realized that even with the blodkyn rune, you couldn't draw power from a corpse?"

"Well, yes, that's technically true," the elder said, having seemingly given up on denial. "And yet, it's at the moment of death that the maximum conveyance of megin occurs."

Reginn sat back on her heels, her heart thudding painfully. "Explain."

"I discovered it by accident," Frodi said. "Obviously, you are familiar with the rune. For months, Trude had been providing me with a trickle of power from her vast supply along with a few tidbits of wisdom from her research. When she died, it released a flood of energy that sustained me for nearly a year, despite the fact that–" He stopped, as if deciding that he'd revealed too much. "Unfortunately, it did not convey the knowledge she'd hidden from me for so long."

"Bastard," Trude whispered.

Reginn released the page from between sweating fingers and watched it spiral down like a late-autumn leaf into Frodi's hands.

"What happened after a year?"

"My power and magical energy dwindled," Frodi said simply. "When I needed more, I found another eager protégé. When it worked a second time, I presented what I had learned to the council." He paused as if expecting some response. Receiving none, he continued. "The council was enthusiastic, to say the least."

It was a challenge for Reginn to maintain her expression of brisk detachment while trying to keep her breakfast where it belonged. "So . . . whenever you are feeling a little low, you–"

"Blood sacrifice is an established tradition here in the northlands. The blodkyn rune ensures that there is an immediate and targeted benefit." After a pause, he added, "That was an answer, by the way."

Reginn released another page into Frodi's eager hands. "So that is why you–and the rest of the council–have lived so long."

"New Jotunheim was dying, once the founder withdrew her support," Frodi said. "Use of the blodkyn rune has led to the rebirth of our sanctuary, and a new era of wisdom accumulated over many lifetimes."

"So–you've become immortal," Reginn said, "at the expense of others."

"In every society there are winners and losers, rulers and ruled. With the death of the Asgardians at Ragnarok, there was a need for a new generation of divine rulers to arise. Why not the jotun?"

Why do we need rulers at all? Reginn thought, dropping another page.

Frodi kept talking, fueled by righteous anger. "Asgard has betrayed us, lied to us, stolen our lands, our women, and our magic since the world tree grew from the body of the jotun Ymir at the founding of the world."

"How do you choose who to sacrifice?"

"Those richest in megin are the very young and the gifted. Those acolytes recruited from the Archipelago come first to the lower school. As they grow older, they can be identified as descendants of the gods or the jotun—our kind."

"Innangard or Utgard," Reginn whispered, her middle heavy with dread. "You use the kynstone pendants left by the founder to sort them."

Frodi nodded. "That's the beauty of it. That way we can cleanse the barbarian lands of the children of Asgard, protect our bloodlines, and prevent our enemies from infiltrating our sanctuary and reestablishing themselves. The jotun advance to the upper school. The others remain at Vesthavn until they are called upon to contribute in a different way.

"You, of course, were a puzzle. You identified as neither Asgardian nor jotun, and yet power flows through you like gold from a crucible. So members of the council assumed that you offered considerable potential—one way or another."

"What about the bondi?"

"Even the bondi have a role to play. While they do not provide the same value as the sacrifice of the gifted, every living thing has megin, especially the young."

"You kill them, too," Reginn whispered. "Is that why you drink so much?"

"Do not presume to assign a motive to what I do," Frodi said
with contempt. "Perhaps I drink because I enjoy it."

Reginn recalled the children she'd seen at Vesthavn with their
bouquets of flowers. The reluctance of the Council of Elders to
accept her at the temple school. The hungry way they looked at
her. Seeing not an aspiring student but a source of power for themselves. She shuddered.

"Are you well, dottir?" Frodi said. "You're looking a bit pale. Are
you sure that you are ready to play in this game?" Somehow, he'd
climbed to the level below her without her noticing. "It also appears
to me that you are out of pages."

He was right. The folio was empty.

"Well!" Reginn said, suddenly short of breath. "Those went
quickly. I'll bring more tomorrow when we discuss future plans.
But now I have to meet with Tyra." She took two steps down toward
him, and Frodi stood to one side to allow her to pass. Just as she
stepped past him, Trude shouted a warning. "Reginn! Look out!"

Something smashed into the side of her head, sending her flying
over the rail and onto the next landing. Reginn wasn't sure if it was
a physical blow or a magical attack, but it left her lying crumpled at
the foot of the stairs, unable to move. At first, she worried that her
back was broken, but it seemed to be some sort of magical paralysis.

Frodi descended the steps toward her, no longer in a hurry, the
light from his staff spilling over her. "Ah," he said when he saw she
was watching him. "I was afraid I'd already killed you, and that
would be a terrible waste."

Kneeling next to her, he drew out a long, thin blade that glittered in the light from the lamps.

"You're making a mistake," Reginn said, struggling to reach for
her own knife and having no luck.

Frodi tried the blade against his thumb. "Actually, I believe you're the one who has made a mistake. What a stupid, ignorant, arrogant child you are to believe that you could force me into some sort of partnership with you." Grasping the neckline of Reginn's tunic, he ripped it down to the waist. A cold draft raised gooseflesh on her bare skin.

"I've shown you the evidence of what I can do," Reginn said. "There's no reason we—"

Frodi backhanded her across the face, splitting her lip so that she could taste the blood on her tongue. "All that you have taught me is that I have been less than thorough in my previous searches of the library. I am centuries old, dottir—too old to believe in ghost stories. Once you are gone, I will have plenty of time to remedy that. The only thing I want from you is what you are going to give me right now." Gripping the hilt of the blade, he made a shallow cut just above her left breast.

With that, something heavy crashed onto the landing, barely missing Frodi's head and sending fragments of stone flying. Reginn recognized it as an elaborate stone carving that had stood on one of the shelves on the upper floors.

Frodi stood, scanning the stacks high above them. "Is someone there?" he said. "Reveal yourself."

There was no response.

Shaking his head, Frodi knelt again and positioned the knife. Halfway through the second cut, he threw up his arms to shield his face as an entire shelf of books flew at him, smacking into his head and shoulders.

Frodi gripped Reginn's chin, his fingers digging into the flesh. "I don't know what you are doing, dottir, but it needs to stop."

"I'm not doing anything, Highest," Reginn said. "You'll have to take it up with Musa."

"*Musa?*"

"You remember—the library mouse. Your pet name for Trude up until you killed her."

"Shut up." Frodi lifted Reginn's shoulders and then slammed her head against the metal stairs so black spots swam before her eyes. Then he pinned her down again and made three quick slashes into the skin of her chest.

"That should suffice," he growled, pushing her chin up and back so that he could get at her neck.

Before he could raise the knife, a brass oil lamp smashed into the side of his head, spilling flaming oil over him and splattering it into his eyes. Screaming, he released his hold on Reginn and blundered blindly about, blood pouring from a gash on his forehead. Reginn rolled to her feet as strength flooded back into her body.

Barreling into the archivist, she slammed him against the railing. Gripping him at knee level, she rolled him up and over. He fell, screaming, like one of the flaming rockets sold by traders from the east. He landed face-first on the floor below and lay motionless, still smoldering.

Reginn leaned back against the railing, breathing hard, head spinning. Not dizzy exactly. Intoxicated, with energy snapping and sparking over her skin. Her hair lifted, a cloud of curls around her head, then settled again.

"You are on *fire*, girl," Trude said. "In a good way."

"What is happening?" Reginn said.

"Frodi tried to kill you, to claim your potential through the blodkyn rune. You killed him instead. And so—" She shrugged. "What was his is now yours."

Reginn shuddered. Briefly, she thought she might be sick. She did not want to share anything with Frodi—not his essence, or his megin, or whatever else was on offer.

"Here," she said, flapping her hands as if she could shake it off. "You take it, I don't want it."

Trude smiled sadly. "I think you'll have more use for it than I will. Now we know the truth. This place is evil—full of evil people doing evil things. And it's all my fault. It makes me kind of glad I'm dead. It's as if I was punished before I knew I'd committed the crime."

Reginn understood. She had no idea what to do with what she had learned. She felt faintly resentful that she'd been put in this position.

"Trude," she said, sitting down on the stairs and wrapping her arms around her knees. "You can always tell what I'm thinking, and whether I'm lying. Can you tell with Frodi? Was he telling the truth?"

Trude nodded. "He was mostly telling the truth, at least as far as he understood it." She hesitated. "He didn't tell all of it, though. All of these images and memories ran through his mind when he was talking to you, some of them totally unfamiliar to me. A robed priest in a stone chamber with oil lamps. Goblets of cherry wine, some kind of ritual." She shrugged. "It could be totally unrelated."

Gingerly, Reginn explored the side of her head with her fingers. Her hair was sticky with blood, but the scalp wound had stopped bleeding, and the pain was dissipating. Her clothing was spattered with blood and oil from the lamp, but the swelling in her lip was already going down.

"Now there's a dead elder in the library," Reginn said, trying to avoid looking at Frodi's body. "That's two down in a matter of weeks. What are we supposed to do with the body?"

"Don't do anything," Trude said. "It's no secret that Elder Frodi drinks. It looks to me like he climbed up the stairs and knocked over an oil lamp, setting himself on fire. A tragedy not unlike what happened to me two hundred years ago. Only I was just sixteen." Clearly, Trude had no sympathy to spare for her one-time mentor.

Reginn cleared her throat. "Is it possible that Modir Tyra wasn't in on this? She's busy with her work at the academy and traveling to the Archipelago. Maybe she doesn't realize what's been going on."

"That's possible, I suppose . . ." Trude said, plucking at her tunic, avoiding Reginn's eyes. "But Tyra was on faculty when I was a dedicate, over two hundred years ago. And according to Brenna's journal, Tyra was already the kennari when the founder left the Midlands two hundred and fifty years ago. She looks remarkably young for her age, don't you think?" Reginn must have looked distraught because Trude added, "It might be that they've found a way to share the gift of long life with others not in on the blodkyn secret."

"Do you think the other dedicates and adepts know what's going on?"

Trude shrugged. "Does it matter?"

"Yes," Reginn said. "It does to me. If even two or three of us could—"

"Remember what I told you," Musa said. "The dedicates are Tyra's—body and soul. Don't confide in them if it's something you don't want the kennari to know."

"I don't know what to do," Reginn said. "I can't just turn a blind eye to what's going on, but I'm just a dedicate. I don't even have a staff."

"Frodi won't be using his," Trude pointed out. "Though it might be incriminating to show up with it under the circumstances."

"I don't want it!" Reginn practically shouted. "Who knows how many people have died because of him? And will continue to die even though he is gone."

"Well," Trude said, "it's possible you will find the help you need in the founder's tomb." She extended her hand, palm up, displaying a symbol. It was a rune. It had a circle at one end and what appeared to be a double-headed arrow at the other.

"This rune is Lykill," Trude said. "The key to the founder's tomb. Here." The library mouse extended her hand and clasped Reginn's. She felt a sting and breathed in the familiar scent of charred flesh, and when Trude let go, the rune was burned into Reginn's palm.

"Modir Brenna told me it was the key to the past," Trude said. "The key to arcane knowledge. She warned me not to go beyond the hall of runes—that it might awaken monsters that are better left alone. So I never did. I hope it opens the door to better fortune than came my way."

"What happens to you now?" Reginn said, knowing that betrayals, grudges, and unfinished business often keep the vaettir from traveling on to the next world.

"That depends on what happens to you," Trude said. "It has been so hard to have so much to say and no one to hear it. You listened, and you believed me, and I believe in you, too. Hatred can keep a spirit tied to this world. But so can love." With that, Trude's lips brushed her forehead.

54

THE HEADMISTRESS

THE ROAD FROM THE ARMY camp on Ithavoll to Eimyrja led through a range of worn, blunted hills down to the coast. Modir Tyra set a rapid pace, which allowed little time for talking. Which was a shame, because Eiric had hoped to use this time to ask questions.

For instance: Who was the council, and why were they so eager to execute him when they didn't even know who he was? Why hadn't they asked him any questions? Who were the bondi? What had Scarlet meant when she said that his presence constituted an unnecessary risk *at this particular time*?

Granted, the boundary was intended to keep people like him out. Why would they think the keeper would lower the boundary to let him in?

What was the "enterprise" Tyra had mentioned that he might be an asset to? Was there a rebellion brewing?

Who was in power here? Most importantly, who controlled the army?

When they reached the crest of the hill, they looked downslope to a black, rocky beach. Across a narrow stretch of water lay a second island, set like an emerald in the blue of the ocean.

Eiric pointed to the other island. "Where are we now, and what's that?"

"We're on Ithavoll, the traditional gathering place of the gods," Shelby said. "That's Eimyrja over there. That's where we're heading."

"Have you ever seen any gods meeting here?" Eiric said.

"All of this happened in a time before memory," Shelby said. "The gods are dead. On the far side of the rift is Vigrid, the site of the last battle of Ragnarok. We call it the deadlands, because to set foot over there is certain death." He eyed Eiric curiously. "Except, apparently, for you."

"Tide's coming in," Katia shouted. "Come on!"

This prompted a breakneck downhill gallop to the beach. If Eiric wasn't already smitten with these horses, their nimble handling of the rocky slope would have convinced him. If he survived his visit to the Grove, he was already scheming to somehow bring one of these horses back with him.

He was going to need a bigger boat.

When Modir Tyra reached the edge of the water, her horse didn't hesitate but plunged right in. The others followed. As they neared the middle of the channel, the water grew deeper, and the force of the current threatened to knock them over. Eiric applied his heels and the horse surged forward. They all made it safely to the other side.

Katia and Shelby grinned at Eiric. "Pretty impressive, huh?" Shelby said.

The rest of the journey passed in a fog of lush greenery, shadowed groves, and the intoxicating scent of flowers. If Vigrid was a battlefield, and Ithavoll an army camp, then Eimyrja was a garden.

They dismounted in a glade at the edge of a clearing. Katia and Shelby took charge of the horses, while Modir Tyra ushered Eiric through what appeared to be the rear entrance of a large hall, built of oak and cherry and other fine woods. Once inside, she put her finger to her lips. "Shh. Be very quiet. If the council or the keeper find you here, they will kill you."

"Where are we?" Eiric whispered.

"This is the Lundhof, the Temple at the Grove, where our religious ceremonies take place," Modir Tyra said. "No one comes here except on feast days. They will never look for you here."

Eiric had expected to be taken straight to another guardhouse or lockup. Was this some sort of trick? Was he going to be killed "trying to escape"?

The rear door opened into a back corridor. While the building had looked to be several stories high, this hallway had a low ceiling. Great double doors carved with runework centered the corridor. That must be the way into the large hall. Tyra led him to to the left, to a door at one end of the hallway.

It was a small room, and simply furnished, but definitely a cut above the guardhouse at Ithavoll. It had a bed, for one, and a hearth on the wall. A door at the rear led out to a small courtyard privy surrounded by very high walls.

So. A comfortable place for guests that you wanted to stay put.

There came a faint knock. Modir Tyra waved Eiric out into the courtyard before she opened the door. After a murmured conversation, the visitors left and she called him back in.

Trousers and a shirt, both of fine white linen, were laid out on the bed. A platter of food and drink sat on a side table. A fire had been kindled on the hearth, and a large pot of water was heating on the grate. Washing supplies, including a basin, rags, a comb, and pots of soap, were set out as well.

Modir Tyra stood, hands on hips, studying him. "How much of that blood on your clothes is yours?" she said.

Eiric shifted his weight self-consciously. "Some. Not much." His memory of the battle at the rift was beginning to scab over, the pain fading, as if it were a story, a saga about somebody else. He felt well, in fact, stronger than before. It was as if with every soldier he cut down, his own strength grew.

"I could bring in one of the healers, if you like, but I would prefer to keep your presence here quiet until I speak with the council."

"I don't need a healer," Eiric said. And it seemed to be true. The sting of his wounds was already fading. "All I need is a bath and a new shirt before I meet with the keeper."

Tyra ignored the hint. "I hope these clothes are big enough. They are the largest we have. Maybe they'll do until we can have some made."

"I'll rinse out my clothes once I wash up," Eiric said, scraping at the dried blood on his breeches with a fingernail. "They'll be fine." It struck him like a fist in the gut that these were the last clothes his modir or systir would ever make for him.

"Give them to me, and I'll have the servants wash them for you," Modir Tyra said. Again, there came that sensation, like fish nibbling at his mind.

"There's no need," Eiric said, conscious of the weight of the pendants, the dagger at his waist. He did not intend to have those taken away from him. "I'm used to doing my own laundry and mending in the summers."

There was something wistful about the way she gazed at him, as if she was looking at him and seeing someone else. Self-conscious, he squatted next to the hearth, checking the temperature of the water with his palm.

Finally, she said, "I'll leave you to it, then, and come back later."

With that, she left. Eiric heard the sound of a bar coming down on the other side of the door.

Eiric removed the sunstone and rune pendants and his sheathed dagger and set them in the fireplace corner. Sitting on the edge of the hearth, he filled the basin from the pot on the fire and scrubbed his chest and arms and as much of his back as he could reach. Soon, the water in the basin was red with blood.

As he'd thought, most of it was not his. The fight at the edge of the rift had left Eiric relatively untouched, adding just a few gashes and bruises to his collection. He emptied the bloody water in the courtyard and refilled the basin to wash what was left of his clothes. When they were as clean as he could get them he hung them by the fire to dry.

The new shirt was a little tight in the chest and shoulders and the trousers were short, but they would do. Once he'd dressed, he started in on the platter of food. He was ravenously hungry.

The pitcher contained a mead so potent that it set his head to swimming after the first cup. After his second, he collapsed back on the bed, leaving his supper half-finished.

Vaguely, he heard the door to his room open and close. A blue-robed figure stood over him, her face in shadow, her jeweled staff glittering in the firelight. She rolled it between her palms. Spinning.

Something tugged at the margins of his mind. He tossed and turned and tried to pull loose, but eventually it snagged a thread of thought and memory and added to it, plying the new with the old, the real with the unreal, until he couldn't decipher which were his own memories and which belonged to someone else, which were true and which were intended to deceive.

55

DEMONS UNDERGROUND

REGINN STOOD BEFORE THE FOUNDER'S tomb still without a plan for how to go forward.

I am no hero, she thought. Far from it. And yet she had to do something. She preferred to do it with the founder's approval and support.

"Modir Brenna, I am Reginn Eiklund, your dottir, seeking your wise counsel," Reginn said without much hope of getting any. She waited. There was no response.

"I bring a message from your dottir Gertrude Lund. Trude wants you to know that she betrayed her promise to you. As a result, your dream has gone horribly wrong. She has asked my assistance in setting things right. And so I've come to you."

Now, once again, Reginn felt the subtle touch of the founder's attention.

"Trude has been dead for years on years, child," Brenna said. "Leave the dead in peace."

"I speak to the dead," Reginn said. "Just as I am speaking to you. Trude is trapped between worlds, unable to find her place in Helgafjell because of the evil that has resulted from her betrayal of you."

"I loved Trude; I trusted her," Brenna said. "And now, when she can no longer speak for herself, you tell me that she betrayed me?"

"That's the way she sees it," Reginn said. "She showed me your journal. She told me that you gave her the key to your tomb so that she could find the runes needed to unlock it, but she was killed before she could do so."

"So she betrayed me by confiding in you when I asked her to tell no one?"

"No!" Reginn said, her cheeks heating. Then added, "Well, maybe, but the problem is, she shared the blodkyn rune with one of her teachers."

"The blodkyn rune?" Brenna said as if puzzled.

"It can be used to transfer the magical essence—the megin—from one person to another, especially at the point of death," Reginn said. "Now the Council of Elders is sacrificing Asgardian acolytes and the bondi in order to build their own power. New Jotunheim has become a killing ground, not a sanctuary."

"Why should I believe you when you say you speak for Trude? You've still offered no proof. I've been lied to before. I suspect that the members of the council and their allies are manipulating dedicates to achieve what they cannot achieve on their own—the secrets of the runes and access to their power. I won't make that mistake again."

"I am not working for the council, Highest," Reginn said. "I only just arrived from the Archipelago seeking sanctuary. Now it seems I've crossed an ocean to find a world as brutal as the one I left behind."

Desperately, she pulled a page from her carry bag. "I arrived in Eimyrja with some knowledge of the runes, and so I was able to unlock your journal and read it. I know what you were trying to accomplish here in New Jotunheim and the resistance you had from the council. I know that at the end of your days on earth you took steps to protect this sanctuary and the people, gifted or not, who live here." Reginn began to read.

> *Today, representatives from the Council of Elders came to see me in my self-imposed exile and demanded the following:*
>
> *1. The amulets that representatives of the academy use to detect the presence of magic in those we bring back to New Jotunheim.*
>
> *2. A geas that will protect all members of the council and the faculty of the academy from violence and rebellion.*
>
> *3. The gift of immortality.*
>
> *4. Finally, they want me to teach them the secrets of the runes and how to use them.*
>
> *These demands are, of course, impossible, since the members of the council have proven themselves unworthy of wielding that much power.*

"Highest, you were right," Reginn said. "And Trude and I are hoping that you will help us put a stop to it."

Brenna laughed, a whisper of sound. "At long last, the journal comes to light, too late to help anyone." After a pause, she continued. "I made mistakes during my time in New Jotunheim," Brenna said. "I believed that, freed from mistrust and persecution by the remnants in the Midlands, the jotnar would thrive. They would build a paradise that could serve as an example of what could be accomplished through the principled use of magic.

"I was blinded by idealism. I had sworn to serve as counselor, not as ruler. I did not foresee the intoxicating effect that power would have on the formerly powerless. I underestimated the poisonous desire for revenge. I should have cut off all contact with the Archipelago, but I could not give up my dream of sanctuary and service. In retrospect, I should have either stayed out of the Midlands, or taken a stronger hand in managing it.

"My greatest fear was a reprise of the Last Battle and the incessant wars among the gods and between gods and the jotnar," the founder said. "As you may know, prophesy tells us that the Asgardians will rise again. I sited the sanctuary here in order to prevent access to the place where so many fell. I fortified Ithavoll and proclaimed the battlefield of Vigrid to be the deadlands, forbidden to all in New Jotunheim. I erected a shield wall to protect us from mischief from the Midlands, and to protect the Midlands from us. I was disappointed in the behavior of the council and others, but at the end of my journey here, I believed that I had at least secured the gathering place of the gods and prevented their return to power.

"I never anticipated the arrival of a dedicate capable of speaking to the dead. I did not prepare for how tempting it would be to respond when she reached out to me—to have a student again. I was weak. As you can see, the result was disastrous for all involved. If what you say is true, the evil you describe resulted from my allowing Trude into the tomb.

"Trude, more than anyone, should understand why I am done with meddling in the Midlands."

"She does understand, Highest," Reginn said, "but she hopes that you will reconsider. She believes that a solution may lie in the chambers beyond your tomb."

The silence between them thickened and grew, until finally, the founder spoke.

"Ah," she said. "Now, at last, I see who you really are."

"I beg your pardon?" Reginn said.

"You have no stake in this game, Aldrnari," Brenna said, her voice cold as glacier melt. "Why are you here?"

"Aldr . . . nari?" Reginn shook her head. "I don't know what you mean. The—the kennari, Modir Tyra, and the keeper, Amma Inger, brought me here from the Archipelago."

"Had Inger understood what you really are, she never would have done that," Brenna said.

She didn't want me to come here, Reginn thought. Was this the reason?

"What makes you think I am dangerous?" Reginn said, not counting on getting a response.

"You are an elemental," Brenna said. "By that I mean that your magic is older than that wielded by any of the peoples of the original Nine Worlds, even the jotun, who were the first among the gifted. It originated with the first collision between fire and ice, Muspelheim and Niflheim. Life-bringer and life-destroyer. Because it is elemental to all other magics, it is the most powerful."

"If I am so powerful, can't I just put a stop to all of this?" Reginn waved her hand toward the entrance of the tomb.

"You could easily do that, dottir," Brenna said dryly, "by destroying the Midlands." After a pause, she explained. "Elemental magic is unstable and so is the most difficult to control. I don't know of anyone who could teach you to use it safely."

This isn't helpful, Reginn thought. "So you are telling me that I have a gift that I cannot use because it is too dangerous?"

"What exactly is it that you hope to find beyond the tomb, dottir?"

"Answers," Reginn said. "Some way to fight back against the council and protect everyone—acolytes, dedicates, adepts, and bondi. Maybe a rune, maybe a weapon, or maybe the truth."

"You see yourself as a savior, but your presence here puts all of New Jotunheim in danger. You are the factor that could unravel everything." She paused. "Raising the dead is an elemental gift," Brenna said. "One Ragnarok is enough."

Compared with what Reginn was facing in New Jotunheim, the risk of Ragnarok seemed remote.

You don't know me. You don't know anything about me.

"With all due respect, Highest, I do not see myself as a savior or a kingmaker. I can tell from your journal that you care deeply about the people of the Midlands—or you used to. This place was supposed to be a sanctuary. Instead, I find it's a slaughterhouse. I don't intend to disturb the dead, but forgive me if I don't want to leave things as they are."

In the ensuing silence, Reginn stood frozen, knowing that she had crossed a line.

Now you've done it. Calling out the gods is never a good idea.

"Hear me, Aldrnari," Brenna said finally. "I will never give you the key to the hall of the dead. The risk is too great. Tell Trude that I am sorry."

Was she supposed to meekly return to her sleeping quarters and wait for the next disaster? Waiting for someone in need of a boost to come for her? Which would happen sooner rather than later when it became clear that she would not give the kennari what she wanted.

Maybe Brenna was done with the Midlands, but Reginn had to continue living here.

"Thank you for your time, Highest," Reginn said. "I had hoped to have your help and your blessing, but if I have to, I'll do this on my own. You see, Trude already gave me the key."

Quickly, so she wouldn't lose courage, Reginn pressed her palm—the one emblazoned with Lykill—against the cool stone of the tomb. Silently, smoothly, the stone slid aside, revealing an opening so narrow Reginn had to turn sideways to pass through.

Once she was inside, the door slid shut behind her.

Reginn took deep breaths, trying to quell her rising panic, the feeling of being buried alive, the worry about being struck dead by a vengeful god.

You know I'm not good with tight spaces.

Inside, the air was cool and moist, and tasted of stone. Ancient sconces lined the walls, scattering light and shadow. How could they possibly have burned for so long?

When her heart finally slowed to a reasonable cadence, she looked around.

Amber and other gemstones had been embedded in the floor in the shape of a ship. At the center of the ship stood a dais that held a small casket. Lamps burned at either end of the vessel.

Arrayed within the ship were grave goods—jewelry, glass, weapons, pots of precious oils and medicinals. Fine silks and embroidery threads in all colors. Combs and carvings of bone and ivory. Weapons of all kinds. Food for the journey, untouched after more than two centuries.

As a sometime thief, Reginn couldn't help thinking that it was a shame to have all those fine things hidden away underground, where they were no good to anybody.

At the far end of the room, a massive oak-and-iron door was set into the wall. *That must be the way to the passages beyond.*

Reginn crossed the chamber and stood before the casket. Next to the dais, there was a small pallet on the floor, as if a mourner might want to have a rest during a siege of grieving.

Brenna spoke. "Aldrnari, please. Do not go any further."

"Highest," Reginn said. "I hear your concern, but I do intend to go on. You say that my magic is dangerous because it is unstable. Tell me this—is there anything I can do to make it safer for myself and others?"

After a long pause, Brenna spoke. "The right staff may be your best protection because it can control and direct your megin. Just choose carefully."

From the time she'd laid eyes on Tyra's staff, Reginn had lusted for one of her own. This might be her opportunity. She turned back toward the door and fumbled with the latch.

"Be careful, dottir. No one has passed through the tunnels between Eimyrja and Ithavoll for hundreds of years. I don't know what manner of creatures you might find there—alive or dead."

"These tunnels lead to Ithavoll?" Reginn said.

"They once did," Brenna said. "It's unlikely they are still open."

"I'll be careful," Reginn said, thinking that *careful* would mean taking the advice of the founder and leaving the catacombs entirely.

Seizing hold of the latch, Reginn pushed at the door. It didn't budge. Setting her shoulder against it, she pushed again. Nothing. Then she remembered she had a key. As she had at the door to the tomb, she pressed her palm inscribed with Lykill against the door. This time, it opened easily. She drew a rune on her other palm with her forefinger—Kenaz, bringing light into darkness. She took a step forward, then leaped back, smothering a shriek of fright.

In the light from the rune, she could see that she was surrounded by heaps of bones, as if dozens of people had gotten this far and then died here.

Brenna's warning echoed in her ears. *I don't know what manner of creatures you might find there—alive or dead.*

Reginn took a breath, then another, and walked forward.

The tunnel that led away from the founder's tomb was straight and level, the kind of tunnel used to get from one place to another efficiently. At the time it was built, it must have been a remarkable feat of engineering. Now the way ahead was littered with heaps of rubble and rockfalls. She was glad that she wouldn't have to navigate them in the dark.

In places, the walls of the tunnel had collapsed, leaving only a narrow pathway.

Eventually, the passage opened into a larger room—so large that she couldn't see the walls around her, only feel a sense of space.

Kenaz provided enough illumination so that she could make her way around the perimeter of the room.

Barrels and bins were lined up against the wall. As Reginn approached, rats scattered in all directions.

Rats were familiar, at least.

The containers appeared to be empty, their contents long since dried up or blown away or eaten.

In one corner, she saw an array of weapons and magical artifacts—an entire bin of pendants and spinner staffs piled against the wall.

Many of the pendants were inscribed with runes. Some were the traditional web-footed pendants worn by the volva.

You may find a staff that suits you.

Methodically, she sorted through the staffs, leaning them against the wall so that she could compare one with another. It would help if she knew what to look for.

The jeweled distaffs drew Reginn's eye. There were three, in different lengths, fashioned of precious metals, elaborate works of exquisite artistry. She ran her fingers over the gemstones in their gold and silver settings.

Any one of these would be worth a fortune in the markets at Langvik, if someone showed up with the means to pay for it.

The smallest of the three looked to be just the right size. She reached for it, then pulled her hand back, empty.

Choose carefully.

Reginn looked them over again. Many of the others were traditional forged iron with silver and brass fittings, most tall enough to lean on. Some were topped with a figure of a spinner or a small chair, representing the high seat of the seeress. Despite centuries under the stone, none of them had rusted.

Leaning against the wall behind the rest was a distaff, a tortured twist of wrought iron, smaller than the rest. The size suited her better than the rest. Reginn could see traces of silver and bronze on the basket that said the staff had seen better days. Within the basket, a chunk of raw amber glowed like warm honey. She reached a finger out to touch it, and power thrummed through her.

When she gripped it just below the basket, it settled into her hand as if it belonged there.

She jumped when she heard Brenna's voice in her ear. "You have taken up my staff, dottir," Brenna said. "It is a good choice for a difficult journey. I only hope it will help you find your way."

"Raidho," Reginn murmured, tracing the rune on her arm with her finger. The head of Brenna's staff kindled, spilling light into the darkness. Eyes glittered ahead of her, and light reflected off metal. When she moved forward to take a closer look, she all but stumbled over a heap of rubble.

No. Not rubble. More bones, still shrouded in remnants of cloth—fine silk cloth, from the looks of it, but it had been charred almost beyond recognition. A staff lay next to the clawlike hand and a web-footed pendant still hung around the neck.

A spinner.

Carefully, Reginn stepped over the body and went on.

On instinct, she used the key again to open a door into a side tunnel, leading to a small chamber. In the light from her staff, she could see that the walls were covered with runes. Carefully, she circled the room, studying the designs, some scratched into stone, others hastily applied with some sort of ink. Some she recognized—Thurisaz, for destruction of enemies; Eihwaz, for strength. Victory runes; runes to confuse the enemy, steal his courage, weaken his weapons, send him astray. She traced several of the unknown runes with her forefinger, knowing she would need to return and record them.

But how would she know their purpose?

She imagined Trude exploring this chamber for the very first time. All the runes would have been unfamiliar to her. An image came to her—of Trude and Frodi, their heads together over a table in the library, poring over the sketches she'd made.

Reginn returned to the main corridor and walked on, passing into the next chamber, which was so large that the light from her staff couldn't reach the far walls.

Nearby, Reginn saw more piles of untended bones.

The remains of the dead, apparently undisturbed for centuries, since their enemies had chosen this tomb for them. Some had been hacked apart. Others lay as if in repose, still encased in the mail shirts that had not protected them in life, their fine swords beside them. The flesh had been sculpted away by time and those creatures that tend to the dead in the dark, but their silver armbands and bits of jewelry remained. Whatever expressions they'd worn at the point of death, they were all grinning now.

The poets said that Odin the One-Eyed had prowled the Midlands, searching out the very best warriors and marking them for death so that they would join his hall in Valhalla, ready to fight with him at the end of the world.

Not all of them were human. Some appeared to be the skeletons of monsters. One skull in particular had teeth like broadswords. Others had horns as long as Reginn was tall. They were creatures out of the old sagas.

Had there been a running battle in this tunnel? If so, who were they, and what were they fighting for? Had there been a winner, or only losers in the end?

Ragnarok—the last battle between the gods and the jotun. From what Brenna had said, Reginn did not belong to either side. She had no natural allies.

Having served as a healer in the Archipelago, Reginn was not squeamish. Having braved the issvagr and trolls of the forests of Muckleholm, she was not easily spooked. But it wasn't difficult to imagine that those who had died violently, trapped underground, might still haunt this place. It was also possible that other monsters had moved in long after the carnage of the past.

When she had first arrived in New Jotunheim, she would have questioned the existence of monsters in Eimyrja. But now, since Alva, she knew that they existed.

As if called by the thought, voices rose all around her, sending shivers running down her spine. At first it sounded like howling or wailing, but eventually she made out words in the clamor.

"Hear us, Aldrnari. We would rise."

"Raise us, Aldrnari, that we may blood our blades again."

"Lead us, Aldrnari. We would march once more."

She remembered Brenna's warning.

Leave the dead in peace.

She'd found the runes. That was enough for now. Keeping a white-knuckled grip on her staff, Reginn turned to go back the way she had come. The voices behind her grew louder. Then someone began to scream.

She couldn't help it. She swung around. Whatever was happening was farther down the corridor, out of sight. The screaming continued, along with what sounded like snorting and squealing and the clatter of hooves on rock.

Gradually, she became aware of a new scent—a musky, wild odor mingled with something familiar—the smell of char.

Reginn's heart flopped like a fish. She could not seem to get her breath. Only her grip on the staff kept her upright. Of all the dangers in this world, this one frightened her the most.

No. It isn't him. It couldn't be.

She took a step back, then another. Nearly stumbled. Every instinct screamed at her to turn and run.

Like a fool, Reginn sprinted forward, into trouble.

When she rounded the corner, she saw a young woman covered in blood, crab-scrambling backward while Asger Eldr kept a pack of wild boars at bay, his whip snapping and flaming as it cut through the darkness.

These boars were the size of draft horses. She'd never seen anything like them, not even in the forests of the Archipelago.

Whenever the lash connected, the boars screamed in pain, but it seemed to enrage them more than discourage them. Their razor-sharp tusks glittered in the light from Reginn's staff.

It was tempting to stand by and watch Asger meet the end he so richly deserved, but the beasts kept trying to circle around him to get to the injured girl, who was down on the floor, frantically looking for something.

Reginn thumped the butt of her staff into the floor of the tunnel, hoping to draw the attention of the boars away from their intended victims. It worked too well, as the pack turned as one and charged toward her.

Desperately, Reginn scratched a stave into the dust at her feet. She was aiming for a shield rune, but her staff seemed to have a will of its own.

It ended as Vakti. To awaken.

Leave the dead in peace, Brenna had said.

Reginn heard a rumbling behind her, and a vibration under her feet. Dust sifted down from the ceiling.

She realized her danger just in time. She lunged sideways as three large beasts thundered past. They were aurochs—three times the size of the spavined creatures that haunted the forests of the Archipelago—with shaggy hair and long silver horns.

They smashed into the pack of boars, flinging them into the air with their horns, trampling them underfoot, driving the survivors around the corner and out of sight. Gradually, the sound of the hunt died away, leaving only the stench of blood and the carcasses of pigs behind.

Speaking of pigs.

Asger stood staring at her, his lash trailing on the ground like the tail of a dead creature. He was wounded in several places. His blood steamed as it hit the floor.

"Meyla," he whispered. The astonishment on his face was nearly worth the heavy price she'd paid for it.

"Keep your distance, demon," Reginn said, struggling to keep her voice from shaking, trying to keep down the bile rising in her throat. She took one step back, and then another, her staff thrust out in front of her.

"I take it you two have met?" The voice was weak, but threaded through with steel.

They both turned to look at the girl, who now sat propped against the wall, a staff lying across her lap.

"Perhaps you could settle this later?" she said. "I could use a little help here."

Reginn crossed to where the girl lay and knelt next to her. There was a dangerous pallor beneath her coppery skin. One side of her face was covered with knotted black scars, as if she had been badly burned sometime in the distant past. Other scars appeared to be more recent.

Her clothing had been ripped all up one side. Underneath, she had a gash that reached from just below her rib cage to her hip, likely caused by a tusk. It was bleeding freely, but it didn't appear that any major blood vessels had been cut.

Bleeding was good, up to a point. It helped clear out the wound.

"What's your name?" Reginn said.

"Heidin."

"Take a breath, Heidin," Reginn said, "and let it out."

Heidin did as she was told. Her lungs sounded clear, and there were no bubbles coming up in the wound or entrails visible beneath. Reginn could feel the buzz of strong magic under the girl's skin.

Out of the corner of her eye, she saw Asger edging nearer.

"Don't come any closer or I'll cut your heart out," Reginn spat. Why she chose that particular threat, she couldn't say. But it worked. He edged away.

Heidin snorted in amusement.

Was this Asger's new thrall? Someone else he could leech on to and drain of magic whenever he needed it?

She didn't seem the type to be taken advantage of.

Reginn used the water from her waterskin to rinse the visible grit and dirt from the wound. These kinds of injuries often got infected. She wished she'd come better prepared.

Heidin was shivering, her teeth chattering.

"You!" Reginn said to Asger, who sat brooding in the corner, watching the proceedings with anxious eyes. "Give me your coat."

He blinked at her as if she'd begun to speak a new language. Then he stood and carefully removed his coat, crossed the room, dangled it from his fingertips a moment, as if taunting her, then dropped it within arm's reach.

Reginn laid the coat over Heidin, lining side up. Then she tossed her waterskin at Asger. He plucked it out of the air before it hit him in the face. He'd always had good reflexes.

"I'm going to need some clean water."

For a long moment, he didn't move, his eyes like windows into the cauldrons beneath the earth. Then he inclined his head slightly and turned back the way he'd come.

"How do you know Asger?" Heidin said as soon as he was out of hearing distance.

"My modir and I were healers and seers in the Archipelago. When I was just a child, Asger bought me from my modir and took me as his thrall. I've been with him ever since—until three months ago."

Understanding kindled in Heidin's eyes, as if she had fit together two pieces of a puzzle.

Reginn ripped the linen lining out of Asger's coat and wrapped it around Heidin's middle to hold the edges of the gash together.

"What happened three months ago?" Heidin said after such a long pause that Reginn had thought the conversation was over.

"Modir Tyra rescued me from the Archipelago and brought me here, to the temple."

"Modir... Tyra," Heidin whispered as if Reginn had invoked the name of the goddess. "You've seen her? You know her?"

"Yes," Reginn said. "Why?"

"I would speak with her," Heidin said in a manner suggesting that Reginn should rush off and arrange it. It was as if her patient was two people at once—a girl who might be a friend and also the imperial empress of all the Nine Worlds.

"How did you get here?" Reginn said.

"My brodir and I sailed from Muckleholm in our ship, with Asger as crew," Liv said. "We ran into a storm, and Asger and I were swept overboard. We swam ashore here."

"What about your brodir?" Reginn said.

Heidin shook her head. "I hoped we'd find him here, but so far I've seen no sign of him or his ship. I'm afraid he may be lost." Her voice shook.

"I hope you find him," Reginn said. "Where were you heading when you were blown off course?"

"We weren't blown off course," Heidin said. "This was our destination all along."

"But . . . how did you find your way?" Reginn said.

"I was born here," Heidin said, shifting her eyes away. "I always knew that I would come home."

Reginn wanted to dig deeper on that, but she could tell that her patient was finished with that topic.

"Did Asger tell you why he wanted to come here?" she asked, trying for a neutral voice.

"He came looking for you," Heidin said.

"If he comes anywhere near me, I'll gut him," Reginn said.

"I think he knows better than to try that now," Heidin said, looking amused. "It appears that you've gained considerable strength since he last saw you." She shrugged. "Still, once a demon, always a demon."

"So . . . what is your arrangement with Asger?" Reginn said. "He seems unusually . . . deferential."

"He has agreed to serve me," Heidin said. "In exchange, I have agreed to do what I can to restore his homeland of Muspelheim. Failing that, I have offered him a powerful role in New Jotunheim." She said this with an easy, peremptory confidence.

Reginn was lost. What did she mean "restore his homeland"? "You've offered a powerful role to a son of Muspel?"

Heidin shrugged. "Demons are what they are," she said. "But they can be useful."

"What makes you think that you'll be in a position to do that?" Reginn said. "I mean, restore Muspelheim and rule New Jotunheim?"

"Wait and see," Heidin said with a faint smile. She closed her eyes.

Was this confidence or arrogance? Reginn wondered. Whichever it was, her patient wouldn't be doing much of anything if she didn't survive. Guilt pricked her. She shouldn't have kept her talking so long. When she picked up Heidin's wrist, the pulse was weak and thready. Her forehead was cold and clammy, not a good sign. She had to get her to Brenna's House, where they'd have the supplies she needed. She didn't really want to take the two of them back through Brenna's tomb, but she didn't really have a choice.

Well. There *was* one thing she could do right away.

She dug into her remedy bag, sorting through the contents by feel until she found what she wanted. She hadn't risked using healing runes since the episode with Alva, but this seemed to be the time. Making a little pocket in Heidin's makeshift bandage, she slipped a runestone inside. Eihwaz, for strength.

Heidin came instantly awake. "What's that?" she asked, twisting around to look.

"Nothing. Lie back now, so you don't start bleeding again."

Heidin complied.

Reginn heard a boot scraping over rock. She spun around, her hand on her dagger. It was Asger, the fat waterskin dangling from his hand.

"Where have you been?" Reginn said.

"It was farther back than I thought."

Reginn took the waterskin and slung it over her shoulder. "We've got to get her to the healers at the temple," she said. "You'll need to carry her. And *don't* suck any magic from her. She'll need everything she's got."

56

FEVER DREAMS

EIRIC KEPT TRYING TO FIGHT his way to the surface, but each time he was sucked down into a maelstrom of dreams.

An image surfaced. An elaborate chamber, with rich cherry paneling and a table carved from a single slab of oak. Nine solemn-faced spinners gathered around it, men and women dressed in the finest silks and linens. A servant walked around the table with an alabaster jar, and each person dropped something into it.

A man in yellow silk and green stoles dumped the jar out and counted. Nine black stones.

"It's decided, then," the man said. "The chance child must die."

"This gift will be most pleasing to the gods," a woman said. Eiric recognized her—it was Scarlet Lund, who'd been so eager to see him slaughtered at the rift.

On a moonless night, a little girl raced across the beach to where a man waited, his faering drawn up on the sand.

It was Liv, as she was when she arrived at Sundgard.

"Fadir!" she cried. "You came back!"

Leif knelt, arms flung wide to receive her. When she reached him, he pulled her close and kissed her on top of the head. Then, gripping her shoulders, he held her out at arm's length and studied her.

"Gods, dottir," he muttered, his voice shaking. "What have they done to you?"

"They'll be sorry," the little girl said, in a surprisingly grown-up voice. "They'll all be sorry."

"Heidin! Wait!"

The man looked up to see two women running toward him, both in spinner blue, the younger of the two in the lead.

Grimly, Leif lifted Liv into the faering and pushed it out into the shallows. Giving it one final shove, he leaped aboard himself and took up the oars, pulling hard for the open sea.

The first spinner had reached the waterline. Without hesitating, she waded into the waves, shouting after the boat.

"No! You can't have her! She's mine."

Leif kept rowing, but Liv hung over the stern of the boat. "That's my modir," she cried. "Maybe she wants to come with us."

"She can't come with us this time," Leif said.

The spinner waded out until the water was too deep to go farther. She held out her arms. "Jump, Heidin," she cried. "I'll catch you."

But Heidin was afraid. She huddled in the stern, shrieking and crying, "Modir!"

The older spinner called from the edge of the water. "Let her go, dottir. It's for the best. Maybe in a different setting, she will thrive."

"No! I will not let her go. She belongs with me."

"It is not safe, for her or anyone else."

"I'll keep her safe."

"Something you have not done so far."

Seeing that there was no way to reach the boat, the spinner lifted her overdress and strode back toward shore.

For the first time, Eiric could see her face. It was Tyra—a much younger Tyra.

"Bring her back, Modir," the dedicate said. "Turn the winds and waves against them and send her back to me."

The old woman shook her head. "I will not. You were wrong to tamper with fate. You have abused your gifts, and my indulgence. Let it be."

The young woman stepped forward until she towered over the elder. "Why would we be given these gifts if not to use them? Now. Bring them back."

"Has it occurred to you that Heidin is using you? That the consequences of bringing her back might be catastrophic?"

The young woman slammed the butt of her staff into the sand. "Bring them back or—or I'll make you swim out after them."

"That is not within your power, dottir, and you know it," the spinner said.

"Don't try my patience, old woman."

"Listen to yourself," the elder said. "This is not like you. Can't you see how she has changed you?"

"She's just a little girl," the dedicate said. "She needs her modir."

By now, the little boat was nearly out of sight.

The old woman sighed. "If you insist, I will raise the seas. But I make no promises about the outcome. The fates are not as easily manipulated as you think." She waved the dedicate back, then lifted her staff with both hands. Light collected around the head and began to spin.

The wind began to blow, an offshore gale. Eventually, the sea began to rise, higher and higher, forming a funnel of water resembling the waterspouts Eiric had seen at sea in the Westlands. It grew broader, too, until he could no longer see the horizon. It sucked up so much water that the sea actually receded, leaving a strip of wet sand, as if the tide were going out.

The young woman watched this, shifting nervously. "Modir," she said. "That's enough." And then: "Don't you think that's enough?"

All at once, the elder brought the head of her staff down, and the waterspout collapsed, sending a wall of water seaward. It rolled on until it reached the horizon and was gone.

There was no sign of the faering.

The dedicate screamed, hands fisted in frustration. Then turned on the elder. "You drowned her! You murdered her. You did it on purpose." Her eyes narrowed. "You're the one who let him in."

"Dottir, a little reflection will tell you that it was your obstinance that has put the academy and our mission at risk."

"The academy. Our mission," the dedicate spat. "It's a joke to everyone but you. I will never forgive you. Never ever."

"I hope you will, one day, dottir," the old woman said. "Forgiveness is a gift you give yourself. Now. Come back to my office and warm up." She extended her hand, but the dedicate slapped it away.

Slowly, shoulders rounded with grief, the spinner walked away from the water. The dedicate sat on the sand all night. When the sun rose, bits of the faering washed up on the beach.

She murdered Liv. Liv is dead.

No. That little girl was Heidin. Liv is alive. Liv was at Sundgard. She wove your sails. She saved your life on Muckleholm.

No. Liv is dead. She was swept away in the storm.

Eiric's mind felt like a bowstring being plucked over and over again until the threads of his own memories snapped, and the only ones remaining were someone else's.

He woke, sweat soaking his fine new clothes, to find the blue-robed sorceress standing before him, staff in hand. She looked pale, distraught.

"Get up," she said. "Hurry."

Eiric pressed the heels of his hands into his aching forehead. "What's going on?"

"I am so sorry," Tyra said. "Despite my arguments and entreaties, the keeper and the council mean to give you to the gods."

Eiric sat up, planting his feet on the floor, his mind a melee of competing thoughts and memories. "I don't understand."

Tyra's breath hissed out through gritted teeth. "They mean to cut your throat in the hof and hang your body in the sacrificial grove."

By now Eiric was alert, at least in the way of someone who'd been thrown into glacier melt after a night of heavy drinking. "They're going to kill me?" he said. "Again?"

"Indeed they are, unless we stop them," Modir Tyra said, as if gratified that he'd finally caught on.

We?

"Why me?" he said.

"The elders have been building their power through blood sacrifice for years. What better sacrifice could they offer than a warrior of Asgardian lineage?"

"You keep saying that." Eiric couldn't seem to corral the thoughts and images clamoring in his head. "What makes you think I'm descended from the gods?"

Tyra took hold of the crystal pendant hanging at her neck and extended it toward him. It glowed deep red purple. "This reveals your divine nature. They hope that spilling your blood will assure them victory in the coming war."

"War?" he said. "What war?"

"The war with the barbarians." When Eiric didn't respond, she said, "You saw the encampment on Ithavoll. The Council of Elders has built an army of thousands and a swarm of ships to carry it to the Archipelago. It is contrary to all of the founding principles of the sanctuary and the intent of the founder."

Through the open doorway to the corridor, Eiric could hear voices from the hall beyond, a cadenced chanting.

Modir Tyra nodded. "They are waiting for you in the temple. The guards will be here at any moment to escort you to the altar."

"I'll go out the back, then," Eiric said, turning toward the rear door.

"They have a guard outside already," Tyra said. "There is only one way out—through the hall itself. I have hidden your weapons under the altar stone. They believe that I have rendered you docile. You must allow them to take you forward to the altar. Then lift the stone, retrieve your weapons, and end it."

"End it?"

"Kill them all," Modir Tyra said. "If you do not, you will live to regret it, but not for very long." The head of her staff glowed, and once again Eiric could feel that tickling sensation at the boundaries of his mind.

End it.

In the back of his head, Eiric could hear another voice—Bjorn's voice—calling out a warning. Eiric was tired of hearing voices in his head. He just wanted them to stop.

They both jumped as the double doors leading into the temple banged open, and four massive soldiers marched into the corridor. They stopped just inside the doors and eyed Eiric warily.

They must have heard about what happened on Ithavoll, Eiric thought.

Two of them reached out to take hold of him, but Modir Tyra smacked the butt of her staff into the floor to get their attention. "There is no need for force, gentlemen." She turned to Eiric. "Come," she said. "The gods await."

Eiric followed her through the doorway like any sheep to slaughter.

The Lundhof was cavernous—several stories high at its center, with the far side open to the grove beyond. Beeswax candles lined the nave, warming the wooden beams to the color of honey and creating flickering pools of light amid the darkness. Bonefires blazed in the clearing outside, under-lighting the massive trees of the grove.

Armed guards stood to either side, weapons at the ready, their eyes following Eiric all the way to the raised platform that centered the temple.

To either side of the dais were carved wooden statues, apparently spinners, since none were familiar. By far the largest icon, and the only one not made of wood, was a large statue of a spinner cunningly crafted of gold and silver, recognizable by her elaborate staff.

Atop the platform was an altar, on a slight slant, topped with an iron slab, stained brown with the leavings of previous blots, inlaid with silver channels to carry the sacrificial blood to an ornate copper bowl. It was surrounded by small cups.

Six figures in hooded robes of forest-green silk surrounded the altar. They all swiveled to look as Modir Tyra approached with her charge. They all wore amulets carved from amber. Their right fronts were emblazoned with the familiar crosshatched mark.

The hooded figures shifted and wavered, looming larger. As they turned toward Eiric, the faces within the hoods were monstrous, with cadaverous skin and burning eyes. Eiric nearly missed a step, and Tyra took his elbow to steady him.

The only person Eiric recognized was Scarlet, from the field at Ithavoll. She stood next to the altar, a bandage around her neck, her face blotchy with bruises against the pallor, matching the red-purple crystal at her throat.

Scarlet watched him come, tipping back her hood to get a better look, licking her lips. Was it nervousness or anticipation?

As Eiric approached the altar, Scarlet took a quick step back. "Is he tamed, Modir Tyra?" she said.

"He is," Modir Tyra said. "He is prepared to serve."

Scarlet looked up at Eiric. "It is a shame," she said, "to sacrifice such a man."

"Perhaps," one of the other elders murmured, "but he is worth much more dead than alive."

"Kneel," Elder Scarlet said.

Eiric knelt next to the altar, gripping the iron cap on either side. Elder Scarlet came up next to him, the silk of her robe brushing against his face. He heard the hiss as she drew an ornate seax from its sheath.

She grabbed a fistful of his hair and pulled his head back, exposing his throat. He could see Tyra's pale face floating behind him.

"May our hands be strengthened by the blood we spill here today in honor of the jotnar who have died at the hands of Asgard," Scarlet said. "May our enemies be weakened in equal measure."

Eiric felt Scarlet's body shift as she positioned the blade.

Gripping the cap of the altar, he ripped it free, swinging it back over his head so that the blade clattered against it as it came down. As the iron slammed into her head, Elder Scarlet screamed and fell backward, taking a handful of his hair with her.

Eiric reached into the base beneath the altar, feeling the welcome shape of Bjorn's axe under his hand. He pulled it free, groping for his sword with the other hand, spinning away from the altar and burying his blade in another robed figure.

Death finds a man when he stops moving, Leif had always said. So Eiric never stopped. He laid about himself with both weapons, focusing on those nearest to him. He assumed he'd be dead at the end of it, but he'd sacrifice some of them first.

Staffs clattered to the stone floor as the elders went down. Why aren't they fighting back? Eiric thought. This shouldn't be an easy win.

Is it that they've never had an offering that fought back?

For their part, the guards appeared to be standing down, simply watching as the mayhem went on.

Finally, when Eiric stopped to catch his breath, the floor was littered with bodies, and there were no elders still standing.

He looked for Tyra. She was walking from body to body, touching each one with the tip of her staff, the head glowing brighter and brighter as she did so until it was so bright that it illuminated the entire temple.

"You've done well, Eiric Halvorsen," she said. "They are all dead." She turned to the silent guardsmen. "Clean this up." And to Eiric: "Come with me."

They walked out of the open front of the temple and into the clearing. By now, the bonefires had died down. A handful of long-dead corpses hung in the surrounding trees, swaying gently in the wind. Small corpses.

As Tyra had said, the temple was surrounded by a ring of soldiers in their now-familiar uniforms. They came to attention as the two of them passed by.

Whose army is this? Eiric thought, looking over his shoulder. Tyra had said it was loyal to the council, but that didn't seem to be true.

"Where are we going?" Eiric said. Despite his long legs, he had to hurry to keep up.

"You said that you wanted to see Amma Inger," Modir Tyra said. "Now is the time."

57

MOURNER'S TEARS

TYRA LED THE WAY DOWN a well-worn path through the sacred grove. The woods around them swarmed with phantom armies and ravenous beasts. Again and again, Eiric planted his feet, sword in hand to fight them off, but again and again, they vanished.

"Halvorsen," Tyra said. "Don't worry. They won't hurt you while you're under my protection." She put her hand on his shoulder. "I know this isn't easy, but trust me—the world is better off with them gone. They've been exploiting children and the bondi for years. They've turned the academy into a factory producing adepts who can support their enterprises."

Eiric's thoughts were swirling again, his misgivings easing. Who could deny that the elders had done their best to slaughter him, twice? He had the evidence of his own eyes to confirm it.

"Now," Tyra said, "there is one more task you must complete before we are safe again. You are the only one who can do this."

The trail ended at the edge of a great clearing crisscrossed with walkways leading to buildings of all sizes. Even in the dark, Eiric could see that they were palaces compared to anything he'd seen in Muckleholm.

Tyra led him around to the rear of the largest hall, opening a gate into a small courtyard.

She pointed at a door in the face of the building. "Modir Inger is in there," she said. "She is the greatest threat of all. She has ruled this land with an iron hand ever since the founder died. You must kill her. When she is gone, we will be able to return magic to the Archipelago."

Eiric looked at the door, then back at Tyra. "But . . . she's an old woman?"

"Don't let that fool you. She is the most powerful sorceress in these islands." Tyra planted her staff between them, spun it again between her hands. "You can be a hero, Eiric Halvorsen. You can save us all. But—and this is very important—it is dangerous to allow her to speak." She paused. "She has a ring, set with garnet. When it is done, take the ring as a token, return to your room at the sacred grove, and wait for me there. I need to go back to the council house and make some arrangements."

She turned away, crossed the small courtyard, and exited through the gate.

He turned and looked back at the door.

You can be a hero, Eiric Halvorsen. You can save us all.

To Eiric's surprise, the door was unlocked. He eased it open.

A woman in a blue silk dressing gown sat reading by the fire, her gray hair gathered into a single braid that reached her waist. Eiric recognized her as the spinner from the beach.

On the table beside her stood a vase of yellow and purple flowers.

The firelight flickered, the shadows changed, and now she appeared monstrous, with burning eyes, hollow cheeks, and a cruel slash of a mouth. Eiric blinked, and once again she was simply an old woman so thin that her bones were all but visible through her skin.

He must have made some small sound because she looked up, startled, as he came toward her again. Her gaze traveled down to the weapons in his hands, then up to his face. "Ah," she said. "A true son of Asgard. My dottir Tyra has finally found someone to carry out her revenge."

"Do you blame her?" Eiric said. "You drowned her dottir."

"I did not," the keeper said. "You will realize that when your mind is clear of sorcery, but it will be too late."

What was it he'd seen? How much of it was real? His vision seemed to flicker as she shifted from old woman to monster and back again.

It is dangerous to allow her to speak.

Eiric raised his axe, tightened his grip. He was sweating, the axe handle slippery in his hands.

"You remind me so much of your fadir," Modir Inger said.

That gutted him as effectively as a quick blade under the rib cage.

"No more talking," Eiric growled.

"But it's true," the keeper said. "He was such a handsome man." She eyed Eiric. "You're bigger than him, of course, but your fair hair, that shadow of reddish beard—it is so like his." She paused. "But I see something of your grandfadir, too—at least I hope I do. Isn't it daunting to be descended from two such different and extraordinary men?"

Tyra had warned him. The keeper was getting to him. And he had nothing to say.

"Your grandfadir demonstrated to me that there was truth on both sides, and good hearts, even in the Archipelago. That all voices should be heard. Bjorn was always worth listening to. Had it been up to the two of us, I think we could have reached an amicable peace."

"People keep talking like there's a war going on," Eiric said. "Calling me 'Aesir warrior' and 'son of Asgard.' I'm not at war with anyone, and I didn't sign on to fight for dead gods."

She ran her eyes over his blood-spattered clothing and the blades in his hands. "And yet—here we are."

She sighed. "I should not have allowed Bjorn to return here as often as he did, but I was too weak to say no. I was debating with him when I should have kept a better eye on Tyra and Leif." Her face clouded with regret. "I have made so many mistakes. But know this—I could never kill a child. That's one thing my dear Brenna and I had in common—our love for children. I know that you view yourself as a grown man, but in my eyes, you are still young enough to benefit from guidance."

Monster. Keeper. Monster. Keeper. Monster.

"It is wrong to allow mortals to live forever," the keeper said. "They go on and on, carrying forward old ideas, wounds, and grudges and stifling necessary change in the world."

She studied him, her chin propped on her laced fingers, then nodded sharply, as if coming to a decision. "Your fadir could not say no to Tyra, either. Her mind magic is so very strong. You will do what you must do. Before you carry out your orders, would it be all right if I had a cup of wine to settle my nerves?"

Eiric shifted restlessly, wanting to escape this conversation and finish the work before him. Still, under the circumstances, he could not deny that reasonable request. He nodded.

The keeper stood, went to the sideboard, and brought back a cask of wine and one cup. The cask was dusty, as if it had been sitting on that shelf for some time.

"It's rude to drink without offering you some, but you would be foolish to accept wine from me. And I can tell that you are no fool." She uncorked the cask, poured herself a cup, and drank deeply.

"It's good," she said as if surprised. "I always wondered if it was worth keeping." She sipped again. "Now. As you probably know, the council has sentenced you to death. If you do not perform this task for Tyra, you will be of no use to her, and she will allow them to proceed."

"The council is already dead," Eiric said bluntly.

The keeper was downing the last of the cup of wine, and she choked a bit, coughing until tears came to her eyes. When she could speak again, she said, "Oh. Well then. Tyra chose well." She huffed a laugh. "You'd think a woman of my age would be beyond surprising. Leave it to the young to find a way. Well, don't dwell on it. I have never seen a more repulsive pack of hyenas in my life."

Abruptly, she changed the subject. "Did Tyra ask you to bring her a token?"

"Your ring," Eiric said, shifting from foot to foot. He felt as if he'd been given a role in a play, each character speaking the lines they had been assigned.

She held up her hand, displaying a gold ring set with a blood-red almandine garnet. "Well. Thank goodness she didn't demand that you bring her my head." It took some effort, but the keeper managed to work the ring free. "Here," she said, pushing it across the table toward Eiric. "She's coveted this for a long time. It is not as powerful as she thinks it is."

Eiric slid the ring into his pocket. The keeper poured more wine, her hand shaking, then drank it down again. "Ah," she said. "I do believe it is working. Tyra gifted me this wine, you know," she said, rolling the cup between her hands. "It was in Langvik, in the Archipelago. I think she hoped that outside of New Jotunheim, it might work." She smiled fondly. "That was the last time she tried to kill me.

"You see, Brenna left a geas over the Midlands to protect me from harm. That is the only reason I have stayed alive this long. But it has no power over those who carry the blood of the gods. And it does not prevent me from doing what I need to do."

While Eiric's muddled mind grappled with this, the keeper attempted to refill her cup, but most of it splashed onto the table. When she tried to raise it to her lips, Eiric knocked it from her hands, sending it rolling up against the hearth, spilling red wine like blood on the floor.

He could not have said why he did that. But the keeper, of course, had the answer.

"You see? It is not in your nature to kill old women by the fire. That will not get you into Valhalla. So I have saved you the trouble. The poison is called mourner's tears, and it's quite potent. Considering the enemies you have already made, I recommend that you avoid drinking anything that smells like cherries."

She leaned forward, supporting herself with her forearms. "Now, quickly. This is a period of grave danger for you. Tyra may put the blame for everything that has happened on your shoulders and proceed with your execution. Or she may draft you into her army."

Eiric stared at her. "Her army? But it's your army."

"Not mine," the keeper said. "Never mine. I'm not even supposed to know about it. Maybe it was the council's. It's Tyra's now."

"Have you planned for this? Did you know this would happen?"

"I knew it was a possibility, but teaching is by its nature the work of optimists. In founding the academy, Brenna and I hoped to train up a new generation that could resolve the tension between those with magic and those without, between those who care for the earth and those who see it as something to be conquered. Six centuries would seem to be enough time to do that, and yet we have failed."

Eiric no longer saw any vestige of a monster. Only an old woman, dying. "I'm sorry," he said.

"We should be apologizing to you," the keeper said. "We've left you a world on the brink of war. We've left you another mess to clean up.

"If you want my advice, son of Asgard, your best course is to leave this place as soon as you can. Don't go back to Tyra. She will have you tied in knots again in short order. Leave Eimyrja. Cross over to Ithavoll and make your way to the deadlands. They cannot follow you there. Find your way back to the Archipelago and prepare for war."

With that, the keeper took a last breath, slumped onto the table, and was gone.

58

INCIDENT

WHEN REGINN AND ASGER ARRIVED at Brenna's House with an unconscious Heidin, Reginn was relieved to find Bryn in the healing halls. She hadn't seen him since before Alva died.

After hearing a hurried explanation, he led them to one of the private care cottages, similar to the one that had housed Alva. Asger set Heidin down on a sleeping bench and laid her staff beside her while Bryn and Reginn washed their hands.

"I'm glad to see you here," Reginn said as they soaped up, side by side. "I was afraid that, after what happened with Alva and Naima, you might be in trouble."

"No," he said. He pretended to be totally focused on scrubbing.

"Have you heard anything about Naima?" Reginn said. "Where she's being held and whether–whether she's still alive?"

He shook his head.

"Do you have any idea how Skarde found out that she–"

"Reginn," Bryn said, finally swinging around to face her. "I feel terrible about what happened. I just don't want to talk about it, understand? I just want to move on."

"I see," Reginn said, though she didn't. She rinsed soap from her hands, dried them on a cloth, and returned to Heidin's bench without another word. Yes, she understood the topic was painful, but she believed that it was a conversation that needed to be had.

"Wild boars attacked her?" Bryn said, coming up beside her.

"Yes."

"When?"

"Earlier today," Reginn said, glancing at Asger, who'd retreated to a dark corner. All she could see were his ember eyes.

"Where did this happen?"

"Between here and the crossing to Ithavoll," Reginn said, intentionally vague.

"Really?" Bryn said. "Nobody's mentioned seeing wild boars."

Reginn said nothing.

When Bryn unwrapped the linen binding Heidin's wound, the runestone Eihwaz fell onto the floor. Reginn quickly scooped it up and returned it to her remedy bag.

"What was that?" Bryn said.

"Good-luck charm," she said.

"Huh," Bryn said. "It must've worked. From the way you described the wound, I thought we might need to stitch it, but it looks like it's coming together nicely." He looked up at Reginn. "Do you think we should wrap it up again or leave it open?"

Bryn knew she was irritated, and he was trying to smooth things over by seeking her advice.

You're the healer, Reginn wanted to say. But she'd noticed that Heidin's eyes were open, and she was looking from Reginn to Bryn in puzzlement. So she said, "If it were up to me, I'd apply a little honey so it doesn't fester and wrap it so it doesn't get all over her clothes."

"Good idea," Bryn said, and went to fetch some.

Looking momentarily panicked, Heidin groped around until her hand closed on her staff. With her other hand, she found the pendant at her neck. She visibly relaxed.

"How do you feel?" Reginn said, testing her forehead for fever with the back of her hand.

"Much better," Heidin said. "Thank you. I believe your good-luck charm worked." She sat up just as Bryn returned with a pot of honey.

"Wait," he said, frowning. "I was going to put this on your—"

"I'm all right," Heidin said, then plucked at her ripped and bloody shirt. "Would you have something else I could put on?"

Bryn motioned to one of the healers, who looked Heidin up and down, measuring with his eyes, then left.

"Could you send word to Modir Tyra that Heidin is here?" Heidin said, as if Bryn had a flock of couriers at his beck and call. "I am hungry, too. Would it be possible to get something to eat?"

"Of course," Bryn said, choosing to answer the second question. "We have porridge, and skyr, honey and oat bread—"

"I was thinking of a roast chicken," Heidin said, a dreamy look on her face, "with leeks and lamb's-quarters."

Reginn realized that she was starving, too. How long had she been underground? When had she eaten last? She'd entered Brenna's tomb on a quest for the truth and had been sidetracked by the appearance of Heidin and Asger. She needed to hand this problem off and get back to business.

"I'll ask one of the servants to—" Bryn began, but Reginn cut him off.

"I'll go," she said. "I can't promise a roast chicken, though."

Before anyone could object, Reginn fled through the door and hurried across the quad toward the council building. The only people in sight were armed soldiers crossing the lawn or running through the trees, weapons at the ready. What was going on?

There was a cordon of soldiers around the council house. When she tried to approach the front door, two guards barred her way.

Reginn recognized one of them as Svend, who had attended some of the concerts in the Grove.

"No one is allowed in the council house, Highest," Svend said. "Everyone is to go back to their domiciles and wait."

"What's going on? What's happened?"

"There has been an incident," the other guardsman said. "Everyone is to go back to their domiciles and wait."

"Is Modir Tyra in there? I need to speak with her."

"Modir Tyra is not available right now," Svend said.

"What about the keeper?"

Pain flickered across Svend's face. "She is not available either."

Reginn fastened on that. "Did something happen to Modir Inger?"

"Go back to your domicile, Highest," the other guard said.

"I'll escort you," Svend said abruptly. "It's not safe for you to be out here on your own."

That won't be necessary, Reginn was going to say, then changed her mind. "Thank you," she said. "I'm actually at Brenna's House, tending to a patient."

When Reginn was sure they were out of earshot of the council house, she said, "What's going on, Svend?"

"The keeper is dead, Highest," Svend said. "I'm told she was found in her chambers, stabbed to death. I don't know if anyone else was killed." He waved his hand, taking in the quad, with soldiers everywhere. "There's obviously been some sort of attack. We've been told to look for a fair-haired barbarian with a flaming sword. He's said to be twice the size of most men. If seen, he's to be killed on sight."

"Well," Reginn said skeptically, "at least he ought to be easy to pick out. Have you seen Modir Tyra since this happened? Or anyone from the council?"

Svend shook his head. "That doesn't mean much, though. I'm

not usually assigned to duty at the council house."

What if the council had chosen this moment to deal with the problem of the academy once and for all? What if they'd murdered Amma Inger and Modir Tyra, and blamed it on this giant barbarian?

Reginn had intended to go straight back to Brenna's House, but on impulse, she decided to go past the upper-school dormitory. She hoped that she would find someone who could tell her more.

"Wait here," Reginn said to Svend. "I'll just be a minute."

The dormitory was deserted, save for a handful of bondi assigned there.

"Where is everyone?" Reginn asked Brigida, one of the maids that she knew.

Brigida shrugged. "Nobody was here when I arrived this morning," she said. "Usually there are at least a few dedicates here."

Reginn's skin prickled with dread. What had happened while she was underground?

"If any of them come back, let them know that I'm at Brenna's House," Reginn said. "If Modir Tyra comes, tell her the same thing, and that I need to speak with her as soon as possible."

There was nothing to be done but to return to the healing halls and wait. Svend walked her to the main building. "I have to get back," he said.

"I know," Reginn said. "One more question—do you know if Naima is still alive?"

For a long moment, Svend said nothing, just looked at her, his face unreadable.

"It's all right if you don't know, or you don't want to say," Reginn said, giving him an out. "I just thought—"

"As far as I know, she still lives," Svend said. He answered her second question without her having to ask it. "They've been holding her in the prison under the council house. I think they're still interrogating her, trying to find out if she–if she had any co-conspirators. Then they'll execute her."

Reginn nodded. "Thank you, Svend. If you do see Modir Tyra, tell her where I am. Tell her that I have a new patient that she should meet."

When Reginn returned to the cottage, Heidin and Bryn looked up hopefully.

"No roast chicken, I'm afraid," she said. "You're going to have to learn to love porridge and skyr for now."

59

MIND GAMES

EIRIC'S THOUGHTS CIRCLED LIKE A boat in an eddy. Part of him
wanted to return to his room as Modir Tyra had directed, to confirm that what she'd said was true, that what he'd done was right,
and that he'd prevented a greater wrong.

But the keeper's advice resonated, too.

Leave Eimyrja.

And the instincts that had kept him alive in the dangerous
world of the Archipelago were telling him that he'd been played.

If Modir Inger was right, then he'd just slaughtered six people
he had no quarrel with—seven, if he counted the keeper. Fine hero
he turned out to be.

Sylvi's words came back to him. *Fighting is not the only way to win.*

He was still muddleheaded, from wine or witchery. He couldn't
seem to sort things out in order to come up with a plan. He had to
get away from Eimyrja if only to clear his head.

Eiric decided to head for the crossing to Ithavoll now and hope
that the tide was out. Somehow, he'd have to get back across the
rift. When he reached his ship, he would—reflexively, he reached
for the sunstone.

It was gone. The pendant, too.

He swore softly, sorting back through memory. He'd removed them when he washed up. He must have forgotten to put them back on before he sat down to dinner. Then he'd passed out after drinking Tyra's mead. They must be still in his room at the temple, on the hearth where he'd left them. He had to get them back, unless he wanted to live out his days as a hermit in the deadlands of Ithavoll.

If he moved quickly, perhaps he could get in and out before the alarm was raised. He ghosted across the deserted quad, then trotted down the woodland path as quickly as he dared, hoping not to meet any of the soldiers returning from the temple.

But when he arrived in the sacred grove, all was quiet. The fires were out, leaving only the scent of woodsmoke in the air. He circled around to the back, avoiding the temple hall itself, hoping to be in and out without revisiting the scene of carnage. Or alerting any posted guards.

He waited a few moments at the edge of the trees, watching for activity. Seeing nothing, he ran to the rear door and eased it open.

The corridor was deserted, and when he put his ear to the door of his room, he heard nothing.

Carefully, his axe in one hand, he eased the door open. The room looked to be just as he'd left it. Quickly, he crossed to the hearth.

Eiric had time to realize that neither the sunstone nor the pendant was there when he felt a sting on the side of his neck. He reached up and pulled a tiny, feathered dart from his skin.

He stared at it dumbly for a moment, then turned and saw a figure in the doorway wearing a hooded cloak and a half mask, holding a long, slender object.

Eiric took a step forward, then sagged onto his knees, his vision blurring, his fingers and toes tingling. He tried to lift his arms, but they were too heavy.

His assailant walked toward him, gripped him by the hair, and pulled his head back in order to look him in the face. Despite the mask and despite his confusion, Eiric noticed something right away.

"You're a girl!" he said. It came out sounding garbled, but she understood.

"Ah," she said. "See how clever you are. But I am the girl who bites." She bent close and kissed him on the lips, but then bit down hard on his lower lip so that he tasted salty blood. "I always wanted to spill the blood of a hero," she said, drawing back. "I'm not allowed to kill you now. But soon. And when I do, I will be unstoppable." Releasing her grip on his hair, she gave him a little push. The last thing he remembered was his head hitting the stone floor.

60

REGIME CHANGE

THE LONGER REGINN WAS PENNED up in the cottage at Brenna's House, the more impatient she became. Impatient and worried, feeling as if the hammer of doom was about to fall. She considered throwing the bones to see what they foretold, but she was afraid of what she might see.

No one else seemed similarly afflicted.

Asger had curled up in the corner and gone to sleep. He was like an animal in that way—he could sleep anywhere and usually did when there was nobody to torment or kill and nothing else to do.

Bryn had found Heidin a long tunic and breeches, which fit fairly well, and she'd tied back her hair with a scrap of red linen. The two of them played hnefatafl over and over again. Heidin won every single time.

Finally, Reginn walked out onto the porch. She discovered that there were now two guards posted there, neither of whom was Svend.

They did not object to her being on the porch, but once, when she tried to step off onto the path, they shooed her back.

"We'll let you know when it's safe to be out, Highest," one of them said.

So she sat on a bench on the porch and watched soldiers combing the forests around the quad and searching buildings, calling their findings to each other.

Finally, the bell in the council house tower began to clamor. Everyone in sight visibly relaxed, some collecting in little groups to chat. Soon a soldier in the livery of the temple guards arrived and walked from group to group.

Heidin, Bryn, and Asger came out on the porch to hear the news.

"What happened?" Reginn asked the temple guard when he came their way.

"The bells mean that the barbarian has been captured," he said. "The Grove is safe. Everyone is to gather in the courtyard in front of the council house to hear the news."

"What about Modir Tyra?" Heidin said, suddenly pale and trembling. "Is she all right?"

"They'll know at the council house," the temple guard said.

"I've come so far," Heidin whispered.

Reginn stood and extended her hand to Heidin. "Let's go to the House of Elders," she said. "We'll see her there. I'll introduce you, if need be."

They joined the throngs of dedicates, adepts, soldiers, and others walking toward the council house.

It was obvious that security had been tightened. Reginn saw more soldiers than ever before, all in buff with the crosshatch wyrd emblem. Where had they all come from? Shelby had mentioned settlements on nearby islands. Was there a military camp on one of them, in addition to fields and orchards?

Soldiers had cordoned off the plaza in front of the council house. Beyond the ropes, the quad was already crowded. They worked their way up to the front, ushering Heidin forward, with Asger cutting through the crowd like a blade through silk. They ended up right behind the ropes, where they had an excellent view.

The plaza began to fill with adepts in deep blue, most of whom Reginn had never seen before. There were a few familiar faces. She spotted Katia, Shelby, Stian, Erland, Grima, and Eira, all in adept blue.

When had they been promoted?

She slid a look at Bryn, who was staring at the ground, cheeks flaming. The two of them appeared to be the only dedicates left. In her case, it made sense, since she was so late coming to the academy.

She touched his arm. "I'm sure they'll tell us what's going on," she said.

Surrounding the blue of the adepts was a thick layer of bondi buff, like a beach bordering a blue lake. The buff was spotted with yellow and blue. Taking a second look, Reginn realized that the bondi were holding flowers—the elderflower orchids that Amma Inger loved. Their sweet fragrance perfumed the air.

There was a stir on the porch, and the adepts and guards moved aside to make a path from the door.

Reginn heard Heidin's quick intake of breath as Modir Tyra stepped forward, dressed in a white robe trimmed in the deep blue of the temple, her staff in one hand. Reginn squeezed Heidin's hand. "There she is," she whispered.

"Welcome, everyone," Modir Tyra said. "It is with a heavy heart that I tell you that the Grove and the academy have suffered a murderous attack and grievous losses. Our keeper, Amma Inger, is dead, as well as every member of the Council of Elders."

A murmur of fear and disbelief rolled through the crowd.

Reginn felt flattened. How was that possible? Security was usually tight at the council house.

Who could have done this? Was it the giant barbarian Svend had mentioned?

Could it have been a bondi uprising, and now they're trying to keep it a secret?

If it had been, she would have expected Svend to know something about it.

Why would she doubt that it was true?

"Who did this?" somebody shouted from the outskirts of the crowd. "Who murdered Amma Inger?"

Reginn noted that nobody inquired after the elders.

"How could this happen?" somebody else cried.

"The investigation is still ongoing," Modir Tyra said, "but this is what we know so far. A lone barbarian, the first to have penetrated our defenses in years, appeared at the army camp on Ithavoll. He claimed he was lost. A fight broke out, and a number of our soldiers were killed. The commander contacted the council, and they asked that he be brought before them. With these two dedicates"–she gestured toward Katia and Shelby–"I traveled to Ithavoll and brought him back to the Grove.

"Somehow, he broke out of the prison beneath the council house. It may be that he had accomplices who provided the weapons he used. He went straight to the sacred grove, where the Council of Elders was holding a service. He slaughtered everyone present–the council, the guards, and the presiding priests."

Modir Tyra closed her eyes and took a breath, looking positively haggard. "I blame myself. This has always been a place of safety–of sanctuary. I never should have brought him back here." She brushed at her robes with her free hand, as if she could wipe the guilt away.

There was something about this detailed explanation that felt like a puzzle carefully assembled.

Stop it, Reginn thought. That's probably exactly what it was–assembled from the available evidence.

Reginn glanced at Heidin, to see how she was reacting to all this. She was staring up at Modir Tyra, lips tight, her face unreadable. But she was trembling.

What a time for Heidin to return to Eimyrja, Reginn thought, given everything else that has happened to her.

"When I discovered what happened to the council, I realized that we all might be targets. I posted guards in my room and hurried to warn Amma Inger." She blotted at her eyes with the backs of her hands. "She was already dead—stabbed to death. Meanwhile, the barbarian showed up in my quarters, where he was surprised and subdued by the guards.

"Under interrogation, this man admitted that he was an assassin sent by the jarls in the Archipelago to destroy Eimyrja's leadership. He nearly succeeded." She paused, her voice catching. "What we have lost is irreplaceable. Modir Inger was the institutional memory of the Grove. We will need time for grieving and remembrance, and yet we must act quickly to address this imminent danger."

Tyra straightened, squared her shoulders, and lifted her chin.

"Intelligence gathered during our visits to the Archipelago has led us to believe that the jarls and chieftains there are no longer satisfied with a desperate existence void of magic. We believe that this attack was the first step in a coming invasion. If one man got through, others will follow. We cannot allow them to succeed.

"The Grove has been a refuge for the gifted from the time Brenna Wayfinder landed on these shores centuries ago. We have come to rely on the measures she and others put in place to keep us safe, but clearly they are no longer enough. The world is changing, and we must be ready with new leadership and a new plan.

"To that end, I have spent the day in meetings with our adepts and dedicates. The new council will be made up entirely of adepts from our own academy. Not a council of elders, but a council of the young. They are the ones who have the most to gain and lose by what we do now. That way we will know that they have received the proper training and have a commitment to New Jotunheim. I have promoted all remaining upper-school dedicates to adept."

Reginn and Bryn exchanged glances. They'd been absent during those meetings. Did this include the two of them?

"Rather than an at-large council, each member will have an area of responsibility suitable to their talents. I will introduce a few of the new council members now."

Each adept stepped forward as Tyra called his or her name. "Shelby Lund will be in charge of agriculture and plant science. Stian Lund will be coordinating animal science and resources, both for farming and military purposes. Eira Lund will continue to lead manufacturing initiatives and productivity, only now as a council member. Katia Lund will coordinate the use of our magical defense with the military team. Erland Lund will lead strategic planning and foretelling. Grima Lund will be responsible for security and intelligence services. Bryn Lund will oversee medical and healing services. Reginn Lund will serve as my counselor and strategist."

Bryn released a deep breath and smiled. "Congratulations, Counselor," he whispered.

Though Reginn was glad to be promoted, her mind swirled with questions. Why would Tyra choose her for such a powerful role when she scarcely knew her way to the privy? Or was it an empty title meant to keep her under Tyra's eye?

Tyra was still speaking. "I will have overall responsibility for educational, military, and domestic affairs, uniting the academy and the commerce enterprises for the first time. Many adepts will continue to serve in their current capacities. I will be making more announcements in the coming days.

"I know we're all reeling from this news, but I intend to see that justice is done sooner rather than later. Justice deferred is justice denied." She paused, then commanded, "Brodir Jorik, Systir Grima, fetch the prisoner."

Jorik was tall, thickset, and well muscled, unusual for an adept. He must have been recruited from one of the out islands because Reginn didn't know him. He and Grima walked into the House of Elders followed by a squadron of soldiers.

I hope that's enough, Reginn thought, shivering. She had no affection for the Council of Elders, but they were powerful, and bloodshed on this scale was terrifying. She wanted to have a look at this assassin who had single-handedly destroyed the leadership of the Grove.

Other soldiers carried out an executioner's block and set it in the middle of the plaza.

They're going to execute him right here? Reginn felt a little queasy. She glanced at Heidin, who seemed to have lost the veneer of confidence she'd displayed at the healing halls.

"It may take some time for them to return with the prisoner," Modir Tyra said, "as he is being held in the most secure part of the lockup. So in the meantime, are there any questions?"

61

FAMILY REUNION

THE FIRST SEVERAL QUESTIONS WERE about when a list of the dead would be made available and whether arrangements were being made for a memorial service.

Reginn nudged Heidin. "This is your chance," she whispered. "Say something!"

Despite her bold talk earlier, now Heidin shook her head. "This isn't the right time," she said. "I should go."

Reginn guessed that Heidin was worried that she'd been forgotten, that her memory of her childhood couldn't be trusted, that she'd be rejected.

She guessed this because she'd often felt that way herself.

"Maybe, if we wait until the end, there will be an opportunity to—"

"I'm not feeling well," Heidin said, and it must have been true because she was pale, trembling, her forehead beaded with sweat. Was it possible Reginn had overlooked something? Was her patient bleeding inside? She'd seemed well until now.

Heidin turned back toward the healer's quad. "I'm going back to Brenna's House. I'll see you back there."

Reginn put her arm around Heidin's shoulders, supporting her.

"I'll go back with you," she said. But this time, even with Asger leading the way, the crowd was packed in so tightly there was nowhere to go. It was like sailing into the wind.

"Systir Reginn!" Tyra said, apparently spotting the source of the disturbance near the edge of the dais. "I was worried when we couldn't find you. I was afraid you'd been caught up in these murders somehow."

"No, Modir," Reginn said. "I've been down in the catacombs, so I didn't know about any of this until now."

"Come, dottir," Tyra said, motioning for Reginn to join them on the dais. "We have much to discuss. I'll want to speak with you after the—"

Just then, the doors to the House of Elders banged open, and Modir Tyra swung around. A troop of soldiers marched out with Grima in the lead. Unlike the other adepts, Grima was clad in a black overshirt and breeches, edged in adept blue.

A fair-haired warrior stumbled along in their midst, bound with chains, but standing head and shoulders above the rest.

This must be the barbarian that everyone is talking about, Reginn thought. He was certainly big enough and strong enough to have done what he was accused of.

The soldiers parted in order to give the crowd a good view. He was dressed in a linen shirt and breeches, both stained brown with blood. All of his visible flesh was mottled with bruises, and one eye was nearly swollen shut.

But something wasn't right.

He didn't have the look of a ruthless killer. He looked frightened and confused. He looked like a person who'd been dropped into somebody else's nightmare.

He looked familiar.

Then Asger, standing next to her, muttered, "Halvorsen?"

Asger was right. It *was* Eiric Halvorsen, the coaster who had intervened at the tavern in Langvik when Asger was torturing her, who'd paid dearly for that, who'd shown her how kissing is done.

But how did Asger know his name?

Next to her, Heidin whispered, "No. That's impossible."

"You know him?"

Heidin shushed her with a gesture.

Modir Tyra faced the coaster, standing tall, looking more like a queen than a teacher. Grima stood by, her axe at the ready.

Eiric's eyes focused on Tyra's face. "Modir Tyra," he whispered through swollen lips. "What's happening?"

Something's wrong, Reginn thought. He's not himself. And how does he know Tyra's name?

"Do not speak!" Tyra commanded. "Eiric Halvorsen, you stand before us assassin and spy, murderer of our esteemed council, and dozens of our loyal bondi soldiers. Most egregious of all, you stabbed our beloved Amma Inger as she prayed in her study."

"I never stabbed her," Eiric said so softly that only those closest to the dais could hear.

If she heard, Tyra ignored it. "For those crimes and others unnamed and undiscovered, you are sentenced to death by beheading."

The crowd cheered, all except Reginn, Heidin, and Asger, who stood stunned and speechless.

Soldiers on either side forced Eiric to his knees. He didn't resist.

Grima lined up next to him, axe in hand. Tyra took several paces back, obviously not wanting to be spattered.

Just then, Heidin squeezed past Reginn, pushing toward the stage. "No!" she shouted. "Do not touch him!"

Asger again intervened, pushing people aside, his lash convincing the unconvinced.

When Heidin reached the steps to the dais, soldiers blocked her path.

"Get out of my way!" she screamed, pounding the butt of her staff into the ground.

Somehow, Eiric heard Heidin's shout. He turned his head toward her. His eyes lit up when he saw her.

"Liv!" he cried. "You're alive!"

The soldiers shoved Eiric's head down on the block.

"No! Stop—this is a mistake!" Flinging soldiers out of her path, Heidin climbed the stairs to the dais and strode toward the block.

Grima quickly raised her axe. As it came whistling down, Heidin pointed her staff toward the would-be executioner, and Grima went flying off the dais and into the crowd of onlookers.

Heidin stood over Eiric like a lioness defending her cub. "I don't care what he's done. You will not touch him," she said, looking around the plaza, daring anyone to try. Several guards rushed toward her, and she drove them back with gouts of flame.

Only Modir Tyra stood her ground, staff in hand, grim fury on her face. "Whoever you are, you are making a grave mistake."

Heidin gripped Eiric's arm and helped him to his feet. The two of them stood side by side. "Don't you know me, Modir?" she said.

Tyra stared at her, taking in her dedicate's tunic, bare feet, the mark of the flame on her face.

Heidin spoke again, quoting the passage that Reginn had read at her quarterly review.

Three times they slew her in Odin's Hall.
They stabbed her and burned her, and yet
Still she lived and took their bloody answer back to the Utangard.
This was the beginning of the end of the world.

Tyra's eyes narrowed, and the blood left her face. She would have staggered if not for her grip on her staff. Katia and Shelby hurried to support her, one on either side.

"My name is Heidin," Heidin said, "but you always called me Firebird."

Modir Tyra still shook her head, eyes wide in disbelief. "But— that's impossible. You—you're dead. You drowned." Tears spilled from her eyes and ran down her cheeks. "I tend your shrine in the catacombs."

"My shrine may be there," Heidin said, "but I am not. My fadir carried me off to Muckleholm, where I've lived all this time."

It was only then that Reginn finally caught on.

She looked from Heidin to Tyra and back again, comparing. Heidin's coloring reminded her of Tyra's, with her comb-honey-colored hair and golden skin. They were both tall, but Heidin was taller, larger boned, more imposing. But there was something about the shape of their noses and mouths that said they were related.

That said they were of the same blood.

Bryn had somehow appeared at Reginn's shoulder. "Do you know anything about this?" Reginn whispered without taking her eyes off the scene before her.

"I heard that Modir Tyra had a dottir who died," he whispered back. "I was never sure if there was anything to that."

Finally, Modir Tyra turned and faced the crowd, her cheeks wet with tears, but a smile on her face. "The Norns give and they take in ways beyond our understanding," she said. "At times the world appears to be badly out of balance, and then it rights itself. We have suffered grievous harm, grief, and loss in this sad season, but now there is also reason for celebration." She put her arm around Heidin. "This is my dottir, Heidin, ripped from my arms eleven years ago, taken by the sea. Her body was never found. I have honored her memory ever since.

"Now we learn that she was stolen from us by coasters from the Archipelago and held captive on the island of Muckleholm all this time. This is just one more in a series of crimes they have committed against us. Now she has returned to stand at our sides as we plan revenge on those responsible."

Some in the crowd seemed confused at this change of agenda, but others cheered and clapped at this news.

Modir Tyra and Heidin/Liv/Firebird almost seemed to have forgotten Eiric Halvorsen. Grima had returned to the dais, axe in hand, perhaps still hoping to put it to use. Eiric stood as if in a trance, scarcely aware of what was going on. Now he leaned toward Heidin and said, "What is happening, Liv?"

Alarm chased the joy from Tyra's face. "Heidin! Be careful. He's a murderer."

"He may be a murderer," Heidin said, "but I will allow no one to harm him. He's my brodir."

62

WAITING FOR THE
RECKONING

IN THE DAYS FOLLOWING THE massacre of Eimyrja's Council of Elders, the suspicious death of the keeper, and the aborted (delayed?) execution of Eiric Halvorsen, Reginn still wasn't getting any answers.

She hadn't spoken to Modir Tyra since the day the headmistress announced the news of the massacre of the elders and the formation of a new council. Since the day Reginn had found Heidin Halvorsen, Tyra's long-lost dottir, dying in the catacombs.

Rumor had it that the kennari had been cloistered up with Heidin all day every day. After all, they'd been apart for eleven years. It made sense that they'd have a lot of ground to cover.

No doubt, by now, Tyra had convinced Heidin that Eiric Halvorsen was too dangerous to stay alive. Likely he was already dead. Reginn knew from experience that Modir Tyra could be very convincing.

She knew that, sooner or later, she'd be called to account. Tyra must know that Reginn had gained access to the founder's tomb, since she'd brought Heidin back through the catacombs. Perhaps she also knew that Reginn had knowledge of the runes of magic. What would that mean for her future?

She recalled what Trude had said.

Let me give you a word of advice. Don't ever tell anyone here that you know those runes.

Reginn walked to the library, hoping to find the library mouse and ask for advice. She was half-afraid that Frodi's body was still lying at the base of the stairs. To her relief, it was not. Apparently, his death had been blamed on the ever-blamable barbarian Eiric Halvorsen.

Reginn called Trude's name, but there was no answer. Though she thoroughly searched both niches, there was nothing new.

She scribbled out a note.

Amma Inger dead. The Council of Elders slaughtered. Modir Tyra's long-lost dottir returned. Please advise.

She studied it a moment, then added,

Are you familiar with the word Aldrnari? What does it mean?

She stowed the note in the bovine niche and walked back toward the House of Elders. She was halfway there when someone stepped into her path, bringing with him the scent of embers and ash.

Reginn's staff ignited, sending light and shadow racing along the path between them. "Keep your distance, Asger," she said.

"Of course," he said, tilting his head as if puzzled by her reaction. "I am not your enemy."

He wore his usual black, but the sleeves and hem of his tunic were now embroidered with a flame emblem. It suited him.

"I'll choose my own enemies, and my own friends," Reginn said. "Get out of my way."

"Heidin asked me to find you," Asger said. "She wishes to see you at your earliest convenience. It would be best to come now."

Reginn's mouth went dry. Was this the reckoning she'd anticipated? Would it be Heidin alone or would Tyra be there? "Did she
say why?"

"She did not confide in me, but I believe it might have to do
with the coaster. Halvorsen."

Reginn's heart stumbled, recovered. "He still lives, then?"

"Apparently so. Come." He turned and walked toward the House
of Elders as if confident she would follow.

Reginn did.

Heidin had chosen Elder Skarde's suite of rooms for herself, with
the kennari next door and Asger close enough to provide security.
Soldiers were posted at the private entrance. Asger spoke to them,
and they stepped aside.

Inside, a servant in buff-and-flame livery announced them.

The room was sparsely furnished, plain and functional, with a
rope bed, a writing desk, and a table and benches for dining.

Heidin was seated on a low stool before an upright loom,
surrounded by baskets of spun yarn. As they watched from the
doorway, she rocked to and fro, sliding the shuttle carrying the
weft through the warp and back again.

Finally, with a sigh, she set the shuttle down. Without turning
around, she said, "Thank you for coming, Reginn. That will be all,
Asger. You are free for the evening."

He hesitated a moment, looked from Heidin to Reginn, then
inclined his head and said, "Good night, Lady Heidin."

After the door closed behind him, Heidin said, "I think he
hoped I'd ask him to stay."

"I'm glad you didn't," Reginn said. She paused, then added, "I
didn't know that you were a weaver."

"Time at the loom soothes me," Heidin said, her voice catching.
"We are all weavers, after all."

"How can I help you, Highest?"

Heidin stood and turned to face Reginn. She'd been crying.

"It's about my brodir," Heidin said. "He's not himself. I'm afraid he's gone mad."

Reginn recalled the clever, arrogant coaster she'd met in Langvik. Eiric Halvorsen, would-be hero. Very different from the lost, confused boy at the block.

"I'm sorry to hear that, Highest," Reginn said. "Your brodir was kind to me in Langvik, though it cost him dearly."

"My modir believes his time in the deadlands has destroyed his mind. She says that the kindest thing we could do is to just . . . send him on to Helgafjell." Heidin brushed her hands together.

"What do you think?" Reginn said, feeling as if she were picking her way barefoot over shattered glass.

"I think she doesn't know my brodir," Heidin snapped. "He is the strongest man I know. We have saved each other so many times, I've lost count. I will not let him go without a fight."

"And if you do save him, what role do you have in mind for him?" As soon as the words were out of her mouth, Reginn wished that she could stuff them back in.

To her surprise, Heidin laughed. "That's why I like you, Reginn. You don't hold back. To answer your question, that remains to be seen. He has no love of Muckleholm. Perhaps he'll agree to join us in defending this sanctuary."

She paused. "You saved my life in the catacombs. You healed Eiric in Langvik. You have knowledge and skills and tools as a healer that no one else can match. I hope that you are willing to try to heal my brodir now."

"Of course," Reginn said. "I will do my best."

Heidin sighed and blotted her eyes with her sleeve. "Good. Let's go see him."

63

HEALER

A DOOR HIDDEN BEHIND A panel in Heidin's sitting room opened to a narrow, twisting staircase leading down. They descended, the light from their staffs spilling down the steps, sending shadows swarming on the stone walls. The ceiling was so low that Heidin had to duck several times.

The staircase ended in a vestibule crowded with soldiers in buff-and-flame uniforms. When they saw Heidin, they bowed deeply and stood aside.

Eiric's cell was small, furnished only with a bed, a washbasin on a stand, several chairs, and a trunk. A fire was laid on the hearth at one end, but it had not been lit. As they entered, an attendant stood.

"Reginn!" she said, surprised. And then, bowing: "Highest."

"You know each other?" Heidin said.

"Sibba and I worked together at Brenna's House," Reginn said.

"I see," Heidin said. "Has there been any change, Sibba?"

Sibba shook her head. "He sleeps; he thrashes; he dreams and mumbles and screams and shouts. When he's awake, nothing he says makes any sense. He calms down, sometimes, after Modir Tyra visits."

"Modir Tyra visits him?" Reginn said.

Sibba nodded. "Nearly every day."

"Why?"

"As you know, my modir uses mind magic to help the dedicates succeed," Heidin said. "She hopes that it will help my brodir recover. She knows how important he is to me."

Reginn approached the bedside. Eiric slept, his bedclothes snarled around him. Movement under his eyelids and the way his hands clenched and unclenched told her that he was dreaming.

Her practiced eye told her that he'd been well cared for—the dirt and blood scrubbed from his skin, his hair washed and combed. Even his battered hands had been treated, and the nails trimmed and buffed. He was dressed in a snowy linen bed shirt that contrasted with his sun-kissed skin.

Reginn stripped back the bedclothes and examined his wounds for infection. They all appeared clean and healing, even—she froze, then leaned closer to examine the rune newly carved into the skin of his chest. The blodkyn rune. The rune she was beginning to hate.

Who would have put it there and when? But she didn't want to raise the issue until she was sure of her footing with Heidin.

"Have you been tending him, Sibba?" Reginn said.

Sibba nodded, then added, blushing, "Well, mostly. Some of the others have helped, and of course, Lady Heidin and Modir Tyra."

"Has he eaten anything? Had anything to drink?"

"Some, when he's been awake," Sibba said. "Not enough."

"Where does the food come from?"

"From—from the main kitchen. The usual place," Sibba said, frowning. "Was that wrong?"

"Of course not," Reginn said. "I can tell you've done an excellent job." Straightening the blankets around him, she untied the neck of his shirt. As she'd expected, his pendants were gone.

Licking her finger, she traced a rune just above his collarbone. Thurisaz. His fadir's rune.

Eiric's eyes flew open, his gaze fixed on Reginn's face. He seized both her wrists, his grip so tight that she knew it would leave bruises.

"Please," he said hoarsely, tears pooling in his eyes, then spilling over. "Make it stop."

"I will try," Reginn said. "But you must let me go."

"Don't leave," he said, as if she were a raft in a killing flood.

"I will stay awhile," Reginn said, "but you must let go. You're hurting me."

Understanding kindled in his eyes, kindling hope in her heart. He let go, holding her gaze for a few moments longer, as if to make sure she kept her promise, then closed his eyes and slept.

Reginn stood and turned to Heidin and Sibba, who were gaping at her as if they had just witnessed a miracle.

"Thank you, Reginn," Heidin whispered.

"It's a start, that's all," Reginn said. "Now, would you excuse us, Sibba? I need to talk to Lady Heidin privately."

Sibba bowed her head and backed from the room. Reginn knew that she was still worried she'd be blamed for the prisoner's lack of improvement.

When Sibba had gone, Reginn motioned to the chairs by the bed. "Please—let's sit," she said.

They sat, Heidin lacing her fingers together nervously and sneaking glances at her brodir in the bed.

"When I met your brodir in Langvik, he told me about you," Reginn said. "He said that you were the one who killed your uncle, that you saved his life."

"Eiric started the fight. I finished it," Heidin said. "As I said, that's what we do—we save each other."

"He called you Liv, though."

Heidin nodded. "My real name is Heidin, the name my modir gave me. My fadir insisted on calling me Liv. That's the name Eiric knows."

"Eiric intervened when Asger was tormenting me in an ale-house. He wanted me to leave Asger and come back to Sundgard with him. He said he thought that you and I would get along, but maybe he was just trying to lure me aboard his ship. He has quite the reputation, your brodir."

"He does," Heidin said, smiling through tears, "but he's never brought a girl home with him. And he won't make promises he cannot keep."

"And now you want to save him again," Reginn said.

Heidin nodded.

"Physically, he's all but healed. You and your brodir are remark-able that way. As for the rest—I'll do everything I can to restore him, but I'll need your help."

"Whatever you need, I will make sure you have it," Heidin said.

"Where are his belongings?" Reginn said. "His weapons and the pendants he was wearing?"

"They are locked away for safekeeping," Heidin said. "Why do you ask?"

"Anything that can be restored to him would help," Reginn said. "The pendants especially."

"You know I can't return the sunstone," Heidin said. "I can't take that risk. Besides, we'll need every one we have when we sail for the Archipelago."

"Sunstone? I didn't know he had one," Reginn said. "I was think-ing of his fadir's amulet. It means a lot to him, and I believe it may have some healing or protective qualities."

Heidin touched the amulet at her neck as if verifying that it was still there. "Of course," she said. "He was wearing the runestick you gave him as well. I'll have them returned to him."

"Thank you," Reginn said. "I know you've been busy, conferencing with Modir Tyra and other members of the Council of Elders. But have you seen the purple and yellow flowers everywhere?"

Heidin nodded. "I remember seeing them in the crowd all around the dais on the day Eiric was to be beheaded. I've seen some since then, as well, pinned above doorways and on people's clothing."

"Amma Inger was very popular among the people here on Eimyrja. The elderflower orchid was her favorite flower. People are wearing them in memory of her. There is considerable ill will toward Eiric, as Inger's murderer."

"I still find it hard to believe that he would kill an old woman he'd never met," Heidin said. "It's just not in him."

"Maybe he'll have more to say about that when he recovers," Reginn said noncommittally. "In the meantime, I think it's best to be careful about who is preparing his food. No one should know that it's intended for him."

"That makes sense," Heidin said. She hesitated, then said, "Though I wonder if you see threats where none exist."

"Maybe it's my upbringing on Muckleholm," Reginn said. She took a breath. "May I speak plainly?"

"Don't you always?" Heidin said dryly.

"Your modir wants your brodir dead—you know that, don't you?"

Heidin laced and unlaced her fingers. "I don't know if it's so much that she wants him dead, as—"

"She tried to execute him, and would have, if you'd not stopped her. She's still trying to convince you to let him go. Aren't you at least a little afraid that she might take matters into her own hands?"

Heidin stiffened. "You mean poison him?"

"I know that she has access to, and a knowledge of, poisons," Reginn said.

Seeing storm clouds gathering on Heidin's face, Reginn hurried to add, "I'm sure it's because she's worried about you. You saw how she reacted when you stood up with your brodir on the dais. She thinks he's dangerous and might harm you or get in the way of–of your plans. The fact that he's recovering may force her hand."

"No," Heidin said. "She wouldn't do that. Anyway, I told her that if anything happened to Eiric, I would put the blame at her doorstep."

"So you do recognize that she might be capable of–" Reginn said.

"Stop it!" Heidin shouted. "I was stolen away from my modir when I was just a child. I haven't seen her in eleven years. To see her again, to be with her is a dream come true. If you think I'm going to go to her and accuse her of–"

"I would never ask you to do that," Reginn said gently. She could tell from Heidin's expression that she needed to back off. "I'm just saying to be careful is all. Maybe don't allow any visitors, including Tyra, unless you're here."

Heidin nodded grudgingly. "I will do that."

"Thank you," Reginn said. "With your permission, I will come to see him at least twice a day. I'll do everything in my power to help him recover. I think we'll know within a week or two whether I can help him or not. Then you can decide what you want to do."

"You would do that?" Impulsively, Heidin gripped her hands. "But you were just raised to adept, and my modir has appointed you her counselor and advisor. With war coming, I know that there will be much for you to do."

"I'm honored to be chosen for that role," Reginn said. "But I can tell how close you are with your brodir. I never had that in my life.

I want to do this." She paused. "Just promise that you will not allow unsupervised visitors."

Heidin considered this, running her fingertips over the scars on her left hand. "I'll do it," she said. "Thank you, Reginn. With every passing day, my debt to you grows. Make a list of what you need, and I'll make sure you have it. Don't forget that my suite of rooms is just upstairs."

I hope we're still friends a few weeks from now, Reginn thought. "Just remember—I can't promise a cure, but I'll do my best."

Later, back in her new quarters in the House of Elders, Reginn sank into the chair next to her bed, sipping wine, weighed down by the gravity of the risk she'd taken on. Eiric Halvorsen was the only one who could knit together the story of what had happened the night the council died. With Amma Inger and the council gone, Tyra would be calling all the shots, with the support of a docile council of her former students. Reginn had no doubt that given the opportunity, Tyra would make sure that Eiric didn't live long enough to tell tales to anyone.

Reginn and Heidin were the only two people in New Jotunheim who wanted to keep Eiric alive. There was no telling how long that alliance would last. Heidin must be at least somewhat resistant to Tyra's mind magic or Eiric would be dead already. Did she know about the blodkyn rune—the bloody foundation of the temple's power? Did she realize that someone had carved that rune into Eiric Halvorsen's chest, meaning to take his power for herself?

As a healer in the hellhole that was Muckleholm, Reginn had learned to celebrate the small victories because those were all she had. A child recovered from the sweating sickness, a festering wound healed, a fractured bone straightened and splinted, a baby safely delivered. Maybe that baby would drown or starve to death before reaching adulthood, but she'd bought a little time.

Reginn had come to realize that there is no such thing as a sanctuary beyond the one you create yourself. All you can do is choose the battles you can win. Taking up her healer's knife, she cut a straight line into the flesh of her forearm. Isa, for concentration, will, and focus.

This she knew—whatever the cost, she would find a way to save Eiric Halvorsen. That, at least, might be within her power.

ACKNOWLEDGMENTS

This saga has sailed an exceptionally long way from inspiration to the page, through an ocean of obstacles and distractions, from fire and pestilence to shutdowns, lockdowns, cancellations, personal and political storms, and swarms of longships bristling with weapons.

Well, okay, maybe not that last thing. But the rest is true.

There is always research to be done, even for high fantasy. The Midlands, where the story takes place, is modeled on Midgard, from the Norse sagas. Research provides the foundation that supports the world and the characters and make them real. I needed to get the critical details right with regards to life in medieval Scandinavia in order to embed readers in the story and avoid cranky emails.

It is especially challenging to find reliable resources about pagan Scandinavia, because theirs was an oral tradition, passing information through the generations with stories and poetry. No central church came between pre-Christians and their gods to approve and preserve canon. The first written histories were recorded by Christians centuries after the conversion.

As always, books have been incredibly helpful, including Daniel

McCoy's *The Viking Spirit* and Jackson Crawford's translations of The Poetic Edda and The Saga of the Volsungs. Neil Gaiman's *Norse Mythology* is a reader-friendly and faithful retelling of the stories in the Poetic Edda. The Viking Ship Museum site (*www.vikingeskibsmuseet .dk/en*) was endlessly helpful when it came to ship construction, types of ships, navigation, and sailing in the Viking age. Ross Arthur's English-Old Norse dictionary at York University, Ontario, Canada, was useful in creating terminology for my fictional world (*www.yorku.ca/inpar/language/English-Old_Norse.pdf*).

Pre-pandemic visits to the Jorvik Viking Centre in York, UK, and to Viking museums and heritage sites in Norway, Iceland, Greenland, Ireland, Britain, Newfoundland, and Nova Scotia grounded me in that world and its many challenges.

Many thanks to the editorial team at Balzer+Bray, Donna Bray and Tiara Kittrell. Donna helped me resist the temptation to dump everything I've learned about Viking history, language, mythology, housing, agriculture, textiles, weaponry, and boat-building into the text. Do readers really need to know details about njalbinding, a form of one-needle knitting used in the viking age? Maybe not, but they do need to know about Viking-age poisons, herblore, runes, warfare, and wound care, because those are the kinds of stories I write.

Production editor Laura Harshberger and managing editor Mark Rifkin helped keep things on track, along with production managers Meghan Pettit and Allison Brown. Designers Laura Mock and Joel Tipple created an eye-catching physical package, and artist Kim Ekdahl produced a brilliant cover. Readers of high fantasy expect a detailed map, and map artist Kevin Sheehan of Manuscript Maps did not disappoint. I especially appreciate his creative input and attention to detail.

I look forward to working with Sabrina Abballe in marketing

and personnel in publicity, who will help bring these stories to readers.

Thank you to my literary agent, the tenacious Christopher Schelling, who believed in this story from the time he read the partial and championed it in a way an author never can. And thanks to Chris Lotts and Lara Allen at the Lotts Agency, who sell my books in places I've never been and would like to go to.

As always, I want to thank my husband, Rod, who should have the title Manager of Logistics and Problem Solving, smoother of paths, travel companion and webmaster, and finder of lost things. My sons are always thoughtful early readers, although they tell me they are now a long way from being teens.

Thanks to everyone in the reading and writing community who have made this difficult journey alongside me. I look forward to raising a glass with you in person very soon.